Charles James Lever

The Fortunes of Glencore

Charles James Lever

The Fortunes of Glencore

ISBN/EAN: 9783337272388

Printed in Europe, USA, Canada, Australia, Japan

Cover: Foto ©Andreas Hilbeck / pixelio.de

More available books at **www.hansebooks.com**

THE NOVELS OF CHARLES LEVER.

With an Introduction by Andrew Lang.

THE

FORTUNES OF GLENCORE.

ILLUSTRATED BY E. J. WHEELER.

BOSTON:

LITTLE, BROWN, AND COMPANY.

1891.

PREFACE.

I AM unwilling to suffer this tale to leave my hands without a word of explanation to my reader. If I have never disguised from myself the grounds of any humble success I have attained to as a writer of fiction; if I have always had before me the fact that to movement and action, the stir of incident, and a certain light-heartedness and gayety of temperament, more easy to impart to others than to repress in one's self, I have owed much, if not all, of whatever popularity I have enjoyed, — I have yet felt, or fancied that I felt, that it would be in the delineation of very different scenes, and the portraiture of very different emotions, that I should reap what I would reckon as a real success. This conviction, or impression if you will, has become stronger with years and with the knowledge of life; years have imparted, and time has but confirmed me in, the notion that any skill I possess lies in the detection of character, and the unravelment of that tangled skein which makes up human motives.

I am well aware that no error is more common than to mistake one's own powers; nor does anything more contribute to this error than a sense of self-depreciation for what the world has been pleased to deem successful in us. To test my conviction, or to abandon it as a delusion forever, I have written the present story of "Glencore."

I make but little pretension to the claim of interesting; as little do I aspire to the higher credit of instructing. All I have attempted — all I have striven to accomplish — is the faithful portraiture of character, the close analysis of motives, and correct observation as to some of the manners and modes of thought which mark the age we live in.

Opportunities of society as well as natural inclination have alike disposed me to such studies. I have stood over the game of life very patiently for many a year, and though I may have grieved over the narrow fortune which has prevented me from "cutting in," I have consoled myself by the thought of all the anxieties defeat might have cost me, all the chagrin I had suffered were I to have risen a loser. Besides this, I have learned to know and estimate what are the qualities which win success in life, and what the gifts by which men dominate above their fellows.

If in the world of well-bred life the incidents and events be fewer, because the friction is less than in the classes where vicissitudes of fortune are more frequent, the play of passion, the moods of temper, and the changeful varieties of nature are often very strongly developed, shadowed and screened though they be by the polished conventionalities of society. To trace and mark these has long constituted one of the pleasures of my life : if I have been able to impart even a portion of that gratification to my reader, I will not deem the effort in vain, nor the " Fortunes of Glencore " a failure.

Let me add that although certain traits of character in some of the individuals of my story may seem to indicate sketches of real personages, there is but one character in the whole book drawn entirely from life,

This is Billy Traynor. Not only have I had a sitter for this picture, but he is alive and hearty at the hour I am writing. For the others, they are purely, entirely fictitious. Certain details, certain characteristics, I have of course borrowed, — as he who would mould a human face must needs have copied an eye, a nose, or a chin from some existent model; but beyond this I have not gone, nor, indeed, have I found, in all my experience of life, that fiction ever suggests what has not been implanted unconsciously by memory; originality in the delineation of character being little beyond a new combination of old materials derived from that source.

I wish I could as easily apologize for the faults and blemishes of my story as I can detect and deplore them; but, like the failings in one's nature, they are very often difficult to correct, even when acknowledged. I have, therefore, but to throw myself once more upon the indulgence which, " old offender " that I am, has never forsaken me, and subscribe myself,

Your devoted friend and servant,

C. L.

CONTENTS.

ILLUSTRATIONS.

———◆———

Original Designs by E. J. Wheeler.

PHOTO-ENGRAVED BY WALTER L. COTTS.

THE

FORTUNES OF GLENCORE.

CHAPTER I.

A LONELY LANDSCAPE.

WHERE that singularly beautiful inlet of the sea known in the west of Ireland as the Killeries, after narrowing to a mere strait, expands into a bay, stands the ruin of the ancient Castle of Glencore. With the bold steep sides of Ben Creggan behind, and the broad blue Atlantic in front, the proud keep would seem to have occupied a spot that might have bid defiance to the boldest assailant. The estuary itself here seems entirely landlocked, and resembles, in the wild, fantastic outline of the mountains around, a Norwegian fiord, rather than a scene in our own tamer landscape. The small village of Leenane, which stands on the Galway shore, opposite to Glencore, presents the only trace of habitation in this wild and desolate district, for the country around is poor, and its soil offers little to repay the task of the husbandman. Fishing is then the chief, if not the sole, resource of those who pass their lives in this solitary region; and thus in every little creek or inlet of the shore may be seen the stout craft of some hardy venturer, and nets, and tackle, and such-like gear, lie drying on every rocky eminence. We have said that Glencore was a ruin; but still its vast proportions, yet traceable in massive fragments of masonry, displayed specimens of various eras of architecture, from the rudest tower of the twelfth century to the more ornate style of a later period; while artificial embankments and sloped sides of grass showed the remains of

1

what once had been terrace and "parterre," the successors,
it might be presumed, of fosse and parapet. Many a tale of
cruelty and oppression, many a story of suffering and sorrow,
clung to those old walls, for they had formed the home of a
haughty and a cruel race, the last descendant of which died
at the close of the past century. The Castle of Glencore,
with the title, had now descended to a distant relation of the
house, who had repaired and so far restored the old residence
as to make it habitable, — that is to say, four bleak and lofty
chambers were rudely furnished, and about as many smaller
ones fitted for servant accommodation; but no effort at em-
bellishment, not even the commonest attempt at neatness,
was bestowed on the grounds or the garden; and in this
state it remained for some five-and-twenty or thirty years,
when the tidings reached the little village of Leenane that
his lordship was about to return to Glencore, and fix his
residence there.

Such an event was of no small moment in such a locality,
and many were the speculations as to what might be the
consequence of his coming. Little, or indeed nothing, was
known of Lord Glencore; his only visit to the neighborhood
had occurred many years before, and lasted but for a day.
He had arrived suddenly, and, taking a boat at the ferry, as
it was called, crossed over to the Castle, whence he returned
at nightfall, to depart as hurriedly as he came.

Of those who had seen him in this brief visit the accounts
were vague and most contradictory. Some called him handsome and well built; others said he was a dark-looking,
downcast man, with a sickly and forbidding aspect. None,
however, could record one single word he had spoken, nor
could even gossips pretend to say that he gave utterance
to any opinion about the place or the people. The mode in
which the estate was managed gave as little insight into the
character of the proprietor. If no severity was displayed
to the few tenants on the property, there was no encouragement given to their efforts at improvement; a kind of cold
neglect was the only feature discernible, and many went so
far as to say that if any cared to forget the payment of his
rent, the chances were it might never be demanded of him;
the great security against such a venture, however, lay in

the fact that the land was held at a mere nominal rental, and few would have risked his tenure by such an experiment.

It was little to be wondered at that Lord Glencore was not better known in that secluded spot, since even in England his name was scarcely heard of. His fortune was very limited, and he had no political influence whatever, not possessing a seat in the Upper House; so that, as he spent his life abroad, he was almost totally forgotten in his own country.

All that Debrett could tell of him was comprised in a few lines, recording simply that he was sixth Viscount Glencore and Loughdooner; born in the month of February, 180-, and married in August, 18—, to Clarissa Isabella, second daughter of Sir Guy Clifford, of Wytchley, Baronet; by whom he had issue, Charles Conyngham Massey, born 6th June, 18—. There closed the notice.

Strange and quaint things are these short biographies, with little beyond the barren fact that " he had lived " and " he had died; " and yet, with all the changes of this work-a-day world, with its din, and turmoil, and gold-seeking, and " progress," men cannot divest themselves of reverence for birth and blood, and the veneration for high descent remains an instinct of humanity. Sneer as men will at " heaven-born legislators," laugh as you may at the " tenth transmitter of a foolish face," there is something eminently impressive in the fact of a position acquired by deeds that date back to centuries, and preserved inviolate to the successor of him who fought at Agincourt or at Cressy. If ever this religion shall be impaired, the fault be with those who have derogated from their great prerogative, and forgotten to make illustrious by example what they have inherited illustrious by descent.

When the news first reached the neighborhood that a lord was about to take up his residence in the Castle, the most extravagant expectations were conceived of the benefits to arise from such a source. The very humblest already speculated on the advantages his wealth was to diffuse, and the thousand little channels into which his affluence would be directed. The ancient traditions of the place spoke of a time of boundless profusion, when troops of mounted fol-

lowers used to accompany the old barons, and when the
lough itself used to be covered with boats, with the armorial
bearings of Glencore floating proudly from their mastheads.
There were old men then living who remembered as many as
two hundred laborers being daily employed on the grounds
and gardens of the Castle; and the most fabulous stories
were told of fortunes accumulated by those who were lucky
enough to have saved the rich earnings of that golden
period.

Colored as such speculations were with all the imaginative warmth of the west, it was a terrible shock to such
sanguine fancies when they beheld a middle-aged, sad-looking man arrive in a simple postchaise, accompanied by his
son, a child of six or seven years of age, and a single servant, — a grim-looking old dragoon corporal, who neither
invited intimacy nor rewarded it. It was not, indeed, for
a long time that they could believe that this was " my lord,"
and that this solitary attendant was the whole of that great
retinue they had so long been expecting; nor, indeed, could
any evidence less strong than Mrs. Mulcahy's, of the Post-
office, completely satisfy them on the subject. The address
of certain letters and newspapers to the Lord Viscount Glencore was, however, a testimony beyond dispute; so that
nothing remained but to revenge themselves on the unconscious author of their self-deception for the disappointment
he gave them. This, it is true, required some ingenuity, for
they scarcely ever saw him, nor could they ascertain a single
fact of his habits or mode of life.

He never crossed the " Lough," as the inlet of the sea,
about three miles in width, was called. He as rigidly excluded the peasantry from the grounds of the Castle; and,
save an old fisherman, who carried his letter-bag to and fro,
and a few laborers in the spring and autumn, none ever in-
vaded the forbidden precincts.

Of course, such privacy paid its accustomed penalty; and
many an explanation, of a kind little flattering, was circulated
to account for so ungenial an existence. Some alleged that
he had committed some heavy crime against the State, and
was permitted to pass his life there, on the condition of perpetual imprisonment; others, that his wife had deserted him,

and that in his forlorn condition he had sought out a spot to live and die in, unnoticed and unknown; a few ascribed his solitude to debt; while others were divided in opinion between charges of misanthropy and avarice, — to either of which accusations his lonely and simple life fully exposed him.

In time, however, people grew tired of repeating stories to which no new evidence added any features of interest. They lost the zest for a scandal which ceased to astonish, and "my lord" was as much forgotten, and his existence as unspoken of, as though the old towers had once again become the home of the owl and the jackdaw.

It was now about eight years since "the lord" had taken up his abode at the Castle, when one evening, a raw and gusty night of December, the little skiff of the fisherman was seen standing in for shore, — a sight somewhat uncommon, since she always crossed the "Lough" in time for the morning's mail.

"There's another man aboard, too," said a bystander from the little group that watched the boat, as she neared the harbor; "I think it's Mr. Craggs."

"You're right enough, Sam, — it's the Corporal; I know his cap, and the short tail of hair he wears under it. What can bring him at this time of night?"

"He's going to bespeak a quarter of Tim Healey's beef, maybe," said one, with a grin of malicious drollery.

"Mayhap it's askin' us all to spend the Christmas he'd be," said another.

"Whisht! or he'll hear you," muttered a third; and at the same instant the sail came clattering down, and the boat glided swiftly past, and entered a little natural creek close beneath where they stood.

"Who has got a horse and a jaunting-car?" cried the Corporal, as he jumped on shore. "I want one for Clifden directly."

"It's fifteen miles — devil a less," cried one.

"Fifteen! no, but eighteen! Kiely's bridge is bruck down, and you'll have to go by Gortnamuck."

"Well, and if he has, can't he take the cut?"

"He can't."

" Why not?   Did n't I go that way last week?"

" Well, and if you did, did n't you lame your baste?"

" 'T was n't the cut did it."

" It was — sure I know better — Billy Moore tould me."

" Billy's a liar!"

Such and such-like comments and contradictions were very rapidly exchanged, and already the debate was waxing warm, when Mr. Craggs's authoritative voice interposed with —

" Billy Moore be blowed!   I want to know if I can have a car and horse?"

" To be sure! why not? — who says you can't?" chimed in a chorus.

" If you go to Clifden under five hours my name is n't Terry Lynch," said an old man in rabbitskin breeches.

" I 'll engage, if Barny will give me the blind mare, to drive him there under four."

" Bother!" said the Rabbitskin, in a tone of contempt.

" But where 's the horse?" cried the Corporal.

" Ay, that 's it," said another; " where 's the horse?"

" Is there none to be found in the village?" asked Craggs, eagerly.

" Divil a horse, barrin' an ass. Barny's mare has the staggers the last fortnight, and Mrs. Kyle's pony broke his two knees on Tuesday carrying sea-weed up the rocks."

" But I must go to Clifden; I must be there to-night," said Craggs.

" It 's on foot, then, you 'll have to do it," said the Rabbitskin.

" Lord Glencore 's dangerously ill, and needs a doctor," said the Corporal, bursting out with a piece of most uncommon communicativeness. " Is there none of you will give his horse for such an errand?"

" Arrah, musha! — it 's a pity!" and such-like expressions of compassionate import, were muttered on all sides; but no more active movement seemed to flow from the condolence, while in a lower tone were added such expressions as, " Sorra mend him — if he was n't a naygar, would n't he have a horse of his own? It 's a droll lord he is, to be begging the loan of a baste!"

Something like a malediction arose to the Corporal's lips; but restraining it, and with a voice thick from passion, he said, —

" I 'm ready to pay you — to pay you ten times over the worth of your — "

" You need n't curse the horse, anyhow," interposed Rabbitskin, while with a significant glance at his friends around him, he slyly intimated that it would be as well to adjourn the debate, — a motion as quickly obeyed as it was mooted; for in less than five minutes Craggs was standing beside the quay, with no other companion than a blind beggar-woman, who, perfectly regardless of his distress, continued energetically to draw attention to her own.

" A little fivepenny bit, my lord — the last trifle your honor's glory has in the corner of your pocket, that you 'll never miss, and that 'll sweeten ould Molly's tay to-night? There, acushla, have pity on 'the dark,' and that you may see glory — "

But Craggs did not wait for the remainder, but, deep in his own thoughts, sauntered down towards the village. Already had the others retreated within their homes; and now all was dark and cheerless along the little straggling street.

" And this is a Christian country! — this a land that people tell you abounds in kindness and good-nature!" said he, in an accent of sarcastic bitterness.

" And who 'll say the reverse?" answered a voice from behind, and, turning, he beheld the little hunchbacked fellow who carried the mail on foot from Oughterard, a distance of sixteen miles, over a mountain, and who was popularly known as " Billy the Bag," from the little leather sack which seemed to form part of his attire. " Who 'll stand up and tell me it 's not a fine country in every sense, — for natural beauties, for antiquities, for elegant men and lovely females, for quarries of marble and mines of gould?"

Craggs looked contemptuously at the figure who thus declaimed of Ireland's wealth and grandeur, and, in a sneering tone, said, —

" And with such riches on every side, why do you go barefoot — why are you in rags, my old fellow?"

"Is n't there poor everywhere? If the world was all gould and silver, what would be the precious metals — tell me that? Is it because there 's a little cripple like myself here, that them mountains yonder is n't of copper and iron and cobalt? Come over with me after I lave the bags at the office, and I 'll show you bits of every one I speak of."

"I 'd rather you 'd show me a doctor, my worthy fellow," said Craggs, sighing.

"I 'm the nearest thing to that same going," replied Billy. "I can breathe a vein against any; man in the barony. I can't say, that for any articular congestion of the aortic valves, or for a sero-pulmonic diathesis — d'ye mind? — that there is n't as good as me; but for the ould school of physic, the humoral diagnostic touch, who can beat me?"

"Will you come with me across the lough, and see my lord, then?" said Craggs, who was glad even of such aid in his emergency.

"And why not. when I lave the bags?" said Billy, touching the leather sack as he spoke.

If the Corporal was not without his misgivings as to the skill and competence of his companion, there was something in the fluent volubility of the little fellow that overawed and impressed him, while his words were uttered in a rich mellow voice, that gave them a sort of solemn persuasiveness.

"Were you always on the road?" asked the Corporal, curious to learn some particulars of his history.

"No, sir; I was twenty things before I took to the bags. I was a poor scholar for four years; I kept school in Erris; I was 'on' the ferry in Dublin with my fiddle for eighteen months; and I was a bear in Liverpool for part of a winter."

"A bear!" exclaimed Craggs.

"Yes, sir. It was an Italian — one Pipo Chiassi by name — that lost his beast at Manchester. and persuaded me, as I was about the same stature. to don the sable, and perform in his place. After that I took to writin' for the papers — 'The Skibbereen Celt' — and supported myself very well till it broke. But here we are at the office, so I 'll step in. and get my fiddle, too, if you 've no objection."

The Corporal's meditations scarcely were of a kind to re-
assure him, as he thought over the versatile character of his
new friend; but the case offered no alternative — it was
Billy or nothing — since to reach Clifden on foot would be
the labor of many hours, and in the interval his master
should be left utterly alone. While he was thus musing,
Billy reappeared, with a violin under one arm and a much-
worn quarto under the other.

"This," said he, touching the volume, "is the 'Whole
Art and Mystery of Physic,' by one Fabricius, of Aqua-
pendente; and if we don't find a cure for the case down
here, take my word for it, it's among the *morba ignota*, as
Paracelsus says."

"Well, come along," said Craggs, impatiently, and set off
at a speed that, notwithstanding Billy's habits of foot-travel,
kept him at a sharp trot. A few minutes more saw them, with
canvas spread, skimming across the lough, towards Glencore.

"Glencore — Glencore!" muttered Billy once or twice to
himself, as the swift boat bounded through the hissing surf.
"Did you ever hear Lady Lucy's Lament?" And he
struck a few chords with his fingers as he sang : —

> "'I care not for your trellised vine,
> I love the dark woods on the shore,
> Nor all the towers along the Rhine
> Are dear to me as old Glencore.
> The rugged cliff, Ben Creggan high,
> Re-echoing the Atlantic roar,
> Are mingling with the seagull's cry
> My welcome back to old Glencore.'

And then there's a chorus."

"That's a signal to us to make haste," said the Corporal, pointing to a bright flame which suddenly shot up on
the shore of the lough. "Put out an oar to leeward there,
and keep her up to the wind."

And Billy, perceiving his minstrelsy unattended to, consoled himself by humming over, for his own amusement, the
remainder of his ballad.

The wind freshened as the night grew darker, and heavy
seas repeatedly broke on the bow, and swept over the boat
in sprayey showers.

"It's that confounded song of yours has got the wind up," said Craggs, angrily; "stand by the sheet, and stop your croning!"

"That's an *error vulgaris*, attributing to music marine disasters," said Billy, calmly; "it arose out of a mistake about one Orpheus."

"Slack off there!" cried Craggs, as a squall struck the boat, and laid her almost over.

Billy, however, had obeyed the mandate promptly, and she soon righted, and held on her course.

"I wish they'd show the light again on shore," muttered the Corporal; "the night is black as pitch."

"Keep the top of the mountain a little to windward, and you're all right," said Billy. "I know the lough well; I used to come here all hours, day and night, once, spearing salmon."

"And smuggling, too!" added Craggs.

"Yes, sir; brandy, and tay, and pigtail, for Mister Sheares, in Oughterard."

"What became of him?" asked Craggs.

"He made a fortune and died, and his son married a lady!"

"Here comes another; throw her head up in the wind," cried Craggs.

This time the order came too late; for the squall struck her with the suddenness of a shot, and she canted over till her keel lay out of water, and, when she righted, it was with the white surf boiling over her.

"She's a good boat, then, to stand that," said Billy, as he struck a light for his pipe, with all the coolness of one perfectly at his ease; and Craggs, from that very moment, conceived a favorable opinion of the little hunchback.

"Now we're in the smooth water, Corporal," cried Billy; "let her go a little free."

And, obedient to the advice, he ran the boat swiftly along till she entered a small creek, so sheltered by the highlands that the water within was still as a mountain tarn.

"You never made the passage on a worse night, I'll be bound," said Craggs, as he sprang on shore.

" Indeed and I did, then," replied Billy. " I remember
— it was two days before Christmas — we were blown out to
say in a small boat, not more than the half of this, and we
only made the west side of Arran Island after thirty-six
hours' beating and tacking. I wrote an account of it for
the 'Tyrawly Regenerator,' commencing with —

" ' The elemential conflict that with tremendious violence
raged, ravaged, and ruined the adamantine foundations of
our western coast, on Tuesday, the 23rd of December — ' "

" Come along, come along," said Craggs; " we've something else to think of."

And with this admonition, very curtly bestowed, he
stepped out briskly on the path towards Glencore.

CHAPTER II.

WHEN the Corporal, followed by Billy, entered the gloomy hall of the Castle, they found two or three country people conversing in a low but eager voice together, who speedily turned towards them, to learn if the doctor had come.

" Here's all I could get in the way of a doctor," said Craggs, pushing Billy towards them as he spoke.

" Faix, and ye might have got worse," muttered a very old man; " Billy Traynor has the ' lucky hand.' "

" How is my lord, now, Nelly?" asked the Corporal of a woman who, with bare feet, and dressed in the humblest fashion of the peasantry, appeared.

" He's getting weaker and weaker, sir; I believe he's sinking. I'm glad it's Billy is come; I'd rather see him than all the doctors in the country."

" Follow me," said Craggs, giving a signal to step lightly; and he led the way up a narrow stone stair, with a wall on either hand. Traversing a long, low corridor, they reached a door, at which having waited for a second or two to listen, Craggs turned the handle and entered. The room was very large and lofty, and, seen in the dim light of a small lamp upon the hearthstone, seemed even more spacious than it was. The oaken floor was uncarpeted, and a very few articles of furniture occupied the walls. In one corner stood a large bed, the heavy curtains of which had been gathered up on the roof, the better to admit air to the sick man.

As Billy drew nigh with cautious steps, he perceived that, although worn and wasted by long illness, the patient was a man still in the very prime of life. His dark hair and beard, which he wore long, were untinged with gray, and his forehead showed no touch of age. His dark eyes were wide open, and his lips slightly parted, his whole features exhibiting an expression of energetic action, even to wildness. Still he was sleeping; and, as Craggs whispered, he seldom slept otherwise, even when in health. With all the quietness of a trained practitioner, Billy took down the watch that was pinned to the curtain and proceeded to count the pulse.

"A hundred and thirty-eight," muttered he, as he finished; and then, gently displacing the bedclothes, laid his hand upon the heart.

With a long-drawn sigh, like that of utter weariness, the sick man moved his head round and fixed his eyes upon him.

"The doctor!" said he, in a deep-toned but feeble voice. "Leave me, Craggs — leave me alone with him."

And the Corporal slowly retired, turning as he went to look back towards the bed, and evidently going with reluctance.

"Is it fever?" asked the sick man, in a faint but unfaltering accent.

"It's a kind of cerebral congestion, — a matter of them membranes that's over the brain, with, of course, *febrilis generalis*."

The accentuation of these words, marked as it was by the strongest provincialism of the peasant, attracted the sick man's attention, and he bent upon him a look at once searching and severe.

"What are you — who are you?" cried he, angrily.

"What I am is n't so aisy to say; but who I am is clean beyond me."

"Are you a doctor?" asked the sick man, fiercely.

"I 'm afear'd I 'm not, in the sense of a *gradum Universitatis*, — a diplomia; but sure maybe Paracelsus himself just took to it, like me, having a vocation, as one might say."

"Ring that bell," said the other, peremptorily.

And Billy obeyed without speaking.

"What do you mean by this, Craggs?" said the Viscount, trembling with passion. "Who have you brought me? What beggar have you picked off the highway? Or is he the travelling fool of the district?"

But the anger that supplied strength hitherto now failed to impart energy, and he sank back wasted and exhausted. The Corporal bent over him, and spoke something in a low whisper, but whether the words were heard or not, the sick man now lay still, breathing heavily.

" Can you do nothing for him?" asked Craggs, peevishly — " nothing but anger him?"

" To be sure I can if you let me," said Billy, producing a very ancient lancet-case of boxwood tipped with ivory. " I 'll just take a dash of blood from the temporial artery, to relieve the cerebrum, and then we 'll put cowld on his head, and keep him quiet."

And with a promptitude that showed at least self-confidence, he proceeded to accomplish the operation, every step of which he effected skilfully and well.

" There, now," said he, feeling the pulse, as the blood continued to flow freely, " the circulation is relieved at once; it 's the same as opening a sluice in a mill-dam. He 's better already."

" He looks easier," said Craggs.

" Ay, and he feels it," continued Billy. " Just notice the respiratory organs, and see how easy the intercostials is doing their work now. Bring me a bowl of clean water, some vinegar, and any ould rags you have."

Craggs obeyed, but not without a sneer at the direction.

" All over the head," said Billy; " all over it, — back and front, — and with the blessing of the Virgin, I 'll have that hair off of him if he is n't cooler towards evening."

So saying, he covered the sick man with the wetted cloths, and bathed his hands in the cooling fluid.

" Now to exclude the light and save the brain from stimulation and excitation," said Billy, with a pompous enunciation of the last syllables; " and then *quies* — rest — peace !"

And with this direction, imparted with a caution to enforce its benefits, he moved stealthily towards the door and passed out.

" What do you think of him?" asked the Corporal, eagerly.

" He 'll do — he 'll do," said Billy. " He 's a sanguineous

temperament, and he'll bear the lancet. It's just like weatherin' a point at say. If you have a craft that will carry canvas, there's always a chance for you."

" He perceived that you were not a doctor," said Craggs, when they reached the corridor.

" Did he, faix?" cried Billy, half indignantly. " He might have perceived that I did n't come in a coach; that I had n't my hair powdered, nor gold knee-buckles in my smallcloths; but, for all that, it would be going too far to say that I was n't a doctor! 'T is the same with physic and poetry — you take to it, or you don't take to it! There's chaps, ay, and far from stupid ones either, that could n't compose you ten hexameters if ye'd put them on a hot griddle for it; and there's others that would talk rhyme rather than rayson! And so with the *ars medicatrix* — everybody has n't an eye for a hectic, or an ear for a cough — *non contigit cuique adire Corintheam.* 'T is n't every one can toss pancakes, as Horace says."

" Hush — be still!" muttered Craggs, " here's the young master." And as he spoke, a youth of about fifteen, well grown and handsome, but poorly, even meanly clad, approached them.

" Have you seen my father? What do you think of him?" asked he, eagerly.

" 'T is a critical state he's in, your honor," said Billy, bowing; " but I think he'll come round — *deplation, deplation, deplation — actio, actio, actio* ; relieve the gorged vessels, and don't drown the grand hydraulic machine, the heart — them's my sentiments."

Turning from the speaker with a look of angry impatience, the boy whispered some words in the Corporal's ear.

" What could I do, sir?" was the answer; " it was this fellow or nothing."

" And better, a thousand times better, nothing," said the boy, " than trust his life to the coarse ignorance of this wretched quack." And in his passion the words were uttered loud enough for Billy to overhear them.

" Don't be hasty, your honor," said Billy, submissively, " and don't be unjust. The realms of disaze is like an unknown tract of country, or a country that's only known

a little, just round the coast, as it might be; once ye 're
beyond that, one man is as good a guide as another, *cæteris
paribus*, that is, with · equal lights.' "

" What have you done? Have you given him anything? "
broke in the boy, hurriedly.

" I took a bleeding from him, little short of sixteen
ounces, from the temporial," said Billy, proudly, " and I 'll
give him now a concoction of meadow saffron with a pinch
of saltpetre in it, to cause diaphoresis, d' ye mind? Meanwhile, we 're disgorging the arachnoid membranes with
cowld applications, and we 're relievin' the cerebellum by
repose. I challenge the Hall," added Billy, stoutly, " to
say is n't them the grand principles of · traitment.' Ah!
young gentleman," said he, after a few seconds' pause,
" don't be hard on me, because I 'm poor and in rags, nor
think manely of me because I spake with a brogue, and
maybe bad grammar, for, you see, even a crayture of my
kind can have a knowledge of disaze, just as he may have
a knowledge of nature, by observation. What is sickness,
after all, but just one of the phenomenons of all organic
and inorganic matter — a regular sort of shindy in a man's
inside, like a thunderstorm, or a hurry-cane outside?
Watch what 's coming, look out and see which way the
mischief is brewin', and make your preparations. That 's
the great study of physic."

The boy listened patiently and even attentively to this
speech, and when Billy had concluded, he turned to the
Corporal and said, " Look to him, Craggs, and let him
have his supper, and when he has eaten it send him to
my room."

Billy bowed an acknowledgment, and followed the
Corporal to the kitchen.

" That 's my lord's son, I suppose," said he, as he seated
himself, " and a fine young crayture too — *puer ingenuus*,
with a grand frontal development." And with this reflection he addressed himself to the coarse but abundant
fare which Craggs placed before him, and with an appetite
that showed how much he relished it.

" This is elegant living ye have here, Mr. Craggs," said
Billy, as he drained his tankard of beer, and placed it

with a sigh on the table; "many happy years of it to ye —
I could n't wish ye anything better."

"The life is not so bad," said Craggs, "but it's lonely
sometimes."

"Life need never be lonely so long as a man has health
and his faculties," said Billy; "give me nature to admire,
a bit of baycon for dinner, and my fiddle to amuse me, and
I would n't change with the King of Sugar 'Candy.'"

"I was there," said Craggs, "it's a fine island."

"My lord wants to see the doctor," said a woman,
entering hastily.

"And the doctor is ready for him," said Billy, rising
and leaving the kitchen with all the dignity he could
assume.

2

CHAPTER III.

"Didn't I tell you how it would be?" said Billy, as he re-entered the kitchen, now crowded by the workpeople, anxious for tidings of the sick man. "The head is re-leaved, the congestive symptoms is allayed, and when the artarial excitement subsides, he'll be out of danger."

"Musha, but I'm glad," muttered one; "he'd be a great loss to us."

"True for you, Patsey; there's eight or nine of us here would miss him if he was gone."

"Troth, he doesn't give much employment, but we couldn't spare him," croaked out a third, when the entrance of the Corporal cut short further commentary; and the party gathered around the cheerful turf fire with that instinctive sense of comfort impressed by the swooping wind and rain that beat against the windows.

"It's a dreadful night outside; I wouldn't like to cross the lough in it," said one.

"Then that's just what I'm thinking of this minit," said Billy. "I'll have to be up at the office for the bags at six o'clock."

"Faix, you'll not see Leenane at six o'clock to-morrow."

"Sorra taste of it," muttered another; "there's a sea runnin' outside now that would swamp a life-boat."

"I'll not lose an illigant situation of six pounds ten a year, and a pair of shoes at Christmas, for want of a bit of courage," said Billy; "I'd have my dismissal if I wasn't there as sure as my name is Billy Traynor."

"And better for you than lose your life, Billy," said one.

"And it's not alone myself I'd be thinking of," said Billy; "but every man in this world, high and low, has his duties. *My* duty," added he, somewhat pretentiously, "is to carry the King's mail; and if anything was to obstruckt, or impade, or delay the correspondience, it's on me the blame would lie."

"The letters wouldn't go the faster because you were drowned," broke in the Corporal.

"No, sir," said Billy, rather staggered by the grin of approval that met this remark — "no, sir, what you observe is true; but nobody reflects on the sintry that dies at his post."

"If you must and will go, I'll give you the yawl," said Craggs; "and I'll go with you myself."

"Spoke like a British Grenadier," cried Billy, with enthusiasm.

"Carbineer, if the same to you, master," said the other, quietly; "I never served in the infantry."

"*Tros Tyriusve mihi*," cried Billy; "which is as much as to say, —

> "'To storm the skies, or lay siege to the moon,
> Give me one of the line, or a heavy dragoon,'

it's the same to me, as the poet says."

And a low murmur of the company seemed to accord approval to the sentiment.

"I wish you'd give us a tune, Billy," said one, coaxingly.

"Or a song would be better," observed another.

"Faix," cried a third, "'t is himself could do it, and in Frinch or Latin if ye wanted it."

"The Germans was the best I ever knew for music," broke in Craggs. "I was brigaded with Arentschild's Hanoverians in Spain; and they used to sit outside the tents every evening, and sing. By Jove! how they did sing — all together, like the swell of a church organ."

"Yes, you're right," said Billy, but evidently yielding an unwilling assent to this doctrine. "The Germans has a fine national music, and they're great for harmony. But harmony and melody is two different things."

"And which is best, Billy?" asked one of the company.

"Musha, but I pity your ignorance," said Billy, with a degree of confusion that raised a hearty laugh at his expense.

"Well, but where's the song?" exclaimed another.

"Ay," said Craggs, "we are forgetting the song. Now for it, Billy. Since all is going on so well above stairs, I'll draw you a gallon of ale, boys, and we'll drink to the master's speedy recovery."

It was a rare occasion when the Corporal suffered himself to expand in this fashion, and great was the applause at the unexpected munificence.

Billy at the same moment took out his fiddle and began that process of preparatory screwing and scraping which, no matter how distressing to the surrounders, seems to afford intense delight to performers on this instrument. In the present case, it is but fair to say, there was neither comment nor impatience; on the contrary, they seemed to accept these convulsive throes of sound as an earnest of the grand flood of melody that was coming. That Billy was occupied with other thoughts than those of tuning was, however, apparent, for his lips continued to move rapidly; and at moments he was seen to beat time with his foot, as though measuring out the rhythm of a verse.

"I have it now, ladies and gentlemen," he said, making a low obeisance to the company; and so saying, he struck up a very popular tune, the same to which a reverend divine wrote his words of "The night before Larry was Stretched;" and in a voice of a deep and mellow fulness, managed with considerable taste, sang —

> "'A fig for the *chansons* of France,
>   Whose meaning is always a riddle;
> The music to sing or to dance
>   Is an Irish tune played on the fiddle.
> To your songs of the Rhine and the Rhone
>   I'm ready to cry out *jam satis;*
> Just give us something of our own
>   In praise of our Land of Potatoes.
>   Tol lol de lol, etc.

> "'What care I for sorrows of those
>   Who speak of their heart as a *cuore;*
> How expect me to feel for the woes
>   Of him who calls love an *amore!*
> Let me have a few words about home,
>   With music whose strains I'd remember,
> And I'll give you all Florence and Rome,
>   Tho' they have a blue sky in December.
>   Tol lol de lol, etc.

"' With a pretty face close to your own,
I 'm sure there 's no rayson for sighing ;
Nor when walkin' beside her alone,
Why the blazes be talking of dying !
That 's the way tho', in France and in Spain,
Where love is not real, but acted,
You must always purtend you 're insane,
Or at laste that you 're partly distracted.
Tol lol de lol, etc.' "

It is very unlikely that the reader will estimate Billy's impromptu as did the company; in fact, it possessed the greatest of all claims to their admiration, for it was partly incomprehensible, and by the artful introduction of a word here and there, of which his hearers knew nothing, the poet was well aware that he was securing their heartiest approval. Nor was Billy insensible to such flatteries. The *irritabile genus* has its soft side, and can enjoy to the uttermost its own successes. It is possible, if Billy had been in another sphere, with much higher gifts, and surrounded by higher associates, that he might have accepted the homage tendered him with more graceful modesty, and seemed at least less confident of his own merits ; but under no possible change of places or people could the praise have bestowed more sincere pleasure.

" You 're right, there, Jim Morris," said he, turning suddenly round towards one of the company; " you never said a truer thing than that. The poetic temperament is riches to a poor man. Wherever I go — in all weathers, wet and dreary, and maybe footsore, with the bags full, and the mountain streams all flowin' over — I can just go into my own mind, just the way you 'd go into an inn, and order whatever you wanted. I don't need to be a king, to sit on a throne; I don't want ships, nor coaches, nor horses, to convay me to foreign lands. I can bestow kingdoms. When I haven't tuppence to buy tobacco, and without a shoe to my foot, and my hair through my hat, I can be dancin' wid princesses, and handin' empresses in to tay."

" Musha, musha ! " muttered the surrounders, as though they were listening to a magician, who in a moment of unguarded familiarity condescended to discuss his own miraculous gifts.

" And," resumed Billy, " it isn't only what ye are to
yourself and your own heart, but what ye are to others, that
without that sacret bond between you, would n't think of
you at all.   I remember, once on a time, I was in the north
of England travelling. partly for pleasure, and partly with a
view to a small speculation in Sheffield ware — cheap penknives and scissors, pencil-cases, bodkins, and the like —
and I wandered about for weeks through what they call the
Lake Country, a very handsome place, but nowise grand or
sublime, like what we have here in Ireland — more wood,
forest timber, and better-off people, but nothing beyond
that !

" Well, one evening — it was in August — I came down
by a narrow path to the side of a lake, where there was a
stone seat, put up to see the view from, and in front was
three wooden steps of stairs going down into the water,
where a boat might come in.   It was a lovely spot, and well
chosen, for you could count as many as five promontories
running out into the lake ; and there was two islands, all
wooded to the water's edge ; and behind all, in the distance,
was a great mountain, with clouds on the top ; and it was just
the season when the trees is beginnin' to change their colors,
and there was shades of deep gold, and dark olive, and
russet brown, all mingling together with the green, and
glowing in the lake below under the setting sun, and all was
quiet and still as midnight ; and over the water the only
ripple was the track of a water-hen, as she scudded past
between the islands ; and if ever there was peace and tranquillity in the world it was just there !   Well, I put down my
pack in the leaves, for I did n't like to see or think of it,
and I stretched myself down at the water's edge, and I fell
into a fit of musing.   It 's often and often I tried to remember the elegant fancies that came through my head, and the
beautiful things that I thought I saw that night out on the
lake fornint me !   Ye see I was fresh and fastin' ; I never
tasted a bit the whole day, and my brain, maybe, was all
the better ; for somehow janius, real janius, thrives best on a
little starvation.   And from musing I fell off asleep ; and it
was the sound of voices near that first awoke me !   For a minute or two I believed I was dreaming, the words came so softly

to my ear, for they were spoken in a low, gentle voice, and blended in with the slight splash of oars that moved through the water carefully, as though not to lose a word of him that was speakin'.

" It's clean beyond *me* to tell you what he said; and, maybe, if I could, ye would n't be able to follow it, for he was discoorsin' about night and the moon, and all that various poets said about them; ye 'd think that he had books, and was reading out of them, so glibly came the verses from his lips. I never listened to such a voice before, so soft, so sweet, so musical, and the words came droppin' down, like the clear water filterin' over a rocky ledge, and glitterin' like little spangles over moss and wild-flowers.

" It was n't only in English but Scotch ballads, too, and once or twice in Italian that he recited, till at last he gave out, in all the fulness of his liquid voice, them elegant lines out of Pope's Homer : --

> "' As when the moon, refulgent lamp of night,
> O'er heaven's clear azure spreads her sacred light,
> When not a breath disturbs the deep serene,
> And not a cloud o'ercasts the solemn scene,
> Around her throne the vivid planets roll,
> And stars unnumbered gild the glowing pole :
> O'er the dark trees a yellower verdure shed,
> And top with silver every mountain's head ;
> Then shine the vales ; the rocks in prospect rise —
> A flood of glory bursts from all the skies;
> The conscious swains, rejoicing in the sight,
> Eye the blue vault and bless the useful light.'

" The Lord forgive me, but when he came to the last words and said, ' useful light,' I could n't restrain myself, but broke out, ' That 's mighty like a bull, anyhow, and reminds me of the ould song, —

> "' Good luck to the moon, she 's a fine noble creature,
> And gives us the daylight all night in the dark.'

" Before I knew where I was, the boat glided in to the steps, and a tall man, a little stooped in the shoulders, stood before me.

" ' Is it you,' said he, with a quiet laugh, ' that accuses Pope of a bull?'

" 'It is,' says I; 'and, what's more, there isn't a poet
from Horace downwards that I won't show bulls in; there's
bulls in Shakspeare and in Milton; there's bulls in the
ancients; I'll point out a bull in Aristophanes.'

" 'What have we here?' said he, turning to the others.

" 'A poor crayture,' says I, 'like Goldsmith's chest of
drawers, —

" 'With brains reduced a double debt to pay,
        To dream by night, sell Sheffield ware by day.'

" Well, with that he took a fit of laughing, and handing
the rest out of the boat, he made me come along at his side,
discoorsin' me about my thravels, and all I seen, and all I
read, till we reached an elegant little cottage on a bank
right over the lake; and then he brought me in and made
me take tay with the family; and I spent the night there;
and when I started the next morning there wasn't a 'screed'
of my pack that they didn't buy, penknives, and whistles,
and nut-crackers, and all, just, as they said, for keepsakes.
Good luck to them, and happy hearts, wherever they are,
for they made mine happy that day; ay, and for many an
hour afterwards, when I just think over their kind words
and pleasant faces.' "

More than one of the company had dropped off asleep
during Billy's narrative, and of the others, their complaisance
as listeners appeared taxed to the utmost, while the Corporal
snored loudly, like a man who had a right to indulge himself
to the fullest extent.

" There's the bell again," muttered one, " that's from
the 'lord's room;' " and Craggs, starting up by the instinct
of his office, hastened off to his master's chamber.

" My lord says you are to remain here," said he, as he
re-entered a few minutes later; " he is satisfied with your
skill, and I'm to send off a messenger to the post, to let
them know he has detained you."

" I'm obaydient," said Billy, with a low bow; " and now
for a brief repose!"   And so saying, he drew a long woollen
nightcap from his pocket, and putting it over his eyes, resigned himself to sleep with the practised air of one who
needed but very little preparation to secure slumber.

CHAPTER IV.

THE old Castle of Glencore contained but one spacious room, and this served all the purposes of drawing-room, dining-room, and library. It was a long and lofty chamber, with a raftered ceiling, from which a heavy chandelier hung by a massive chain of iron. Six windows, all in the same wall, deeply set and narrow, admitted a sparing light. In the opposite wall stood two fireplaces, large, massive, and monumental, the carved supporters of the richly-chased pediment being of colossal size, and the great shield of the house crowning the pyramid of strange and uncouth objects that were grouped below. The walls were partly occupied by bookshelves, partly covered by wainscot, and here and there displayed a worn-out portrait of some bygone warrior or dame, who little dreamed how much the color of their effigies should be indebted to the sad effects of damp and mildew. The furniture consisted of every imaginable type, from the carved oak and ebony console to the white and gold of Versailles taste, and the modern compromise of comfort with ugliness which chintz and soft cushions accomplish. Two great screens, thickly covered with prints and drawings, most of them political caricatures of some fifty years back, flanked each fireplace, making, as it were, in this case two different apartments.

At one of those, on a low sofa, sat, or rather lay, Lord Glencore, pale and wasted by long illness. His thin hand held a letter, to shade his eyes from the blazing wood-fire, and the other hand hung listlessly at his side. The expression of the sick man's face was that of deep melancholy — not the mere gloom of recent suffering, but the deep-cut traces of a long-carried affliction, a sorrow which had eaten into his very heart, and made its home there.

At the second fireplace sat his son, and, though a mere
boy, the lineaments of his father marked the youth's face
with a painful exactness. The same intensity was in the
eyes, the same haughty character sat on the brow; and
there was in the whole countenance the most extraordinary
counterpart of the gloomy seriousness of the older face. He
had been reading, but the fast-falling night obliged him to
desist, and he sat now contemplating the bright embers of
the wood fire in dreamy thought. Once or twice was he
disturbed from his revery by the whispered voice of an old
serving-man, asking for something with that submissive
manner assumed by those who are continually exposed to
the outbreaks of another's temper; and at last the boy, who
had hitherto scarcely deigned to notice the appeals to him,
flung a bunch of keys contemptuously on the ground, with a
muttered malediction on his tormentor.

"What's that?" cried out the sick man, startled at the
sound.

"'T is nothing, my lord, but the keys that fell out of
my hand," replied the old man, humbly. "Mr. Craggs is
away to Leenane, and I was going to get out the wine for
dinner."

"Where's Mr. Charles?" asked Lord Glencore.

"He's there beyant," muttered the other, in a low voice,
while he pointed towards the distant fireplace; "but he looks
tired and weary, and I did n't like to disturb him."

"Tired! weary! — with what? Where has he been;
what has he been doing?" cried he, hastily. "Charles,
Charles, I say!"

And slowly rising from his seat, and with an air of languid
indifference, the boy came towards him.

Lord Glencore's face darkened as he gazed on him.

"Where have you been?" asked he, sternly.

"Yonder," said the boy, in an accent like the echo of his
own.

"There's Mr. Craggs, now, my lord," said the old butler,
as he looked out of the window, and eagerly seized the
opportunity to interrupt the scene; "there he is, and a
gentleman with him."

"Ha! go and meet him, Charles, — it's Harcourt. Go

and receive him, show him his room, and then bring him here to me."

The boy heard without a word, and left the room with the same slow step and the same look of apathy. Just as he reached the hall the stranger was entering it. He was a tall, well-built man, with the mingled ease and stiffness of a soldier in his bearing; his face was handsome, but somewhat stern, and his voice had that tone which implies the long habit of command.

"You're a Massy, that I'll swear to," said he, frankly, as he shook the boy's hand; "the family face in every lineament. And how is your father?"

"Better; he has had a severe illness."

"So his letter told me. I was up the Rhine when I received it, and started at once for Ireland."

"He has been very impatient for your coming," said the boy; "he has talked of nothing else."

"Ay, we are old friends. Glencore and I have been schoolfellows, chums at college, and messmates in the same regiment," said he, with a slight touch of sorrow in his tone. "Will he be able to see me now? Is he confined to bed?"

"No, he will dine with you. I'm to show you your room, and then bring you to him."

"That's better news than I hoped for, boy. By the way, what's your name?"

"Charles Conyngham."

"To be sure, Charles; how could I have forgotten it! So, Charles, this is to be my quarters; and a glorious view there is from this window. What's the mountain yonder?"

"Ben Creggan."

"We must climb that summit some of these days, Charley. I hope you're a good walker. You shall be my guide through this wild region here, for I have a passion for explorings."

And he talked away rapidly, while he made a brief toilet, and refreshed himself from the fatigues of the road.

"Now, Charley, I am at your orders; let us descend to the drawing-room."

"You'll find my father there," said the boy, as he stopped

short at the door; and Harcourt, staring at him for a second or two in silence, turned the handle and entered.

Lord Glencore never turned his head as the other drew nigh, but sat with his forehead resting on the table, extending his hand only in welcome.

"My poor fellow!" said Harcourt, grasping the thin and wasted fingers, — "my poor fellow, how glad I am to be with you again!" And he seated himself at his side as he spoke. "You had a relapse after you wrote to me?"

Glencore slowly raised his head, and, pushing back a small velvet skull-cap that he wore, said, —

"You'd not have known me, George. Eh? see how gray I am! I saw myself in the glass to-day for the first time, and I really could n't believe my eyes."

"In another week the change will be just as great the other way. It was some kind of a fever, was it not?"

"I believe so," said the other, sighing.

"And they bled you and blistered you, of course. These fellows are like the farriers — they have but the one system for everything. Who was your torturer; where did you get him from?"

"A practitioner of the neighborhood, the wild growth of the mountain," said Glencore, with a sickly smile; "but I must n't be ungrateful; he saved my life, if that be a cause for gratitude."

"And a right good one, I take it. How like you that boy is, Glencore! I started back when he met me. It was just as if I was transported again to old school-days, and had seen yourself as you used to be long ago. Do you remember the long meadow, Glencore?"

"Harcourt," said he, falteringly, "don't talk to me of long ago, — at least not now;" and then, as if thinking aloud, added, "How strange that a man without a hope should like the future better than the past!"

"How old is Charley?" asked Harcourt, anxious to engage him on some other theme.

"He'll be fifteen, I think, his next birthday; he seems older, does n't he?"

"Yes, the boy is well grown and athletic. What has he been doing — have you had him at a school?"

"At a school!" said Glencore, starting; "no, he has lived always here with myself. I have been his tutor; I read with him every day, till that illness seized me."

"He looks clever; is he so?"

"Like the rest of us, George, he may learn, but he can't be taught. The old obstinacy of the race is strong in him, and to rouse him to rebel all you have to do is to give him a task; but his faculties are good, his apprehension quick, and his memory, if he would but tax it, excellent. Here's Craggs come to tell us of dinner; give me your arm, George, we have n't far to go — this one room serves us for everything."

"You 're better lodged than I expected — your letters told me to look for a mere barrack; and the place stands so well."

"Yes, the spot was well chosen, although I suppose its founders cared little enough about the picturesque."

The dinner-table was spread behind one of the massive screens, and, under the careful direction of Craggs and old Simon, was well and amply supplied, — fish and game, the delicacies of other localities, being here in abundance. Harcourt had a traveller's appetite, and enjoyed himself thoroughly, while Glencore never touched a morsel, and the boy ate sparingly, watching the stranger with that intense curiosity which comes of living estranged from all society.

"Charley will treat you to a bottle of Burgundy, Harcourt," said Glencore, as they drew round the fire; "he keeps the cellar key."

"Let us have two, Charley," said Harcourt, as the boy arose to leave the room, "and take care that you carry them steadily."

The boy stood for a second and looked at his father, as if interrogating, and then a sudden flush suffused his face as Glencore made a gesture with his hand for him to go.

"You don't perceive how you touched him to the quick there, Harcourt? You talked to him as to how he should carry the wine; he thought that office menial and beneath him, and he looked at me to know what he should do."

"What a fool you have made of the boy!" said Harcourt, bluntly. "By Jove! it was time I should come here!"

When the boy came back he was followed by the old butler, carefully carrying in a small wicker contrivance, *Hibernicè* called a cooper, three cobwebbed and well-crusted bottles.

" Now, Charley," said Harcourt, gayly, " if you want to see a man thoroughly happy, just step up to my room and fetch me a small leather sack you 'll find there of tobacco, and on the dressing-table you 'll see my meerschaum pipe ; be cautious with it, for it belonged to no less a man than Poniatowski, the poor fellow who died at Leipsic."

The lad stood again irresolute and confused, when a signal from his father motioned him away to acquit the errand.

" Thank you," said Harcourt, as he re-entered ; " you see I am not vain of my meerschaum without reason. The carving of that bull is a work of real art ; and if you were a connoisseur in such matters, you 'd say the color was perfect. Have you given up smoking, Glencore? — you used to be fond of a weed."

" I care but little for it," said Glencore, sighing.

" Take to it again, my dear fellow, if only that it is a bond 'tween yourself and every one who whiffs his cloud. There are wonderfully few habits — I was going to say enjoyments, and I might say so, but I 'll call them habits — that consort so well with every condition and every circumstance of life, that become the prince and the peasant, suit the garden of the palace and the red watch-fire of the bivouac, relieve the weary hours of a calm at sea, or refresh the tired hunter in the prairies."

" You must tell Charley some of your adventures in the West. — The Colonel has passed two years in the Rocky Mountains," said Glencore to his son.

" Ay, Charley, I have knocked about the world as much as most men, and seen, too, my share of its wonders. If accidents by sea and land can interest you, if you care for stories of Indian life and the wild habits of a prairie hunter, I 'm your man. Your father can tell you more of *salons* and the great world, of what may be termed the high game of life —"

" I have forgotten it, as much as if I had never seen it,"

said Glencore, interrupting, and with a severity of voice that showed the theme displeased him. And now a pause ensued, painful perhaps to the others, but scarcely felt by Harcourt, as he smoked away peacefully, and seemed lost in the windings of his own fancies.

" Have you shooting here, Glencore?" asked he at length.

" There might be, if I were to preserve the game."

" And you do not. Do you fish?"

" No; never."

" You give yourself up to farming, then?"

" Not even that; the truth is, Harcourt, I literally do nothing. A few newspapers, a stray review or so, reach me in these solitudes, and keep me in a measure informed as to the course of events; but Charley and I con over our classics together, and scrawl sheets of paper with algebraic signs, and puzzle our heads over strange formulas, wonderfully indifferent to what the world is doing at the other side of this little estuary."

" You of all men living to lead such a life as this! a fellow that never could cram occupation enough into his short twenty-four hours," broke in Harcourt.

Glencore's pale cheek flushed slightly, and an impatient movement of his fingers on the table showed how ill he relished any allusion to his own former life.

" Charley will show you to-morrow all the wonders of our erudition, Harcourt," said he, changing the subject; " we have got to think ourselves very learned, and I hope you'll be polite enough not to undeceive us."

" You'll have a merciful critic, Charley," said the Colonel, laughing, " for more reasons than one. Had the question been how to track a wolf or wind an antelope, to outmanœuvre a scout party or harpoon a calf-whale, I'd not yield to many; but if you throw me amongst Greek roots or double equations, I'm only Samson with his hair *en crop!*"

The solemn clock over the mantelpiece struck ten, and the boy arose as it ceased.

" That's Charley's bedtime," said Glencore, " and we are determined to make no stranger of you, George. He'll say good-night."

And with a manner of mingled shyness and pride the
boy held out his hand, which the soldier shook cordially,
saying, —

"To-morrow, then, Charley, I count upon you for my
day, and so that it be not to be passed in the library I'll
acquit myself creditably."

"I like your boy, Glencore," said he, as soon as they
were alone. "Of course I have seen very little of him;
and if I had seen more I should be but a sorry judge of
what people would call his abilities. But he is a good stamp:
'Gentleman' is written on him in a hand that any can read;
and, by Jove! let them talk as they will, but that's half the
battle of life!"

"He is a strange fellow; you'll not understand him in a
moment," said Glencore, smiling half sadly to himself.

"Not understand him, Glencore? I read him like print,
man. You think that his shy, bashful manner imposes upon
me; not a bit of it; I see the fellow is as proud as Lucifer.
All your solitude and estrangement from the world haven't
driven out of his head that he's to be a Viscount one of
these days; and somehow, wherever he has picked it up, he
has got a very pretty notion of the importance and rank that
same title confers."

"Let us not speak of this now, Harcourt; I'm far too
weak to enter upon what it would lead to. It is, however,
the great reason for which I entreated you to come here.
And to-morrow — at all events in a day or two — we can
speak of it fully. And now I must leave you. You'll have
to rough it here, George; but as there is no man can do so
with a better grace, I can spare my apologies; only, I beg,
don't let the place be worse than it need be. Give your
orders; get what you can; and see if your tact and knowledge of life cannot remedy many a difficulty which our
ignorance or apathy have served to perpetuate."

"I'll take the command of the garrison with pleasure,"
said Harcourt, filling up his glass, and replenishing the fire.
"And now a good night's rest to you, for I half suspect I
have already jeopardied some of it."

The old campaigner sat till long past midnight. The
generous wine, his pipe, the cheerful wood-fire, were all

companionable enough, and well suited thoughts which took no high or heroic range, but were chiefly reveries of the past, — some sad, some pleasant, but all tinged with the one philosophy, which made him regard the world as a campaign, wherein he who grumbles or repines is but a sorry soldier, and unworthy of his cloth.

It was not till the last glass was drained that he arose to seek his bed, and presently humming some old air to himself, he slowly mounted the stairs to his chamber.

CHAPTER V.

COLONEL HARCOURT'S LETTER.

As we desire throughout this tale to make the actors themselves, wherever it be possible, the narrators, using their words in preference to our own, we shall now place before the reader a letter written by Colonel Harcourt about a week after his arrival at Glencore, which will at least serve to rescue him and ourselves from the task of repetition.

It was addressed to Sir Horace Upton, Her Majesty's Envoy at Stuttgard, one who had formerly served in the same regiment with Glencore and himself, but who left the army early to follow the career of diplomacy, wherein, still a young man, he had risen to the rank of a minister. It is not important, at this moment, to speak more particularly of his character, than that it was in almost every respect the opposite of his correspondent's. Where the one was frank, open, and unguarded, the other was cold, cautious, and reserved; where one believed, the other doubted; where one was hopeful, the other had nothing but misgivings. Harcourt would have twenty times a day wounded the feelings, or jarred against the susceptibility, of his best friend; Upton could not be brought to trench upon the slightest prejudice of his greatest enemy. We might continue this contrast to every detail of their characters; but enough has now been said, and we proceed to the letter in question:

GLENCORE CASTLE.

DEAR UPTON, — True to my promise to give you early tidings of our old friend, I sit down to pen a few lines, which if a rickety table and some infernal lampblack for ink should make illegible, you'll have to wait for the elucidation till my arrival. I found Glencore terribly altered; I'd not have known him. He used to be muscular and rather full in habit; he is now a mere skeleton. His hair and mustache were coal black; they are a motley gray.

He was straight as an arrow — pretentiously erect, many thought; he is stooped now, and bent nearly double. His voice, too, the most clear and ringing in the squadron, is become a hoarse whisper. You remember what a passion he had for dress, and how heartily we all deplored the chance of his being colonel, well knowing what precious caprices of costly costume would be the consequence; well, a discharged corporal in a cast-off mufti is stylish compared to him. I don't think he has a hat — I have only seen an oilskin cap; but his coat, his one coat, is a curiosity of industrious patchwork; and his trousers are a pair of our old overalls, the same pattern we wore at Hounslow when the King reviewed us.

Great as these changes are, they are nothing to the alteration in the poor fellow's disposition. He that was generous to munificence is now an absolute miser, descending to the most pitiful economy and moaning over every trifling outlay. He is irritable, too, to a degree. Far from the jolly, light-hearted comrade, ready to join in the laugh against himself, and enjoy a jest of which he was the object, he suspects a slight in every allusion, and bristles up to resent a mere familiarity as though it were an insult.

Of course I put much of this down to the score of illness, and of bad health before he was so ill; but, depend upon it, he's not the man we knew him. Heaven knows if he ever will be so again. The night I arrived here he was more natural, more like himself, in fact, than he has ever been since. His manner was heartier, and in his welcome there was a touch of the old jovial good fellow, who never was so happy as when sharing his quarters with a comrade. Since that he has grown punctilious, anxiously asking me if I am comfortable, and teasing me with apologies for what I don't miss, and excuses about things that I should never have discovered wanting.

I think I see what is passing within him; he wants to be confidential, and he does n't know how to go about it. I suppose he looks on me as rather a rough father to confess to; he is n't quite sure what kind of sympathy, if any, he 'll meet with from me, and he more than half dreads a certain careless, outspoken way in which I have now and then addressed his boy, of whom more anon.

I may be right, or I may be wrong, in this conjecture; but certain it is, that nothing like confidential conversation has yet passed between us, and each day seems to render the prospect of such only less and less likely. I wish from my heart you were here; you are just the fellow to suit him, — just calculated to nourish the susceptibilities that *I* only shock. I said as much t' other day, in a half-careless way, and he immediately caught it up, and said,

"Ay, George, Upton is a man one wants now and then in life, and when the moment comes, there is no such thing as a substitute for him." In a joking manner, I then remarked, "Why not come over to see him?" "Leave this!" cried he; "venture in the world again; expose myself to its brutal insolence, or still more brutal pity!" In a torrent of passion, he went on in this strain, till I heartily regretted that I had ever touched this unlucky topic.

I date his greatest reserve from that same moment; and I am sure he is disposed to connect me with the casual suggestion to go over to Stuttgard, and deems me, in consequence, one utterly deficient in all true feeling and delicacy.

I need n't tell you that my stay here is the reverse of a pleasure. I'm never what fine people call bored anywhere; and I could amuse myself gloriously in this queer spot. I have shot some half-dozen seals, hooked the heaviest salmon I ever saw rise to a fly, and have had rare coursing, — not to say that Glencore's table, with certain reforms I have introduced, is very tolerable, and his cellar unimpeachable. I'll back his chambertin against your Excellency's, and I have discovered a bin of red hermitage that would convert a whole vineyard of the smallest Lafitte into Sneyd's claret; but with all these seductions, I can't stand the life of continued restraint I 'm reduced to. Glencore evidently sent for me to make some revelations, which, now that he sees me, he cannot accomplish. For aught I know, there may be as many changes in *me* to *his* eyes as to *mine* there are in *him*. I only can vouch for it, that if I ride three stone heavier, I have n't the worse place, and I don't detect any striking falling off in my appreciation of good fare and good fellows.

I spoke of the boy: he is a fine lad, — somewhat haughty, perhaps; a little spoiled by the country people calling him the young lord; but a generous fellow, and very like Glencore when he first joined us at Canterbury. By way of educating him himself, Glencore has been driving Virgil and decimal fractions into him; and the boy, bred in the country, — never out of it for a day, — can't load a gun or tie a hackle. Not the worst thing about the lad is his inordinate love for Glencore, whom he imagines to be about the greatest and most gifted being that ever lived. I can scarcely help smiling at the implicitness of this honest faith; but I take good care not to smile: on the contrary, I give every possible encouragement to the belief. I conclude the disenchantment will arrive only too early at last.

You 'll not know what to make of such a lengthy epistle from me, and you 'll doubtless torture that fine diplomatic intelligence of yours to detect the secret motive of my long-windedness; but the simple fact is, it has rained incessantly for the last three days, and promises the same cheering weather for as many more. Glencore does n't fancy that the boy's lessons should be broken in upon, and *hinc istæ litteræ*, — that 's classical for you.

I wish I could say when I am likely to beat my retreat. I 'd stay — not very willingly, perhaps, but still I 'd stay — if I thought myself of any use; but I cannot persuade myself that I am such. Glencore is now about again, feeble of course, and much pulled down, but able to go about the house and the garden. I can contribute nothing to his recovery, and I fear as little to his comfort. I even doubt if he desires me to prolong my visit ; but such is my fear of offending him, that I actually dread to allude to my departure, till I can sound my way as to how he 'll take it. This fact alone will show you how much he is changed from the Glencore of long ago. Another feature in him, totally unlike his former self, struck me the other evening. We were talking of old messmates — Croydon, Stanhope, Loftus, and yourself — and instead of dwelling, as he once would have done, exclusively on your traits of character and disposition, he discussed nothing but your abilities, and the capacity by which you could win your way to honors and distinction. I need n't say how, in such a valuation, you came off best. Indeed, he professes the highest esteem for your talents, and says, " You 'll see Upton either a cabinet minister or ambassador at Paris yet ; " and this he repeated in the same words last night, as if to show it was not dropped as a mere random observation.

I have some scruples about venturing to offer anything bordering on a suggestion to a great and wily diplomatist like yourself ; but if an illustrious framer of treaties and protocols would condescend to take a hint from an old dragoon colonel, I 'd say that a few lines from your crafty pen might possibly unlock this poor fellow's heart, and lead him to unburthen to *you* what he evidently cannot persuade himself to reveal to *me.* I can see plainly enough that there is something on his mind ; but I know it just as a stupid old hound feels there is a fox in the cover, but cannot for the life of him see how he 's to "draw" him.

A letter from you would do him good, at all events ; even the little gossip of your gossiping career would cheer and amuse him. He said very plaintively, two nights ago, " They 've all forgotten me. When a man retires from the world he begins to die, and the great event, after all, is only the *coup de grace* to a long agony of torture." Do write to him, then ; the address is "Glencore Castle, Leenane, Ireland," where, I suppose, I shall be still a resident for another fortnight to come.

Glencore has just sent for me ; but I must close this for the post, or it will be too late.

Yours ever truly,
GEORGE HARCOURT.

I open this to say that he sent for me to ask your address, — whether through the Foreign Office, or direct to Stuttgard. You'll probably not hear for some days, for he writes with extreme difficulty, and I leave it to your wise discretion to write to him or not in the interval.

Poor fellow, he looks very ill to-day. He says that he never slept the whole night, and that the laudanum he took to induce drowsiness only excited and maddened him. I counselled a hot jorum of mulled porter before getting into bed; but he deemed me a monster for the recommendation, and seemed quite disgusted besides. Could n't you send him over a despatch? I think such a document from Stuttgard ought to be an unfailing soporific.

CHAPTER VI.

QUEER COMPANIONSHIP.

WHEN Harcourt repaired to Glencore's bedroom, where he still lay, wearied and feverish after a bad night, he was struck by the signs of suffering in the sick man's face. The cheeks were bloodless and fallen in, the lips pinched, and in the eyes there shone that unnatural brilliancy which results from an over-wrought and over-excited brain.

"Sit down here, George," said he, pointing to a chair beside the bed; "I want to talk to you. I thought every day that I could muster courage for what I wish to say; but somehow, when the time arrived, I felt like a criminal who entreats for a few hours more of life, even though it be a life of misery."

"It strikes me that you were never less equal to the effort than now," said Harcourt, laying his hand on the other's pulse.

"Don't believe my pulse, George," said Glencore, smiling faintly. "The machine may work badly, but it has wonderful holding out. I've gone through enough," added he, gloomily, "to kill most men, and here I am still, breathing and suffering."

"This place doesn't suit you, Glencore. There are not above two days in the month you can venture to take the air."

"And where would you have me go, sir?" he broke in, fiercely. "Would you advise Paris and the Boulevards, or a palace in the Piazza di Spagna at Rome; or perhaps the Chiaja at Naples would be public enough? Is it that I may parade disgrace and infamy through Europe that I should leave this solitude?"

" I want to see you in a better climate, Glencore, — in a place where the sun shines occasionally."

" This suits me," said the other, bluntly; " and here I have the security that none can invade, — none molest me. But it is not of myself I wish to speak, — it is of my boy."

Harcourt made no reply, but sat patiently to listen to what was coming.

" It is time to think of him," added Glencore, slowly. " The other day, — it seems but the other day, — and he was a mere child; a few years more, — to seem when past like a long dreary night, — and he will be a man."

" Very true," said Harcourt; " and Charley is one of those fellows who only make one plunge from the boy into all the responsibilities of manhood. Throw him into a college at Oxford, or the mess of a regiment to-morrow, and this day week you'll not know him from the rest."

Glencore was silent; if he had heard, he never noticed Harcourt's remark.

" Has he ever spoken to you about himself, Harcourt?" asked he, after a pause.

" Never, except when I led the subject in that direction; and even then reluctantly, as though it were a topic he would avoid."

" Have you discovered any strong inclination in him for a particular kind of life, or any career in preference to another?"

" None; and if I were only to credit what I see of him, I'd say that this dull monotony and this dreary uneventful existence is what he likes best of all the world."

" You really think so?" cried Glencore, with an eagerness that seemed out of proportion to the remark.

" So far as I see," rejoined Harcourt, guardedly, and not wishing to let his observation carry graver consequences than he might suspect.

" So that you deem him capable of passing a life of a quiet, unambitious tenor, — neither seeking for distinctions nor fretting after honors?"

" How should he know of their existence, Glencore?

What has the boy ever heard of life and its struggles? It's not in Homer or Sallust he'd learn the strife of parties and public men."

" And why need he ever know them?" broke in Glencore, fiercely.

" If he does n't know them now, he's sure to be taught them hereafter. A young fellow who will succeed to a title and a good fortune — "

" Stop, Harcourt!" cried Glencore, passionately. " Has anything of this kind ever escaped you in intercourse with the boy?"

" Not a word — not a syllable."

" Has he himself ever, by a hint, or by a chance word, implied that he was aware of — "

Glencore faltered and hesitated, for the word he sought for did not present itself. Harcourt, however, released him from all embarrassment by saying, —

" With me the boy is rarely anything but a listener; he hears me talk away of tiger-shooting and buffalo-hunting, scarcely ever interrupting me with a question. But I can see in his manner with the country people, when they salute him, and call him ' my lord ' — "

" But he is not ' my lord.'" broke in Glencore.

" Of course he is not; that I am well aware of."

" He never will — never shall be," cried Glencore, in a voice to which a long pent-up passion imparted a terrible energy.

" How! — what do you mean, Glencore?" said Harcourt, eagerly. " Has he any malady; is there any deadly taint?"

" That there is. by Heaven!" cried the sick man. grasping the curtain with one hand, while he held the other firmly clenched upon his forehead, — " a taint, the deadliest that can stain a human heart! Talk of station, rank, title — what are they, if they are to be coupled with shame, ignominy, and sorrow? The loud voice of the herald calls his father Sixth Viscount of Glencore, but a still louder voice proclaims his mother a — "

With a wild burst of hysteric laughter, he threw himself, face downwards, on the bed; and now scream after scream burst from him, till the room was filled by the servants, in the midst of whom appeared Billy, who had only that same day returned from Leenane, whither he had gone to make a formal resignation of his functions as letter-carrier.

"This is nothing but an '*accessio nervosa*,'" said Billy; "clear the room, ladies and gentlemen, and lave me with the patient." And Harcourt gave the signal for obedience by first taking his departure.

Lord Glencore's attack was more serious than at first it was apprehended, and for three days there was every threat of a relapse of his late fever; but Billy's skill was once more successful, and on the fourth day he declared that the danger was past. During this period, Harcourt's attention was for the first time drawn to the strange creature who officiated as the doctor, and who, in despite of all the detracting influences of his humble garb and mean attire, aspired to be treated with the deference due to a great physician.

"If it's the crown and the sceptre makes the king," said he, "'t is the same with the science that makes the doctor; and no man can be despised when he has a rag of ould Galen's mantle to cover his shoulders."

"So you're going to take blood from him?" asked Harcourt, as he met him on the stairs, where he had awaited his coming one night when it was late.

"No, sir; 't is more a disturbance of the great nervous centres than any derangement of the heart and arteries," said Billy, pompously; "that's what shows a real doctor, — to distinguish between the effects of excitement and inflammation, which is as different as fireworks is from a bombardment."

"Not a bad simile, Master Billy; come in and drink a glass of brandy-and-water with me," said Harcourt, right glad at the prospect of such companionship.

Billy Traynor, too, was flattered by the invitation, and seated himself at the fire with an air at once proud and submissive.

"You've a difficult patient to treat there," said Harcourt, when he had furnished his companion with a pipe, and twice filled his glass; "he's hard to manage, I take it?"

" Yer' right," said Billy; " every touch is a blow, every breath of air is a hurricane with him. There's no such thing as traitin' a man of that timperament; it's the same with many of them ould families as with our racehorses, — they breed them too fine."

" Egad! I think you are right," said Harcourt, pleased with an illustration that suited his own modes of thinking.

" Yes, sir," said Billy, gaining confidence by the approval; " a man is a mã-chine, and all the parts ought to be balanced, and, as the ancients say, *in equilibrio*. If pre-ponderance here or there, whether it be brain or spinal marrow, cardiac functions or digestive ones, you disthroy him, and make that dangerous kind of constitution that, like a horse with a hard mouth, or a boat with a weather helm, always runs to one side."

" That's well put, well explained," said Harcourt, who really thought the illustration appropriate.

" Now, my lord there," continued Billy, " is all out of balance, every bit of him. Bleed him, and he sinks; stimulate him, and he goes ragin' mad. 'T is their physical conformation makes their character; and to know how to cure them in sickness, one ought to have some knowledge of them in health."

" How came you to know all this? You are a very remarkable fellow, Billy."

" I am, sir; I'm a phenumenon in a small way. And many people thinks, when they see and convarse with me, what a pity it is I hav' n't the advantages of edication and instruction; and that's just where they're wrong, — complately wrong."

" Well, I confess I don't perceive that."

" I'll show you, then. There's a kind of janius natural to men like myself, — in Ireland I mean, for I never heerd of it elsewhere, — that's just like our Irish emerald or Irish diamond, — wonderful if one considers where you find it, astonishin' if you only think how azy it is to get, but a regular disappointment, a downright take-in, if you intend to have it cut and polished and set. No, sir; with all the care and culture in life, you'll never make a precious stone of it!"

"You've not taken the right way to convince me, by using such an illustration, Billy."

"I'll try another, then," said Billy. "We are like Willy-the-Whisps, showing plenty of light where there's no road to travel, but of no manner of use on the highway, or in the dark streets of a village where one has business."

"Your own services here are the refutation to your argument, Billy," said Harcourt, filling his glass.

"'T is your kindness to say so, sir," said Billy, with gratified pride; "but the sacrat was, he thrusted me, — that was the whole of it. All the miracles of physic is confidence, just as all the magic of eloquence is conviction."

"You have reflected profoundly, I see," said Harcourt.

"I made a great many observations at one time of my life, — the opportunity was favorable."

"When and how was that?"

"I travelled with a baste caravan for two years, sir; and there's nothing taches one to know mankind like the study of bastes!"

"Not complimentary to humanity, certainly," said Harcourt, laughing.

"Yes, but it is, though; for it is by a con-sideration of the *feræ naturæ* that you get at the raal nature of mere animal existence. You see there man in the rough, as a body might say, just as he was turned out of the first workshop, and before he was infiltrated with the *divinus afflatus*, the ethereal essence, that makes him the first of creation. There's all the qualities, good and bad, — love, hate, vengeance, gratitude, grief, joy, ay, and mirth, — there they are in the brutes; but they're in no subjection, except by fear. Now, it's out of man's motives his character is moulded, and fear is only one amongst them. D'ye apprehend me?"

"Perfectly; fill your pipe." And he pushed the tobacco towards him.

"I will; and I'll drink the memory of the great and good man that first intro-duced the weed amongst us — Here's Sir Walter Raleigh! By the same token, I was in his house last week."

"In his house! where?"

"Down at Greyhall. You Englishmen, savin' your presence, always forget that many of your celebrities lived years in Ireland; for it was the same long ago as now, — a place of decent banishment for men of janius, a kind of straw-yard where ye turned out your intellectual hunters till the sayson came on at home."

" I 'm sorry to see, Billy, that, with all your enlightenment, you have the vulgar prejudice against the Saxon."

" And that 's the rayson I have it, because it is vulgar," said Billy, eagerly. " Vulgar means popular, common to many; and what 's the best test of truth in anything but universal belief, or whatever comes nearest to it? I wish I was in Parliament — I just wish I was there the first night one of the nobs calls out ' That 's vulgar; ' and I 'd just say to him, ' Is there anything as vulgar as men and women? Show me one good thing in life that is n't vulgar! Show me an object a painter copies, or a poet describes, that is n't so!' Ayeh," cried he, impatiently, " when they wanted a hard word to fling at us, why did n't they take the right one?"

" But you are unjust, Billy; the ungenerous tone you speak of is fast disappearing. Gentlemen nowadays use no disparaging epithets to men poorer or less happily cir-cumstanced than themselves."

" Faix," said Billy, " it is n't sitting here at the same table with yourself that I ought to gainsay that remark."

And Harcourt was so struck by the air of good breeding in which he spoke, that he grasped his hand, and shook it warmly.

" And what is more," continued Billy, " from this day out I 'll never think so."

He drank off his glass as he spoke, giving to the libation all the ceremony of a solemn vow.

" D' ye hear that? — them 's oars; there 's a boat coming in."

" You have sharp hearing, master," said Harcourt, laughing.

" I got the gift when I was a smuggler," replied he. " I could put my ear to the ground of a still night, and tell you the tramp of a revenue boot as well as if I seen it. And now I 'll lay sixpence it 's Pat Morissy is at the bow oar there; he rows with a short jerking stroke there's no timing. That's himself, and it must be something urgent from the post-office that brings him over the lough to-night."

The words were scarcely spoken when Craggs entered with a letter in his hand.

"This is for you, Colonel," said he; "it was marked 'immediate,' and the post-mistress despatched it by an express."

The letter was a very brief one; but, in honor to the writer, we shall give it a chapter to itself.

CHAPTER VII.

A GREAT DIPLOMATIST.

My dear Harcourt, — I arrived here yesterday, and by good fortune caught your letter at F. O., where it was awaiting the departure of the messenger for Germany.

Your account of poor Glencore is most distressing. At the same time, my knowledge of the man and his temper in a measure prepared me for it. You say that he wishes to see me, and intends to write. Now, there is a small business matter between us, which his lawyer seems much disposed to push on to a difficulty, if not to worse. To prevent this, if possible, — at all events to see whether a visit from me might not be serviceable, — I shall cross over to Ireland on Tuesday, and be with you by Friday, or at latest Saturday. Tell him that I am coming, but only for a day. My engagements are such that I must be here again early in the following week. On Thursday I go down to Windsor.

There is wonderfully little stirring here, but I keep that little for our meeting. You are aware, my dear friend, what a poor, shattered, broken-down fellow I am; so that I need not ask you to give me a comfortable quarter for my one night, and some shell-fish, if easily procurable, for my one dinner.

Yours, ever and faithfully,

H. U.

We have already told our reader that the note was a brief one, and yet was it not altogether uncharacteristic. Sir Horace Upton — it will spare us both some repetition if we present him at once — was one of a very composite order of human architecture; a kind of being, in fact, of which many would deny the existence, till they met and knew them, so full of contradictions, real and apparent, was his nature. Chivalrous in sentiment and cunning in action, noble in aspiration and utterly sceptical as regards motives, one half of his temperament was the antidote to the other. Fastidious to a painful extent in matters of taste, he was simplicity itself in all the requirements of his life; and with all a courtier's love of great people, not only tolerating, but actually preferring the society of men beneath him. In person he was tall, and with that air of distinction in his manner that belongs only to those who unite natural graces with long habits of high society. His features were finely formed, and would have been strikingly handsome, were the expression not spoiled by a look of astuteness, — a something that implied a tendency to overreach, — which marred their repose and injured their uniformity. Not that his manner ever betrayed this weakness; far from it, — his was a most polished courtesy. It was impossible to conceive an address more bland or more conciliating. His very gestures, his voice, languid by a slight habit of indisposition, seemed as though exerted above their strength in the desire to please, and making the object of his attentions to feel himself the mark of peculiar honor. There ran through all his nature, through everything he did or said or thought, a certain haughty humility, which served, while it assigned an humble place to himself, to mark out one still more humble for those about him. There were not many things he could not do; indeed, he had actually done most of those which win honor and distinction in life. He had achieved a very gallant but brief military career in India, made a most brilliant opening in Parliament, where his abilities at once marked him out for office, was suspected to be the writer of the cleverest political satire, and more than suspected to be the author of " the novel " of the day. With all this, he had great social success. He was deep enough for a ministerial dinner, and " fast " enough for a party of young Guardsmen at Greenwich. With women, too, he was especially a favorite; there was a Machiavelian subtlety which he could throw into small things, a mode of making the veriest trifles little Chinese puzzles of ingenuity, that flattered and amused them. In a word, he had great adaptiveness, and it was a quality he indulged less for the gratification of others than for the pleasure it afforded himself.

He had mixed largely in society, not only of his own, but of every country of Europe. He knew every chord of that complex instrument which people call the world, like a master; and although a certain jaded and wearied look, a tone of exhaustion and fatigue, seemed to say that he was tired of it all, that he had found it barren and worthless, the real truth was, he enjoyed life to the full as much as on the first day in which he entered it; and for this simple reason, — that he had started with an humble opinion of mankind, their hopes, fears, and ambitions, and so he continued, not disappointed, to the end.

The most governing notion of his own life was an impression that he had a disease of the chest, some subtle and mysterious affection which had defied the doctors, and would go on to defy them to the last. He had been dangerously wounded in the Burmese war, and attributed the origin of his malady to this cause. Others there were who said that the want of recognition to his services in that campaign was the direst of all the injuries he had received. And true it was, a most brilliant career had met with neither honors nor advancement, and Upton left the service in disgust, carrying away with him only the lingering sufferings of his wound. To suggest to him that his malady had any affinity to any known affection was to outrage him, since the mere supposition would reduce him to a species of equality with some one else, — a thought infinitely worse than any mere physical suffering; and, indeed, to avoid this shocking possibility, he vacillated as to the locality of his disorder, making it now in the lung, now in the heart, at one time in the bronchial tubes, at another in the valves of the aorta. It was his pleasure to consult for this complaint every great physician of Europe, and not alone consult, but commit himself to their direction, and this with a credulity which he could scarcely have summoned in any other cause.

It was difficult to say how far he himself believed in this disorder, — the pressure of any momentous event, the necessity of action, never finding him unequal to any effort, no matter how onerous. Give him a difficulty, — a minister to outwit, a secret scheme to unravel, a false move to profit by, — and he rose above all his pulmonary symptoms, and could exert himself with a degree of power and perseverance that very few men could equal, none surpass. Indeed it

4

seemed as though he kept this malady for the pastime of idle
hours, as other men do a novel or a newspaper, but would
never permit it to interfere with the graver business of life.

We have, perhaps, been prolix in our description; but we
have felt it the more requisite to be thus diffuse, since the
studious simplicity which marked all his manner might have
deceived our reader, and which the impression of his mere
words have failed to convey.

"You will be glad to hear Upton is in England, Glencore," said Harcourt, as the sick man was assisted to his
seat in the library, "and, what is more, intends to pay you a
visit."

"Upton coming here!" exclaimed Glencore, with an
expression of mingled astonishment and confusion; "how
do you know that?"

"He writes me from Long's to say that he'll be with us
by Friday, or, if not, by Saturday."

"What a miserable place to receive him!" exclaimed
Glencore. "As for you, Harcourt, you know how to rough
it, and have bivouacked too often under the stars to care
much for satin curtains. But think of Upton here! How is
he to eat, where is he to sleep?"

"By Jove! we'll treat him handsomely. Don't you fret
yourself about his comforts; besides, I've seen a great deal
of Upton, and, with all his fastidiousness and refinement,
he's a thorough good fellow at taking things for the best.
Invite him to Chatsworth, and the chances are he'll find
fault with twenty things,—with the place, the cookery, and
the servants; but take him down to the Highlands, lodge
him in a shieling, with bannocks for breakfast and a Fyne
herring for supper, and I'll wager my life you'll not see a
ruffle in his temper, nor hear a word of impatience out of his
mouth."

"I know that he is a well-bred gentleman," said Glencore, half pettishly; "but I have no fancy for putting his
good manners to a severe test, particularly at the cost of my
own feelings."

"I tell you again he shall be admirably treated; he shall
have my room; and, as for his dinner, Master Billy and I
are going to make a raid amongst the lobster-pots. And

what with turbot, oysters, grouse-pie, and mountain mutton, I'll make the diplomatist sorrow that he is not accredited to some native sovereign in the Arran islands, instead of some 'mere German Hertzog.' He can only stay one day."

"One day!"

"That's all; he is over head and ears in business, and he goes down to Windsor on Thursday, so that there is no help for it."

"I wish I may be strong enough; I hope to Heaven that I may rally —" Glencore stopped suddenly as he got thus far, but the agitation the words cost him seemed most painful.

"I say again, don't distress yourself about Upton, — leave the care of entertaining him to *me*. I'll vouch for it that he leaves us well satisfied with his welcome."

"It was not of *that* I was thinking," said he, impatiently; "I have much to say to him, — things of great importance. It may be that I shall be unequal to the effort; I cannot answer for my strength for a day, — not for an hour. Could you not write to him, and ask him to defer his coming till such time as he can spare me a week, or at least some days?"

"My dear Glencore, you know the man well, and that we are lucky if we can have him on his *own* terms, not to think of imposing *ours*; he is sure to have a number of engagements while he is in England."

"Well, be it so," said Glencore, sighing, with the air of a man resigning himself to an inevitable necessity.

CHAPTER VIII.

"Not come, Craggs!" said Harcourt, as late on the Saturday evening the Corporal stepped on shore, after crossing the lough.

"No, sir, no sign of him. I sent a boy away to the top of 'the Devil's Mother,' where you have a view of the road for eight miles, but there was nothing to be seen."

"You left orders at the post-office to have a boat in readiness if he arrived?"

"Yes, Colonel," said he, with a military salute; and Harcourt now turned moodily towards the Castle.

Glencore had scarcely ever been a very cheery residence, but latterly it had become far gloomier than before. Since the night of Lord Glencore's sudden illness, there had grown up a degree of constraint between the two friends which to a man of Harcourt's disposition was positive torture. They seldom met, save at dinner, and then their reserve was painfully evident.

The boy, too, in unconscious imitation of his father, grew more and more distant; and poor Harcourt saw himself in that position, of all others the most intolerable, — the unwilling guest of an unwilling host.

"Come or not come," muttered he to himself, "I'll bear this no longer. There is, besides, no reason why I should bear it. I'm of no use to the poor fellow; he does not want, he never sees me. If anything, my presence is irksome to him; so that, happen what will, I'll start to-morrow, or next day at farthest."

He was one of those men to whom deliberation on any subject was no small labor, but who, once that they have come to a decision, feel as if they had acquitted a debt, and

need give themselves no further trouble in the matter. In
the enjoyment of this newly purchased immunity he entered
the room where Glencore sat impatiently awaiting him.

"Another disappointment!" said the Viscount, anxiously.

"Yes; Craggs has just returned, and says there's no sign
of a carriage for miles on the Oughterard road."

"I ought to have known it," said the other, in a voice of
guttural sternness. "He was ever the same; an appointment with him was an engagement meant only to be binding
on those who expected him."

"Who can say what may have detained him? He was
in London on business, — public business, too; and even if
he had left town, how many chance delays there are in
travelling."

"I have said every one of these things over to myself,
Harcourt; but they don't satisfy me. This is a habit
with Upton. I've seen him do the same with his Colonel,
when he was a subaltern; I've heard of his arrival late to
a Court dinner, and only smiling at the dismay of the
horrified courtiers."

"Egad," said Harcourt, bluntly, "I don't see the advantage of the practice. One is so certain of doing fifty
things in this daily life to annoy one's friends, through
mere inadvertence or forgetfulness, that I think it is but
sorry fun to incur their ill-will by malice prepense."

"That is precisely why he does it."

"Come, come, Glencore; old Rixson was right when he
said, 'Heaven help the man whose merits are canvassed
while they wait dinner for him.' I'll order up the soup, for
if we wait any longer we'll discover Upton to be the most
graceless vagabond that ever walked."

"I know his qualities, good and bad," said Glencore,
rising, and pacing the room with slow, uncertain steps;
"few men know him better. None need tell me of his
abilities; none need instruct me as to his faults. What
others do by accident, *he* does by design. He started in
life by examining how much the world would bear from
him; he has gone on, profiting by the experience, and
improving on the practice."

"Well, if I don't mistake me much, he'll soon appear to

plead his own cause. I hear oars coming speedily in this direction."

And so saying, Harcourt hurried away to resolve his doubts at once. As he reached the little jetty, over which a large signal-fire threw a strong red light, he perceived that he was correct, and was just in time to grasp Upton's hand as he stepped on shore.

"How picturesque all this, Harcourt," said he, in his soft, low voice; "a leaf out of 'Rob Roy.' Well, am I not the mirror of punctuality, eh?"

"We looked for you yesterday, and Glencore has been so impatient."

"Of course he has; it is the vice of your men who do nothing. How is he? Does he dine with us? Fritz, take care those leather pillows are properly aired, and see that my bath is ready by ten o'clock. Give me your arm, Harcourt; what a blessing it is to be such a strong fellow!"

"So it is, by Jove! I am always thankful for it. And you — how do you get on? You look well."

"Do I?" said he, faintly, and pushing back his hair with an almost fine-ladylike affectation. "I'm glad you say so. It always rallies me a little to hear I'm better. You had my letter about the fish?"

"Ay, and I'll give you such a treat."

"No, no. my dear Harcourt; a fried mackerel, or a whiting and a few crumbs of bread, — nothing more."

"If you insist, it shall be so; but I promise you I'll not be of your mess, that's all. This is a glorious spot for turbot — and such oysters!"

"Oysters are forbidden me, and don't let me have the torture of temptation. What a charming place this seems to be! — very wild, very rugged."

"Wild — rugged! I should think it is," muttered Harcourt.

"This pathway, though, does not bespeak much care. I wish our friend yonder would hold his lantern a little lower. How I envy you the kind of life you lead here, — so tranquil, so removed from all bores! By the way, you get the newspapers tolerably regularly?"

"Yes, every day."

"That's all right. If there be a luxury left to any man

after the age of forty, it is to be let alone. It's the best thing I know of. What a terrible bit of road! They might have made a pathway."

" Come, don't grow faint-hearted. Here we are; this is Glencore."

" Wait a moment. Just let him raise that lantern. Really this is very striking — a very striking scene altogether. The doorway excellent, and that little watch-tower, with its lone-star light, a perfect picture."

" You 'll have time enough to admire all this; and we are keeping poor Glencore waiting," said Harcourt, impatiently.

" Very true; so we are."

" Glencore's son, Upton," said Harcourt, presenting the boy, who stood, half pride, half bashfulness, in the porch.

" My dear boy, you see one of your father's oldest friends in the world," said Upton, throwing one arm on the boy's shoulder, apparently caressing, but as much to aid himself in ascending the stair. " I'm charmed with your old Schloss here, my dear," said he, as they moved along. " Modern architects cannot attain the massive simplicity of these structures. They have a kind of confectionery style with false ornament, and inappropriate decoration, that bears about the same relation to the original that a suit of Drury Lane tinfoil does to a coat of Milanese mail armor. This gallery is in excellent taste."

And as he spoke, the door in front of him opened, and the pale, sorrow-struck, and sickly figure of Glencore stood before him. Upton, with all his self-command, could scarcely repress an exclamation at the sight of one whom he had seen last in all the pride of youth and great personal powers; while Glencore, with the instinctive acuteness of his morbid temperament, as quickly saw the impression he had produced, and said, with a deep sigh, —

" Ay, Horace, a sad wreck."

" Not so, my dear fellow," said the other, taking the thin, cold hand within both his own; " as seaworthy as ever, after a little dry-docking and refitting. It is only a craft like that yonder," and he pointed to Harcourt, " that can keep the sea in all weathers, and never care for the carpenter. You and I are of another build."

" And you — how are you?" asked Glencore, relieved to turn attention away from himself, while he drew his arm within the other's.

" The same poor ailing mortal you always knew me," said Upton, languidly; " doomed to a life of uncongenial labor, condemned to climates totally unsuited to me, I drag along existence, only astonished at the trouble I take to live, knowing pretty well as I do what life is worth."

" 'Jolly companions every one!' By Jove!" said Harcourt, " for a pair of fellows who were born on the sunny side of the road, I must say you are marvellous instances of gratitude."

" That excellent hippopotamus," said Upton, " has no thought for any calamity if it does not derange his digestion! How glad I am to see the soup! Now, Glencore, you shall witness no invalid's appetite."

As the dinner proceeded, the tone of the conversation grew gradually lighter and pleasanter. Upton had only to permit his powers to take their free course to be agreeable, and now talked away on whatever came uppermost, with a charming union of reflectiveness and repartee. If a very rigid purist might take occasional Gallicisms in expression, and a constant leaning to French modes of thought, none could fail to be delighted with the graceful ease with which he wandered from theme to theme, adorning each with some trait of that originality which was his chief characteristic. Harcourt was pleased without well knowing how or why, while to Glencore it brought back the memory of the days of happy intercourse with the world, and all the brilliant hours of that polished circle in which he had lived. To the pleasure, then, which his powers conferred, there succeeded an impression of deep melancholy, so deep as to attract the notice of Harcourt, who hastily asked, —

" If he felt ill?"

" Not worse," said he, faintly, " but weak — weary; and I know Upton will forgive me if I say good-night."

" What a wreck indeed!" exclaimed Upton, as Glencore left the room with his son. " I'd not have known him."

" And yet until the last half-hour I have not seen him so

well for weeks past. I 'm afraid something you said about Alicia Villars affected him," said Harcourt.

"My dear Harcourt, how young you are in all these things," said Upton, as he lighted his cigarette. "A poor heart-stricken fellow, like Glencore, no more cares for what *you* would think a painful allusion, than an old weather-beaten sailor would for a breezy morning on the Downs at Brighton. His own sorrows lie too deeply moored to be disturbed by the light winds that ruffle the surface. And to think that all this is a woman's doing! Is n't that what's passing in your mind, eh, most gallant Colonel?"

"By Jove, and so it was! They were the very words I was on the point of uttering," said Harcourt, half nettled at the ease with which the other read him.

"And of course you understand the source of the sorrow?"

"I 'm not quite so sure of that," said Harcourt, more and more piqued at the tone of bantering superiority with which the other spoke.

"Yes, you do, Harcourt; I know you better than you know yourself. Your thoughts were these: Here 's a fellow with a title, a good name, good looks, and a fine fortune, going out of the world of a broken heart, and all for a woman!"

"You knew her," said Harcourt, anxious to divert the discussion from himself.

"Intimately. Ninetta della Torre was the belle of Florence — what am I saying? of all Italy — when Glencore met her, about eighteen years ago. The Palazzo della Torre was the best house in Florence. The old Prince, her grandfather, — her father was killed in the Russian campaign, — was spending the last remnant of an immense fortune in every species of extravagance. Entertainments that surpassed those of the Pitti Palace in splendor, fêtes that cost fabulous sums, banquets voluptuous as those of ancient Rome, were things of weekly occurrence. Of course every foreigner, with any pretension to distinction, sought to be presented there, and we English happened just at that moment to stand tolerably high in Italian estimation. I am speaking of some eighteen or twenty years back, before we sent out that swarm of domestic economists who, under the somewhat erroneous notion of foreign cheapness, by a system of incessant higgle and bargain, cutting down every one's demand to the measure of their own pockets, end by making the word 'Englishman' a synonym for all that is mean, shabby, and contemptible. The English of that day were of another class; and assuredly their characteristics, as regards munificence and high dealing, must have been strongly impressed upon the minds of foreigners, seeing how their successors, very different people, have contrived to trade upon the mere memory of these qualities ever since."

"Which all means that 'my lord' stood cheating better than those who came after him," said Harcourt, bluntly.

"He did so; and precisely for that very reason he conveyed the notion of a people who do not place money in the first rank of all their speculations, and who aspire to no luxury that they have not a just right to enjoy. But to come back to Glencore. He soon became a favored guest at the Palazzo della Torre. His rank, name, and station, combined with very remarkable personal qualities, obtained for him a high place in the old Prince's favor, and Ninetta deigned to accord him a little more notice than she bestowed on any one else. I have, in the course of my career, had occasion to obtain a near view of royal personages and their habits, and I can say with certainty that never in any station, no matter how exalted, have I seen as haughty a spirit as in that girl. To the pride of her birth, rank, and splendid mode of life were added the consciousness of her surpassing beauty, and the graceful charm of a manner quite unequalled. She was incomparably superior to all around her, and, strangely enough, she did not offend by the bold assertion of this superiority. It seemed her due, and no more. Nor was it the assumption of mere flattered beauty. Her house was the resort of persons of the very highest station, and in the midst of them — some even of royal blood — she exacted all the deference and all the homage that she required from others."

"And they accorded it?" asked Harcourt, half contemptuously.

"They did; and so had you also if you had been in

their place! Believe me, most gallant Colonel, there is a wide difference between the empty pretension of mere vanity and the daring assumption of conscious power. This girl saw the influence she wielded. As she moved amongst us she beheld the homage, not always willing, that awaited her. She felt that she had but to distinguish any one man there, and he became for the time as illustrious as though touched by the sword or ennobled by the star of his sovereign. The courtier-like attitude of men, in the presence of a very beautiful woman, is a spectacle full of interest. In the homage vouchsafed to mere rank there enters always a sense of humiliation, and in the observances of respect men tender to royalty, the idea of vassalage presents itself most prominently; whereas in the other case, the chivalrous devotion is not alloyed by this meaner servitude, and men never lift their heads more haughtily than after they have bowed them in lowly deference to loveliness."

A thick, short snort from Harcourt here startled the speaker, who, inspired by the sounds of his own voice and the flowing periods he uttered, had fallen into one of those paroxysms of loquacity which now and then befell him. That his audience should have thought him tiresome or prosy, would, indeed, have seemed to him something strange; but that his hearer should have gone off asleep, was almost incredible.

"It is quite true," said Upton to himself; "he snores 'like a warrior taking his rest.' What wonderful gifts some fellows are endowed with! and, to enjoy life, there is none of them all like dulness. Can you show me to my room?" said he, as Craggs answered his ring at the bell.

The Corporal bowed an assent.

"The Colonel usually retires early, I suppose?" said Upton.

"Yes, sir; at ten to a minute."

"Ah! it is one — nearly half-past one — now, I perceive," said he, looking at his watch. "That accounts for his drowsiness," muttered he, between his teeth. "Curious vegetables are these old campaigners. Wish him good night for me when he awakes, will you?"

And so saying, he proceeded on his way, with all that lassitude and exhaustion which it was his custom to throw into every act which demanded the slightest exertion.

" Any more stairs to mount, Mr. Craggs?" said he, with a bland but sickly smile.

" Yes, sir; two flights more."

" Oh, dear! could n't you have disposed of me on the lower floor? — I don't care where or how, but something that requires no climbing. It matters little, however, for I'm only here for a day."

" We could fit up a small room, sir, off the library."

" Do so, then. A most humane thought; for if I *should* remain another night — Not at it yet?" cried he, peevishly, at the aspect of an almost perpendicular stair before him.

" This is the last flight, sir; and you'll have a splendid view for your trouble, when you awake in the morning."

" There is no view ever repaid the toil of an ascent, Mr. Craggs, whether it be to an attic or the Righi. Would you kindly tell my servant, Mr. Schöfer, where to find me, and let him fetch the pillows, and put a little rosemary in a glass of water in the room, — it corrects the odor of the night-lamp. And I should like my coffee early, — say at seven, though I don't wish to be disturbed afterwards. Thank you, Mr. Craggs, — good-night. Oh! one thing more. You have a doctor here: would you just mention to him that I should like to see him to-morrow about nine or half-past? Good night, good night."

And with a smile worthy of bestowal upon a court beauty, and a gentle inclination of the head, the very ideal of gracefulness, Sir Horace dismissed Mr. Craggs, and closed the door.

CHAPTER IX.

Mr. Schöfer moved through the dimly lighted chamber with all the cat-like stealthiness of an accomplished valet, arranging the various articles of his master's wardrobe, and giving, so far as he was able, the semblance of an accustomed spot to this new and strange locality. Already, indeed, it was very unlike what it had been during Harcourt's occupation. Guns, whips, fishing-tackle, dog-leashes, and landing-nets had all disappeared, as well as uncouth specimens of costume for boating or the chase; and in their place were displayed all the accessories of an elaborate toilet, laid out with a degree of pomp and ostentation somewhat in contrast to the place. A richly embroidered dressing-gown lay on the back of a chair, before which stood a pair of velvet slippers worked in gold. On the table in front of these, a whole regiment of bottles, of varied shape and color, were ranged, the contents being curious essences and delicate odors, every one of which entered into some peculiar stage of that elaborate process Sir Horace Upton went through, each morning of his life, as a preparation for the toils of the day.

Adjoining the bed stood a smaller table, covered with various medicaments, tinctures, essences, infusions, and extracts, whose subtle qualities he was well skilled in, and but for whose timely assistance he would not have believed himself capable of surviving throughout the day. Beside these was a bulky file of prescriptions, the learned documents of doctors of every country of Europe, all of whom had enjoyed their little sunshine of favor, and all of whom had ended by "mistaking his case." These had now been placed in readiness for the approaching consultation with "Glencore's doctor;" and Mr. Schöfer still glided noiselessly from place to place, preparing for that event.

" I'm not asleep, Fritz," said a weak, plaintive voice from the bed. " Let me have my aconite, — eighteen drops; a full dose to-day, for this journey has brought back the pains."

" Yes, Excellenz," said Fritz, in a voice of broken accentuation.

" I slept badly," continued his master, in the same complaining tone. " The sea beat so heavily against the rocks, and the eternal plash, plash, all night irritated and worried me. Are you giving me the right tincture?"

" Yes, Excellenz," was the brief reply.

" You have seen the doctor, — what is he like, Fritz?"

A strange grimace and a shrug of the shoulders were Mr. Schöfer's only answer.

" I thought as much," said Upton, with a heavy sigh. " They called him the wild growth of the mountains last night, and I fancied what that was like to prove. Is he young?"

A shake of the head implied not.

" Nor old?"

Another similar movement answered the question.

" Give me a comb, Fritz, and fetch the glass here." And now Sir Horace arranged his silky hair more becomingly, and having exchanged one or two smiles with his image in the mirror, lay back on the pillow, saying, " Tell him I am ready to see him."

Mr. Schöfer proceeded to the door, and at once presented the obsequious figure of Billy Traynor, who, having heard some details of the rank and quality of his new patient, made his approaches with a most deferential humility. It was true, Billy knew that my Lord Glencore's rank was above that of Sir Horace, but to his eyes there was the far higher distinction of a man of undoubted ability, — a great speaker, a great writer, a great diplomatist; and Billy Traynor, for the first time in his life, found himself in the presence of one whose claims to distinction stood upon the lofty basis of personal superiority. Now, though bashfulness was not the chief characteristic of his nature, he really

felt abashed and timid as he drew near the bed, and shrank
under the quick but searching glance of the sick man's cold
gray eyes.

"Place a chair, and leave us, Fritz," said Sir Horace;
and then, turning slowly round, smiled as he said, "I'm
happy to make your acquaintance, sir. My friend, Lord
Glencore, has told me with what skill you treated him, and
I embrace the fortunate occasion to profit by your profes-
sional ability."

"I'm your humble slave, sir," said Billy, with a deep,
rich brogue; and the manner of the speaker, and his accent,
seemed so to surprise Upton that he continued to stare at
him fixedly for some seconds without speaking.

"You studied in Scotland, I believe?" said he, with one
of the most engaging smiles, while he hazarded the question.

"Indeed, then, I did not, sir," said Billy, with a heavy
sigh; "all I know of the *ars medicātrix* I picked up, —
currendo per campos, — as one may say, vagabondizing
through life, and watching my opportunities. Nature gave
me the Hippocratic turn, and I did my best to improve it."

"So that you never took out a regular diploma?" said Sir
Horace, with another and still blander smile.

"Sorra one, sir! I'm a doctor just as a man is a poet, —
by sheer janius! 'T is the study of nature makes both one
and the other; that is, when there's the raal stuff, — the
divinus afflatus, — inside. Without you have that, you're
only a rhymester or a quack."

"You would, then, trace a parallel between them?" said
Upton, graciously.

"To be sure, sir! Ould Heyric says that the poet and the
physician is one: —

> "'For he who reads the clouded skies,
> And knows the utterings of the deep,
> Can surely see in human eyes
> The sorrows that so heart-locked sleep.'

The human system is just a kind of universe of its own;
and the very same faculties that investigate the laws of
nature in one case is good in the other."

"I don't think the author of 'King Arthur' supports your
theory," said Upton, gently.

" Blackmoor was an ass; but maybe he was as great a bosthoon in physic as in poetry," rejoined Billy, promptly.

" Well, Doctor," said Sir Horace, with one of those plaintive sighs in which he habitually opened the narrative of his own suffering, " let us descend to meaner things, and talk of myself. You see before you one who, in some degree, is the reproach of medicine. That file of prescriptions beside you will show that I have consulted almost every celebrity in Europe; and that I have done so unsuccessfully, it is only necessary that you should look on these worn looks — these wasted fingers — this sickly, feeble frame. Vouchsafe me a patient hearing for a few moments, while I give you some insight into one of the most intricate cases, perhaps, that has ever engaged the faculty."

It is not our intention to follow Sir Horace through his statement, which in reality comprised a sketch of half the ills that the flesh is heir to. Maladies of heart, brain, liver, lungs, the nerves, the arteries, even the bones, contributed their aid to swell the dreary catalogue, which, indeed, contained the usual contradictions and exaggerations incidental to such histories. We could not assuredly expect from our reader the patient attention with which Billy listened to this narrative. Never by a word did he interrupt the description; not even a syllable escaped him as he sat; and even when Sir Horace had finished speaking, he remained with slightly drooped head and clasped hands in deep meditation.

" It's a strange thing," said he, at last; " but the more I see of the aristocracy, the more I 'm convinced that they ought to have doctors for themselves alone, just as they have their own tailors and coachmakers, — chaps that could devote themselves to the study of physic for the peerage, and never think of any other disorders but them that befall people of rank. Your mistake, Sir Horace, was in consulting the regular middle-class practitioner, who invariably imagined there must be a disease to treat."

" And you set me down as a hypochondriac, then," said Upton, smiling.

" Nothing of the kind! You have a malady, sure enough, but nothing organic. 'T is the oceans of tinctures, the

sieves full of pills, the quarter-casks of bitters you're takin',
has played the divil with you. The human machine is like
a clock, and it depends on the proportion the parts bear to
each other, whether it keeps time. You may make the
spring too strong, or the chain too thick, or the balance too
heavy for the rest of the works, and spoil everything just by
over security. That's what your doctors was doing with
their tonics and cordials. They didn't see, here's a poor
washy frame, with a wake circulation and no vigor. If we
nourish him, his heart will go quicker, to be sure; but what
will his brain be at? There's the rub! His brain will
begin to go fast too, and already it's going the pace. 'T is
soothin' and calmin' you want; allaying the irritability of
an irrascible, fretful nature, always on the watch for self-
torment. Say-bathin', early hours, a quiet mopin' kind of
life. that would, maybe, tend to torpor and sleepiness, —
them's the first things you need; and for exercise, a little
work in the garden that you'd take interest in."

"And no physic?" asked Sir Horace.

"Sorra screed! not as much as a powder or a draught,
—barrin'," said he, suddenly catching the altered expression of the sick man's face. "a little mixture of hyoscya-
mus I'll compound for you myself. This, and friction over
the region of the heart, with a mild embrocation, is all my
tratement!"

"And you have hopes of my recovery?" asked Sir
Horace, faintly.

"My name isn't Billy Traynor if I'd not send you out
of this hale and hearty before two months. I read you like
a printed book."

"You really give me great confidence. for I perceive you
understand the tone of my temperament. Let us try this
same embrocation at once; I'll most implicitly obey you
in everything."

"My head on a block, then, but I'll cure you," said
Billy, who determined that no scruples on his side should
mar the trust reposed in him by the patient. "But you
must give yourself entirely up to me: not only as to your
eatin' and drinkin', but your hours of recreation and study,
exercise, amusement, and all, must be at my biddin'. It is

5

the principle of harmony between the moral and physical
nature constitutes the whole secret of my system. To be
stimulatin' the nerves, and lavin' the arteries dormant, is
like playing a jig to minuet time, — all must move in simul-
taneous action; and the cerebellum, the great flywheel of
the whole, must be made to keep orderly time. D'ye
mind?"

"I follow you with great interest," said Sir Horace, to
whose subtle nature there was an intense pleasure in the
thought of having discovered what he deemed a man of
original genius under this unpromising exterior. "There is
but one bar to these arrangements: I must leave this at
once; I ought to go to-day. I must be off to-morrow."

"Then I'll not take the helm when I can't pilot you
through the shoals," said Billy. "To begin my system,
and see you go away before I developed my grand invigo-
ratin' arcanum, would be only to destroy your confidence in
an elegant discovery."

"Were I only as certain as you seem to be ——" began
Sir Horace, and then stopped.

"You'd stay and be cured, you were goin' to say. Well,
if you didn't feel that same trust in me, you'd be right to
go; for it is that very confidence that turns the balance.
Ould Babbington used to say that between a good physician
and a bad one there was just the difference between a pound
and a guinea. But between the one you trust and the one
you don't, there's all the way between Billy Traynor and
the Bank of Ireland!"

"On that score every advantage is with you," said Upton,
with all the winning grace of his incomparable manner;
"and I must now bethink me how I can manage to prolong
my stay here." And with this he fell into a musing fit, letting drop occasionally some stray word or two, to mark the
current of his thoughts: "The Duke of Headwater's on
the thirteenth; Ardroath Castle the Tuesday after; More-
hampton for the Derby day. These easily disposed of.
Prince Boratinsky, about that Warsaw affair, must be attended to; a letter, yes, a letter, will keep that question
open. Lady Grencliffe *is* a difficulty; if I plead illness,
she'll say I'm not strong enough to go to Russia. I'll think

it over." And with this he rested his head on his hands, and sank into profound reflection. " Yes, Doctor," said he, at length, as though summing up his secret calculations, "health is the first requisite. If you can but restore me, you will be — I am above the mere personal consideration — you will be the means of conferring an important service on the King's Government. A variety of questions, some of them deep and intricate, are now pending, of which I alone understand the secret meaning. A new hand would infallibly spoil the game ; and yet, in my present condition, how could I hear the fatigues of long interviews, ministerial deliberations, incessant note-writing, and evasive conversations ? "

" Utterly unpossible ! " exclaimed the doctor.

" As you observe, it is utterly impossible," rejoined Sir Horace, with one of his own dubious smiles ; and then, in a manner more natural, resumed : " We public men have the sad necessity of concealing the sufferings on which others trade for sympathy. We must never confess to an ache or a pain, lest it be rumored that we are unequal to the fatigues of office ; and so is it that we are condemned to run the race with broken health and shattered frame, alleging all the while that no exertion is too much, no effort too great for us."

" And maybe, after all, it 's that very struggle that makes you more than common men," said Billy. " There 's a kind of irritability that keeps the brain at stretch, and renders it equal to higher efforts than ever accompany good everyday health. Dyspepsia is the soul of a prose-writer, and a slight ossification of the aortic valves is a great help to the imagination."

" Do you really say so ? " asked Sir Horace, with all the implicit confidence with which he accepted any marvel that had its origin in medicine.

" Don't you feel it yourself, sir ? " asked Billy. " Do you ever pen a reply to a knotty state-paper as nately as when you 've the heartburn ? — are you ever as epigrammatic as when you 're driven to a listen slipper ? — and when do you give a minister a jobation as purtily as when you are laborin' under a slight indigestion ? Not that it would sarve a man to be permanently in gout or the colic; but for a spurt like a cavalry charge, there's nothing like eatin' something that disagrees with you."

"An ingenious notion," said the diplomatist, smiling.

"And now I'll take my lave," said Billy, rising. "I'm going out to gather some mountain-colchicum and sorrel, to make a diaphoretic infusion; and I've to give Master Charles his Greek lesson; and blister the colt, — he's thrown out a bone spavin; and, after that, Handy Carr's daughter has the shakin' ague, and the smith at the forge is to be bled, — all before two o'clock, when ' the lord' sends for me. But the rest of the day, and the night too, I'm your honor's obaydient."

And with a low bow, repeated in a more reverential manner at the door, Billy took his leave and retired.

CHAPTER X.

A DISCLOSURE.

"HAVE you seen Upton?" asked Glencore eagerly of Harcourt as he entered his bedroom.

"Yes; he vouchsafed me an audience during his toilet, just as the old kings of France were accustomed to honor a favorite with one."

"And is he full of miseries at the dreary place, the rough fare and deplorable resources of this wild spot?"

"Quite the reverse; he is charmed with everything and everybody. The view from his window is glorious; the air has already invigorated him. For years he has not break-fasted with the same appetite; and he finds that of all the places he has ever chanced upon, this is the one veritable exact spot which suits him."

"This is very kind on his part," said Glencore, with a faint smile. "Will the humor last, Harcourt? That is the question."

"I trust it will, — at least it may well endure for the short period he means to stay; although already he has extended that, and intends remaining till next week."

"Better still," said Glencore, with more animation of voice and manner. "I was already growing nervous about the brief space in which I was to crowd in all that I want to say to him; but if he will consent to wait a day or two, I hope I shall be equal to it."

"In his present mood there is no impatience to be off; on the contrary, he has been inquiring as to all the available means of locomotion, and by what convenience he is to make various sea and land excursions."

"We have no carriage, — we have no roads, even," said Glencore, peevishly.

" He knows all that; but he is concerting measures about
a certain turf-kish, I think they call it, which, by the aid of
pillows to lie on, and donkeys to drag, can be made a most
useful vehicle; while, for longer excursions, he has suggested a ' conveniency ' of wheels and axles to the punt,
rendering it equally eligible on land or water.   Then he has
been designing great improvements in horticulture, and giving orders about a rake, a spade, and a hoe for himself.
I 'm quite serious," said Harcourt, as Glencore smiled with a
kind of droll incredulity.   " It is perfectly true; and as he
hears that the messenger occasionally crosses the lough to
the post, when there are no letters there, he hints at a
little simple telegraph for Leenane, which should announce
what the mail contains, and which might be made useful to
convey other intelligence.   In fact, all *my* changes here will
be as for nothing to *his* reforms, and between us you 'll not
know your own house again, if you even be able to live
in it."

" You have already done much to make it more habitable,
Harcourt," said Glencore, feelingly; " and if I had not the
grace to thank you for it, I 'm not the less grateful.   To say
truth, my old friend, I half doubted whether it was an act
of friendship to attach me ever so lightly to a life of which
I am well weary.   Ceasing as I have done for years back to
feel interest in anything, I dread whatever may again recall
me to the world of hopes and fears, — that agitated sea of
passion wherein I have no longer vigor to contend.   To
speak to me, then, of plans to carry out, schemes to accomplish, was to point to a future of activity and exertion; and
I " — here he dropped his voice to a deep and mournful
tone — " can have but one future, — the dark and dreary
one before the grave!"

Harcourt was too deeply impressed by the solemnity of
these words to venture on a reply, and he sat silently contemplating the sorrow-struck but placid features of the sick
man.

" There is nothing to prevent a man struggling, and successfully too, against mere adverse fortune," continued
Glencore.   " I feel at times that if I had been suddenly
reduced to actual beggary, — left without a shilling in the

world, — there are many ways in which I could eke out
subsistence. A great defeat to my personal ambition I
could resist. The casualty that should exclude me from a
proud position and public life, I could bear up against with
patience, and I hope with dignity. Loss of fortune, loss
of influence, loss of station, loss of health even, dearer
than them all, can be borne. There is but one intolerable
ill, one that no time alleviates, no casuistry diminishes, —
loss of honor! Ay, Harcourt, rank and riches do little for
him who feels himself the inferior of the meanest that elbows
him in a crowd; and the man whose name is a scoff and a
jibe has but one part to fill, — to make himself forgotten."

"I hope I'm not deficient in a sense of personal honor,
Glencore," said Harcourt; "but I must say that I think
your reasoning on this point is untenable and wrong."

"Let us not speak more of it," said Glencore, faintly.
"I know not how I have been led to allude to what it is
better to bear in secret than to confide even to friendship;"
and he pressed the strong fingers of the other as he spoke,
in his own feeble grasp. "Leave me now, Harcourt, and
send Upton here. It may be that the time is come when I
shall be able to speak to him."

"You are too weak to-day, Glencore, — too much agitated.
Pray defer this interview."

"No, Harcourt; these are my moments of strength.
The little energy now left to me is the fruit of strong excitement. Heaven knows how I shall be to-morrow."

Harcourt made no further opposition, but left the room in
search of Upton.

It was full an hour later when Sir Horace Upton made his
appearance in Glencore's chamber, attired in a purple dressing-gown, profusely braided with gold, loose trousers as
richly brocaded, and a pair of real Turkish slippers, resplen-
dent with costly embroidery; a small fez of blue velvet, with
a deep gold tassel, covered the top of his head, at either side
of which his soft silky hair descended in long massy waves,
apparently negligently, but in reality arranged with all the
artistic regard to effect of a consummate master. From the
gold girdle at his waist depended a watch, a bunch of keys,
a Turkish purse, an embroidered tobacco-bag, a gorgeously

chased smelling-bottle, and a small stiletto, with a topaz handle. In one hand he carried a meerschaum, the other leaned upon a cane, and with all the dependence of one who could not walk without its aid. The greeting was cordial and affectionate on both sides; and when Sir Horace, after a variety of preparations to ensure his comfort, at length seated himself beside the bed, his features beamed with all their wonted gentleness and kindness.

"I'm charmed at what Harcourt has been telling me, Upton," said Glencore; "and that you really can exist in all the savagery of this wild spot."

"I'm in ecstasy with the place, Glencore. My memory cannot recall the same sensations of health and vigor I have experienced since I came here. Your cook is first-rate; your fare is exquisite; the quiet is a positive blessing; and that queer creature, your doctor, is a very remarkable genius."

"So he is," said Glencore, gravely.

"One of those men of original mould who leave cultivation leagues behind, and arrive at truth by a bound."

"He certainly treated me with considerable skill."

"I'm satisfied of it; his conversation is replete with shrewd and intelligent observation, and he seems to have studied his art more like a philosopher than a mere physician of the schools. And depend upon it, Glencore, the curative art must mainly depend upon the secret instinct which divines the malady, less by the rigid rules of acquired skill than by that prerogative of genius, which, however exerted, arrives at its goal at once. Our conversation had scarcely lasted a quarter of an hour, when he revealed to me the exact seat of all my sufferings, and the most perfect picture of my temperament. And then his suggestions as to treatment were all so reasonable, so well argued."

"A clever fellow, no doubt of it," said Glencore.

"But he is far more than that, Glencore. Cleverness is only a manufacturing quality, — that man supplies the raw article also. It has often struck me as very singular that such heads are not found in *our* class, — they belong to another order altogether. It is possible that the stimulus of necessity engenders the greatest of all efforts, calling to the operations of the mind the continued strain for contrivance;

and thus do we find the most remarkable men are those, every step of whose knowledge has been gained with a struggle."

"I suspect you are right," said Glencore, "and that our old system of school education, wherein all was rough, rugged, and difficult, turned out better men than the present-day habit of everything-made-easy and everybody-made-anything. Flippancy is the characteristic of our age, and we owe it to our teaching."

"By the way, what do you mean to do with Charley?" said Upton. "Do you intend him for Eton?"

"I scarcely know. — I make plans only to abandon them," said Glencore, gloomily.

"I'm greatly struck with him. He is one of those fellows, however, who require the nicest management, and who either rise superior to all around them, or drop down into an indolent, dreamy existence, conscious of power, but too bashful or too lazy to exert it."

"You have hit him off, Upton, with all your own subtlety; and it was to speak of that boy I have been so eager to see you."

Glencore paused as he said these words, and passed his hand over his brow, as though to prepare himself for the task before him.

"Upton," said he, at last, in a voice of deep and solemn meaning, "the resolution I am about to impart to you is not unlikely to meet your strenuous opposition; you will be disposed to show me strong reasons against it on every ground; you may refuse me that amount of assistance I shall ask of you to carry out my purpose; but if your arguments were all unanswerable, and if your denial to aid me was to sever the old friendship between us, I'd still persist in my determination. For more than two years the project has been before my mind. The long hours of the day, the longer ones of the night, have found me deep in the consideration of it. I have repeated over to myself everything that my ingenuity could suggest against it; I have said to my own heart all that my worst enemy could utter, were he to read the scheme and detect my plan; I have done more. — I have struggled with myself to abandon it; but in vain. My heart is linked to it; it forms the one sole tie that attaches me to life. Without it, the apathy that I feel stealing over me would be complete, and my existence become a mournful dream. In a word, Upton, all is passionless within me, save one sentiment; and I drag on life merely for a ' *Vendetta.*' "

Upton shook his head mournfully, as the other paused here, and said, —

" This is disease, Glencore! "

" Be it so; the malady is beyond cure," said he, sternly.

" Trust me it is not so," said Upton, gently; " you listened to my persuasions on a more — "

" Ay, that I did! " cried Glencore, interrupting; " and have I ever ceased to rue the day I did so? But for *your* arguments, and I had not lived this life of bitter, self-reproaching misery; but for you, and my vengeance had been sated ere this! "

" Remember, Glencore," said the other, " that you had obtained all the world has decreed as satisfaction. He met you and received your fire; you shot him through the chest, — not mortally, it is true, but to carry to his grave a painful, lingering disease. To have insisted on his again meeting you would have been little less than murder. No man could have stood your friend in such a quarrel. I told you so then, I repeat it now, *he* could not fire at you; what, then, was it possible for you to do? "

" Shoot him, — shoot him like a dog! " cried Glencore, while his eyes gleamed like the glittering eyes of an enraged beast. " You talk of his lingering life of pain: think of *mine;* have some sympathy for what *I* suffer! Would all the agony of *his* whole existence equal one hour of the torment he has bequeathed to me, its shame and ignominy? "

" These are things which passion can never treat of, my dear Glencore."

" Passion alone can feel them," said the other, sternly. " Keep subtleties for those who use like weapons. As for me, no casuistry is needed to tell me I am dishonored, and just as little to tell me I must be avenged! If *you* think differently, it were better not to discuss this question further between us; but I did think I could have reckoned upon you, for I felt you had barred my first chance of a vengeance."

"Now, then, for your plan, Glencore," said Upton, who, with all the dexterity of his calling, preferred opening a new channel in the discussion, to aggravating difficulties by a further opposition.

"I must rid myself of her! There's my plan!" cried Glencore, savagely. "You have it all in that resolution. Of no avail is it that I have separated my fortune from hers, so long as she bears my name, and renders it infamous in every city of Europe. Is it to *you*, who live in the world, — who mix with men of every country, — that I need tell this? If a man cannot throw off such a shame, he must sink under it."

"But you told me you had an unconquerable aversion to the notion of seeking a divorce."

"So I had; so I have! The indelicate, the ignominious course of a trial at law, with all its shocking exposure, would be worse than a thousand deaths! To survive the suffering of all the licensed ribaldry of some gowned coward aspersing one's honor, calumniating, inventing, and, when invention failed, suggesting motives, the very thought of which in secret had driven a man to madness! To endure this — to read it — to know it went published over the wide globe, till one's shame became the gossip of millions — and then — with a verdict extorted from pity, damages awarded to repair a broken heart and a sullied name — to carry this disgrace before one's equals, to be again discussed, sifted, and cavilled at! No, Upton; this poor shattered brain would give way under such a trial; to compass it in mere fancy is already nigh to madness! It must be by other means than these that I attain my object!"

The terrible energy with which he spoke actually frightened Upton, who fancied that his reason had already begun to show signs of decline.

"The world has decreed," resumed Glencore, "that in these conflicts all the shame shall be the husband's; but it shall not be so here! *She* shall have her share, ay, and, by Heaven, not the smaller share either!"

" Why, what would you do?" asked Upton, eagerly.

" Deny my marriage; call her my mistress!" cried Glencore, in a voice shaken with passion and excitement.

" But your boy, — your son, Glencore!"

" He shall be a bastard! You may hold up your hands in horror, and look with all your best got-up disgust at such a scheme; but if you wish to see me swear to accomplish it, I'll do so now before you, ay, on my knees before you! When we eloped from her father's house at Castellamare, we were married by a priest at Capri; of the marriage no trace exists. The more legal ceremony was performed before you, as Chargé d'Affaires at Naples, — of that I have the registry here; nor, except my courier, Sanson, is there a living witness. If you determine to assert it, you will do so without a fragment of proof, since every document that could substantiate it is in my keeping. You shall see them for yourself. She is, therefore, in my power; and will any man dare to tell me how I should temper that power?"

" But your boy, Glencore, your boy!"

" Is my boy's station in the world a prouder one by being the son of the notorious Lady Glencore, or as the offspring of a nameless mistress? What avail to him that he should have a title stained by *her* shame? Where is he to go? In what land is he to live, where her infamy has not reached? Is it not a thousand times better that he enter life ignoble and unknown, — to start in the world's race with what he may of strength and power, — than drag on an unhonored existence, shunned by his equals, and only welcome where it is disgrace to find companionship?"

" But you surely have never contemplated all the consequences of this rash resolve. It is the extinction of an ancient title, the alienation of a great estate, when once you have declared your boy illegitimate."

" He is a beggar: I know it; the penalty he must pay is a heavy one. But think of *her*, Upton, — think of the haughty Viscountess, revelling in splendor, and, even in all her shame, the flattered, welcomed guest of that rotten, corrupt society she lives in. Imagine her in all the pride of wealth and beauty, sought after, adulated, worshipped as she is, suddenly struck down by the brand of this disgrace, and left upon the world without fortune, without rank, without even a name. To be shunned like a leper by the very meanest of those it had once been an honor when she recognized them. Picture to yourself this woman, degraded to the position of all that is most vile and contemptible. She, that scarcely condescended to acknowledge as her equals the best-born and the highest, sunk down to the hopeless infamy of a mistress. They tell me she laughed on the day I fainted at seeing her entering the San Carlos at Naples, — laughed as they carried me down the steps into the fresh air! Will she laugh now, think you? Shall I be called ' Le Pauvre Sire ' when she hears this? Was there ever a vengeance more terrible. more complete?"

" Again, I say, Glencore, you have no right to involve others in the penalty of her fault. Laying aside every higher motive, you can have no more right to deny your boy's claim to his rank and fortune than I or any one else. It cannot be alienated nor extinguished; by his birth he became the heir to your title and estates."

" He has no birth, sir, he is a bastard: who shall deny it? *You* may," added he, after a second's pause; " but where's your proof? Is not every probability as much against you as all documentary evidence, since none will ever believe that I could rob myself of the succession, and make over my fortune to Heaven knows what remote relation?"

" And do you expect me to become a party to this crime?" asked Upton, gravely.

" You balked me in one attempt at vengeance, and I think you owe me a reparation!"

" Glencore," said Upton, solemnly. " we are both of us men of the world, — men who have seen life in all its varied aspects sufficiently to know the hollowness of more than half the pretension men trade upon as principle; we have witnessed mean actions and the very lowest motives amongst the highest in station; and it is not for either of us to affect any overstrained estimate of men's honor and good faith; but I say to you, in all sincerity, that not alone do I refuse you all concurrence in the act you meditate. but I hold myself open to denounce and frustrate it."

" You do!" cried Glencore, wildly, while with a bound he sat up in his bed, grasping the curtain convulsively for support.

" Be calm, Glencore, and listen to me patiently."

" You declare that you will use the confidence of this morning against me!" cried Glencore, while the lines in his face became indented more deeply, and his bloodless lips quivered with passion. " You take your part with *her!*"

" I only ask that you would hear me."

" You owe me four thousand five hundred pounds, Sir Horace Upton," said Glencore, in a voice barely above a whisper, but every accent of which was audible.

" I know it, Glencore," said Upton, calmly. " You helped me by a loan of that sum in a moment of great difficulty. Your generosity went farther, for you took, what nobody else would, my personal security."

Glencore made no reply, but, throwing back the bed-clothes, slowly and painfully arose, and with tottering and uncertain steps approached a table. With a trembling hand he unlocked a drawer, and taking out a paper, opened and scanned it over.

" There's your bond, sir," said he, with a hollow, cavernous voice, as he threw it into the fire, and crushed it down into the flames with a poker. " There is now nothing between us. You are free to do your worst!" And as he spoke, a few drops of dark blood trickled from his nostril, and he fell senseless upon the floor.

CHAPTER XI.

THERE is a trait in the lives of great diplomatists of which it is just possible some one or other of my readers may not have heard, which is, that none of them have ever attained to any great eminence without an attachment — we can find no better word for it — to some woman of superior understanding who has united within herself great talents for society with a high and soaring ambition.

They who only recognize in the world of politics the dry details of ordinary parliamentary business, poor-law questions, sanitary rules, railroad bills, and colonial grants can form but a scanty notion of the excitement derived from the high interests of party, and the great game played by about twenty mighty gamblers, with the whole world for the table, and kingdoms for counters. In this "grand rôle" women perform no ignoble part; nay, it were not too much to say that theirs is the very motive-power of the whole vast machinery.

Had we any right to step beyond the limits of our story for illustration, it would not be difficult to quote names enough to show that we are speaking not at hazard, but "from book," and that great events derive far less of their impulse from "the lords" than from "the ladies of creation." Whatever be the part they take in these contests, their chief attention is ever directed, not to the smaller battle-field of home questions, but to the greater and wider campaign of international politics. Men may wrangle and hair-split, and divide about a harbor bill or a road cession; but women occupy themselves in devising how thrones may be shaken and dynasties disturbed, — how frontiers may be changed, and nationalities trafficked; for, strange as it may seem, the stupendous incidents which mould human destinies are more under the influence of passion and intrigue than the commonest events of every-day life.

Our readers may, and not very unreasonably, begin to suspect that it was in some moment of abstraction we wrote " Glencore" at the head of these pages, and that these speculations are but the preface to some very abstruse reflections upon the political condition of Europe. But no; they are simply intended as a prelude to the fact that Sir Horace Upton was not exempt from the weakness of his order, and that he, too, reposed his trust upon a woman's judgment.

The name of his illustrious guide was the Princess Sabloukoff, by birth a Pole, but married to a Russian of vast wealth and high family, from whom she separated early in life, to mingle in the world with all the " prestige" of position, riches, and — greater than either — extreme beauty, and a manner of such fascination as made her name of European celebrity.

When Sir Horace first met her, he was the junior member of our Embassy at Naples, and she the distinguished leader of fashion in that city. We are not about to busy ourselves with the various narratives which professed to explain her influence at Court, or the secret means to which she owed her ascendency over royal highnesses, and her sway over cardinals. Enough that she possessed such, and that the world knew it. The same success attended her at Vienna and at Paris. She was courted and sought after everywhere; and if her arrival was not fêted with the public demonstrations that await royalty, it was assuredly an event recognized with all that could flatter her vanity or minister to her self-esteem.

When Sir Horace was presented to her as an Attaché, she simply bowed and smiled. He renewed his acquaintance some ten years later as a Secretary, when she vouchsafed to say she remembered him. A third time, after a lapse of years, he came before her as a Chargé d'Affaires, when she conversed with him; and lastly, when time had made him a Minister, and with less generosity had laid its impress upon herself, she gave him her hand, and said, —

"My dear Horace, how charming to see an old friend, if you will be good enough to let me call you so."

And he was so; he accepted the friendship as frankly as it was proffered. He knew that time was when he could have no pretension to this distinction: but the beautiful Princess was no longer young; the fascinations she had wielded were already a kind of Court tradition; archdukes and ambassadors were no more her slaves; nor was she the terror of jealous queens and Court favorites. Sir Horace knew all this; but he also knew that, she being such, his ambition had never dared to aspire to her friendship, and it was only in her days of declining fortune that he could hope for such distinction.

All this may seem very strange and very odd, dear reader; but we live in very strange and very odd times, and more than one-half the world is only living on "second-hand,"— second-hand shawls and second-hand speeches, second-hand books, and Court suits and opinions are all rife; and why not second-hand friendships?

Now, the friendship between a bygone beauty of forty— and we will not say how many more years—and a hack-neyed, half-disgusted man of the world, of the same age, is a very curious contract. There is no love in it; as little is there any strong tie of esteem: but there is a wonderful bond of self-interest and mutual convenience. Each seems to have at last found "one that understands him;" similarity of pursuit has engendered similarity of taste. They have each seen the world from exactly the same point of view, and they have come out of it equally heart-wearied and tired, stored with vast resources of social knowledge, and with a keen insight into every phase of that complex machinery by which one-half the world cheats the other.

Madame de Sabloukoff was still handsome; she had far more than what is ill-naturedly called the remains of good looks. She had a brilliant complexion, lustrous dark eyes, and a profusion of the most beautiful hair. She was, besides, a most splendid dresser. Her toilet was the very perfection of taste, and if a little inclining to over-magnificence, not the less becoming to one whose whole air and bearing assumed something of queenly dignity.

G

In the world of society there is a very great prestige attends those who have at some one time played a great part in life. The deposed king, the ex-minister, the banished general, and even the bygone beauty, receive a species of respectful homage, which the wider world without-doors is not always ready to accord them. Good breeding, in fact, concedes what mere justice might deny; and they who have to fall back upon "souvenirs" for their greatness, always find their advantage in associating with the class whose prerogative is good manners.

The Princess Sabloukoff was not, however, one of those who can live upon the interest of a bygone fame. She saw that, when the time of coquetry and its fascinations has passed, still, with faculties like hers, there was yet a great game to be played. Hitherto she had only studied characters; now she began to reflect upon events. The transition was an easy one, to which her former knowledge contributed largely its assistance. There was scarcely a royalty, hardly a leading personage, in Europe she did not know personally and well. She had lived in intimacy with ministers, and statesmen, and great politicians. She knew them in all that "life of the *salon*" where men alternately expand into frankness, and practise the wily devices of their crafty callings. She had seen them in all the weaknesses, too, of inferior minds, eager after small objects, tormented by insignificant cares. They who habitually dealt with these mighty personages only beheld them in their dignity of station, or surrounded by the imposing accessories of office. What an advantage, then, to regard them closer and nearer, —to be aware of their shortcomings, and acquainted with the secret springs of their ambitions!

The Princess and Sir Horace very soon saw that each needed the other. When Robert Macaire accidentally met an accomplished gamester who "turned the king" as often as he did, and could reciprocate every trick and artifice with him, he threw down the cards, saying, "Embrassons-nous, nous sommes frères!" Now, the illustration is a very ignoble one, but it conveys no very inexact idea of the bond which united these two distinguished individuals.

Sir Horace was one of those fine, acute intelligences which may be gapped and blunted if applied to rough work, but are splendid instruments where you would cut cleanly and cut deep. She saw this at once. He, too, recognized in her a wonderful knowledge of life, joined to vast powers of employing it with profit. No more was wanting to establish a friendship between them. Dispositions must be, to a certain degree, different between those who are to live together as friends, but tastes must be alike. Theirs were so. They had the same veneration for the same things, the same regard for the same celebrities, and the same contempt for the small successes which were engaging the minds of many around them. If the Princess had a real appreciation of the fine abilities of Sir Horace, he estimated at their full value all the resources of her wondrous tact and skill, and the fascinations which even yet surrounded her.

Have we said enough to explain the terms of this alliance, or must we make one more confession, and own that her insidious praise — a flattery too delicate and fine ever to be committed to absolute eulogy — convinced Sir Horace that she alone, of all the world, was able to comprehend the vast stores of his knowledge, and the wide measure of his capacity as a statesman?

In the great game of statecraft, diplomatists are not above looking into each other's hands; but this must always be accomplished by means of a confederate. How terribly alike are all human rogueries, whether the scene be a conference at Vienna, or the tent of a thimblerig at Ascot! La Sabloukoff was unrivalled in the art. She knew how to push raillery and *persiflage* to the very frontiers of truth, and even peep over and see what lay beyond. Sir Horace traded on the material with which she supplied him, and acquired the reputation of being all that was crafty and subtle in diplomacy.

How did Upton know this? Whence came he by that? What mysterious source of information is he possessed of? Who could have revealed such a secret to him? were questions often asked in that dreary old drawing-room of Downing Street, where men's destinies are shaped, and the fate of millions decided, from four o'clock to six of an afternoon.

Often and often were the measures of the Cabinet shaped by the tidings which arrived with all the speed of a foreign courier; over and over again were the speeches in Parliament based upon information received from him. It has even happened that the news from his hand has caused the telegraph of the Admiralty to signalize the "Thunderer" to put to sea with all haste. In a word, he was the trusted agent of our Government, whether ruled by a Whig or a Tory, and his despatches were ever regarded as a sure warranty for action.

The English Minister at a Foreign Court labors under one great disadvantage, which is, that his policy, and all the consequences that are to follow it, are rarely, if ever, shaped with any reference to the state of matters then existing in his own country. Absorbed as he is in great European questions, how can he follow with sufficient attention the course of events at home, or recognize, in the signs and tokens of the division list, the changeful fortunes of party? He may be advising energy when the cry is all for temporizing; counselling patience and submission, when the nation is eager for a row; recommend religious concessions in the very week that Exeter Hall is denouncing toleration; or actually suggesting aid to a Government that a popular orator has proclaimed to be everything that is unjust and ignominious.

It was Sir Horace Upton's fortune to have fallen into one of these embarrassments. He had advised the Home Government to take some measures, or at least look with favor on certain movements of the Poles in Russia, in order the better to obtain some concessions then required from the Cabinet of the Czar. The Premier did not approve of the suggestion, nor was it like to meet acceptance at home. We were in a pro-Russian fever at the moment. Some mob disturbances at Norwich, a Chartist meeting at Stockport, and something else in Wales, had frightened the nation into a hot stage of conservatism; and never was there such an ill-chosen moment to succor Poles or awaken dormant nationalities.

Upton's proposal was rejected. He was even visited with one of those disagreeable acknowledgments by which the

Foreign Office reminds a speculative minister that he is going *ultra crepidam*. When an envoy is snubbed, he always asks for leave of absence. If the castigation be severe, he invariably, on his return to England, goes to visit the Leader of the Opposition. This is the ritual. Sir Horace, however, only observed it in half. He came home ; but after his first morning's attendance at the Foreign Office, he disappeared ; none saw or heard of him. He knew well all the value of mystery, and he accordingly disappeared from public view altogether.

When, therefore, Harcourt's letter reached him, proposing that he should visit Glencore, the project came most opportunely ; and that he only accepted it for a day, was in the spirit of his habitual diplomacy, since he then gave himself all the power of an immediate departure, or permitted the option of remaining gracefully, in defiance of all pre-engagements, and all plans to be elsewhere. We have been driven, for the sake of this small fact, to go a great way round in our history ; but we promise our readers that Sir Horace was one of those people whose motives are never tracked without a considerable *détour*. The reader knows now why he was at Glencore. — he already knew how.

The terrible interview with Glencore brought back a second relapse of greater violence than the first, and it was nigh a fortnight ere he was pronounced out of danger. It was a strange life that Harcourt and Upton led in that dreary interval. Guests of one whose life was in utmost peril, they met in that old gallery each day to talk, in half-whispered sentences, over the sick man's case, and his chances of recovery.

Harcourt frankly told Upton that the first relapse was the consequence of a scene between Glencore and himself. Upton made no similar confession. He reflected deeply, however, over all that had passed, and came to the conclusion that, in Glencore's present condition, opposition might prejudice his chance of recovery, but never avail to turn him from his project. He also set himself to study the boy's character, and found it, in all respects, the very type of his father's. Great bashfulness, united to great boldness, timidity, and distrust, were there side by side with a rash, impetuous nature that would hesitate at nothing in pursuit of an object. Pride, however, was the great principle of his being, — the good and evil motive of all that was in him. He had pride on every subject. His name, his rank, his station, a consciousness of natural quickness, a sense of aptitude to learn whatever came before him, — all gave him the same feeling of pride.

" There's a deal of good in that lad," said Harcourt to Upton, one evening, as the boy had left the room; " I like his strong affection for his father, and that unbounded faith he seems to have in Glencore's being better than every one else in the world."

" It is an excellent religion, my dear Harcourt, if it could only last! " said the diplomat, smiling amiably.

" And why should n't it last? " asked the other, impatiently.

" Just because nothing lasts that has its origin in ignorance. The boy has seen nothing of life, has had no opportunity for forming a judgment or instituting a comparison between any two objects. The first shot that breaches that same fortress of belief, down will come the whole edifice ! "

" You 'd give a lad to the Jesuits, then, to be trained up in every artifice and distrust? "

" Far from it, Harcourt. I think their system a mistake all through. The science of life must be self-learned, and it is a slow acquisition. All that education can do is to prepare the mind to receive it. Now, to employ the first years of a boy's life by storing him with prejudices, is just to encumber a vessel with a rotten cargo that she must throw overboard before she can load with a profitable freight."

" And is it in that category you 'd class his love for his father? " asked the Colonel.

" Of course not; but any unnatural or exaggerated estimate of him is a great error, to lead to an equally unfair depreciation when the time of deception is past. To be plain, Harcourt, is that boy fitted to enter one of our great public schools, stand the hard, rough usage of his own equals, and buffet it as you or I have done? "

" Why not? or, at least, why should n't he become so after a month or two?"

"Just because in that same month or two he'd either die broken-hearted, or plunge his knife into the heart of some comrade who insulted him."

"Not a bit of it. You don't know him at all. Charley is a fine give-and-take fellow; a little proud, perhaps, because he lives apart from all that are his equals. Let Glencore just take courage to send him to Harrow or Rugby, and my life on it, but he 'll be the manliest fellow in the school."

" I 'll undertake, without Harrow or Rugby, that the boy should become something even greater than that," said Upton, smiling.

"Oh, I know you sneer at my ideas of what a young fellow ought to be," said Harcourt; "but, somehow, you did not neglect these same pursuits yourself. You can shoot as well as most men, and you ride better than any I know of."

"One likes to do a little of everything, Harcourt," said Upton, not at all displeased at this flattery; "and somehow it never suits a fellow, who really feels that he has fair abilities, to do anything badly; so that it comes to this: one does it well, or not at all. Now, you never heard me touch the piano?"

"Never."

"Just because I 'm only an inferior performer, and so I only play when perfectly alone."

"Egad, if I could only master a waltz, or one of the melodies, I 'd be at it whenever any one would listen to me."

"You 're a good soul, and full of amiability, Harcourt," said Upton; but the words sounded very much as though he said, "You 're a dear, good, sensible creature, without an atom of self-respect or esteem."

Indeed, so conscious was Harcourt that the expression meant no compliment that he actually reddened and looked away. At last he took courage to renew the conversation, and said, —

"And what would you advise for the boy, then?"

"I'd scarcely lay down a system; but I'll tell you what
I would not do. I'd not bore him with mathematics; I'd
not put his mind on the stretch in any direction; I'd not
stifle the development of any taste that may be struggling
within him, but rather encourage and foster it, since it is
precisely by such an indication you'll get some clew to his
nature. Do you understand me?"

"I'm not quite sure I do; but I believe you'd leave him
to something like utter idleness."

"What to *you*, my dear Harcourt, would be utter idleness, I've no doubt; but not to *him*, perhaps."

Again the Colonel looked mortified, but evidently knew
not how to resent this new sneer.

"Well," said he, after a pause, "the lad will not require
to be a genius."

"So much the better for him, probably; at all events, so
much the better for his friends, and all who are to associate
with him."

Here he looked fixedly at Upton, who smiled a most courteous acquiescence in the opinion, — a politeness that made
poor Harcourt perfectly ashamed of his own rudeness, and
he continued hurriedly, —

"He'll have abundance of money. The life Glencore
leads here will be like a long minority to him. A fine old
name and title, and the deuce is in it if he can't rub through
life pleasantly enough with such odds."

"I believe you are right, after all, Harcourt," said Upton,
sighing, and now speaking in a far more natural tone; "it
is 'rubbing through' with the best of us, and no more!"

"If you mean that the process is a very irksome one, I
enter my dissent at once," broke in Harcourt. "I'm not
ashamed to own that I like life prodigiously; and if I be
spared to say so, I'm sure I'll have the same story to tell
fifteen or twenty years hence; and yet I'm not a genius!"

"No," said Upton, smiling a bland assent.

"Nor a philosopher either," said Harcourt, irritated at
the acknowledgment.

"Certainly not," chimed in Upton, with another smile.

"Nor have I any wish to be one or the other," rejoined
Harcourt, now really provoked. "I know right well that

if I were in trouble or difficulty to-morrow, — if I wanted a friend to help me with a loan of some thousand pounds, — it is not to a genius or a philosopher I'd look for the assistance."

It is ever a chance shot that explodes a magazine, and so is it that a random speech is sure to hit the mark that has escaped all the efforts of skilful direction.

Upton winced and grew pale at these last words, and he fixed his penetrating gray eyes upon the speaker with a keenness all his own. Harcourt, however, bore the look without the slightest touch of uneasiness. The honest Colonel had spoken without any hidden meaning, nor had he the slightest intention of a personal application in his words. Of this fact Upton appeared soon to be convinced, for his features gradually recovered their wonted calmness.

"How perfectly right you are, my dear Harcourt," said he, mildly. "The man who expects to be happier by the possession of genius is like one who would like to warm himself through a burning-glass."

"Egad, that is a great consolation for us slow fellows," said Harcourt, laughing; "and now what say you to a game at écarté; for I believe it is just the one solitary thing I am more than your match in?"

"I accept inferiority in a great many others," said Upton, blandly; "but I must decline the challenge, for I have a letter to write, and our post here starts at daybreak."

"Well, I'd rather carry the whole bag than indite one of its contents," said the Colonel, rising; and, with a hearty shake of the hand, he left the room.

A letter was fortunately not so great an infliction to Upton, who opened his desk at once, and with a rapid hand traced the following lines: —

My DEAR PRINCESS, — My last will have told you how and when I came here; I wish I but knew in what way to explain why I still remain! Imagine the dreariest desolation of Calabria in a climate of fog and sea-drift: sunless skies, leafless trees, impassable roads, the out-door comforts; the joys within depending on a gloomy old house, with a few gloomier inmates, and a host on a sick bed. Yet, with all this, I believe I am better: the doctor, a strange, unsophisticated creature, a cross between Galen and

Caliban, seems to have hit off what the great dons of science never could detect, — the true seat of my malady. He says — and he really reasons out his case ingeniously — that the brain has been working for the inferior nerves, not limiting itself to cerebral functions, but actually performing the humbler office of muscular direction, and so forth: in fact, a field-marshal doing duty for a common soldier! I almost fancy I can corroborate his view, from internal sensations; I have a kind of secret instinct that he is right. Poor brain! why it should do the work of another department, with abundance of occupation of its own, I cannot make out. But to turn to something else. This is not a bad refuge just now. They cannot make out where I am, and all the inquiries at my club are answered by a vague impression that I have gone back to Germany, which the people at F. O. are aware is not the case. I have already told you that my suggestion has been negatived in the Cabinet: it was ill-timed, Allington says; but I ventured to remind his Lordship that a policy requiring years to develop, and more years still to push to a profitable conclusion, is not to be reduced to the category of mere à propos measures. He was vexed, and replied weakly and angrily. I rejoined, and left him. Next day he sent for me, but my reply was, "I was leaving town;" and I left. I don't want the Bath, because it would be "ill-timed;" so that they must give me Vienna, or be satisfied to see me in the House and the Opposition!

Your tidings of Brekenoff came exactly in the nick. Allington said pompously that they were sure of him; so I just said, "Ask him if they would like our sending a Consular Agent to Cracow?" It seems that he was so flurried by a fancied detection that he made a full acknowledgment of all. But even at this, Allington takes no alarm. The malady of the Treasury benches is deafness, with a touch of blindness. What a cumbrous piece of bungling machinery is this boasted "representative government" of ours! No promptitude, no secrecy! Everything debated, and discussed, and discouraged, before begun: every blot-hit for an antagonist to profit by! Even the characters of our public men exposed, and their weaknesses displayed to view, so that every state of Europe may see where to wound us, and through whom! There is no use in the Countess remaining here any longer; the King never noticed her at the last ball: she is angry at it, and if she shows her irritation she'll spoil all. I always thought Josephine would fail in England. It is, indeed, a widely different thing to succeed in the small Courts of Germany, and our great whirlpool of St. James. You could do it, my dear friend; but where is the other dare attempt it?

Until I hear from you again I can come to no resolution. One thing is clear, — they do not, or they will not, see the danger I have pointed out to them. All the home policy of our country is drifting, day by day, towards a democracy : how, in the name of common sense, then, is our foreign policy to be maintained at the standard of the Holy Alliance ? What an absurd juxtaposition is there between popular rights and an alliance with the Czar ! This peril will overtake them one day or another, and then, to escape from national indignation, the minister, whoever he may be, will be driven to make war. But I can't wait for this ; and yet, were I to resign, my resignation would not embarrass them, — it would irritate and annoy, but not disconcert. Brekenoff will surely go home on leave. You ought to meet him : he is certain to be at Ems. It is the refuge of disgraced diplomacy. Try if something cannot be done with him. He used to say formerly yours were the only dinners now in Europe. He hates Allington. This feeling, and his love for white truffles, are, I believe, the only clews to the man. Be sure, however, that the truffles are Piedmontese ; they have a slight flavor of garlic, rather agreeable than otherwise. Like Josephine's lisp, it is a defect that serves for a distinction. The article in the "Beau Monde" was clever, prettily written, and even well worked out ; but state affairs are never really well treated save by those who conduct them. One must have played the game himself to understand all the nice subtleties of the contest. These, your mere reviewer or newspaper scribe never attains to ; and then he has no reserves, — none of those mysterious concealments that are to negotiations like the eloquent pauses of conversation : the moment when dialogue ceases, and the real interchange of ideas begins.

The fine touch, the keen *aperçu*, belongs alone to those who have had to exercise these same qualities in the treatment of great questions : and hence it is that though the Public be often much struck, and even enlightened, by the powerful "article" or the able "leader," the Statesman is rarely taught anything by the journalist, save the force and direction of public opinion.

I had a deal to say to you about poor Glencore, whom you tell me you remember ; but, how to say it ? He is broken-hearted — literally broken-hearted — by her desertion of him. It was one of those ill-assorted leagues which cannot hold together. Why they did not see this, and make the best of it, — sensibly, dispassionately, even amicably, — it is difficult to say. An Englishman, it would seem, must always hate his wife if she cannot love him ; and, after all, how involuntary are all affections, and what a severe penalty is this for an unwitting offence !

He ponders over this calamity just as if it were the crushing stroke by which a man's whole career was to be finished forever.

The stupidity of all stupidities is in these cases to fly from the world and avoid society. By doing this a man rears a barrier he never can repass; he proclaims aloud his sentiment of the injury, quite forgetting all the offence he is giving to the hundred and fifty others who, in the same predicament as himself, are by no means disposed to turn hermits on account of it. Men make revolutionary governments, smash dynasties, transgress laws, but they cannot oppose *convenances!*

I need scarcely say that there is nothing to be gained by reasoning with him. He has worked himself up to a chronic fury, and talks of vengeance all day long, like a Corsican. For company here I have an old brother officer of my days of tinsel and pipe-clay, — an excellent creature, whom I amuse myself by tormenting. There is also Glencore's boy, — a strange, dreamy kind of haughty fellow, an exaggeration of his father in disposition, but with good abilities. These are not the elements of much social agreeability; but you know, dear friend, how little I stand in need of what is called company. Your last letter, charming as it was, has afforded me all the companionship I could desire. I have re-read it till I know it by heart. I could almost chide you for that delightful little party in my absence, but of course it was, as all you ever do is, perfectly right; and, after all, I am, perhaps, not sorry that you had those people when I was away, so that we shall be more *chez nous* when we meet. But when is that to be? Who can tell? My medico insists upon five full weeks for my cure. Allington is very likely, in his present temper, to order me back to my post. You seem to think that you must be in Berlin when Seckendorf arrives, so that — But I will not darken the future by gloomy forebodings. I *could* leave this — that is, if any urgency required it — at once; but, if possible, it is better I should remain at least a little longer. My last meeting with Glencore was unpleasant. Poor fellow! his temper is not what it used to be, and he is forgetful of what is due to one whose nerves are in the sad state of mine. You shall hear all my complainings when we meet, dear Princess; and with this I kiss your hand, begging you to accept all "*mes hommages*" *et mon estime.*

H. U.

Your letter must be addressed "Leenane, Ireland." Your last had only "Glencore" on it, and not very legible either, so that it made what I wished *I* could do, "the tour of Scotland," before reaching me.

Sir Horace read over his letter carefully, as though it had been a despatch, and, when he had done, folded it up with an air of satisfaction. He had said nothing that he wished unsaid, and he had mentioned a little about everything he desired to touch upon. He then took his " drops " from a queer-looking little phial he carried about with him, and having looked at his face in a pocket-glass, he half closed his eyes in revery.

Strange, confused visions were they that flitted through his brain. Thoughts of ambition the most daring, fancies about health, speculations in politics, finance, religion, literature, the arts, society, — all came and went. Plans and projects jostled each other at every instant. Now his brow would darken, and his thin lips close tightly, as some painful impression crossed him ; now again a smile, a slight laugh even, betrayed the passing of some amusing conception. It was easy to see how such a nature could suffice to itself, and how little he needed of that give-and-take which companionship supplies. He could — to steal a figure from our steam language — he could " bank his fires," and await any emergency, and, while scarcely consuming any fuel, prepare for the most trying demand upon his powers. A hasty movement of feet overhead, and the sound of voices talking loudly, aroused him from his reflections, while a servant entered abruptly to say that Lord Glencore wished to see him immediately.

" Is his Lordship worse? " asked Upton.

" No, sir ; but he was very angry with the young lord this evening about something, and they say that with the passion he opened the bandage on his head, and set the vein a-bleeding again. Billy Traynor is there now trying to stop it."

" I 'll go upstairs," said Sir Horace, rising, and beginning to fortify himself with caps, and capes, and comforters, — precautions that he never omitted when moving from one room to the other.

CHAPTER XII.

A NIGHT AT SEA.

GLENCORE'S chamber presented a scene of confusion and dismay as Upton entered. The sick man had torn off the bandage from his temples, and so roughly as to reopen the half-closed artery, and renew the bleeding. Not alone the bedclothes and the curtains, but the faces of the attendants around him, were stained with blood, which seemed the more ghastly from contrast with their pallid cheeks. They moved hurriedly to and fro, scarcely remembering what they were in search of, and evidently deeming his state of the greatest peril. Traynor, the only one whose faculties were unshaken by the shock, sat quietly beside the bed, his fingers firmly compressed upon the orifice of the vessel, while with the other hand he motioned to them to keep silence.

Glencore lay with closed eyes, breathing long and labored inspirations, and at times convulsed by a slight shivering. His face, and even his lips, were bloodless, and his eyelids of a pale, livid hue. So terribly like the approach of death was his whole appearance that Upton whispered in the doctor's ear, —

" Is it over? Is he dying?"

" No. Upton," said Glencore; for, with the acute hearing of intense nervousness, he had caught the words. " It is not so easy to die."

" There, now, — no more talkin', — no discoorsin' — azy and quiet is now the word."

" Bind it up and leave me, — leave me with *him;*" and Glencore pointed to Upton.

" I dar' n't move out of this spot," said Billy, addressing Upton. " You'd have the blood coming out, *per saltim*, if I took away my finger."

"You must be patient, Glencore," said Upton, gently; "you know I'm always ready when you want me."

"And you'll not leave this, — you'll not desert me?" cried the other, eagerly.

"Certainly not; I have no thought of going away."

"There, now, hould your prate, both of ye, or, by my conscience, I'll not take the responsibility upon me, — I will not!" said Billy, angrily. "'T is just a disgrace and a shame that ye haven't more discretion."

Glencore's lips moved with a feeble attempt at a smile, and in his faint voice he said, —

"We must obey the doctor, Upton; but don't leave me."

Upton moved a chair to the bedside, and sat down without a word.

"Ye think an artery is like a canal, with a lock-gate to it, I believe," said Billy, in a low, grumbling voice, to Upton, "and you forget all its vermicular motion, as ould Fabricius called it, and that it is only by a coagalum, a kind of barrier, like a mud breakwater, that it can be plugged. Be off out of that, ye spalpeens! be off, every one of yez, and leave us tranquil and paceable!"

This summary command was directed to the various servants, who were still moving about the room in imaginary occupation. The room was at last cleared of all save Upton and Billy, who sat by the bedside, his hand still resting on the sick man's forehead. Soothed by the stillness, and reduced by the loss of blood, Glencore sank into a quiet sleep, breathing softly and gently as a child.

"Look at him now," whispered Billy to Upton, "and you'll see what philosophy there is in ascribin' to the heart the source of all our emotions. He lies there azy and comfortable just because the great bellows is working smoothly and quietly. They talk about the brain, and the spinal nerves, and the soliar plexus; but give a man a wake, washy circulation, and what is he? He's just like a chap with the finest intentions in the world, but not a sixpence in his pocket to carry them out! A fine well-regulated, steady-batin' heart is like a credit on the bank, — you draw on it, and your draft is n't dishonored!"

" What was it brought on this attack?" asked Upton, in a whisper.

" A shindy he had with the boy. I was n't here; there was nobody by. But when I met Master Charles on the stairs, he flew past me like lightning, and I just saw by a glimpse that something was wrong. He rushed out with his head bare, and his coat all open, and it sleetin' terribly! Down he went towards the lough, at full speed, and never minded all my callin' after him."

" Has he returned?" asked Upton.

" Not as I know, sir. We were too much taken up with the lord to ask for him."

" I 'll just step down and see," said Sir Horace, who arose, and left the room on tiptoe.

To Upton's inquiry all made the same answer. None had seen the young lord. — none could give any clew as to whither he had gone. Sir Horace at once hastened to Harcourt's room, and, after some vigorous shakes, succeeded in awakening the Colonel, and by dint of various repetitions at last put him in possession of all that had occurred.

" We must look after the lad," cried Harcourt, springing from his bed, and dressing with all haste. " He is a rash, hot-headed fellow; but even if it were nothing else, he might get his death in such a night as this."

The wind dashed wildly against the window-panes as he spoke, and the old timbers of the frame rattled fearfully.

" Do you remain here, Upton. I 'll go in search of the boy. Take care Glencore hears nothing of his absence." And with a promptitude that bespoke the man of action, Harcourt descended the stairs and set out.

The night was pitch dark; sweeping gusts of wind bore the rain along in torrents, and the thunder rolled incessantly, its clamor increased by the loud beating of the waves as they broke upon the rocks. Upton had repeated to Harcourt that Billy saw the boy going towards the sea-shore, and in this direction he now followed. His frequent excursions had familiarized him with the place, so that even at night Harcourt found no difficulty in detecting the path and keeping it. About half an hour's brisk walking brought him to the side of the lough, and the narrow flight of steps cut in the rock, which descended to the little boat-quay. Here he halted, and called out the boy's name several times. The sea, however, was running mountains high, and an immense drift, sweeping over the rocks, fell in sheets of scattered foam beyond them; so that Harcourt's voice was drowned by the uproar. A small shealing under the shelter of the rock formed the home of a boatman; and at the crazy door of this humble cot Harcourt now knocked violently.

The man answered the summons at once, assuring him that he had not heard or seen any one since the night closed in; adding, at the same time, that in such a tempest a boat's crew might have landed without his knowing it.

"To be sure," continued he, after a pause, "I heard a chain rattlin' on the rock soon after I went to bed, and I'll just step down and see if the yawl is all right."

Scarcely had he left the spot, when his voice was heard calling out from below, —

"She's gone! the yawl is gone! the lock is broke with a stone, and she's away!"

"How could this be? No boat could live in such a sea," cried Harcourt, eagerly.

"She could go out fast enough, sir. The wind is north-east, due; but how long she'll keep the say is another matter."

"Then he'll be lost!" cried Harcourt, wildly.

"Who, sir. — who is it?" asked the man.

"Your master's son!" cried he, wringing his hands in anguish.

"Oh, murther! murther!" screamed the boatman; "we'll never see him again. 'T is out to say, into the wild ocean, he'll be blown!"

"Is there no shelter, — no spot he could make for?"

"Barrin' the islands, there's not a spot between this and America."

"But he could make the islands, — you are sure of that?"

"If the boat was able to live through the say. But sure I know him well; he'll never take in a reef or sail, but sit there, with the helm hard up, just never carin' what came of him! Oh, musha! musha! what druv him out such a night as this!"

7

"Come, it's no time for lamenting, my man; get the launch ready, and let us follow him. Are you afraid?"

"Afraid!" replied the man, with a touch of scorn in his voice; "faix, it's little fear troubles me. But, may be, you won't like to be in her yourself when she's once out. I've none belongin' to me, — father, mother, chick or child; but you may have many a one that's near to you."

"My ties, are, perhaps, as light as your own," said Harcourt. "Come, now, be alive. I'll put ten gold guineas in your hand if you can overtake him."

"I'd rather see his face than have two hundred," said the man, as, springing into the boat, he began to haul out the tackle from under the low half-deck, and prepare for sea.

"Is your honor used to a boat, or ought I to get another man with me?" asked the sailor.

"Trust me, my good fellow; I have had more sailing than yourself, and in more treacherous seas too," said Harcourt, who, throwing off his cloak, proceeded to help the other, with an address that bespoke a practised hand.

The wind blew strongly off the shore, so that scarcely was the foresail spread than the boat began to move rapidly through the water, dashing the sea over her bows, and plunging wildly through the waves.

"Give me a hand now with the halyard," said the boat-man; "and when the mainsail is set, you'll see how she'll dance over the top of the waves, and never wet us."

"She's too light in the water, if anything," said Harcourt, as the boat bounded buoyantly under the increased press of canvas.

"Your honor's right; she'd do better with half a ton of iron in her. Stand by, sir, always, with the peak halyards; get the sail aloft in, when I give you the word."

"Leave the tiller to me, my man," said Harcourt, taking it as he spoke. "You'll soon see that I'm no new hand at the work."

"She's doing it well," said the man. "Keep her up! keep her up! there's a spit of land runs out here; in a few minutes more we'll have say room enough."

The heavier roll of the waves, and the increased force of the wind, soon showed that they had gained the open sea; while the atmosphere, relieved of the dark shadows of the mountain, seemed lighter and thinner than in shore.

" We 're to make for the islands, you say, sir?"

" Yes. What distance are they off?"

" About eighteen miles. Two hours, if the wind lasts, and we can bear it."

" And could the yawl stand this?" said Harcourt, as a heavy sea struck the bow, and came in a cataract over them.

" Better than ourselves, if she was manned. Luff! luff! — that's it!" And as the boat turned up to wind, sheets of spray and foam flew over her. " Master Charles has n't his equal for steerin', if he was n't alone. Keep her there! — now! steady, sir!"

" Here 's a squall coming," cried Harcourt; " I hear it hissing."

Down went the peak, but scarcely in time, for the wind, catching the sail, laid the boat gunwale under. After a struggle, she righted, but with nearly one-third of her filled with water.

" I 'd take in a reef, or two reefs," said the man; " but if she could n't rise to the say, she 'll fill and go down. We must carry on, at all events."

" So say I. It 's no time to shorten sail, with such a sea running."

The boat now flew through the water, the sea itself impelling her, as with every sudden gust the waves struck the stern.

" She 's a brave craft," said Harcourt, as she rose lightly over the great waves, and plunged down again into the trough of the sea; " but if we ever get to land again, I 'll have combings round her to keep her dryer."

" Here it comes! — here it comes, sir!"

Nor were the words well out, when, like a thunder-clap, the wind struck the sail, and bent the mast over like a whip. For an instant it seemed as if she were going down by the prow; but she righted again, and, shivering in every plank, held on her way.

" That 's as much as she could do," said the sailor; " and I would not like to ax her to do more."

"I agree with you," said Harcourt, secretly stealing his feet back again into his shoes, which he had just kicked off.

"It's fresh'ning it is every minute," said the man; "and I'm not sure that we could make the islands if it lasts."

"Well. — what then?"

"There's nothing for it but to be blown out to say," said he, calmly, as, having filled his tobacco-pipe, he struck a light and began to smoke.

"The very thing I was wishing for," said Harcourt, touching his cigar to the bright ashes. "How she labors! Do you think she can stand this?"

"She can, if it's no worse, sir."

"But it looks heavier weather outside."

"As well as I can see, it's only beginnin'."

Harcourt listened with a species of admiration to the calm and measured sentiment of the sailor, who, fully conscious of all the danger, yet never, by a word or gesture, showed that he was flurried or excited.

"You have been out on nights as bad as this, I suppose?" said Harcourt.

"Maybe not quite, sir, for it's a great say is runnin'; and, with the wind off shore, we could n't have this, if there was n't a storm blowing farther out."

"From the westward, you mean?"

"Yes, sir, — a wind coming over the whole ocean, that will soon meet the land wind."

"And does that often happen?"

The words were but out, when, with a loud report like a cannon-shot, the wind reversed the sail, snapping the strong sprit in two, and bringing down the whole canvas clattering into the boat. With the aid of a hatchet, the sailor struck off the broken portion of the spar, and soon cleared the wreck, while the boat, now reduced to a mere foresail, labored heavily, sinking her prow in the sea at every bound. Her course, too, was now altered, and she flew along parallel to the shore, the great cliffs looming through the darkness, and seeming as if close to them.

"The boy! — the boy!" cried Harcourt; "what has become of him? He never could have lived through that squall."

" If the spar stood, there was an end of us, too," said the sailor; " she 'd have gone down by the stern, as sure as my name is Peter."

" It is all over by this time," muttered Harcourt, sorrowfully.

" Pace to him now ! " said the sailor, as he crossed himself, and went over a prayer.

The wind now raged fearfully; claps, like the report of cannon, struck the frail boat at intervals, and laid her nearly keel uppermost; while the mast bent like a whip, and every rope creaked and strained to its last endurance. The deafening noise close at hand told where the waves were beating on the rock-bound coast, or surging with the deep growl of thunder through many a cavern. They rarely spoke, save when some emergency called for a word. Each sat wrapped up in his own dark reveries, and unwilling to break them. Hours passed thus, — long, dreary hours of darkness, that seemed like years of suffering, so often in this interval did life hang in the balance.

As morning began to break with a grayish blue light to the westward, the wind slightly abated, blowing more steadily, too, and less in sudden gusts; while the sea rolled in large round waves, unbroken above, and showing no crest of foam.

" Do you know where we are ? " asked Harcourt.

" Yes, sir; we 're off the Rooks' Point, and if we hold on well, we 'll soon be in slacker water."

" Could the boy have reached this, think you ? "

The man shook his head mournfully, without speaking.

" How far are we from Glencore ? "

" About eighteen miles, sir; but more by land."

" You can put me ashore, then, somewhere hereabouts."

" Yes, sir, in the next bay; there 's a creek we can easily run into."

" You are quite sure he could n't have been blown out to sea ? "

" How could he, sir? There 's only one way the wind could drive him. If he is n't in the Clough Bay, he 's in glory."

All the anxiety of that dreary night was nothing to what

Harcourt now suffered, in his eagerness to round the Rooks' Point, and look in the bay beyond it. Controlling it as he would, still would it break out in words of impatience and even anger.

"Don't curse the boat, yer honor," said Peter, respectfully, but calmly; "she's behaved well to us this night, or we'd not be here now."

"But are we to beat about here forever?" asked the other, angrily.

"She's doin' well, and we ought to be thankful," said the man; and his tone, even more than his words, served to reprove the other's impatience. "I'll try and set the mainsail on her with the remains of the spirit."

Harcourt watched him, as he labored away to repair the damaged rigging; but though he looked at him, his thoughts were far away with poor Glencore upon his sick bed, in sorrow and in suffering, and perhaps soon to hear that he was childless. From these he went on to other thoughts. What could have occurred to have driven the boy to such an act of desperation? Harcourt invented a hundred imaginary causes, to reject them as rapidly again. The affection the boy bore to his father seemed the strongest principle of his nature. There appeared to be no event possible in which that feeling would not sway and control him. As he thus ruminated, he was aroused by the sudden cry of the boatman.

"There's a boat, sir, dismasted, ahead of us, and drifting out to say."

"I see her! — I see her!" cried Harcourt; "out with the oars, and let's pull for her."

Heavily as the sea was rolling, they now began to pull through the immense waves, Harcourt turning his head at every instant to watch the boat, which now was scarcely half a mile ahead of them.

"She's empty! — there's no one in her!" said Peter, mournfully, as, steadying himself by the mast, he cast a look seaward.

"Row on. — let us get beside her," said Harcourt.

"She's the yawl! I know her now," cried the man.

"And empty?"

"Washed out of her with a say, belike," said Peter, resuming his oar, and tugging with all his strength.

A quarter of an hour's hard rowing brought them close to the dismasted boat, which, drifting broadside on the sea, seemed at every instant ready to capsize.

"There's something in the bottom, — in the stern-sheets!" screamed Peter. "It's himself! O blessed Virgin, it's himself!" And, with a bound, he sprang from his own boat into the other.

The next instant he had lifted the helpless body of the boy from the bottom of the boat, and, with a shout of joy, screamed out, —

"He's alive! — he's well! — it's only fatigue!"

Harcourt pressed his hands to his face, and sank upon his knees in prayer.

CHAPTER XIII.

A "VOW" ACCOMPLISHED.

JUST as Upton had seated himself at that frugal meal of weak tea and dry toast he called his breakfast, Harcourt suddenly entered the room, splashed and road-stained from head to foot, and in his whole demeanor indicating the work of a fatiguing journey.

"Why, I thought to have had my breakfast with you," cried he, impatiently, "and this is like the diet of a convalescent from fever. Where is the salmon — where the grouse pie — where are the cutlets — and the chocolate — and the poached eggs — and the hot rolls, and the cherry bounce?"

"Say, rather, where are the disordered livers, worn-out stomachs, fevered brains, and impatient tempers, my worthy Colonel?" said Upton, blandly. "Talleyrand himself once told me that he always treated great questions starving."

"And he made a nice mess of the world in consequence," blustered out Harcourt. "A fellow with an honest appetite and a sound digestion would never have played false to so many masters."

"It is quite right that men like you should read history in this wise," said Upton, smiling, as he dipped a crust in his tea and ate it.

"Men like me are very inferior creatures, no doubt," broke in Harcourt, angrily; "but I very much doubt if men like you had come eighteen miles on foot over a mountain this morning, after a night passed in an open boat at sea, — ay, in a gale, by Jove, such as I sha' n't forget in a hurry."

"You have hit it perfectly, Harcourt; *suum cuique;* and if only we could get the world to see that each of us has his speciality, we should all of us do much better."

By the vigorous tug he gave the bell, and the tone in which he ordered up something to eat, it was plain to see that he scarcely relished the moral Upton had applied to his speech. With the appearance of the good cheer, however, he speedily threw off his momentary displeasure, and as he ate and drank, his honest, manly face lost every trace of annoyance. Once only did a passing shade of anger cross his countenance. It was when, suddenly looking up, he saw Upton's eyes settled on him, and his whole features expressing a most palpable sensation of wonderment and compassion.

"Ay," cried he, "I know well what's passing in your mind this minute. You are lost in your pitying estimate of such a mere animal as I am; but, hang it all, old fellow, why not be satisfied with the flattering thought that *you* are of another stamp, — a creature of a different order?"

"It does not make one a whit happier," sighed Upton, who never shrunk from accepting the sentiment as his own.

"I should have thought otherwise," said Harcourt, with a malicious twinkle of the eye; for he fancied that he had at last touched the weak point of his adversary.

"No, my dear Harcourt, the *crassæ naturæ* have rather the best of it, since no small share of this world's collisions are actually physical shocks; and that great strong pipkin that encloses your brains will stand much that would smash the poor egg-shell that shrouds mine."

"Whenever you draw a comparison in my favor, I always find at the end I come off worst," said Harcourt, bluntly; and Upton laughed one of his rich, musical laughs, in which there was indeed nothing mirthful, but something that seemed to say that his nature experienced a sense of enjoyment higher, perhaps, than anything merely comic could suggest.

"You came off best this time, Harcourt," said he, good-humoredly; and such a thorough air of frankness accompanied the words that Harcourt was disarmed of all distrust at once, and joined in the laugh heartily.

"But you have not yet told me, Harcourt," said the other, "where you have been, and why you spent your night on the sea."

"The story is not a very long one," replied he; and at once gave a full recital of the events, which our reader has already had before him in our last chapter, adding, in conclusion,

" I have left the boy in a cabin at Belmullet ; he is in a high
fever, and raving so loud that you could hear him a hundred yards away. I told them to keep cold water on his
head, and give him plenty of it to drink, — nothing more,
— till I could fetch our doctor over, for it will be impossible
to move the boy from where he is for the present."

" Glencore has been asking for him already this morning.
He did not desire to see him, but he begged of me to go to
him and speak with him."

" And have you told him that he was from home, — that
he passed the night away from this ? "

" No ; I merely intimated that I should look after him,
waiting for your return to guide myself afterwards."

" I don't suspect that when we took him from the boat the
malady had set in ; he appeared rather like one overcome
by cold and exhaustion. It was about two hours after, — he
had taken some food and seemed stronger, — when I said to
him, ' Come, Charley, you'll soon be all right again ; I have
sent a fellow to look after a pony for you, and you'll be able
to ride back, won't you ? '

" ' Ride where ? ' cried he, eagerly.

" ' Home, of course,' said I, ' to Glencore.'

" ' Home ! I have no home,' cried he ; and the wild scream
he uttered the words with, I'll never forget. It was just as
if that one thought was the boundary between sense and
reason, and the instant he had passed it, all was chaos and
confusion ; for now his raving began, — the most frantic
imaginations ; always images of sorrow, and with a rapidity of utterance there was no following. Of course in such
cases the delusions suggest no clew to the cause, but all his
fancies were about being driven out of doors an outcast and
a beggar, and of his father rising from his sick bed to curse
him. Poor boy ! Even in this his better nature gleamed
forth as he cried, ' Tell him ' — and he said the words in a
low whisper — ' tell him not to anger himself ; he is ill, very
ill, and should be kept tranquil. Tell him, then, that I am
going — going away forever, and he'll hear of me no
more.' " As Harcourt repeated the words, his own voice
faltered, and two heavy drops slowly coursed down his
bronzed cheeks. " You see," added he, as if to excuse the

emotion, " that was n't like raving, for he spoke this just as
he might have done if his very heart was breaking."

" Poor fellow ! " said Upton : and the words were uttered
with real feeling.

" Some terrible scene must have occurred between them,"
resumed Harcourt ; " of that I feel quite certain."

" I suspect you are right," said Upton, bending over his
teacup ; " and *our* part, in consequence, is one of considerable delicacy ; for until Glencore alludes to what has passed,
we, of course, can take no notice of it. The boy is ill ; he
is in a fever : we know nothing more."

" I 'll leave you to deal with the father ; the son shall be
my care. I have told Traynor to be ready to start with me
after breakfast, and have ordered two stout ponies for the
journey. I conclude there will be no objection in detaining
the doctor for the night : what think you, Upton ? "

" Do *you* consult the doctor on that head ; meanwhile, I 'll
pay a visit to Glencore. I 'll meet you in the library." And
so saying, Upton rose, and gracefully draping the folds of
his dressing-gown, and arranging the waving lock of hair
which had escaped beneath his cap, he slowly set out towards
the sick man's chamber.

Of all the springs of human action, there was not one in
which Sir Horace Upton sympathized so little as passion.
That any man could adopt a line of conduct from which no
other profit could result than what might minister to a feeling of hatred, jealousy, or revenge, seemed to him utterly
contemptible. It was not, indeed, the morality of such a
course that he called in question, although he would not have
contested that point. It was its meanness, its folly, its
insufficiency. His experience of great affairs had imbued
him with all the importance that was due to temper and mod-
eration. He scarcely remembered an instant where a false
move had damaged a negotiation that it could not be traced
to some passing trait of impatience, or some lurking spirit
of animosity biding the hour of its gratification.

He had long learned to perceive how much more temperament has to do, in the management of great events,
than talent or capacity, and his opinion of men was chiefly
founded on this quality of their nature. It was, then, with

an almost pitying estimate of Glencore that he now entered the room where the sick man lay.

Anxious to be alone with him, Glencore had dismissed all the attendants from his room, and sat, propped up by pillows, eagerly awaiting his approach.

Upton moved through the dimly lighted room like one familiar to the atmosphere of illness, and took his seat beside the bed with that noiseless quiet which in *him* was a kind of instinct.

It was several minutes before Glencore spoke, and then, in a low, faint voice, he said, " Are we alone, Upton ? "

" Yes," said the other, gently pressing the wasted fingers which lay on the counterpane before him.

" You forgive me, Upton," said he, — and the words trembled as he uttered them, — " You forgive me, Upton, though I cannot forgive myself."

" My dear friend, a passing moment of impatience is not to breach the friendship of a lifetime. Your calmer judgment would, I know, not be unjust to me."

" But how am I to repair the wrong I have done you?"

" By never alluding to it, — never thinking of it again, Glencore."

" It is so unworthy, so ignoble in me!" cried Glencore, bitterly; and a tear fell over his eyelid and rested on his wan and worn cheek.

" Let us never think of it, my dear Glencore. Life has real troubles enough for either of us, not to dwell on those which we may fashion out of our emotions. I promise you, I have forgotten the whole incident."

Glencore sighed heavily, but did not speak; at last he said, " Be it so, Upton," and, covering his face with his hand, lay still and silent. " Well," said he, after a long pause, " the die is cast, Upton: I have told him ! "

" Told the boy?" said Upton.

He nodded an assent. " It is too late to oppose me now, Upton, — the thing is done. I didn't think I had strength for it; but revenge is a strong stimulant, and I felt as though once more restored to health, as I proceeded. Poor fellow! he bore it like a man. Like a man, do I say? No, but better than man ever bore such crushing tidings.

He asked me to stop once, while his head reeled, and said, ' In a minute I shall be myself again,' and so he was, too; you should have seen him, Upton, as he rose to leave me. So much of dignity was there in his look that my heart misgave me; and I told him that still, as my son, he should never want a friend and a protector. He grew deadly pale, and caught at the bed for support. Another moment, and I 'd not have answered for myself. I was already relenting; but I thought of *her*, and my resolution came back in all its force. Still, I dared not look on him. The sight of that wan cheek, those quivering lips and glassy eyes, would certainly have unmanned me. I turned away. When I looked round, he was gone!" As he ceased to speak, a clammy perspiration burst forth over his face and forehead, and he made a sign to Upton to wet his lips.

"It is the last pang she is to cost me, Upton, but it is a sore one!" said he, in a low, hoarse whisper.

"My dear Glencore, this is all little short of madness; even as revenge it is a failure, since the heaviest share of the penalty recoils upon yourself."

"How so?" cried he, impetuously.

"Is it thus that an ancient name is to go out forever? Is it in this wise that a house noble for centuries is to crumble into ruin? I will not again urge upon you the cruel wrong you are doing. Over that boy's inheritance you have no more right than over mine,—you cannot rob him of the protection of the law. No power could ever give you the disposal of his destiny in this wise."

"I have done it, and I will maintain it, sir," cried Glencore; "and if the question is, as you vaguely hint, to be one of law —"

"No, no, Glencore; do not mistake me."

"Hear me out, sir," said he, passionately. "If it is to be one of law, let Sir Horace Upton give his testimony,— tell all that he knows,—and let us see what it will avail him. You may—it is quite open to you—place us front to front as enemies. You may teach the boy to regard me as one who has robbed him of his birthright, and train him up to become my accuser in a court of justice. But my cause is a strong one, it cannot be shaken; and where you hope to brand *me* with tyranny, you will but visit bastardy upon *him*. Think twice, then, before you declare this combat. It is one where all your craft will not sustain you."

"My dear Glencore, it is not in this spirit that we can speak profitably to each other. If you will not hear my reasons calmly and dispassionately, to what end am I here? You have long known me as one who lays claim to no more rigid morality than consists with the theory of a worldly man's experiences. I affect no high-flown sentiments. I am as plain and practical as may be; and when I tell you that you are wrong in this affair. I mean to say that what you are about to do is not only bad, but impolitic. In your pursuit of a victim, you are immolating yourself."

"Be it so; I go not alone to the stake; there is another to partake of the torture," cried Glencore, wildly; and already his flushed cheek and flashing eyes betrayed the approach of a feverish access.

"If I am not to have any influence with you, then," resumed Upton. "I am here to no purpose. If to all that I say — to arguments you cannot answer — you obstinately persist in opposing an insane thirst for revenge. I see not why you should desire my presence. You have resolved to do this great wrong?"

"It is already done, sir," broke in Glencore.

"Wherein, then, can I be of any service to you?"

"I am coming to that. I had come to it before, had you not interrupted me. I want you to be guardian to the boy. I want you to replace me in all that regards authority over him. You know life well, Upton. You know it not alone in its paths of pleasure and success, but you understand thoroughly the rugged footway over which humble men toil wearily to fortune. None can better estimate a man's chances of success, nor more surely point the road by which he is to attain it. The provision which I destine for him will be an humble one, and he will need to rely upon his own efforts. You will not refuse me this service, Upton. I ask it in the name of our old friendship."

"There is but one objection I could possibly have, and yet that seems to be insurmountable."

"And what may it be?" cried Glencore.

"Simply, that in acceding to your request, I make myself

an accomplice in your plan, and thus aid and abet the very scheme I am repudiating."

"What avails your repudiation if it will not turn me from my resolve? That it will not, I'll swear to you as solemnly as ever an oath was taken. I tell you again, the thing is done. For the consequences which are to follow on it you have no responsibility; these are my concern."

"I should like a little time to think over it," said Upton, with the air of one struggling with irresolution. "Let me have this evening to make up my mind; to-morrow you shall have my answer."

"Be it so, then," said Glencore; and, turning his face away, waved a cold farewell with his hand.

We do not purpose to follow Sir Horace as he retired, nor does our task require that we should pry into the secret recesses of his wily nature; enough if we say that in asking for time, his purpose was rather to afford another opportunity of reflection to Glencore than to give himself more space for deliberation. He had found, by the experience of his calling, that the delay we often crave for, to resolve a doubt, has sufficed to change the mind of him who originated the difficulty.

"I'll give him some hours, at least," thought he, "to ponder over what I have said. Who knows but the argument may seem better in memory than in action? Such things have happened before now." And having finished this reflection, he turned to peruse the pamphlet of a quack doctor who pledged himself to cure all disorders of the circulation by attending to tidal influences, and made the moon herself enter into the *materia medica*. What Sir Horace believed, or did not believe, in the wild rhapsodies of the charlatan, is known only to himself. Whether his credulity was fed by the hope of obtaining relief, or whether his fancy only was aroused by the speculative images thus suggested, it is impossible to say. It is not altogether improbable that he perused these things as Charles Fox used to read all the trashiest novels of the Minerva Press, and find, in the very distorted and exaggerated pictures, a relief and a relaxation which more correct views of life had failed to impart. Hard-headed men require strange indulgences.

CHAPTER XIV.

BILLY TRAYNOR AND THE COLONEL.

It was a fine breezy morning as the Colonel set out with Billy Traynor for Belmullet. The bridle-path by which they travelled led through a wild and thinly inhabited tract, — now dipping down between grassy hills, now tracing its course along the cliffs over the sea. Tall ferns covered the slopes, protected from the west winds, and here and there little copses of stunted oak showed the traces of what once had been forest. It was, on the whole, a silent and dreary region, so that the travellers felt it even relief as they drew nigh the bright blue sea, and heard the sonorous booming of the waves as they broke along the shore.

" It cheers one to come up out of those dreary dells, and hear the pleasant plash of the sea," said Harcourt; and his bright face showed that he felt the enjoyment.

" So it does, sir," said Billy. " And yet Homer makes his hero go heavy-hearted as he hears the ever-sounding sea."

" What does that signify, Doctor?" said Harcourt, impatiently. " Telling me what a character in a fiction feels affects me no more than telling me what he does. Why, man, the one is as unreal as the other. The fellow that created him fashioned his thoughts as well as his actions."

"To be sure he did; but when the fellow is a janius, what he makes is as much a crayture as either you or myself."

" Come, come, Doctor, no mystification."

" I don't mean any," broke in Billy. " What I want to say is this, that as we read every character to elicit truth, — truth in the working of human motives, truth in passion.

truth in all the struggles of our poor weak natures, —
why would n't a great janius like Homer, or Shakspeare, or
Milton, be better able to show us this in some picture drawn
by themselves, than you or I be able to find it out for
ourselves?"

Harcourt shook his head doubtfully.

"Well, now," said Billy, returning to the charge, "did
you ever see a waxwork model of anatomy? Every nerve
and siny of a nerve was there, — not a vein nor an artery
wanting. The artist that made it all just wanted to show
you where everything was; but he never wanted you to
believe it was alive, or ever had been. But with janius
it 's different. He just gives you some traits of a character,
he points him out to you passing, — just as I would to a
man going along the street, — and there he is alive for ever
and ever; not like you and me, that will be dead and
buried to-morrow or next day, and the most known of us
three lines in a parish registhry, but he goes down to
posterity an example, an illustration — or a warning, maybe
— to thousands and thousands of living men. Don't talk
to me about fiction! What *he* thought and felt is truer
than all that you and I and a score like us ever did or
ever will do. The creations of janius are the landmarks
of humanity; and well for us is it that we have such to
guide us!"

"All this may be very fine," said Harcourt, contemptuously, "but give *me* the sentiments of a living man, or one
that has lived, in preference to all the imaginary characters
that have ever adorned a story."

"Just as I suppose that you 'd say that a soldier in
the Blues, or some big, hulking corporal in the Guards,
is a finer model of the human form than ever Praxiteles
chiselled."

"I know which I 'd rather have alongside of me in a
charge, Doctor," said Harcourt, laughing; and then, to
change the topic, he pointed to a lone cabin on the sea-shore,
miles away, as it seemed, from all other habitations.

"That 's Michel Cady's, sir," said Traynor; "he lives
by birds, — hunting them saygulls and cormorants through
the crevices of the rocks, and stealing the eggs. There

8

is n't a precipice that he won't climb, not a cliff that he
won't face."

" Well, if that be his home, the pursuit does not seem a
profitable one."

" 'T is as good as breaking stones on the road for four-
pence a day, or carrying sea-weed five miles on your back
to manure the potatoes," said Billy, mournfully.

" That 's exactly the very thing that puzzles me," said
Harcourt, " why, in a country so remarkable for fertility,
every one should be so miserably poor ! "

" And you never heard any explanation of it? "

" Never; at least, never one that satisfied me."

" Nor ever will you," said Billy, sententiously.

" And why so? "

" Because," said he, drawing a long breath, as if preparing for a discourse, — " because there 's no man capable of
going into the whole subject; for it 's not merely an eco-
nomical question or a social one, but it is metaphysical, and
religious, and political, and ethnological, and historical, —
ay, and geographical too ! You have to consider, first,
who and what are the aborigines. A conquered people that
never gave in they were conquered. Who are the rulers?
A Saxon race that always felt that they were infarior to
them they ruled over ! "

" By Jove, Doctor, I must stop you there ; I never heard
any acknowledgment of this inferiority you speak of."

" I 'd like to get a goold medal for arguin' it out with
you," said Billy.

" And, after all, I don't see how it would resolve the
original doubt," said Harcourt. " I want to know why the
people are so poor, and I don't want to hear of the battle of
Clontarf, or the Danes at Dundalk."

" There it is, you 'd like to narrow down a great question
of race, language, traditions, and laws to a little miserable
dispute about labor and wages. O Manchester, Manchester ! how ye 're in the heart of every Englishman, rich or
poor, gentle or simple ! You say you never heard of any
confession of inferiority. Of course you did n't ; but quite
the reverse, — a very confident sense of being far better than
the poor Irish ; and I 'll tell you how, and why, just as

you, yourself, after a discusshion with me, when you find yourself dead bate, and not a word to reply, you'll go home to a good dinner and a bottle of wine, dry clothes and a bright fire; and no matter how hard my argument pushed you, you'll remember that *I'm* in rags, in a dirty cabin, with potatoes to ate and water to drink, and you'll say, at all events, 'I'm better off than he is;' and there's your superiority, neither more or less, — there it is!   And all the while, *I'm* saying the same thing to *myself*, — 'Sorrow matter for his fine broadcloth, and his white linen, and his very best roast beef that he's atin', — I'm his master!   In all that dignifies the spacies in them grand qualities that makes us poets, rhetoricians, and the like, in those elegant attributes that, as the poet says, —

> " In all our pursuits
>   Lifts us high above brutes,' "

— in these, I say again. I'm his master!'"

As Billy finished his glowing panegyric upon his country and himself, he burst out in a joyous laugh, and cried. " Did ye ever hear conceit like that?   Did ye ever expect to see the day that a ragged poor blackguard like *me* would dare to say as much to one like *you?* And, after all, it's the greatest compliment I could pay you."

" How so, Billy?   I don't exactly see *that*."

" Why, that if you were n't a gentleman, — a raal gentleman, born and bred, — I could never have ventured to tell you what I said now.   It is because, in *your own* refined feelings, you can pardon all the coarseness of *mine*, that I have my safety."

" You 're as great a courtier as you are a scholar. Billy." said Harcourt, laughing; " meanwhile, I'm not likely to be enlightened as to the cause of Irish poverty."

" 'T is a whole volume I could write on the same subject." said Billy; " for there's so many causes in operation, combinin', and assistin', and aggravatin' each other.   But if you want the head and front of the mischief in one word, it is this, that no Irishman ever gave his heart and sowl to his own business, but always was mindin' something else that he had nothin' to say to; and so, ye see, the priest does be

thinkin' of politics, the parson's thinkin' of the priest, the
people are always on the watch for a crack at the agent or
the tithe-proctor, and the landlord, instead of looking after
his property, is up in Dublin dinin' with the Lord-Leftinint
and abusin' his tenants. I don't want to screen myself, nor
say I'm better than my neighbors, for though I have a
larned profession to live by, I'd rather be writin' a ballad,
and singin' it too, down Thomas Street, than I'd be lecturin'
at the Surgeons' Hall."

" You are certainly a very strange people," said Harcourt.

" And yet there's another thing stranger still, which is,
that your countrymen never took any advantage of our
eccentricities, to rule us by; and if they had any wit in
their heads, they'd have seen, easy enough, that all these
traits are exactly the clews to a nation's heart. That's
what Pitt meant when he said, ' Let me make the *songs* of a
people, and I don't care who makes the *laws*.' Look down
now in that glen before you, as far as you can see. There's
Belmullet, and ain't you glad to be so near your journey's
end? for you're mighty tired of all this discoorsin'."

" On the contrary, Billy, even when I disagree with what
you say, I'm pleased to hear your reasons; at the same
time, I'm glad we are drawing nigh to this poor boy, and I
only trust we may not be too late."

Billy muttered a pious concurrence in the wish, and they
rode along for some time in silence. " There's the Bay of
Belmullet now under your feet," cried Billy, as he pulled up
short, and pointed with his whip seaward. " There's five
fathoms, and fine anchoring ground on every inch ye see
there. There's elegant shelter from tempestuous winds.
There's a coast rich in herrings, oysters, lobsters, and crabs;
farther out there's cod, and haddock, and mackerel in the
sayson. There's sea wrack for kelp, and every other con-
vanience any one can require; and a poorer set of devils
than ye'll see when we get down there, there's nowhere to
be found. Well, well! ' if idleness is bliss, it's folly to
work hard.' " And with this paraphrase, Billy made way
for the Colonel, as the path had now become too narrow for
two abreast, and in this way they descended to the shore.

CHAPTER XV.

A SICK BED.

ALTHOUGH the cabin in which the sick boy lay was one of the best in the village, its interior presented a picture of great poverty. It consisted of a single room, in the middle of which a mud wall of a few feet in height formed a sort of partition, abutting against which was the bed, — the one bed of the entire family, — now devoted to the guest. Two or three coarsely fashioned stools, a rickety table, and a still more rickety dresser comprised all the furniture. The floor was uneven and fissured, and the solitary window was mended with an old hat, — thus diminishing the faint light which struggled through the narrow aperture.

A large net, attached to the rafters, hung down in heavy festoons overhead, the corks and sinks dangling in dangerous proximity to the heads underneath. Several spars and oars littered one corner, and a newly painted buoy filled another; but, in spite of all these encumbrances, there was space around the fire for a goodly company of some eight or nine of all ages, who were pleasantly eating their supper from a large pot of potatoes that smoked and steamed in front of them.

"God save all here!" cried Billy, as he preceded the Colonel into the cabin.

"Save ye kindly," was the courteous answer, in a chorus of voices; at the same time, seeing a gentleman at the door, the whole party arose at once to receive him. Nothing could have surpassed the perfect good-breeding with which the fisherman and his wife did the honors of their humble home; and Harcourt at once forgot the poverty-struck aspect of the scene in the general courtesy of the welcome.

"He's no better, your honor, — no better at all," said the man, as Harcourt drew nigh the sick bed. "He does be always ravin', — ravin' on, — beggin' and implorin' that we won't take him back to the Castle; and if he falls asleep, the first thing he says when he wakes up is, 'Where am I? — tell me I'm not at Glencore!' and he keeps on screechin', 'Tell me, tell me so!'"

Harcourt bent down over the bed and gazed at him. Slowly and languidly the sick boy raised his heavy lids and returned the stare.

"You know me, Charley, boy, don't you?" said he, softly.

"Yes," muttered he, in a weak tone.

"Who am I, Charley? Tell me who is speaking to you."

"Yes," said he again.

"Poor fellow!" sighed Harcourt, "he does *not* know me!"

"Where's the pain?" asked Billy, suddenly.

The boy placed his hand on his forehead, and then on his temples.

"Look up! look at *me!*" said Billy. "Ay, there it is! the pupil does not contract, — there's mischief in the brain. He wants to say something to you, sir," said he to Harcourt; "he's makin' signs to you to stoop down."

Harcourt put his ear close to the sick boy's lips, and listened.

"No, my dear child, of course not," said he, after a pause. "You shall remain here, and I will stay with you too. In a few days your father will come — "

A wild yell, a shriek that made the cabin ring, now broke from the boy, followed by another, and then a third; and then with a spring he arose from the bed, and tried to escape. Weak and exhausted as he was, such was the strength supplied by fever, it was all that they could do to subdue him and replace him in the bed; violent convulsions followed this severe access, and it was not till after hours of intense suffering that he calmed down again and seemed to slumber.

"There's more than we know of here, Colonel," said Billy, as he drew him to one side. "There's moral causes as well as malady at work."

" There may be, but I know nothing of them," said Harcourt; and in the frank air of the speaker the other did not hesitate to repose his trust.

" If we hope to save him, we ought to find out where the mischief lies," said Billy; " for, if ye remark, his ravin' is always upon one subject; he never wanders from that."

" He has a dread of home. Some altercation with his father has, doubtless, impressed him with this notion."

" Ah, that is n't enough, we must go deeper; we want a clew to the part of the brain engaged. Meanwhile, here's at him, with the antiphlogistic touch; " and he opened his lancet-case, and tucked up his cuffs. " Houlde the basin, Biddy."

" There, Harvey himself could n't do it nater than that. It's an elegant study to be feelin' a pulse while the blood is flowin'. It comes at first like a dammed-up cataract, a regular out-pouring, just as a young girl would tell her love, all wild and tumultuous; then, after a time, she gets more temperate, the feelings are relieved, and the ardor is moderated, till at last, wearied and worn out, the heart seems to ask for rest; and then ye'll remark a settled faint smile coming over the lips, and a clammy coldness in the face."

" He's fainting, sir," broke in Biddy.

" He is, ma'am, and it's myself done it," said Billy. " Oh, dear, oh, dear! If we could only do with the moral heart what we can with the raal physical one, what wonderful poets we'd be! "

" What hopes have you? " whispered Harcourt.

" The best, the very best. There's youth and a fine constitution to work upon; and what more does a doctor want? As ould Marsden said, ' You can't destroy these in a fortnight, so the patient must live.' But you must help me, Colonel, and you *can* help me."

" Command me in any way, Doctor."

" Here's the *modus*, then. You must go back to the Castle and find out, if you can, what happened between his father and *him*. It does not signify now, nor will it for some days; but when he comes to the convalescent stage, it's then we'll need to know how to manage him, and what

subjects to keep him away from. 'T is the same with the
brain as with a sprained ankle; you may exercise if you
don't twist it; but just come down once on the wrong spot,
and maybe ye won't yell out!' "

" You 'll not quit him, then."

" I 'm a senthry on his post, waiting to get a shot at the
enemy if he shows the top of his head. Ah, sir, if ye only
knew physic, ye 'd acknowledge there 's nothing as treacherous as dizaze. Ye hunt him out of the brain, and then he
is in the lungs. Ye chase him out of that, and he skulks in
the liver. At him there, and he takes to the fibrous membranes, and then it 's regular hide-and-go-seek all over the
body. Trackin' a bear is child's play to it." And so saying, Billy held the Colonel's stirrup for him to mount, and
giving his most courteous salutation, and his best wishes
for a good journey, he turned and re-entered the cabin.

CHAPTER XVI.

THE " PROJECT."

IT was not without surprise that Harcourt saw Glencore enter the drawing-room a few minutes before dinner. Very pale and very feeble, he slowly traversed the room, giving a hand to each of his guests, and answering the inquiries for his health by a sickly smile, while he said, " As you see me."

" I am going to dine with you to-day, Harcourt," said he, with an attempt at gayety of manner. " Upton tells me that a little exertion of this kind will do me good."

" Upton's right," cried the Colonel, " especially if he added that you should take a glass or two of that admirable Burgundy. My life on 't, but that is the liquor to set a man on his legs again."

" I did n't remark that this was exactly the effect it produced upon you t' other night," said Upton, with one of his own sly laughs.

" That comes of drinking it in bad company," retorted Harcourt; " a man is driven to take two glasses for one."

As the dinner proceeded, Glencore rallied considerably, taking his part in the conversation, and evidently enjoying the curiously contrasted temperaments at either side of him. The one, all subtlety, refinement, and finesse; the other, out-spoken, rude, and true-hearted; rarely correct in a question of taste, but invariably right in every matter of honorable dealing. Though it was clear enough that Upton relished the eccentricities whose sallies he provoked, it was no less easy to see how thoroughly he appreciated the frank and manly nature of the old soldier; nor could all the crafty habits of his acute mind overcome the hearty admiration with which he regarded him.

It is in the unrestricted case of these "little dinners," where two or three old friends are met, that social intercourse assumes its most charming form. The usages of the great world, which exact a species of uniformity of breeding and manners, are here laid aside, and men talk with all the bias and prejudices of their true nature, dashing the topics discussed with traits of personality, and even whims, that are most amusing. How little do we carry away of tact or wisdom from the grand banquets of life; and what pleasant stores of thought, what charming memories remain to us, after those small gatherings!

How, as I write this, one little room rises to my recollection, with its quaint old sideboard of carved oak; its dark-brown cabinets, curiously sculptured; its heavy old brocade curtains, and all its queer devices of knick-knackery, where such meetings once were held, and where, throwing off the cares of life, — shut out from them, as it were, by the massive folds of the heavy drapery across the door, — we talked in all the fearless freedom of old friendship, rambling away from theme to theme, contrasting our experiences, balancing our views in life, and mingling through our converse the racy freshness of a boy's enjoyment with the sager counsels of a man's reflectiveness. Alas! how very early is it sometimes in life that we tread "the banquet-hall deserted." But to our story: the evening wore pleasantly on; Upton talked, as few but himself could do, upon the public questions of the day; and Harcourt, with many a blunt interruption, made the discourse but more easy and amusing. The soldier was, indeed, less at his ease than the others. It was not alone that many of the topics were not such as he was most familiar with, but he felt angry and indignant at Glencore's seeming indifference as to the fate of his son. Not a single reference to him even occurred; his name was never even passingly mentioned. Nothing but the careworn, sickly face, the wasted form and dejected expression before him, could have restrained Harcourt from alluding to the boy. He bethought him, however, that any indiscretion on his part might have the gravest consequences. Upton, too, might have said something to quiet Glencore's mind. "At all events, I'll wait," said he to himself; "for wherever

there is much delicacy in a negotiation, I generally make a
mess of it." The more genially, therefore, did Glencore
lend himself to the pleasure of the conversation, the more
provoked did Harcourt feel at his heartlessness, and the more
did the struggle cost him to control his own sentiments.

Upton, who detected the secret working of men's minds
with a marvellous exactness, saw how the poor Colonel was
suffering, and that, in all probability, some unhappy ex-
plosion would at last ensue, and took an opportunity of
remarking that though all this chit-chat was delightful for
them, Glencore was still a sick man.

"We must n't forget, Harcourt," said he, "that a chicken-
broth diet includes very digestible small-talk; and here we
are leading our poor friend through politics, war, diplomacy,
and the rest of it, just as if he had the stomach of an old
campaigner and —"

"And the brain of a great diplomatist! Say it out, man,
and avow honestly the share of excellence you accord to each
of us," broke in Harcourt, laughing.

"I would to Heaven we could exchange," sighed Upton,
languidly.

"The saints forbid!" exclaimed the other; "and it
would do us little good if we were able."

"Why so?"

"I'd never know what to do with that fine intellect if I
had it; and as for *you*, what with your confounded pills and
mixtures, your infernal lotions and embrocations, you'd
make my sound system as bad as your own in three months'
time."

"You are quite wrong, my dear Harcourt: I should treat
the stomach as you would do the brain, — give it next to
nothing to do, in the hopes it might last the longer."

"There now, good night," said Harcourt; "he's always
the better for bitters, whether he gives or takes them."
And with a good-humored laugh he left the room.

Glencore's eyes followed him as he retired; and then, as
they closed, an expression as of long-repressed suffering
settled down on his features so marked that Upton hastily
asked, —

"Are you ill, are you in pain, Glencore?"

" In pain? Yes," said he, " these two hours back I have been suffering intensely; but there's no help for it! Must you really leave this to-morrow, Upton?"

" I must. This letter from the Foreign Office requires my immediate presence in London, with a very great likelihood of being obliged to start at once for the Continent."

" And I had so much to say, — so many things to consult you on," sighed the other.

" Are you equal to it now?" asked Upton.

" I must try, at all events. You shall learn my plan." He was silent for some minutes, and sat with his head resting on his hand, in deep reflection. At last he said, " Has it ever occurred to you, Upton, that some incident of the past, some circumstance in itself insignificant, should rise up, as it were, in after life to suit an actual emergency, just as though fate had fashioned it for such a contingency?"

" I cannot say that I have experienced what you describe, if, indeed, I fully understand it."

" I'll explain better by an instance. You know now," — here his voice became slow, and the words fell with a marked distinctness, — " you know now what I intend by this woman. Well, just as if to make my plan more feasible, a circumstance intended for a very different object offers itself to my aid. When my uncle, Sir Miles Herrick, heard that I was about to marry a foreigner, he declared that he would never leave me a shilling of his fortune. I am not very sure that I cared much for the threat when it was uttered. My friends, however, thought differently; and though they did not attempt to dissuade me from my marriage, they suggested that I should try some means of overcoming this prejudice; at all events, that I should not hurry on the match without an effort to obtain his consent. I agreed, — not very willingly, indeed, — and so the matter remained. The circumstance was well known amongst my two or three most intimate friends, and constantly discussed by them. I need n't tell you that the tone in which such things are talked of as often partakes of levity as seriousness. They gave me all manner of absurd counsels, one more outrageously ridiculous than the other. At last, one day, — we were picnicking at Baia, — Old Clifford, — you

remember that original who had the famous schooner-yacht
' The Breeze,'— well, he took me aside after dinner, and said,
' Glencore, I have it, — I have just hit upon the expedient.
Your uncle and I were old chums at Christ Church fifty
years ago. What if we were to tell him that you were going
to marry a daughter of mine? I don't think he'd object.
I'm half certain he'd not. I have been abroad these five-
and-thirty years. Nobody in England knows much about
me now. Old Herrick can't live forever; he is my senior
by a good ten or twelve years; and if the delusion only
lasts his time —'

" 'But perhaps you have a daughter?' broke I in.

" 'I have, and she is married already, so there is no risk
on that score.' I need n't repeat all that he said for, nor
that I urged against, the project; for though it was after
dinner, and we all had drunk very freely, the deception was
one I firmly rejected. When a man shows a great desire to
serve you on a question of no common difficulty, it is very
hard to be severe upon his counsels, however unscrupulous
they may be. In fact, you accept them as proofs of friendship only the stronger, seeing how much they must have cost
him to offer."

Upton smiled dubiously, and Glencore, blushing slightly,
said, " You don't concur in this, I perceive."

" Not exactly," said Upton, in his silkiest of tones; " I
rather regard these occasions as I should do the generosity
of a man who, filling my hand with base money, should say,
' Pass it if you can !' "

" In this case, however," resumed Glencore, " he took his
share of the fraud, or at least was willing to do so, for I
distinctly said ' No' to the whole scheme. He grew very
warm about it; at one moment appealing to my ' good sense,
not to kick seven thousand a year out of the window;' at
the next, in half-quarrelsome mood, asking ' if it were any
objection I had to be connected with his family.' To get rid
of a very troublesome subject, and to end a controversy that
threatened to disturb a party, I said at last, ' We'll talk it
over to-morrow, Clifford, and if your arguments be as good
as your heart, then perhaps they may yet convince me.'
This ended the theme, and we parted. I started the next

day on a shooting excursion into Calabria, and when I got back it was not of meeting Clifford I was thinking. I hastened to meet the Della Torres, and then came our elopement. You know the rest. We went to the East, passed the winter in Upper Egypt, and came to Cairo in spring, where Charley was born. I got back to Naples after a year or two, and then found that my uncle had just died, and in consequence of my marrying the daughter of his old and attached friend, Sir Guy Clifford, had reversed the intention of his will, and by a codicil left me his sole heir. It was thus that my marriage, and even my boy's birth, became inserted in the Peerage; my solicitor, in his vast eagerness for my interests, having taken care to indorse the story with his own name. The disinherited nephews and nieces, the half-cousins and others, soon got wind of the real facts, and contested the will, on the ground of its being executed under a delusion. I, of course, would not resist their claim, and satisfied myself by denying the statement as to my marriage; and so, after affording the current subject of gossip for a season, I was completely forgotten, the more as we went to live abroad, and never mixed with English. And now, Upton, it is this same incident I would utilize for the present occasion, though, as I said before, when it originally occurred it had a very different signification."

"I don't exactly see how," said Upton.

"In this wise. My real marriage was never inserted in the Peerage. I'll now manage that it shall so appear, to give me the opportunity of formally contradicting it, and alluding to the strange persistence with which, having married me some fifteen years ago to a lady who never existed, they now are pleased to unite me to one whose character might have secured me against the calumny. I'll threaten an action for libel, etc., obtain a most full, explicit, and abject apology, and then, when this has gone the round of all the journals of Europe, her doom is sealed!"

"But she has surely letters, writings, proofs of some sort."

"No, Upton, I have not left a scrap in her possession; she has not a line, not a letter to vindicate her. On the night I broke open her writing-desk, I took away everything that bore the traces of my own hand. I tell you again she is in my power, and never was power less disposed to mercy."

"Once more, my dear friend," said Upton, "I am driven to tell you that I cannot be a profitable counsellor in a matter to every detail of which I object. Consider calmly for one moment what you are doing. See how, in your desire to be avenged upon *her*, you throw the heaviest share of the penalty on your own poor boy. I am not her advocate now. I will not say one word to mitigate the course of your anger towards her, but remember that you are actually defrauding him of his birthright. This is not a question where you have a choice. There is no discretionary power left you."

"I'll do it," said Glencore, with a savage energy.

"In other words, to wreak a vengeance upon one, you are prepared to immolate another, not only guiltless, but who possesses every claim to your love and affection."

"And do you think that if I sacrifice the last tie that attaches me to life, Upton, that I retire from this contest heart-whole? No, far from it; I go forth from the struggle broken, blasted, friendless!"

"And do you mean that this vengeance should outlive you? Suppose, for instance, that she should survive you."

"It shall be to live on in shame, then," cried he, savagely.

"And were she to die first?"

"In that case — I have not thought well enough about that. It is possible, — it is just possible; but these are subtleties, Upton, to detach me from my purpose, or weaken my resolution to carry it through. You would apply the craft of your calling to the case, and, by suggesting emergencies, open a road to evasions. Enough for me the present. I neither care to prejudge the future, nor control it. I know," cried he, suddenly, and with eyes flashing angrily as he spoke, — "I know that if you desire to use the confidence I have reposed in you against me, you can give me trouble and even difficulty; but I defy Sir Horace Upton, with all his skill and all his cunning, to outwit me."

There was that in the tone in which he uttered these words, and the exaggerated energy of his manner, that convinced Upton, Glencore's reason was not intact. It was not

what could amount to aberration in the ordinary sense, but
sufficient evidence was there to show that judgment had become so obscured by passion that the mental power was
weakened by the moral.

"Tell me, therefore, Upton," cried he, "before we part,
do you leave this house my friend or my enemy?"

"It is as your sincere, attached friend that I now dispute
with you, inch by inch, a dangerous position, with a judgment under no influence from passion, viewing this question
by the coldest of all tests, — mere expediency —'

"There it is," broke in Glencore; "you claim an advantage over me, because you are devoid of feeling; but this is
a case, sir, where the sense of injury gives the instinct of
reparation. Is it nothing to me, think you, that I am content to go down dishonored to my grave, but also to be the
last of my name and station? Is it nothing that a whole
line of honorable ancestry is extinguished at once? Is it
nothing that I surrender him who formed my sole solace
and companionship in life? You talk of your calm, un-
biassed mind; but I tell you, till your brain be on fire like
mine, and your heart swollen to very bursting, that you have
no right to dictate to *me!* Besides, it is done! The blow
has fallen," added he, with a deeper solemnity of voice.
"The gulf that separates us is already created. She and I
can meet no more. But why continue this contest? It was
to aid me in directing that boy's fortunes I first sought your
advice, not to attempt to dissuade me from what I will not
be turned from."

"In what way can I serve you?" said Upton, calmly.

"Will you consent to be his guardian?"

"I will."

Glencore seized the other's hand, and pressed it to his
heart, and for some seconds he could not speak.

"This is all that I ask, Upton," said he. "It is the
greatest boon friendship could accord me. I need no more.
Could you have remained here a day or two more, we could
have settled upon some plan together as to his future life; as
it is, we can arrange it by letter."

"He must leave this," said Upton, thoughtfully.

"Of course, — at once!"

"How far is Harcourt to be informed in this matter: have you spoken to him already?"

"No; nor mean to do so. I should have from *him* nothing but reproaches for having betrayed the boy into false hopes of a station he was never to fill. You must tell Harcourt. I leave it to yourself to find the suitable moment."

"We shall need his assistance," said Upton, whose quick faculties were already busily travelling many a mile of the future. "I'll see him to-night, and try what can be done. In a few days you will have turned over in your mind what you yourself destine for him, — the fortune you mean to give — "

"It is already done," said Glencore, laying a sealed letter on the table. "All that I purpose in his behalf you will find there."

"All this detail is too much for you, Glencore," said the other, seeing that a weary, depressed expression had come over him, while his voice grew weaker with every word. "I shall not leave this till late to-morrow, so that we can meet again. And now good night."

9

CHAPTER XVII.

A TÊTE-À-TÊTE.

WHEN Harcourt was aroused from his sound sleep by Upton, and requested in the very blandest tones of that eminent diplomatist to lend him every attention of his " very remarkable faculties," he was not by any means certain that he was not engaged in a strange dream; nor was the suspicion at all dispelled by the revelations addressed to him.

" Just dip the end of that towel in the water, Upton, and give it to me," cried he at last; and then, wiping his face and forehead, said, " Have I heard you aright, — there was no marriage?"

Upton nodded assent.

" What a shameful way he has treated this poor boy, then!" cried the other. " I never heard of anything equal to it in cruelty, and I conclude it was breaking this news to the lad that drove him out to sea on that night, and brought on this brain fever. By Jove, I'd not take *his* title, and *your* brains, to have such a sin on my conscience!"

" We are happily not called on to judge the act," said Upton, cautiously.

" And why not? Is it not every honest man's duty to reprobate whatever he detects dishonorable or disgraceful? I do judge him, and sentence him too, and I say, moreover, that a more cold-blooded piece of cruelty I never heard of. He trains up this poor boy from childhood to fancy himself the heir to his station and fortune; he nurses in him all the pride that only a high rank can cover; and then, when the lad's years have brought him to the period when these things assume all their value, he sends for him to tell him he is a bastard."

" It is not impossible that I think worse of Glencore's conduct than you do yourself," said Upton, gravely.

"But you never told him so, I'll be sworn, — you never said to him it was a rascally action. I'll lay a hundred pounds on it, you only expostulated on the inexpediency, or the inconvenience, or some such trumpery consideration, and did not tell him, in round numbers, that what he had done was an infamy."

"Then I fancy you'd lose your money, pretty much as you are losing your temper, — that is, without getting anything in requital."

"What did you say to him, then?" said Harcourt, slightly abashed.

"A great deal in the same strain as you have just spoken in, doubtless not as warm in vituperation, but possibly as likely to produce an effect; nor is it in the least necessary to dwell upon that. What Glencore has done, and what I have said about it, both belong to the past. They are over, — they are irrevocable. It is to what concerns the present and the future I wish now to address myself, and to interest you."

"Why, the boy's name was in the Peerage, — I read it there myself."

"My dear Harcourt, you must have paid very little attention to me a while ago, or you would have understood how that occurred."

"And here were all the people, the tenantry on the estate, calling him the young lord, and the poor fellow growing up with the proud consciousness that the title was his due."

"There is not a hardship of the case I have not pictured to my own mind as forcibly as you can describe it," said Upton; "but I really do not perceive that any reprobation of the past has in the slightest assisted me in providing for the future."

"And then," murmured Harcourt, — for all the while he was pursuing his own train of thought, quite irrespective of all Upton was saying, — "and then he turns him adrift on the world without friend or fortune."

"It is precisely that he may have both the one and the other that I have come to confer with you now," replied Upton. "Glencore has made a liberal provision for the

boy, and asked me to become his guardian. I have no
fancy for the trust, but I did n't see how I could decline it.
In this letter he assigns to him an income, which shall be
legally secured to him. He commits to *me* the task of
directing his education, and suggesting some future career,
and for both these objects I want your counsel."

"Education, — prospects, — why, what are you talking
about? A poor fellow who has not a name, nor a home,
nor one to acknowledge him, — what need has he of education,
or what chance of prospects? I'd send him to sea, and if
he was n't drowned before he came to manhood, I'd give
him his fortune, whatever it was, and say, 'Go settle in
some of the colonies.' You have no right to train him up to
meet fresh mortifications and insults in life; to be flouted
by every fellow that has a father, and outraged by every cur
whose mother was married."

"And are the colonies especially inhabited by illegitimate
offspring?" said Upton, dryly.

"At least he'd not be met with a rebuff at every step
he made. The rude life of toil would be better than the
polish of a civilization that could only reflect upon him."

"Not badly said, Harcourt," said Upton, smiling; "but
as to the boy, I have other prospects. He has, if I mistake
not, very good faculties. You estimate them even higher.
I don't see why they should be neglected. If he merely
possess the mediocrity of gifts which make men tolerable
lawyers and safe doctors, why, perhaps, he may turn them
into some channel. If he really can lay claim to higher
qualities, they must not be thrown away."

"Which means that he ought to be bred up to diplomacy," said Harcourt.

"Perhaps," said the other, with a bland inclination of the
head.

"And what can an old dragoon like myself contribute to
such an object?" asked Harcourt.

"You can be of infinite service in many ways," said
Upton; "and for the present I wish to leave the boy in your
care, till I can learn something about my own destiny.
This, of course, I shall know in a few days. Meanwhile
you'll look after him, and as soon as his removal becomes

safe you'll take him away from this, — it does not much
matter whither; probably some healthy, secluded spot in
Wales, for a week or two, would be advisable. Glencore
and he must not meet again; if ever they are to do so, it
must be after a considerable lapse of time."

"Have you thought of a name for him, or is his to be
still Massy?" asked Harcourt, bluntly.

"He may take the maternal name of Glencore's family,
and be called Doyle, and the settlements could be drawn up
in that name."

"I'll be shot if I like to have any share in the whole
transaction! Some day or other it will all come out, and
who knows how much blame may be imputed to us, perhaps
for actually advising the entire scheme," said Harcourt.

"You must see, my dear Harcourt, that you are only
refusing aid to alleviate an evil, and not to devise one. If
this boy —"

"Well — well — I give in. I'd rather comply at once
than be preached into acquiescence. Even when you do not
convince me, I feel ashamed to oppose myself to so much
cleverness; so, I repeat, I'm at your orders."

"Admirably spoken," said Upton, with a smile.

"My greatest difficulty of all," said Harcourt, "will be
to meet Glencore again after this. I know — I feel — I
never can forgive him."

"Perhaps he will not ask forgiveness, Harcourt," said
the other, with one of his slyest of looks. "Glencore is a
strange, self-opinionated fellow, and has amongst other odd
notions that of going the road he likes best himself. Besides,
there is another consideration here, and with no man will it
weigh more than with yourself. Glencore has been dangerously ill, — at this moment we can scarcely say that he has
recovered; his state is yet one of anxiety and doubt. You
are the last who would forget such infirmity; nor is it necessary to secure your pity that I should say how seriously the
poor fellow is now suffering."

"I trust he'll not speak to me about this business," said
Harcourt, after a pause.

"Very probably he will not. He will know that I have
already told you everything, so that there will be no need of
any communication from him."

" I wish from my heart and soul I had never come here. I would to Heaven I had gone away at once, as I first intended. I like that boy; I feel he has fine stuff in him; and now — "

" Come, come, Harcourt, it's the fault of all soft-hearted fellows, like yourself, that their kindliness degenerates into selfishness, and they have such a regard for their own feelings that they never agree to anything that wounds them. Just remember that you and I have very small parts in this drama, and the best way we can do is to fill them without giving ourselves the airs of chief characters."

" You're at your old game, Upton; you are always ready to wet yourself, provided you give another fellow a ducking."

" Only if he get a worse one, or take longer to dry after it," remarked Upton, laughing.

"Quite true, by Jove!" chimed in the other; "you take special care to come off best. And now you're going," added he, as Upton rose to withdraw, "and I'm certain that I have not half comprehended what you want from me."

" You shall have it in writing, Harcourt; I'll send you a clear despatch the first spare moment I can command after I reach town. The boy will not be fit to move for some time to come, and so good-bye."

" You don't know where they are going to send you?"

" I cannot frame even a conjecture," sighed Upton, languidly. " I ought to be in the Brazils for a week or so about that slave question; and then the sooner I reach Constantinople the better."

" Sha'n't they want you at Paris?" asked Harcourt, who felt a kind of quiet vengeance in developing what he deemed the weak vanity of the other.

" Yes," sighed he again; " but I can't be everywhere." And so saying, he lounged away, while it would have taken a far more subtle listener than Harcourt to say whether he was mystifying the other, or the dupe of his own self-esteem.

CHAPTER XVIII.

THREE weeks rolled over, — an interval not without its share
of interest for the inhabitants of the little village of Leenane,
since on one morning Mr. Craggs had made his appearance
on his way to Clifden, and after an absence of two days
returned to the Castle. The subject for popular discussion
and surmise had not yet declined, when a boat was seen to
leave Glencore, heavily laden with trunks and travelling
gear; and as she neared the land, the " lord" was detected
amongst the passengers, looking very ill, — almost dying;
he passed up the little street of the village, scarcely noticing
the uncovered heads which saluted him respectfully. Indeed,
he scarcely lifted up his eyes, and, as the acute observers
remarked, never once turned a glance towards the opposite
shore, where the Castle stood.

He had not reached the end of the village, when a chaise
with four horses arrived at the spot. No time was lost in
arranging the trunks and portmanteaus, and Lord Glencore
sat moodily on a bank, listlessly regarding what went forward. At length Craggs came up, and, touching his cap in
military fashion, announced all was ready.

Lord Glencore arose slowly, and looked languidly around
him; his features wore a mingled expression of weariness
and anxiety, like one not fully awakened from an oppressive dream. He turned his eyes on the people, who at a
respectful distance stood around, and in a voice of peculiar
melancholy said, " Good-bye."

" A good journey to you, my Lord, and safe back again
to us," cried a number together.

" Eh — what — what was that?" cried he, suddenly; and
the tones were shrill and discordant in which he spoke.

A warning gesture from Craggs imposed silence on the
crowd, and not a word was uttered.

"I thought they said something about coming back again," muttered Glencore, gloomily.

"They were wishing you a good journey, my Lord," replied Craggs.

"Oh, that was it, was it?" And so saying, with bent-down head he walked feebly forward and entered the carriage. Craggs was speedily on the box, and the next moment they were away.

It is no part of our task to dwell on the sage speculations and wise surmises of the village on this event. They had not, it is true, much "evidence" before them, but they were hardy guessers, and there was very little within the limits of possibility which they did not summon to the aid of their imaginations. All, however, were tolerably agreed upon one point. — that to leave the place while the young lord was still unable to quit his bed, and too weak to sit up, was unnatural and unfeeling; traits which, "after all," they thought "not very surprising, since the likes of them lords never cared for anybody."

Colonel Harcourt still remained at Glencore, and under his rigid sway the strictest blockade of the coast was maintained, nor was any intercourse whatever permitted with the village. A boat from the Castle, meeting another from Leenane, half way in the lough, received the letters and whatever other resources the village supplied. All was done with the rigid exactness of a quarantine regulation; and if the mainland had been scourged with plague, stricter measures of exclusion could scarcely have been enforced.

In comparison with the present occupant of the Castle, the late one was a model of amiability; and the village, as is the wont in the case, now discovered a vast number of good qualities in the "lord," when they had lost him. After a while, however, the guesses, the speculations, and the comparisons all died away, and the Castle of Glencore was as much dreamland to their imaginations as, seen across the lough in the dim twilight of an autumn evening, its towers might have appeared to their eyes.

It was about a month after Lord Glencore's departure, of a fine, soft evening in summer, Billy Traynor suddenly appeared in the village. Billy was one of a class who,

whatever their rank in life, are always what Coleridge would
have called "noticeable men." He was soon, therefore,
surrounded with a knot of eager and inquiring friends, all
solicitous to know something of the life he was leading, what
they were doing " beyant at the Castle."

" It's a mighty quiet studious kind of life," said Billy,
" but agrees with me wonderfully; for I may say that until
now I never was able to give my 'janius' fair play. Pro-
fessional life is the ruin of the student; and being always
obleeged to be thinkin' of the bags destroyed my taste for
letters." A grin of self-approval at his own witticism closed
this speech.

" But is it true, Billy, the lord is going to break up house
entirely, and not come back here?" asked Peter Slevin, the
sacristan, whose rank and station warranted his assuming
the task of cross-questioner.

" There's various ways of breakin' up a house," said Billy.
" Ye may do so in a moral sinse, or in a physical sinse: you
may obliterate, or extinguish, or, without going so far, you
may simply obfuscate, — do you perceave?"

" Yes!" said the sacristan, on whom every eye was now
bent, to see if he was able to follow subtleties that had outwitted the rest.

" And whin I say *obfuscate*," resumed Billy, " I open a
question of disputed etymology, bekase tho' Lucretius thinks
the word *obfuscator* original, there's many supposes it comes
from *ob* and *fucus*, the dye the ancients used in their wool,
as we find in Horace, *lana fuco medicata;* while Cicero employs it in another sense, and says, *facere fucum*, which is
as much as to say, humbuggin' somebody, — do ye mind?"

" Begorra, he might guess that anyhow!" muttered a
shrewd little tailor, with a significance that provoked hearty
laughter.

" And now," continued Billy, with an air of triumph,
" we'll proceed to the next point."

" Ye needn't trouble yerself then," said Terry Lynch,
" for Peter has gone home."

And so, to the amusement of the meeting, it turned out to
be the case: the sacristan had retired from the controversy.

" Come in here to Mrs. Moore's, Billy, and take a glass

with us," said Terry; "it is n't often we see you in these
parts."

"If the honorable company will graciously vouchsafe and
condescind to let me trate them to a half-gallon," said Billy,
"it will be the proudest event of my terrestrial existence."

The proposition was received with a cordial enthusiasm,
flattering to all concerned; and in a few minutes after, Billy
Traynor sat at the head of a long table in the neat parlor of
"The Griddle," with a company of some fifteen or sixteen
very convivially disposed friends around him.

"If I was Cæsar, or Lucretius, or Nebuchadnezzar, I
could n't be prouder," said Billy, as he looked down the
board. "And let moralists talk as they will, there's a
beautiful expansion of sentiment, there's a fine genial
overflowin' of the heart, in gatherin's like this, where we
mingle our feelin's and our philosophy; and our love and
our learning walk hand in hand like brothers — pass the
sperits, Mr. Shea. If we look to the ancient writers, what
do we see! — Lemons! bring in some lemons, Mickey. —
What do we see, I say, but that the very highest enjoyment
of the haythen gods was — Hot wather! why won't they
send in more hot wather?"

"Begorra, if I was a haythen god, I 'd like a little whisky
in it," muttered Terry, dryly.

"Where was I?" asked Billy, a little disconcerted by this
sally, and the laugh it excited. "I was expatiatin' upon
celestial convivialities. The *noctes coenœque deum*, — them
elegant hospitalities where wisdom was moistened with nec-
tar, and wit washed down with ambrosia. It is not, by
coorse, to be expected," continued he, modestly, "that we
mere mortials can compete with them elegant refections.
But, as Ovid says, we can at least *diem jucundum decipere*."

The unknown tongue had now restored to Billy all the
reverence and respect of his auditory, and he continued to
expatiate very eloquently on the wholesome advantages to
be derived from convivial intercourse, both amongst gods
and men; rather slyly intimating that either on the score of
the fluids, or the conversation, his own leanings lay towards
"the humanities."

"For, after all," said he, "'t is our own wakenesses is

often the source of our most refined enjoyments. No, Mrs.
Cassidy, ye need n't be blushin'. I 'm considerin' my subject in a high ethnological and metaphysical sinse." Mrs.
Cassidy's confusion, and the mirth it excited, here interrupted the orator.

"The meeting is never tired of hearin' you, Billy," said
Terry Lynch; "but if it was plazin' to ye to give us a
song, we 'd enjoy it greatly."

"Ah!" said Billy, with a sigh, "I have taken my
partin' kiss with the Muses; *non mihi licet increpare digitis
lyram:* —

> "'No more to feel poetic fire,
> No more to touch the soundin' lyre;
> But wiser coorses to begin,
> I now forsake my violin.'"

An honest outburst of regret and sorrow broke from the
assembly, who eagerly pressed for an explanation of this
calamitous change.

"The thing is this," said Billy: "if a man is a creature
of mere leisure and amusement, the fine arts — and by the
fine arts I mean music, paintin', and the ladies — is an
elegant and very refined subject of cultivation; but when
you raise your cerebrial faculties to grander and loftier considerations, to explore the difficult ragions of polemic or
political truth, to investigate the subtleties of the schools,
and penetrate the mysteries of science, then, take my word
for it, the fine arts is just snares, — devil a more than snares!
And whether it is soft sounds seduces you, or elegant tints,
or the union of both, — women, I mane, — you 'll never arrive
at anything great or tri-um-phant till you wane yourself
away from the likes of them vanities. Look at the haythen
mythology; consider for a moment who is the chap that
represents Music, — a lame blackguard, with an ugly face,
they call Pan. Ay, indeed, Pan! If you wanted to see
what respect they had for the art, it 's easy enough to guess,
when this crayture represints it; and as to Paintin', on my
conscience, they have n't a god at all that ever took to the
brush. — Pass up the sperits, Mickey," said he, somewhat
blown and out of breath by this effort. "Maybe," said he,
"I 'm wearin' you."

" No, no, no," loudly responded the meeting.

" Maybe I 'm imposin' too much of personal details on the house," added he, pompously.

" Not at all; never a bit," cried the company.

" Because," resumed he, slowly, " if I did so, I 'd have at least the excuse of sayin', like the great Pitt, ' These may be my last words from this place.' "

An unfeigned murmur of sorrow ran through the meeting, and he resumed : —

" Ay, ladies and gintlemin, Billy Traynor is takin' his ' farewell benefit ; ' he 's not humbuggin'. I 'm not like them chaps that 's always positively goin', but stays on at the unanimous request of the whole world. No; I 'm really goin' to leave you."

" What for? Where to, Billy?" broke from a number of voices together.

" I 'll tell ye," said he, — " at least so far as I can tell; because it would n't be right nor decent to ' print the whole of the papers for the house,' as they say in parliamint. I 'm going abroad with the young lord; we are going to improve our minds, and cultivate our janiuses, by study and foreign travel. We are first to settle in Germany, where we 're to enter a University, and commince a coorse of modern tongues, French, Sweadish, and Spanish; imbibin' at the same time a smatterin' of science, such as chemistry, conchology, and the use of the globes."

" Oh dear! oh dear! " murmured the meeting, in wonder and admiration.

" I 'm not goin' to say that we 'll neglect mechanics, metaphysics, and astrology; for we mane to be cosmonopolists in knowledge. As for myself, ladies and gintlemin, it 's a proud day that sees me standin' here to say these words. I, that was ragged, without a shoe to my foot, — without breeches, — never mind, I was, as the poet says, *nudus nummis ac cestimentis,* —

> " ' I have n't sixpence in my pack,
>   I have n't small clothes to my back,'

carryin' the bag many a weary mile, through sleet and snow, for six pounds tin per annum, and no pinsion for wounds or superannuation; and now I'm to be — it is n't easy to say what — to the young lord a spacies of humble companion, — not manial, do you mind, nothing manial; what the Latins called a *famulus*, which was quite a different thing from a *servus*. The former bein' a kind of domestic adviser, a deputy-assistant, monitor-general, as a body might say. There, now, if I discoorsed for a month, I could n't tell you more about myself and my future prospects. I own to you that I'm proud of my good luck, and I would n't exchange it to be Emperor of Jamaica, or King of the Bahamia Islands."

If we have been prolix in our office of reporter to Billy Traynor, our excuse is that his discourse will have contributed so far to the reader's enlightenment as to save us the task of recapitulation. At the same time, it is but justice to the accomplished orator that we should say we have given but the most meagre outline of an address which, to use the newspaper phrase. " occupied three hours in the delivery." The truth was, Billy was in vein; the listeners were patient, the punch strong: nor is it every speaker who has had the good fortune of such happy accessories.

CHAPTER XIX.

THE CASCINE AT FLORENCE.

IT was spring, and in Italy! one of those half-dozen days, at very most, when, the feeling of winter departed, a gentle freshness breathes through the air; trees stir softly, and as if by magic; the earth becomes carpeted with flowers, whose odors seem to temper, as it were, the exciting atmosphere. An occasional cloud, fleecy and jagged, sails lazily aloft, marking its shadow on the mountain side. In a few days — a few hours, perhaps — the blue sky will be unbroken, the air hushed, a hot breath will move among the leaves, or pant over the trickling fountains.

In this fast-flitting period, - we dare not call it season, — the Cascine of Florence is singularly beautiful; on one side, the gentle river stealing past beneath the shadowing foliage; on the other, the picturesque mountain towards Fiesole, dotted with its palaces and terraced gardens. The ancient city itself is partly seen, and the massive Duomo and the Palazzo Vecchio tower proudly above the trees! What other people of Europe have such a haunt? — what other people would know so thoroughly how to enjoy it? The day was drawing to a close, and the Piazzone was now filled with equipages. There were the representatives of every European people, and of nations far away over the seas, — splendid Russians, brilliant French, splenetic, supercilious English, and ponderous Germans, mingled with the less marked nationalities of Belgium and Holland, and even America. Everything that called itself Fashion was there to swell the tide; and although a choice military band was performing with exquisite skill the favorite overtures of the day, the noise and tumult of conversation almost drowned their notes. Now, the Cascine is to the world of society

what the Bourse is to the world of trade. It is the great
centre of all news and intelligence, where markets and bar-
gains of intercourse are transacted, and where the scene of
past pleasure is revived, and the plans of future enjoyment
are canvassed. The great and the wealthy are there, to see
and to meet with each other. The proud equipages lie side
by side, like great liners; while phaetons, like fast frigates,
shoot swiftly by, and solitary dandies flit past in varieties of
conveyance to which sea-craft can offer no analogies. All are
busy, eager, and occupied. Scandal holds here its festival,
and the misdeeds of every capital of Europe are now being
discussed. The higher themes of politics occupy but few;
the interests of literature attract still less. It is essentially
of the world they talk, and it must be owned they do it like
adepts. The last witticism of Paris, — the last duel at Berlin, — who has fled from his creditors in England, — who has
run away from her husband at Naples, — all are retailed with
a serious circumstantiality that would lead one to believe that
gossip maintained its "own correspondent" in every city of
the Continent. Moralists might fancy, perhaps, that in the
tone these subjects are treated there would mingle a reprobation of the bad, and a due estimate of the opposite, if it
ever occurred at all; but as surely would they be disappointed. Never were censors more lenient, — never were
critics so charitable. The transgressions against good-
breeding — the "gaucheries" of manner, the solecisms in
dress, language, or demeanor — do indeed meet with sharp
reproof and cutting sarcasm; but, in recompense for such
severity, how gently do they deal with graver offences! For
the felonies they can always discover "the attenuating circumstances;" for the petty larcenies of fashion they have
nothing but whipcord.

Amidst the various knots where such discussions were
carried on, one was eminently conspicuous. It was around
a handsome open carriage, whose horses, harnessing, and
liveries were all in the most perfect taste. The equipage
might possibly have been deemed showy in Hyde Park; but
in the Bois de Boulogne or the Cascine it must be pronounced the acme of elegance. Whatever might have been
the differences of national opinion on this point, there could

assuredly have been none as to the beauty of those who occupied it.

Though a considerable interval of years divided them, the aunt and her niece had a wonderful resemblance to each other. They were both — the rarest of all forms of beauty — blond Italians; that is, with light hair and soft gray eyes. They had a peculiar tint of skin, deeper and mellower than we see in Northern lands, and an expression of mingled seriousness and softness that only pertains to the South of Europe. There was a certain coquetry in the similarity of their dress, which in many parts was precisely alike; and although the niece was but fifteen, and the aunt above thirty, it needed not the aid of flattery to make many mistake one for the other.

Beauty, like all other " Beaux Arts," has its distinctions. The same public opinion that enthrones the sculptor or the musician, confers its crown on female loveliness; and by this acclaim were they declared Queens of Beauty. To any one visiting Italy for the first time, there would have seemed something very strange in the sort of homage rendered them: a reverence and respect only accorded elsewhere to royalties, — a deference that verged on actual humiliation, — and yet all this blended with a subtle familiarity that none but an Italian can ever attain to. The uncovered head, the attitude of respectful attention, the patient expectancy of notice, the glad air of him under recognition, were all there; and yet, through these, there was dashed a strange tone of intimacy, as though the observances were but a thin crust over deeper feelings. " La Contessa " — for she was especially " the Countess," as one illustrious man of our own country was " the Duke " — possessed every gift which claims preeminence in this fair city. She was eminently beautiful, young, charming in her manners, with ample fortune; and, lastly, — ah! good reader, you would surely be puzzled to supply that " lastly," the more as we say that in it lies an excellence without which all the rest are of little worth, and yet with it are objects of worship, almost of adoration, — she was — separated from her husband! There must have been an epidemic, a kind of rot, among husbands at one period; for we scarcely remember a very pretty woman, from five-and-twenty to five-and-thirty, who had not been obliged to leave hers from acts of cruelty or acts of brutality, etc., that only husbands are capable of, or of which their poor wives are ever the victims.

If the moral geography of Europe be ever written, the region south of the Alps will certainly be colored with that tint, whatever it be, that describes the blessedness of a divorced existence. In other lands, especially in our own, the separated individual labors under no common difficulty in his advances to society. The story — there must be a story — of his separation is told in various ways, all, of course, to his disparagement. Tyrant or victim, it is hard to say under which title he comes out best, — so much for the man; but for the woman there is no plea : judgment is pronounced at once, without the merits. Fugitive, or fled from, — who inquires? she is one that few men dare to recognize. The very fact that to mention her name exacts an explanation, is condemnatory. What a boon to all such must it be that there is a climate mild enough for their malady, and a country that will suit their constitution; and not only that, but a region which actually pays homage to their infirmity, and makes of their martyrdom a triumph! As you go to Norway for salmon-fishing, — to Bengal to hunt tigers, — to St. Petersburg to eat caviare, so when divorced, if you really know the blessing of your state, go take a house on the Arno. Vast as are the material resources of our globe, the moral ones are infinitely greater; nor need we despair, some day or other, of finding an island where a certificate of fraudulent bankruptcy will be deemed a letter of credit, and an evidence of insolvency be accepted as qualification to open a bank.

La Contessa inhabited a splendid palace, furnished with magnificence; her gardens were one of the sights of the capital, not only for their floral display, but that they contained a celebrated group by Canova, of which no copy existed. Her gallery was, if not extensive, enriched with some priceless treasures of art; and with all these she possessed high rank, for her card bore the name of La Comtesse de Glencore, née Comtesse della Torre.

The reader thus knows at once, if not actually as much

as we do ourselves, all that we mean to impart to him; and now let us come back to that equipage around which swarmed the fashion of Florence, eagerly pressing forward to catch a word, a smile, or even a look, and actually perched on every spot from which they could obtain a glimpse of those within. A young Russian Prince, with his arm in a sling, had just recited the incident of his late duel; a Neapolitan Minister had delivered a rose-colored epistle from a Royal Highness of his own court. A Spanish Grandee had deposited his offering of camellias, which actually covered the front cushions of the carriage; and now a little lane was formed for the approach of the old Duke de Brignolles, who made his advance with a mingled courtesy and haughtiness that told of Versailles and long ago.

A very creditable specimen of the old *noblesse* of France was the Duke, and well worthy to be the grandson of one who was Grand Maréchal to Louis XIV. Tall, thin, and slightly stooped from age, his dark eye seemed to glisten the brighter beneath his shaggy white eyebrows. He had served with distinction as a soldier, and been an ambassador at the court of the Czar Paul; in every station he had filled sustaining the character of a true and loyal gentleman, — a man who could reflect nothing but honor upon the great country he belonged to. It was amongst the scandal of Florence that he was the most devoted of La Contessa's admirers; but we are quite willing to believe that his admiration had nothing in it of love. At all events, she distinguished him by her most marked notice. He was the frequent guest of her choicest dinners, and the constant visitor at her evenings at home. It was, then, with a degree of favor that many an envious heart coveted, she extended her hand to him as he came forward, which he kissed with all the lowly deference he would have shown to that of his prince.

"*Mon cher Duc*," said she, smiling, "I have such a store of grievances to lay at your door. The essence of violets is not violets, but verbena."

"Charming Comtesse, I had it direct from Pierrot's."

"Pierrot is a traitor, then, that 's all; and where 's Ida's

Arab? is he to be here to-day, or to-morrow? When are we to see him?"

"Why, I only wrote to the Emir on Tuesday last."

"*Mais à quoi bon l'Emir* if he can't do impossibilities? Surely the very thought of him brings up the Arabian Nights and the Calif Haroun. By the way, thank you for the poignard. It is true Damascus, is it not?"

"Of course. I'd not have dared —"

"To be sure not. I told the Archduchess it was. I wore it in my Turkish dress on Wednesday, and you, false man, would n't come to admire me!"

"You know what a sad day was that for me, madam," said he, solemnly. "It was the anniversary of her fate who was your only rival in beauty, as she had no rival in unde-served misfortunes."

"Pauvre Reine!" sighed the Countess, and held her bouquet to her face.

"What great mass of papers is that you have there, Duke?" resumed she. "Can it be a journal?"

"It is an English newspaper, my dear Countess. As I know you do not receive any of his countrymen, I have not asked your permission to present the Lord Selby; but hear-ing him read out your name in a paragraph here, I carried off his paper to have it translated for me. You read Eng-lish, don't you?"

"Very imperfectly, and I detest it," said she, impa-tiently; "but Prince Volkoffsky can, I am sure, oblige you." And she turned away her head, in ill humor.

"It is here somewhere. *Parbleu*, I thought I marked the place," muttered the Duke, as he handed the paper to the Russian. "Is n't that it?"

"This is all about theatres, — Madame Pasta and the Haymarket."

"Ah! well, it is lower down; here, perhaps."

"Court news. The Grand Duke of Saxe-Weimar —"

"No, no; not that."

"Oh, here it is. 'Great Scandal in High Life. — A very singular correspondence has just passed, and will soon, we believe, be made public, between the Heralds' College and Lord Glencore.'" Here the reader stopped, and lowered his voice at the next word.

" Read on, Prince. *C'est mon mari*," said she, coldly, while a very slight movement of her upper lip betrayed what might mean scorn or sorrow, or even both.

The Prince, however, had now run his eyes over the paragraph, and crushing the newspaper in his hand, hurried away from the spot. The Duke as quickly followed, and soon overtook him."

" Who gave you this paper, Duke?" cried the Russian, angrily.

" It was Lord Selby. He was reading it aloud to a friend."

" Then he is an *infame!* and I'll tell him so," cried the other, passionately. " Which is he? the one with the light moustache, or the shorter one?" And, without waiting for reply, the Russian dashed between the carriages, and thrusting his way through the prancing crowd of moving horses, arrived at a spot where two young men, evidently strangers to the scene, were standing, calmly surveying the bright panorama before them.

" The Lord Selby," said the Russian, taking off his hat and saluting one of them.

" That's his Lordship," replied the one he addressed, pointing to his friend.

" I am the Prince Volkoffsky, aide-de-camp to the Emperor," said the Russian; " and hearing from my friend the Duke de Brignolles that you have just given him this newspaper, that he might obtain the translation of a passage in it which concerns Lady Glencore, and have the explanation read out at her own carriage, publicly, before all the world, I desire to tell you that your Lordship is unworthy of your rank; that you are an *infame!* and if you do not resent this, a *polisson!* "

" This man is mad. Selby," said the short man, with the coolest air imaginable.

" Quite sane enough to give your friend a lesson in good manners; and you too, sir, if you have any fancy for it," said the Russian.

" I'd give him in charge to the police. by Jove! if there were police here," said the same one who spoke before; " he can't be a gentleman."

"There's my card, sir," said the Russian; "and for you too, sir," said he, presenting another to him who spoke.

"Where are you to be heard of?" said the short man.

"At the Russian legation," said the Prince, haughtily, and turned away.

"You're wrong, Baynton, he is a gentleman," said Lord Selby, as he pocketed the card, "though certainly he is not a very mild-tempered specimen of his order."

"You did n't give the newspaper as he said —"

"Nothing of the kind. I was reading it aloud to you when the royal carriages came suddenly past; and, in taking off my hat to salute, I never noticed that the old Duke had carried off the paper. I know he can't read English, and the chances are, he has asked this Scythian gentleman to interpret for him."

"So, then, the affair is easily settled," said the other, quietly.

"Of course it is," was the answer; and they both lounged about among the carriages, which already were thinning, and, after a while, set out towards the city.

They had but just reached the hotel, when a stranger presented himself to them as the Count de Marny. He had come as the friend of Prince Volkoffsky, who had fully explained to him the event of that afternoon.

"Well," said Baynton, "we are of opinion your friend has conducted himself exceedingly ill, and we are here to receive his excuses."

"I am afraid, messieurs," said the Frenchman, bowing, "that it will exhaust your patience if you continue to wait for them. Might it not be better to come and accept what he is quite prepared to offer you, — satisfaction?"

"Be it so," said Lord Selby: "he 'll see his mistake some time or other, and perhaps regret it. Where shall it be? — and when?"

"At the Fossombroni Villa, about two miles from this. To-morrow morning, at eight, if that suit you."

"Quite well. I have no other appointment. Pistols, of course?"

"You have the choice, otherwise my friend would have preferred the sword."

"Take him at his word, Selby," whispered Baynton; " you are equal to any of them with the rapier."

" If your friend desire the sword, I have no objection, — I mean the rapier."

" The rapier be it," said the Frenchman; and with a polite assurance of the infinite honor he felt in forming their acquaintance, and the gratifying certainty that they were sure to possess of his highest consideration, he bowed, backed, and withdrew.

" Well-mannered fellow, the Frenchman," said Baynton, as the door closed; and the other nodded assent, and rang the bell for dinner.

CHAPTER XX.

THE grounds of the Villa Fossombroni were, at the time we speak of, the Chalk Farm, or the Fifteen Acres of Tuscany. The villa itself, long since deserted by the illustrious family whose name it bore, had fallen into the hands of an old Piedmontese noble, ruined by a long life of excess and dissipation. He had served with gallantry in the imperial army of France, but was dismissed the service for a play transaction in which his conduct was deeply disgraceful; and the Colonel Count Tasseroni, of the 8th Hussars of the Guards, was declared unworthy to wear the uniform of a Frenchman.

For a number of years he had lived so estranged from the world that many believed he had died; but at last it was known that he had gone to reside in a half-ruined villa near Florence, which soon became the resort of a certain class of gamblers whose habits would have speedily attracted notice if practised within the city. The quarrels and altercations, so inseparable from high play, were usually settled on the spot in which they occurred, until at last the villa became famous for these meetings, and the name of Fossombroni, in a discussion, was the watchword for a duel.

It was of a splendid spring morning that the two Englishmen arrived at this spot, which, even on the unpleasant errand that they had come, struck them with surprise and admiration. The villa itself was one of those vast structures which the country about Florence abounds in. Gloomy, stern, and jail-like without, while within, splendid apartments opened into each other in what seems an endless succession. Frescoed walls and gorgeously ornamented ceilings, gilded mouldings and rich tracery, were on every side;

and these, too, in chambers where the immense proportions
and the vast space recalled the idea of a royal residence.
Passing in by a dilapidated "grille" which once had been
richly gilded, they entered by a flight of steps a great hall
which ran the entire length of the building. Though lighted
by a double range of windows, neglect and dirt had so
dimmed the panes that the place was almost in deep
shadow. Still, they could perceive that the vaulted roof was
a mass of stuccoed tracery, and that the colossal divisions
of the wall were of brilliant Sienna marble. At one end of
this great gallery was a small chapel, now partly despoiled
of its religious decorations, which were most irreverently replaced by a variety of swords and sabres of every possible
size and shape, and several pairs of pistols, arranged with
an evident eye to picturesque grouping.

"What are all these inscriptions here on the walls,
Baynton?" cried Selby, as he stood endeavoring to decipher
the lines on a little marble slab, a number of which were
dotted over the chapel.

"Strange enough this, by Jove!" muttered the other,
reading to himself, half aloud, "'Francesco Ricordi, ucciso
da Gieronimo Gazzi, 29 Settembre, 1818.'"

"What does that mean?" asked Selby.

"It is to commemorate some fellow who was killed here
in '18."

"Are they all in the same vein?" asked the other.

"It would seem so. Here's one: 'Gravamente ferito,'
— badly wounded; with a postscript that he died the same
night."

"What's this large one here, in black marble?" inquired
Selby.

"To the memory of Carlo Luigi Guiccidrini, 'detto il
Carnefice,' called 'the slaughterer:' cut down to the forehead by Pietro Baldasseroni, on the night of July 8th,
1819."

"I confess any other kind of literature would amuse me
as well," said Selby, turning back again into the large
hall. Baynton had scarcely joined him when they saw
advancing towards them through the gloom a short, thickset
man, dressed in a much-worn dressing-gown and slippers.

He removed his skull-cap as he approached, and said, " The Count Tasseroni, at your orders."

" We have come here by appointment," said Baynton.

" Yes, yes. I know it all. Volkoffsky sent me word. He was here on Saturday. He gave that French colonel a sharp lesson. Ran the sword clean through the chest. To be sure, he was wounded too, but only through the arm ; but ' La Marque' has got his passport."

" You'll have him up there soon, then," said Baynton, pointing towards the chapel.

" I think not. We have not done it latterly," said the Count, musingly. " The authorities don't seem to like it ; and, of course, we respect the authorities ! "

" That's quite evident." said Baynton, who turned to translate the observation to his friend.

Selby whispered a word in his ear.

" What does the signore say ? " inquired the Count.

" My friend thinks that they are behind the time."

" *Per Baccho!* Let him be easy as to that. I have known some to think that the Russian came too soon. I never heard of one who wished him earlier ! There they are now : they always come by the garden." And so saying, he hastened off to receive them.

" How is this fellow to handle a sword, if his right arm be wounded ? " said Selby.

" Don't you know that these Russians use the left hand indifferently with the right, in all exercises? It may be awkward for *you;* but, depend upon it, *he'll* not be inconvenienced in the least."

As he spoke, the others entered the other end of the hall. The Prince no sooner saw the Englishmen than he advanced towards them with his hat off. " My lord," said he, rapidly. " I have come to make you an apology, and one which I trust you will accept in all the frankness that I offer it. I have learned from your friend the Duc de Brignolles how the incident of yesterday occurred. I see that the only fault committed was my own. Will you pardon, then, a momentary word of ill-temper, occasioned by what I wrongfully believed to be a great injury?"

" Of course, I knew it was all a mistake on your part.

I told Colonel Baynton, here, you'd see so yourself, — when it is too late, perhaps."

"I thank you sincerely," said the Russian, bowing; "your readiness to accord me this satisfaction makes your forgiveness more precious to me. And now, as another favor, will you permit me to ask you one question?"

"Yes, certainly."

"Why, when you could have so easily explained this misconception on my part, did you not take the trouble of doing so?"

Selby looked confused, blushed, looked awkwardly from side to side, and then, with a glance towards his friend, seemed to say, "Will you try and answer him?"

"I think you have hit it yourself, Prince," said Baynton. "It was the trouble, the bore of an explanation, deterred him. He hates writing, and he thought there would be a shower of notes to be replied to, meetings, discussions, and what not; and so he said, ' Let him have his shot, and have done with it.'"

The Russian looked from one to the other as he listened, and seemed really as if not quite sure whether this speech was uttered in seriousness or sarcasm. The calm, phlegmatic faces of the Englishmen, — the almost apathetic expression they wore, — soon convinced him that the words were truthfully spoken; and he stood actually confounded with amazement before them.

Lord Selby and his friend freely accepted the polite invitation of the Prince to breakfast, and they all adjourned to a small but splendidly decorated room, where everything was already awaiting them. There are few incidents in life which so much predispose to rapid intimacy as the case of an averted duel. The revulsion from animosity is almost certain to lead to, if not actual friendship, what may easily become so. In the present instance, the very diversities of national character gave a zest and enjoyment to the meeting; and while the Englishmen were charmed by the fascination of manners and conversational readiness of their hosts, the Russians were equally struck with a cool imperturbability and impassiveness, of which they had never seen the equal.

By degrees the Russian led the conversation to the question by which their misunderstanding originated. " You know my Lord Glencore, perhaps?" said he.

"Never saw, scarcely ever heard of him," said Selby, in his dry, laconic tone.

" Is he mad, or a fool?" asked the Prince, half angrily.

"I served in a regiment once where he commanded a troop," said Baynton; "and they always said he was a good sort of fellow."

"You read that paragraph this morning, I conclude?" said the Russian. "You saw how he dares to stigmatize the honor of his wife, — to degrade her to the rank of a mistress, — and, at the same time, to bastardize the son who ought to inherit his rank and title?"

"I read it," said Selby, dryly; "and I had a letter from my lawyer about it this morning."

"Indeed!" exclaimed he, anxious to hear more, and yet too delicate to venture on a question.

"Yes; he writes to me for some title-deeds or other. I didn't pay much attention, exactly, to what he says. Glencore's man of business had addressed a letter to him."

The Russian bowed, and waited for him to resume; but, apparently, he had rather fatigued himself by such unusual loquacity, and so he lay back in his chair, and puffed his cigar in indolent enjoyment.

"A goodish sort of thing for *you* it ought to be," said Baynton, between the puffs of his tobacco smoke, and with a look towards Selby.

"I suspect it may," said the other, without the slightest change of tone or demeanor.

"Where is it, — somewhere in the south?"

"Mostly, Devon. There's something in Wales too, if I remember aright."

"Nothing Irish?"

"No, thank Heaven, — nothing Irish;" and his grim Lordship made the nearest advance to a smile of which his unplastic features seemed capable.

"Do I understand you aright, my Lord," said the Prince, "that you receive an accession of fortune by this event?"

"I shall, if I survive Glencore," was the brief reply.

" You are related, then ? "

" Some cousinship, — I forget how it is. Do you remember, Baynton ? "

" I'm not quite certain. I think it was a Coventry married one of Jack Conway's sisters, and she afterwards became the wife of Sir something Massy. Isn't that it ? "

" Yes, that's it," muttered the other, in the tone of a man who was tired of a knotty problem.

" And, according to your laws, this Lord Glencore may marry again ? " cried the Russian.

" I should think so, if he has no wife living," said Selby ; " but I trust, for *my* sake, he'll not."

" And what if he should, and should be discovered the wedded husband of another ? "

" That would be bigamy," said Selby. " Would they hang him, Baynton ? "

" I think not, — scarcely," rejoined the Colonel.

The Prince tried in various ways to obtain some insight into Lord Glencore's habits, his tastes and mode of life, but all in vain. They knew, indeed, very little, but even that little they were too indolent to repeat. Lord Selby's memory was often at fault, too, and Baynton's had ill supplied the deficiency. Again and again did the Russian mutter curses to himself over the apathy of these stony islanders. At moments he fancied that they suspected his eagerness, and had assumed their most guarded caution against him ; but he soon perceived that this manner was natural to them, not prompted in the slightest degree by any distrust whatever.

" After all," thought the Russian, " how can I hope to stimulate a man who is not excited by his own increase of fortune? Talk of Turkish fatalism, these fellows would shame the Moslem."

" Do you mean to prolong your stay at Florence, my Lord ? " asked the Prince, as they arose from the table.

" I scarcely know. What do you say, Baynton ? "

" A week or so, I fancy," muttered the other.

" And then on to Rome, perhaps ? "

The two Englishmen looked at each other with an air of as

much confusion as if subjected to a searching examination in science.

"Well, I shouldn't wonder," said Selby, at last, with a sigh.

"Yes, it may come to that," said Baynton, like a man who had just overcome a difficulty.

"You'll be in time for the Holy Week and all the ceremonies," said the Prince.

"Mind that, Baynton," said his Lordship, who wasn't going to carry what he felt to be another man's load; and Baynton nodded acquiescence.

"And after that comes the season for Naples, — you have a month or six weeks, perhaps, of such weather as nothing in all Europe can vie with."

"You hear, Baynton!" said Selby.

"I've booked it," muttered the other; and so they took leave of their entertainer, and set out towards Florence. Neither you nor I, dear reader, will gain anything by keeping them company, for they say scarcely a word by the way. They stop at intervals, and cast their eyes over the glorious landscape at their feet. Their glances are thrown over the fairest scene of the fairest of all lands; and whether they turn towards the snow-capt Apennines, by Vall'ombrosa, or trace the sunny vineyards along the Val' d' Arno, they behold a picture such as no canvas ever imitated; still, they are mute and uncommunicative. Whatever of pleasure their thoughts suggest, each keeps for himself. Objects of wonder, strange sights and new, may present themselves, but they are not to be startled out of national dignity by so ignoble a sentiment as surprise. And so they jog onward, — doubtless richer in reflection than eloquent in communion; and so we leave them.

Let us not be deemed unjust or ungenerous if we assert that we have met many such as these. They are not individuals, — they are a class; and, strange enough too, a class which almost invariably pertains to a high and distinguished rank in society. It would be presumptuous to ascribe such demeanor to insensibility. There is enough in their general conduct to disprove the assumption. As little is it affectation; it is simply an acquired habit of stoical indifference, supposed to be — why, Heaven knows! — the essential ingredient of the best breeding. If the practice extinguish all emotion, and obliterate all trace of feeling from the heart, we deplore the system. If it only gloss over the working of human sympathy, we pity the men. At all events, they are very uninteresting company, with whom longer dalliance would only be wearisome.

CHAPTER XXI.

SOME TRAITS OF LIFE.

It was the night Lady Glencore received; and, as usual, the street was crowded with equipages, which somehow seemed to have got into inextricable confusion, — some endeavoring to turn back, while others pressed forward, — the court of the palace being closely packed with carriages which the thronged street held in fast blockade. As the apartments which faced the street were not ever used for these receptions, the dark unlighted windows suggested no remark; but they who had entered the courtyard were struck by the gloomy aspect of the vast building: not only that the entrance and the stairs were in darkness, but the whole suite of rooms, usually brilliant as the day, were now in deep gloom. From every carriage window heads were protruded, wondering at this strange spectacle; and eager inquiries passed on every side for an explanation. The explanation of "sudden illness" was rapidly disseminated, but as rapidly contradicted, and the reply given by the porter to all demands quickly repeated from mouth to mouth, "Her Ladyship will not receive."

"Can no one explain this mystery?" cried the old Princess Borinsky, as, heavy with fat and diamonds, she hung out of her carriage window. "Oh, there's Major Scaresby; he is certain to know, if it be anything malicious."

Scaresby was, however, too busy in recounting his news to others to perceive the signals the old Princess held out; and it was only as her chasseur, six feet three of green and gold, bent down to give her Highness's message, that the Major hurried off, in all the importance of a momentary scandal, to the side of her carriage.

"Here I am, all impatience. What is it, Scaresby? Tell me quickly," cried she.

"A smash, my dear Princess, — nothing more or less," said he, in a voice which nature seemed to have invented to utter impertinences, so harsh and grating, and yet so painfully distinct in all its accents, — "as complete a smash as ever I heard of."

"You can't mean that her fortune is in peril?"

"I suppose that must suffer also. It is her character — her station as one of us — that's shipwrecked here."

"Go on, go on," cried she, impatiently; "I wish to hear it all."

"All is very briefly related, then," said he. "The charming Countess, you remember, ran away with a countryman of mine, young Glencore, of the 8th Hussars; I used to know his father intimately."

"Never mind his father."

"That's exactly what Glencore did. He came over here and fell in love with the girl, and they ran off together; but they forgot to get married, Princess. Ha — ha — ha !" And he laughed with a cackle a demon could not have rivalled.

"I don't believe a word of it, — I'll never believe it," cried the Princess.

"That's exactly what I was recommending to the Marquesa Guesteni. I said, you need n't believe it. Why, how do we go anywhere, nowadays, except by 'not believing' the evil stories that are told of our entertainers."

"Yes, yes; but I repeat that this is an infamous calumny. She, a Countess, of a family second to none in all Italy; her father a Grand d'Espagne. I'll go to her this moment."

"She'll not see you. She has just refused to see La Genori," said the Major, tartly. "Though, if a cracked reputation might have afforded any sympathy, she might have admitted *her*."

"What is to be done?" exclaimed the Princess, sorrowfully.

"Just what you suggested a few moments ago, — don't believe it. Hang me, but good houses and good cooks are growing too scarce to make one credulous of the ills that can be said of their owners."

"I wish I knew what course to take," muttered the Princess.

"I'll tell you, then. Get half a dozen of your own set together to-morrow morning, vote the whole story an atrocious falsehood, and go in a body and tell the Countess your mind. You know as well as I, Princess, that social credit is as great a bubble as commercial; we should all of us be bankrupts if our books were seen. Ay, by Jove! and the similitude goes farther too; for when one old established house breaks, there is generally a crash in the whole community around it."

While they thus talked, a knot had gathered around the carriage, all eager to hear what opinion the Princess had formed on the catastrophe.

Various were the sentiments expressed by the different speakers, — some sorrowfully deploring the disaster; others more eagerly inveighing against the infamy of the man who had proclaimed it. Many declared that they had come to the determination to discredit the story. Not one, however, sincerely professed that he disbelieved it.

Can it be, as the French moralist asserts, that we have a latent sense of satisfaction in the misfortunes of even our best friends; or is it, as we rather suspect, that true friendship is a rarer thing than is commonly believed, and has little to do with those conventional intimacies which so often bear its name?

Assuredly, of all this well-bred, well-dressed, and well-born company, now thronging the courtyard of the palace and the street in front of it, the tone was as much sarcasm as sorrow, and many a witty epigram and smart speech were launched over a disaster which might have been spared such levity. At length the space slowly began to thin. Slowly carriage after carriage drove off, — the heaviest grief of their occupants often being over a lost *soirée*, an unprofited occasion to display toilette and jewels; while a few, more reflective, discussed what course was to be followed in future, and what recognition extended to the victim.

The next day Florence sat in committee over the lost Countess. Witnesses were heard and evidence taken as to

11

her case. They all agreed it was a great hardship, — a terrible calamity; but still, if true, what could be done?

Never was there a society less ungenerously prudish, and yet there were cases — this, one of them — which transgressed all conventional rule. Like a crime which no statute had ever contemplated, it stood out self-accused and self-condemned. A few might, perhaps, have been merciful, but they were overborne by numbers. Lady Glencore's beauty and her vast fortune were now counts in the indictment against her, and many a jealous rival was not sorry at this hour of humiliation. The despotism of beauty is not a very mild sway, after all; and perhaps the Countess had exercised her rule right royally. At all events, it was the young and the good-looking who voted her exclusion, and only those who could not enter into competition with her charms who took the charitable side. They discussed and debated the question all day; but while they hesitated over the reprieve, the prisoner was beyond the law. The gate of the palace, locked and barred all day, refused entrance to every one; at night, it opened to admit the exit of a travelling-carriage. The next morning large bills of sale, posted over the walls, declared that all the furniture and decorations were to be sold.

The Countess had left Florence, none knew whither.

"I must really have those large Sèvres jars," said one.

"And I, the small park phaeton," cried another.

"I hope she has not taken Horace with her; he was the best cook in Italy. Splendid hock she had. — I wonder is there much of it left?"

"I wish we were certain of another bad reputation to replace her," grunted out Scaresby; "they are the only kind of people who give good dinners, and never ask for returns."

And thus these dear friends — guests of a hundred brilliant fêtes — discussed the fall of her they once had worshipped.

It may seem small-minded and narrow to stigmatize such conduct as this. Some may say that for the ordinary courtesies of society no pledges of friendship are required, no real gratitude incurred. Be it so. Still, the revulsion, from habits of deference and respect, to disparagement, and even sarcasm, is a sorry evidence of human kindness; and the threshold, over which for years we had only passed as guests, might well suggest sadder thoughts as we tread it to behold desolation.

The fair Countess had been the celebrity of that city for many a day. The stranger of distinction sought her, as much as a matter of course as he sought presentation to the sovereign. Her *salons* had the double eminence of brilliancy in rank and brilliancy in wit; her entertainments were cited as models of elegance and refinement; and now she was gone! The extreme of regret that followed her was the sorrow of those who were to dine there no more; the grief of him who thought he should never have a house like it.

The respectable vagabonds of society are a large family, much larger than is usually supposed. They are often well born, almost always well mannered, invariably well dressed. They do not, at first blush, appear to discharge any very great or necessary function in life; but we must by no means, from that, infer their inutility. Naturalists tell us that several varieties of insect existence we rashly set down as mere annoyances, have their peculiar spheres of usefulness and good; and, doubtless, these same loungers contribute in some mysterious manner to the welfare of that state which they only seem to burden. We are told that but for flies, for instance, we should be infested with myriads of winged tormentors, insinuating themselves into our meat and drink, and rendering life miserable. Is there not something very similar performed by the respectable class I allude to? Are they not invariably devouring and destroying some vermin a little smaller than themselves, and making thus a healthier atmosphere for their betters? If good society only knew the debt it owes to these defenders of its privileges, a " Vagabonds' Home and Aged Asylum " would speedily figure amongst our national charities.

We have been led to these thoughts by observing how distinctly different was Major Scaresby's tone in talking of the Countess when he addressed his betters or spoke in his own class. To the former he gave vent to all his sarcasm and bitterness; they liked it just because they would n't condescend to it themselves. To his own he put on the bullying air of one who said, "How should *you* possibly know what vices such great people have, any more than you know what they have for dinner? *I* live amongst them, — *I* understand them, — *I* am aware that what would be very shocking in *you* is quite permissible to *them*. *They* know how to be wicked: *you* only know how to be gross." And thus Scaresby talked, and sneered, and scoffed, making such a hash of good and evil, such a Maëlstrom of right and wrong, that it were a subtle moralist who could have extracted one solitary scrap of uncontaminated meaning from all his muddy lucubrations.

He, however, effected this much: he kept the memory of her who had gone, alive by daily calumnies. He embalmed her in poisons, each morning appearing with some new trait of her extravagance, till the world, grown sick of himself and his theme, vowed they would hear no more of either; and so she was forgotten.

Ay, good reader, utterly forgotten! The gay world, for so it likes to be called, has no greater element of enjoyment amongst all its high gifts than its precious power of forgetting. It forgets not only all it owes to others, — gratitude, honor, and esteem, — but even the closer obligations it has contracted with itself. The Palazzo della Torre was for a fortnight the resort of the curious and the idle. At the sale crowds appeared to secure some object of especial value to each; and then the gates were locked, the shutters closed, and a large, ill-written notice on the door announced that any letters for the proprietor were to be addressed to "Pietro Arretini, Via del Sole."

CHAPTER XXII.

AN UPTONIAN DESPATCH.

BRITISH LEGATION, NAPLES.

MY DEAR HARCOURT, — It would seem that a letter of mine to you must have miscarried, — a not unfrequent occurrence when entrusted to our Foreign Office for transmission. Should it ever reach you, you will perceive how unjustly you have charged me with neglecting your wishes. I have ordered the Sicilian wine for your friend; I have obtained the Royal leave for you to shoot in Calabria; and I assure you it is rather a rare incident in my life to have forgotten nothing required of me! Perhaps you, who know me well, will do me this justice, and be the more grateful for my present promptitude.

It was quite a mistake sending me here; for anything there is to be done, Spencer or Lonsdale would perfectly suffice. I ought to have gone to Vienna, — and so they know at home; but it's the old game played over again. Important questions! why, my dear friend, there is not a matter between this country and our own that rises above the capacity of a Colonel of Dragoons. Meanwhile really great events are preparing in the East of Europe, — not that I am going to inflict them upon you, nor ask you to listen to speculations which even those in authority turn a deaf ear to.

It is very kind of you to think of my health. I am still a sufferer: the old pains rather aggravated than relieved by this climate. You are aware that, though warm, the weather here has some exciting property, some excess or other of a peculiar gas in the atmosphere, prejudicial to certain temperaments. I feel it greatly; and though the season is midsummer, I am obliged to dress entirely in a light costume of buckskin, and take Marsalla baths, which refresh me, at least for the while. I have also taken to smoke the leaves of the nux vomica, steeped in arrack, and think it agrees with me. The King has most kindly placed a little villa at Ischia at my disposal; but I do not mean to avail myself of the politeness. The Duke of San Giustino has also offered me his palace at Baia ; but I don't fancy leaving this just now, where there is a doctor, a certain Luigi Buffeloni, who really seems to have hit off my case. He calls it arterial arthriticis, — a kind of inflammatory action of one coat of the arterial system ; his notion is highly ingenious, and wonderfully borne out by the symptoms. I wish you would ask Brodie, or any of our best men, whether they have met with this affection ; what class it affects, and what course it usually takes ? My Italian doctor implies that it is the passing malady of men highly excitable, and largely endowed with mental gifts. He may, or may not, be correct in this. It is only nature makes the blunder of giving the sharpest swords the weakest scabbards. What a pity the weapon cannot be worn naked !

You ask me if I like this place. I do, perhaps, as well as I should like anywhere. There is a wonderful sameness over the world just now, preluding, I have very little doubt, some great outburst of nationality from all the countries of Europe, — just as periods of Puritanism succeed intervals of gross licentiousness.

Society here is, therefore, what you see it in London or Paris ; well-bred people, like Gold, are current everywhere. There is really little peculiar to observe. I don't perceive that there is more levity than elsewhere. The difference is, perhaps, that there is less shame about it, since it is under the protection of the Church.

I go out very little ; my notion is, that the Diplomatist, like the ancient Augur, must not suffer himself to be vulgarized by contact. He can only lose, not gain, by that mixed intercourse with the world. I have a few who come when I want them, and go in like manner. They tell me "what is going on," far better and more truthfully than paid employees, and they cannot trace my intentions through my inquiries, and hasten off to retail them at the Ministry of Foreign Affairs. Of my colleagues I see as little as possible, though, when we do meet, I feel an unbounded affection for them. So much for my life, dear Harcourt ; on the whole, a very tolerable kind of existence, which if few would envy, still fewer would care to part with.

I now come to the chief portion of your letter. This boy of Glencore's, I rather like the account you give of him, better than you do yourself. Imaginative and dreamy he may be, but remember what he was, and where we have placed him. A moonstruck, romantic youth at a German University. Is it not painting the lily ?

I merely intended he should go to Gottingen to learn the language, — always a difficulty, if not abstracted from other and more dulcet sounds. I never meant to have him domesticated with some rusty Hochgelehrter, eating sauer-kraut in company with a green-eyed Fräulein, and imbibing love and metaphysics together. Let him "moon away," as you call it, my dear Harcourt. It is wonderfully little consequence what any one does with his intellect till he be three or four and twenty. Indeed, I half suspect that the soil might be left quietly to rear weeds till that time; and as to dreaminess, it signifies nothing if there be a strong "physique." With a weak frame, imagination will play the tyrant, and never cease till it dominates over all the other faculties; but where there is strength and activity, there is no fear of this.

You amuse me with your account of the doctor; and so the Germans have actually taken him for a savant, and given him a degree "honoris causa." May they never make a worse blunder. The man is eminently remarkable, — with his opportunities, miraculous. I am certain, Harcourt, you never felt half the pleasure on arriving at a region well stocked with game, that he did on finding himself in a land of Libraries, Museums, and Collections. Fancy the poor fellow's ecstasy at being allowed to range at will through all ancient literature, of which hitherto a stray volume alone had reached him. Imagine his delight as each day opened new stores of knowledge to him, surrounded as he was by all that could encourage zeal and reward research. The boy's treatment of him pleases me much; it smacks of the gentle blood in his veins. Poor lad, there is something very sad in his case.

You need not have taken such trouble about accounts and expenditure; of course, whatever you have done I perfectly approve of. You say that the boy has no idea of money or its value. There is both good and evil in this. And now as to his future. I should have no objection whatever to having him attached to my Legation here, and perhaps no great difficulty in effecting his appointment; but there is a serious obstacle in his position. The young men who figure at embassies and missions are all "cognate numbers." They each of them know who and what the other is, whence he came, and so on. Now, our poor boy could not stand this ordeal, nor would it be fair he should be exposed to it. Besides this, it was never Glencore's wish, but the very opposite to it, that he should be brought prominently forward in life. He even suggested one of the Colonies as the means of withdrawing him at once, and forever, from public gaze.

You have interested me much by what you say of the boy's progress. His tastes, I infer, lie in the direction which, in a worldly sense, are least profitable; but, after all, Harcourt, every one has brains enough, and to spare, for any career. Let us only decide upon that one most fitted for him, and, depend upon it, his faculties will day by day conform to his duties, and his tastes be merely dissipations, just as play or wine is to coarser natures.

If you really press the question of his coming to me, I will not refuse, seeing that I can take my own time to consider what steps subsequently should be adopted. How is it that you know nothing of Glencore,—can he not be traced?

Lord Selby, whom you may remember in the Blues formerly, dined here yesterday, and mentioned a communication he had received from his lawyer with regard to some property in tail, which, if Glencore should leave no heir male, devolved upon him. I tried to find out the whereabouts and the amount of this heritage; but, with the admirable indifference that characterizes him, he did not know or care.

As to my Lady, I can give you no information whatever. Her house at Florence is uninhabited, the furniture is sold off; but no one seems even to guess whither she has betaken herself. The fast and loose of that pleasant city are, as I hear, actually houseless since her departure. No asylum opens there with fire and cigars. A number of the destitute have come down here in half despair, amongst the rest Scaresby,—Major Scaresby, an insupportable nuisance of flat stories and stale gossip: one of those fellows who cannot make even malevolence amusing, and who speak ill of their neighbors without a single spark of wit. He has left three cards upon me, each duly returned; but I am resolved that our interchange of courtesies shall proceed no farther.

I trust I have omitted nothing in reply to your last despatch, except it be to say that I look for you here about September, or earlier, if as convenient to you; you will, of course, write to me, however, meanwhile.

Do not mention having heard from me, at the clubs or in society. I am, as I have the right to be, on the sick list, and it is as well my rest should remain undisturbed.

I wish you had any means of making it known that the article in the "Quarterly," on our Foreign relations, is not mine. The newspapers have coolly assumed me to be the author, and of course I am not going to give them the *éclat* of a personal denial. The fellow who wrote it must be an ass; since had he known what he pretends, he had never revealed it. He who wants to bag his bird, Colonel, never bangs away at nothing. I have now completed a longer despatch to you than I intend to address to the Noble Secretary at F. O., and am yours, very faithfully,

HORACE UPTON.

Whose Magnesia is it that contains essence of Bark? Tripley's or Chipley's, I think. Find it out for me, and send me a packet through the office; put up Fauchard's pamphlet with it, on Spain, and a small box of those new blisters, — Mouches they are called; they are to be had at Atkinson's. I have got so accustomed to their stimulating power that I never write without one or two on my forehead. They tell me the cautery, if dexterously applied, is better; but I have not tried it.

CHAPTER XXIII.

THE TUTOR AND HIS PUPIL.

We are not about to follow up the correspondence of Sir Horace by detailing the reply which Harcourt sent, and all that thereupon ensued between them.

We pass over, then, some months of time, and arrive at the late autumn.

It is a calm, still morning; the sea, streaked with tinted shadows, is without a ripple; the ships of many nations that float on it are motionless, their white sails hung out to bleach, their ensigns drooping beside the masts. Over the summit of Vesuvius — for we are at Naples — a light blue cloud hangs, the solitary one in all the sky. A mild, plaintive song, the chant of some fishermen on the rocks, is the only sound, save the continuous hum of that vast city, which swells and falls at intervals.

Close beside the sea, seated on a rock, are two figures. One is that of a youth of some eighteen or nineteen years; his features, eminently handsome, wear an expression of gloomy pride as in deep preoccupation he gazes out over the bay; to all seeming, indifferent to the fair scene before him, and wrapped in his own sad thoughts. The other is a short, square-built, almost uncouth figure, overshadowed by a wide straw hat, which seems even to diminish his stature; a suit of black, wide and ample enough for one twice his size, gives his appearance a grotesqueness to which his features contribute their share.

It is, indeed, a strange physiognomy, to which Celt and Calmuc seem equally to contribute. The low, overhanging forehead, the intensely keen eye, sparkling with an almost imp-like drollery, are contrasted by a firmly compressed mouth and a far-projecting under-jaw that imply sternness even to cruelty; a mass of waving black hair, that covers neck and shoulders, adds a species of savagery to a head which assuredly has no need of such aid. Bent down over a large quarto volume, he never lifts his eyes; but, intently occupied, his lips are rapidly repeating the words as he reads them.

"Do you mean to pass the morning here?" asks the youth, at length, "or where shall I find you later on?"

"I'll do whatever you like best," said the other, in a rich brogue; "I'm agreeable to go or stay, — *ad utramque paratus.*" And Billy Traynor, for it was he, shut up his venerable volume.

"I don't wish to disturb you," said the boy, mildly, "you can read. *I* cannot; I have a fretful, impatient feeling over me that perhaps will go off with exercise. I'll set out, then, for a walk, and come back here towards evening, then go and dine at the Rocca, and afterwards whatever you please."

"If you say that, then," said Billy, in a voice of evident delight, "we'll finish the day at the Professor Tadeucci's, and get him to go over that analysis again."

"I have no taste for chemistry. It always seems to me to end where it began," said the boy, impatiently. "Where do all researches tend to? how are you elevated in intellect? how are your thoughts higher, wider, nobler, by all these mixings and manipulations?"

"Is it nothing to know how thunder and lightning is made; to understand electricity; to dive into the secrets of that old crater there, and see the ingredients in the crucible that was bilin' three thousand years ago?"

"These things appeal more grandly to my imagination when the mystery of their forces is unrevealed. I like to think of them as dread manifestations of a mighty will, rather than gaseous combinations or metallic affinities."

"And what prevents you?" said Billy, eagerly. "Is the grandeur of the phenomenon impaired because it is in part intelligible? Ain't you elevated as a reasoning being when you get what I may call a peep into God's workshop, rather than by implicitly accepting results just as any old woman accepts a superstition?"

"There is something ignoble in mechanism," said the boy, angrily.

"Don't say that, while your heart is beatin' and your arteries is contractin'; never say it as long as your lungs dilate or collapse. It's mechanism makes water burst out of the ground, and, swelling into streams, flow as mighty rivers through the earth. It's mechanism raises the sap to the topmost bough of the cedar-tree that waves over Lebanon. 'T is the same power moves planets above, just to show us that as there is nothing without a cause, there is one great and final 'Cause' behind all."

"And will you tell me," said the boy, sneeringly, "that a sunbeam pours more gladness into your heart because a prism has explained to you the composition of light?"

"God's blessings never seemed the less to me because he taught me the beautiful laws that guide them," said Billy, reverently; "every little step that I take out of darkness is on the road, at least, to Him."

In part abashed by the words, in part admonished by the tone of the speaker, the boy was silent for some minutes. "You know, Billy," said he, at length, "that I spoke in no irreverence; that I would no more insult your convictions than I would outrage my own. It is simply that it suits my dreamy indolence to like the wonderful better than the intelligible; and you must acknowledge that there never was so palatable a theory for ignorance."

"Ay, but I don't want you to be ignorant," said Billy, earnestly; "and there 's no greater mistake than supposing that knowledge is an impediment to the play of fancy. Take my word for it, Master Charles, imagination, no more than any one else, does not work best in the dark."

"I certainly am no adept under such circumstances," said the boy. "I have n't told you what happened me in the studio last night. I went in without a candle, and, trying to grope my way to the table, I overturned the large olive jar, full of clay, against my Niobe, and smashed her to atoms."

"Smashed Niobe!" cried Billy, in horror.

"In pieces. I stood over her sadder than ever she felt herself, and I have not had the courage to enter the studio since."

"Come, come, let us see if she couldn't be restored," said Billy, rising. "Let us go down there together."

"You may, if you have any fancy, — there's the key," said the boy. "I'll return there no more till the rubbish be cleared away." And so saying, he moved off, and was soon out of sight.

Deeply grieving over this disaster, Billy Traynor hastened from the spot, but he had only reached the garden of the Chiaja when he heard a faint, weak voice calling him by his name; he turned, and saw Sir Horace Upton, who, seated in a sort of portable arm-chair, was enjoying the fresh air from the sea.

"Quite a piece of good fortune to meet you, Doctor," said he, smiling; "neither you nor your pupil have been near me for ten days or more."

"'T is our own loss then, your Excellency," said Billy, bowing; "even a chance few minutes in your company is like whetting the intellectual razor, — I feel myself sharper for the whole day after."

"Then why not come oftener, man? Are you afraid of wearing the steel all away?"

"'T is more afraid I am of gapping the fine edge of your Excellency by contact with my own ruggedness," said Billy, obsequiously.

"You were intended for a courtier, Doctor," said Sir Horace, smiling.

"If there was such a thing as a court fool nowadays, I'd look for the place."

"The age is too dull for such a functionary. They'll not find ten men in any country of Europe equal to the office," said Sir Horace. "One has only to see how lamentably dull are the journals dedicated to wit and drollery, to admit this fact; though written by many hands, how rare it is to chance upon what provokes a laugh. You'll have fifty metaphysicians anywhere before you'll hit on one Molière. Will you kindly open that umbrella for me? This autumnal sun, they say, gives sunstroke. And now what do you think of this boy? He'll not make a diplomatist, that's clear."

"He'll not make anything, — just for one simple reason, because he could be whatever he pleased."

"An intellectual spendthrift," sighed Sir Horace. "What a hopeless bankruptcy it leads to!"

"My notion is 't would be spoiling him entirely to teach him a trade or a profession. Let his great faculties shoot up without being trimmed or trained; don't want to twist or twine or turn them at all, but just see whether he won't, out of his uncurbed nature, do better than all our discipline could effect. There's no better colt than the one that was never backed till he was a five-year-old."

"He ought to have a career," said Sir Horace, thoughtfully. "Every man ought to have a calling, if only that he may be able to abandon it."

"Just as a sailor has a point of departure," said Billy.

"Precisely," said Sir Horace, pleased at being so well appreciated.

"You are aware, Doctor," resumed he, after a pause, "that the lad will have little or no private fortune. There are family circumstances that I cannot enter into, nor would your own delicacy require it, that will leave him almost dependent on his own efforts. Now, as time is rolling over, we should bethink us what direction it were wisest to give his talents; for he has talents."

"He has genius and talents both," said Billy; "he has the raw material, and the workshop to manufacture it."

"I am rejoiced to hear such an account from one so well able to pronounce," said Sir Horace, blandly; and Billy bowed, and blushed with a sense of happiness that none but humble men, so praised, could ever feel.

"I should like much to hear what you would advise for him," said Upton.

"He's so full of promise," said Billy, "that whatever he takes to he'll be sure to fancy he'd be better at something else. See, now, it isn't a bull I'm sayin', but I'll make a blunder of it if I try to explain."

"Go on; I think I apprehend you."

"By coorse you do. Well, it's that same feelin' makes me cautious of sayin' what he ought to do. For, after all, a variety of capacity implies discursiveness, and discursiveness is the mother of failure."

"You speak like an oracle, Doctor."

"If I do, it's because the priest is beside me," said Billy, bowing. "My notion is this: I'd let him cultivate his fine gifts for a year or two in any way he liked, — in work or idleness; for they'll grow in the fallow as well as in the tilled land. I'd let him be whatever he liked, — striving always, as he's sure to be striving, after something higher, and greater, and better than he'll ever reach; and then, when he has felt both his strength and his weakness, I'd try and attach him to some great man in public life; set a grand ambition before him, and say, 'Go on.'"

"He's scarcely the stuff for public life," muttered Sir Horace.

"He is," said Billy, boldly.

"He'd be easily abashed, — easily deterred by failure."

"Sorra bit. Success might cloy, but failure would never damp him."

"I can't fancy him a speaker."

"Rouse him by a strong theme and a flat contradiction, and you'll see what he can do."

"And then his lounging, idle habits — "

"He'll do more in two hours than any one else in two days."

"You are a warm admirer, my dear Doctor," said Sir Horace, smiling blandly. "I should almost rather have such a friend than the qualities that win the friendship. — Have you a message for me, Antoine?" said he to a servant who stood at a little distance, waiting the order to approach. The man came forward, and whispered a few words. Sir Horace's cheek gave a faint, the very faintest possible, sign of flush as he listened, and uttering a brief "Very well," dismissed the messenger.

"Will you give me your arm, Doctor?" said he, languidly; and the elegant Sir Horace Upton passed down the crowded promenade, leaning on his uncouth companion, without the slightest consciousness of the surprise and sarcasm around him. No man more thoroughly could appreciate conventionalities; he would weigh the effect of appearances to the veriest nicety; but in practice he seemed either to forget his knowledge or despise it. So that, as leaning on the little dwarf's arm he moved along, his very

air of fashionable languor seemed to heighten the absurdity
of the contrast. Nay, he actually seemed to bestow an almost deferential attention to what the other said, bowing
blandly his acquiescence, and smiling with an urbanity all
his own.

Of the crowd that passed, nearly all knew the English
Minister. Uncovered heads were bent obsequiously; graceful salutations met him as he went; while a hundred con-
jectures ran as to who and what might be his companion.

He was a Mesmeric Professor, a Writer in Cipher, a
Rabbi, an Egyptian Explorer, an Alchemist, an African
Traveller, and, at last, Monsieur Thiers! — and so the fine
world of Naples discussed the humble individual whom
you and I, dear reader, are acquainted with as Billy
Traynor.

CHAPTER XXIV.

On the evening of that day the handsome saloons of the great Hôtel " Universo " were filled with a brilliant assemblage to compliment the Princess Sabloukoff on her arrival. We have already introduced this lady to the reader, and have no need to explain the homage and attention of which she was the object. There is nothing which so perfectly illustrates the maxim of *ignotum pro magnifico* as the career of politics; certain individuals obtaining, as they do, a pre-eminence and authority from a species of mysterious prestige about them, and a reputation of having access at any moment to the highest personage in the world of state affairs. Doubtless great ministers are occasionally not sorry to see the public full cry on a false scent, and encourage to a certain extent this mystification; but still it would be an error to deny to such persons as we speak of a knowledge, if not actually an influence, in great affairs.

When the Swedish Chancellor uttered his celebrated sarcasm on the governing capacities of Europe, the political *salon*, as a state engine, was not yet in existence. What additional energy might it have given to his remark, had he known that the tea-table was the chapel of ease to the council-room, and gossip a new power in the state. Despotic governments are always curious about public opinion; they dread while affecting to despise it. They, however, make a far greater mistake than this, for they imagine its true exponent to be the society of the highest in rank and station.

It is not necessary to insist upon an error so palpable, and yet it is one of which nearly every capital of Europe affords example; and the same council-chamber that would

12

treat a popular movement with disdain would tremble at the epigram launched by some "elegant" of society. The theory is, "that the masses *act*, but never *think;* the higher ranks *think*, and set the rest in motion." Whether well or ill founded, one consequence of the system is to inundate the world with a number of persons who, no matter what their station or pretensions, are no other than spies. If it be observed that, generally speaking, there is nothing worth recording; that society, too much engaged with its own vicissitudes, troubles itself little with those of the state, — let it be remembered that the governments which employ these agencies are in a position to judge of the value of what they receive; and as they persevere in maintaining them, they are, doubtless, in some degree, remunerated.

To hold this high detective employ, a variety of conditions are essential. The individual must have birth and breeding to gain access to the highest circles; conciliating manners and ample means. If a lady, she is usually young and a beauty, or has the fame of having once been such. The strangest part of all is, that her position is thoroughly appreciated. She is recognized everywhere for what she is; and yet her presence never seems to impose a restraint or suggest a caution. She becomes, in reality, less a discoverer than a depositary of secrets. Many have something to communicate, and are only at a loss as to the channel. They have found out a political puzzle, hit a state blot, or unravelled a cabinet mystery. Others are in possession of some personal knowledge of royalty. They have marked the displeasure of the Queen Dowager, or seen the anger of the Crown Prince. Profitable as such facts are, they are nothing without a market. Thus it is that these characters exercise a wider sphere of influence than might be naturally ascribed to them, and possess besides a terrorizing power over society, the chief members of which are at their mercy.

It is, doubtless, not a little humiliating that such should be the instruments of a government, and that royalty should avail itself of such agencies; but the fact is so, and perhaps an inquiry into the secret working of democratic institutions might not make one a whit more proud of Popular Sovereignty.

Amongst the proficients in the great science we speak of, the Princess held the first place. Mysterious stories ran of her acquaintance with affairs the most momentous; there were narratives of her complicity in even darker events. Her name was quoted by Savary in his secret report of the Emperor Paul's death; an allusion to her was made by one of the assassins of Murat; and a gloomy record of a celebrated incident in Louis Philippe's life ascribed to her a share in a terrible tragedy. Whether believed or not, they added to the prestige that attended her, and she was virtually a "puissance" in European politics.

To all the intriguists in state affairs her arrival was actually a boon. She could and would give them, out of her vast capital, enough to establish them successfully in trade. To the minister of police she brought accurate descriptions of suspected characters, — the *signalements* of Carbonari that were threatening half the thrones of Europe. To the foreign secretary she brought tidings of the favor in which a great Emperor held him, and a shadowy vision of the grand cross he was one day to have. She had forbidden books for the cardinal confessor, and a case of smuggled cigars for the minister of finance. The picturesque language of a "Journal de Modes" could alone convey the rare and curious details of dress which she imported for the benefit of the court ladies. In a word, she had something to secure her a welcome in every quarter, — and all done with a tact and a delicacy that the most susceptible could not have resisted.

If the tone and manner of good society present little suitable to description, they are yet subjects of great interest to him who would study men in their moods of highest subtlety and astuteness. To mere passing careless observation, the reception of the Princess was a crowded gathering of a number of well-dressed people, in which the men were in far larger proportion than the other sex. There was abundance of courtesy; not a little of that half-flattering compliment which is the small change of intercourse; some — not much — scandal, and a fair share of small-talk. It was late when Sir Horace Upton entered, and, advancing to where the Princess stood, kissed her gloved hand with all the submis-

sive deference of a courtier. The most lynx-eyed observer
could not have detected either in his manner or in hers that
any intimacy existed between them, much less friendship;
least of all, anything still closer. His bearing was a most
studied and respectful homage, — hers a haughty, but condescending, acceptance of it; and yet, with all this, there
was that in those around that seemed to say, "This man is
more master here than any of us." He did not speak long
with the Princess, but, respectfully yielding his place to a
later arrival, fell back into the crowd, and soon after took
a seat beside one of the very few ladies who graced the
reception. In all, they were very few, we are bound to
acknowledge; for although La Sabloukoff was received at
court and all the embassies, they who felt, or affected to
feel, any strictness on the score of morals avoided rather
than sought her intimacy.

She covered over what might have seemed this disparagement of her conduct, by always seeking the society of men,
as though their hardy and vigorous intellects were more in
unison with her own than the graceful attributes of the softer
sex; and in this tone did the few lady friends she possessed
appear also to concur. It was their pride to discuss matters
of state and politics; and whenever they condescended to
more trifling themes, they treated them with a degree of
candor and in a spirit that allowed men to speak as unre-
servedly as though no ladies were present.

Let us be forgiven for prolixity, since we are speaking
less of individuals than of a school, — a school, too, on the
increase, and one whose results will be more widely felt
than many are disposed to believe.

As the evening wore on, the guests bartered the news
and *bons mots;* scraps of letters from royal hands were
read; epigrams from illustrious characters repeated; racy
bits of courtly scandal were related; and shrewd explanations hazarded as to how this was to turn out, and that
was to end. It was a very strange language they talked,
— so much seemed left for inference, so much seemed left
to surmise. There was a shadowy indistinctness, as it were,
over all; and yet their manner showed a perfect and thorough
appreciation of whatever went forward. Through all this

treatment of great questions, one striking feature pre-eminently displayed itself, — a keen appreciation of how much the individual characters, the passions, the prejudices, the very caprices of men in power modified the acts of their governments; and thus you constantly heard such remarks as, "If the Duke of Wellington disliked the Emperor less; or, so long as Metternich has such an attachment to the Queen Dowager; when we get over Carini's dread of the Archduchess; or, if we could only reconcile the Prince to a visit from Nesselrode," — showing that private personal feelings were swaying the minds of those whose contemplation might have seemed raised to a far loftier level. And then what a mass of very small gossip abounded, — incidents so slight and insignificant that they only were lifted into importance by the actors in them being Kings and Kaisers! By what accidents great events were determined; on what mere trifles vast interests depended, — it were, doubtless, no novelty to record; still, it would startle many to be told that a casual pique, a passing word launched at hazard, some petty observance omitted or forgotten, have changed the destinies of whole nations.

It is in such circles as these that incidents of this kind are recounted. Each has some anecdote, trivial and unimportant it may be, but still illustrating the life of those who live under the shadow of Royalty. The Princess herself was inexhaustible in these stores of secret biography; there was not a dynastic ambition to be consolidated by a marriage, not a Coburg alliance to patch up a family compact, that she was not well versed in. She detected in the vaguest movements plans and intentions, and could read the signs of a policy in indications that others would have passed without remark.

One by one the company retired, and at length Sir Horace found himself the last guest of the evening. Scarcely had the door closed on the last departure, when, drawing his arm-chair to the side of the fire opposite to that where the Princess sat, he took out his cigar-case, and, selecting a cheroot, deliberately lighted and commenced to smoke it.

"I thought they'd never go," said she, with a sigh; "but I know why they remained. — they all thought the Prince of

Istria was coming. They saw his carriage stop here this evening, and heard he had sent up to know if I received. I wrote on a card, 'To-morrow at dinner, at eight;' so be sure you are here to meet him."

Sir Horace bowed, and smiled his acceptance.

"And your journey, dear Princess," said he, between the puffs of his smoke, "was it pleasant?"

"It might have been well enough, but I was obliged to make a great *détour*. The Duchess detained me at Parma for some letters, and then sent me across the mountains of Pontremoli — a frightful road — on a secret mission to Massa."

"To Massa! of all earthly places."

"Even so. They had sent down there, some eight or nine months ago, the young Count Wahnsdorf, the Arch-duchess Sophia's son, who, having got into all manner of dissipation at Vienna, and lost largely at play, it was judged expedient to exile him for a season; and as the Duke of Modena offered his aid to their plans, he was named to a troop in a dragoon regiment, and appointed aide-de-camp to his Royal Highness. Are you attending; or has your Excellency lost the clew of my story?"

"I am all ears; only waiting anxiously to hear: who is she?"

"Oh, then, you suspect a woman in the case?"

"I am sure of it, dear Princess. The very accents of your voice prepared me for a bit of romance."

"Yes, you are right; he has fallen in love, — so desperately in love that he is incessant in his appeals to the Duchess to intercede with his family and grant him leave to marry."

"To marry whom?" asked Sir Horace.

"That's the very question which he cannot answer himself; and when pressed for information, can only reply that 'she is an angel.' Now, angels are not always of good family; they have sometimes very humble parents, and very small fortunes."

"*Hélas!*" sighed the diplomatist, pitifully.

"This angel, it would seem, is untraceable. She arrived with her mother, or what is supposed to be her mother, from Corsica; they landed at Spezzia, with an English passport, calling them Madame and Mademoiselle Harley. On arriving at Massa they took a villa close to the town, and established themselves with all the circumstance of people well-off as to means. They, however, neither received visits nor made acquaintance with any one. They even so far withdrew themselves from public view that they rarely left their own grounds, and usually took their carriage-airing at night. You are not attending, I see."

"On the contrary, I am an eager listener; only, it is a story one has heard so often. I never heard of any one preserving the incognito except where disclosure would have revealed a shame."

"Your Excellency mistakes," replied she; "the incognito is sometimes, like a feigned despatch in diplomacy, a means of awakening curiosity."

"*Ces ruses ne se font plus*, Princess, — they were the fashion in Talleyrand's time; now we are satisfied to mystify by no meaning."

"If the weapons of the old school are not employed, there is another reason, perhaps," said she, with a dubious smile.

"That modern arms are too feeble to wield them, you mean," said he, bowing courteously. "Ah! it is but too true, Princess;" and he sighed what might mean regret over the fact, or devotion to herself, — perhaps both. At all events, his submission served as a treaty of peace, and she resumed.

"And now, *revenons à nos moutons*," said she, "or at least to our lambs. This Wahnsdorf is quite capable of contracting a marriage without any permission, if they appear inclined to thwart him; and the question is, What can be done? The Duke would send these people away out of his territory, only that, if they be English, as their passports imply, he knows that there will be no end of trouble with your amiable Government, which is never paternal till some one corrects one of her children. If Wahnsdorf be sent away, where are they to send him? Besides, in all these cases the creature carries his malady with him, and is sure to marry the first who sympathizes with him. In a word, there were difficulties on all sides, and the Duchess sent me over, in observation, as they say, rather than with any direct plan of extrication."

"And you went?"

"Yes; I passed twenty-four hours. I couldn't stay longer, for I promised the Cardinal Caraffa to be in Rome on the 18th, about those Polish nunneries. As to Massa, I gathered little more than I had heard beforehand. I saw their villa; I even penetrated as far as the orangery in my capacity of traveller, — the whole a perfect Paradise. I'm not sure I did not get a peep at Eve herself, — at a distance, however. I made great efforts to obtain an interview, but all unsuccessfully. The police authorities managed to summon two of the servants to the Podestà, on pretence of some irregularity in their papers, but we obtained nothing out of them; and, what is more, I saw clearly that nothing could be effected by a *coup de main*. The place requires a long siege, and I had not time for that."

"Did you see Wahnsdorf?"

"Yes; I had him to dinner with me alone at the hotel, for, to avoid all observation, I only went to the Palace after nightfall. He confessed all his sins to me, and, like every other scapegrace, thought marriage was a grand absolution for past wickedness. He told me, too, how he made the acquaintance of these strangers. They were crossing the Magra with their carriage on a raft, when the cable snapped, and they were all carried down the torrent. He happened to be a passenger at the time, and did something very heroic, I've no doubt, but I cannot exactly remember what; but it amounted to either being, or being supposed to be, their deliverer. He thus obtained leave to pay his respects at the villa. But even this gratitude was very measured; they only admitted him at rare intervals, and for a very brief visit. In fact, it was plain he had to deal with consummate tacticians, who turned the mystery of their seclusion and the honor vouchsafed him to an ample profit."

"He told them his name and his rank?"

"Yes; and he owned that they did not seem at all impressed by the revelation. He describes them as very haughty, very condescending in manner, *très grandes dames*, in fact, but unquestionably born to the class they represent. They never dropped a hint of whence they had come, or any circumstance of their past lives, but seemed entirely engrossed by the present, which they spent principally in cultivating the arts; they both drew admirably, and the young lady had become a most skilful modellist in clay, her whole day being passed in a studio which they had just built. I urged him strongly to try and obtain permission for me to see it, but he assured me it was hopeless, — the request might even endanger his own position with them.

"I could perceive that, though very much in love, Wahnsdorf was equally taken with the romance of this adventure. He had never been a hero to himself before, and he was perfectly enchanted by the novelty of the sensation. He never affected to say that he had made the least impression on the young lady's heart; but he gave me to understand that the nephew of an Emperor need not trouble his head much on that score. He is a very good-looking, well-mannered, weak boy, who, if he only reach the age of thirty without some great blunder, will pass for a very dignified Prince for the rest of his life."

"Did you give him any hopes?"

"Of course, if he only promised to follow my counsels; and as these same counsels are yet in the oven, he must needs wait for them. In a word, he is to write to me everything, and I to him; and so we parted."

"I should like to see these people," said Upton, languidly.

"I'm sure of it," rejoined she; "but it is perhaps unnecessary;" and there was that in the tone which made the words very significant.

"Chelmsford — he's now Secretary at Turin — might perhaps trace them," said he; "he always knows everything of those people who are secrets to the rest of the world."

"For the present, I am disposed to think it were better not to direct attention towards them," replied she. "What we do here must be done adroitly, and in such a way as that it can be disavowed if necessary, or abandoned if unsuccessful."

" Said with all your own tact, Princess," said Sir Horace, smiling. " I can perceive, however, that you have a plan in your head already.   Is it not so?"

" No," said she, with a faint sigh; " I took wonderfully little interest in the affair.   It was one of those games where the combinations are so few you don't condescend to learn it.   Are you aware of the hour?"

" Actually three o'clock," said he, standing up.   " Really, Princess, I am quite shocked."

" And so am I," said she, smiling; "*on se compromet si facilement dans ce bas monde.*   Good night."   And she courtesied and withdrew before he had time to take his hat and retire.

CHAPTER XXV.

A DUKE AND HIS MINISTER.

In this age of the world, when everybody has been everywhere, seen everything, and talked with everybody, it may savor of an impertinence if we ask of our reader if he has ever been at Massa. It may so chance that he has not, and, if so, as assuredly has he yet an untasted pleasure before him.

Now, to be sure, Massa is not as it once was. The little Duchy, whose capital it formed, has been united to a larger state. The distinctive features of a metropolis, and the residence of a sovereign prince, are gone. The life and stir and animation which surround a court have subsided; grass-grown streets and deserted squares replace the busy movement of former days; a dreamy weariness seems to have fallen over every one, as though life offered no more prizes for exertion, and that the day of ambition was set forever. Yet are there features about the spot which all the chances and changes of political fortune cannot touch. Dynasties may fall, and thrones crumble, but the eternal Apennines will still rear their snow-clad summits towards the sky. Along the vast plain of ancient olives the perfumed wind will still steal at evening, and the blue waters of the Mediterranean plash lazily among the rocks, over which the myrtle and the arbutus are hanging. There, amidst them all, half hid in clustering vines, bathed in soft odors from orange-groves, with plashing fountains glittering in the sun, and foaming streams gushing from the sides of marble mountains, — there stands Massa, ruined, decayed, and deserted, but beautiful in all its desolation, and fairer to gaze on than many a scene where the tide of human fortune is at the flood.

As you wander there now, passing the deep arch over which, hundreds of feet above you, the ancient fortress

frowns, and enter the silent streets. you would find it somewhat difficult to believe how, a very few years back, this
was the brilliant residence of a court, — the gay resort of
strangers from every land of Europe, — that showy equipages traversed these weed-grown squares, and highborn
dames swept proudly beneath these leafy alleys. Hard,
indeed, to fancy the glittering throng of courtiers, the
merry laughter of light-hearted beauty, beneath these trel-
lised shades, where, moodily and slow, some solitary figure
now steals along, " pondering sad thoughts over the
bygone!"

But a few, a very few years ago, and Massa was in the
plenitude of its prosperity. The revenues of the state
were large, — more than sufficient to have maintained all
that such a city could require, and nearly enough to gratify
every caprice of a prince whose costly tastes ranged over
every theme, and found in each a pretext for reckless expenditure. He was one of those men whom Nature, having
gifted largely, " takes out" the compensation by a disposition of instability and fickleness that renders every acquire-
ment valueless. He could have been anything, — orator,
poet, artist, soldier, statesman ; and yet, in the very diversity of his abilities there was that want of fixity of purpose
that left him ever short of success, till he himself, wearied
by repeated failures, distrusted his own powers, and ceased
to exert them.

Such a man, under the hard pressure of a necessity, might
have done great things ; as it was, born to a princely station,
and with a vast fortune, he became a reckless spendthrift, —
a dreamy visionary at one time, an enthusiastic dilettante
at another. There was not a scheme of government he had
not eagerly embraced and abandoned in turn. He had
attracted to his little capital all that Europe could boast of
artistic excellence, and as suddenly he had thrown himself
into the most intolerant zeal of Papal persecution, — denouncing every species of pleasure, and ordaining a more
than monastic self-denial and strictness. There was only
one mode of calculating what he might be, which was, by
imagining the very opposite to what he then was. Extremes
were his delight, and he undulated between Austrian tyranny

and democratic licentiousness in politics. just as he vacillated between the darkest bigotry of his church and open infidelity.

At the time when we desire to present him to our readers (the exact year is not material), he was fast beginning to weary of an interregnum of asceticism and severity. He had closed theatres, and suppressed all public rejoicings; and for an entire winter he had sentenced his faithful subjects to the unbroken sway of the Priest and the Friar, — a species of rule which had banished all strangers from the Duchy, and threatened, by the injury to trade, the direst consequences to his capital. To have brought the question formally before him in all its details would have ensured the downfall of any minister rash enough for such daring. There was, indeed, but one man about the court who had courage for the enterprise; and to him we would devote a few lines as we pass. He was an Englishman, named Stubber. He had originally come out to Italy with horses for his Highness, and been induced, by good offers of employment, to remain. He was not exactly stable-groom, nor trainer, nor was he of the dignity of master of the stables; but he was something whose attributes included a little of all, and something more. One thing he assuredly was, — a consummately clever fellow, who could apply all his native Yorkshire shrewdness to a new sphere, and make of his homespun faculties the keen intelligence by which he could guide himself in novel and difficult circumstances.

A certain freedom of speech, with a bold hardihood of character, based, it is true, upon a conscious sense of honor, had brought him more than once under the notice of the Prince. His Highness felt such pleasure in the outspoken frankness of the man that he frequently took opportunities of conversing with him, and even asking his advice. Never deterred by the subject, whatever it was, Stubber spoke out his mind; and by the very force of strong native sense, and an unswerving power of determination, soon impressed his master that his best counsels were to be had from the Yorkshire jockey, and not from the decorated and gilded throng who filled the antechambers.

To elevate the groom to the rank of personal attendant, to create him a Chevalier, and then a Count, were all easy steps to such a Prince. At the time we speak of, Stubber was chief of the Cabinet, — the trusted adviser of his master in knottiest questions of foreign politics, the arbiter of the most difficult points with other states, the highest authority in home affairs, and the absolute ruler over the Duke's household and all who belonged to it. He was one of those men of action who speedily distinguish themselves wherever the game of life is being played. Smart to discern the character of those around him, prompt to avail himself of their knowledge, little hampered by the scruples which conventionalities impose on men bred in a higher station, he generally attained his object before others had arranged their plans to oppose him. To these qualities he added a rugged, unflinching honesty, and a loyal attachment to the person of his Prince. Strong in his own conscious rectitude, and in the confiding regard of his sovereign, Stubber stood alone against all the wiles and machinations of his formidable rivals.

Were we giving a history of this curious court and its intrigues, we could relate some strange stories of the mechanism by which states are ruled. We have, however, no other business with the subject than as it enters into the domain of our own story, and to this we return.

It was a calm evening of the early autumn, as the Prince, accompanied by Stubber alone, and unattended by even a groom, rode along one of the alleys of the olive wood which skirts the sea-shore beneath Massa. His Highness was unusually moody and thoughtful, and as he sauntered carelessly along, seemed scarcely to notice the objects about him.

" What month are we in, Stubber? " asked he, at length.

" September, Altezza," was the short reply.

" *Per Bacco!* so it is; and in this very month we were to have been in Bohemia with the Archduke Stephen, — the best shooting in all Europe, and the largest stock of pheasants in the whole world, perhaps; and I, that love field-sports as no man ever loved them! Eh, Stubber? " and he turned abruptly round to seek a confirmation of what he asserted. Either Stubber did not fully agree in the judgment, or did not deem it necessary to record his concurrence; but the Prince was obliged to reiterate his statement, adding, "I might say, indeed, it is the one solitary dissipation I have ever permitted myself."

Now, this was a stereotyped phrase of his Highness, and employed by him respecting music, literature, field-sports, picture-buying, equipage, play, and a number of other pursuits not quite so pardonable, in each of which, for the time, his zeal would seem to be exclusive.

A scarcely audible ejaculation — a something like a grunt — from Stubber, was the only assent to this proposition.

"And here I am," added the Prince, testily, "the only man of my rank in Europe, perhaps, without society, amusement, or pleasure, condemned to the wearisome details of a petty administration, and actually a slave, — yes, sir, I say, a slave — What the deuce is this? My horse is sinking above his pasterns. Where are we, Stubber?" and with a vigorous dash of the spurs he extricated himself from the deep ground.

"I often told your Highness that these lands were ruined for want of drainage. You may remark how poor the trees are along here; the fruit, too, is all deteriorated, — all for want of a little skill and industry. And, if your Highness remarked the appearance of the people in that village, every second man has the ague on him."

"They did look very wretched. And why is it not drained? Why is n't everything done as it ought, Stubber, eh?"

"Why is n't your Highness in Bohemia?"

"Want of means, my good Stubber; no money. My man, Landelli, tells me the coffer is empty; and until this new tax on the Colza comes in, we shall have to live on our credit or our wits. — I forget which, but I conclude they are about equally productive."

"Landelli is a *ladro*," said Stubber. "He has money enough to build a new wing to his château in Serravezza, and to give fifty thousand scudi of fortune to his daughter, though he can't afford your Highness the common necessaries of your station."

"*Per Bacco!* Billy, you are right; you must look into these accounts yourself. They always confuse me."

"I *have* looked into them, and your Highness shall have two hundred thousand francs to-morrow on your dressing-table, and as much more within the week."

"Well done, Billy! you are the only fellow who can un-mask these rogueries. If I had only had you with me long ago! Well! well! well! it is too late to think of it. What shall we do with this money? Bohemia is out of the ques-tion now. Shall we rebuild the San Felice? It is really too small; the stage is crowded with twenty people on it. There's that gate towards Carrara, when is it to be com-pleted? There's a figure wanted for the centre pedestal. As for the fountain, it must be done by the municipality. It is essentially the interest of the townspeople. You'd advise me to spend the money in draining these low lands, or in a grant to that new company for a pier at Marina; but I'll not; I have other thoughts in my head. Why should not this be the centre of art to the whole Peninsula? Carrara is a city of sculptors. Why not concentrate their efforts here — by a gallery? I have myself some glorious things, — the best group Canova ever modelled; the original Ariadne too, — far finer than the thing people go to see at Frankfort. Then there's Tanderini's Shepherd with the Goats. — Who lives yonder, Stubber? What a beautiful garden it is!" And he drew up short in front of a villa whose grounds were ter-raced in a succession of gardens down to the very margin of the sea. Plants and shrubs of other climates were min-gled with those familiar to Italy, making up a picture of singular beauty, by diversity of color and foliage. "Is n't this the 'Ombretta,' Stubber?"

"Yes, Altezza; but the Morelli have left it. It is let now to a stranger, — a French lady. Some call her English, I believe."

"To be sure; I remember. There was a demand about a formal permission to reside here. Landelli advised me not to sign it, — that she might turn out English, or have some claim upon England, which was quite equivalent to placing the Duchy, and all within it, under that blessed thing they call British protection."

"There are worse things than even that," muttered Stubber.

" British occupation, perhaps you mean; well, you may be right. At all events, I did not take Landelli's advice, for I gave the permission, and I have never heard more of her. She must be rich, I take it. See what order this place is kept in; that conservatory is very large indeed, and the orange-trees are finer than ours."

" They seem very fine indeed," said Stubber.

" I say, sir, that we have none such at the Palace. I'll wager a zecchino they have come from Naples. And look at that magnolia: I tell you, Stubber, this garden is very far superior to ours."

" Your Highness has not been in the Palace gardens lately, perhaps. I was there this morning, and they are really in admirable order."

" I'll have a peep inside of these grounds, Stubber," said the Duke, who, no longer attentive to the other, only followed out his own train of thought. At the same instant he dismounted, and, without giving himself any trouble about his horse, made straight for a small wicket which lay invitingly open in front of him. The narrow skirting of copse passed, the Duke at once found himself in the midst of a lovely garden, laid out with consummate skill and taste, and offering at intervals the most beautiful views of the surrounding scenery. Although much of what he beheld around him was the work of many years, there were abundant traces of innovation and improvement. Some of the statues were recently placed, and a small temple of Grecian architecture seemed to have been just restored. A heavy curtain hung across the doorway; drawing back which, the Duke entered what he at once perceived to be a sculptor's studio. Casts and models lay carelessly about, and a newly begun group stood enshrouded in the wetted drapery with which artists clothe their unfinished labors. No mean artist himself, the Duke examined critically the figures before him; nor was he long in perceiving that the artist had committed more than one fault in drawing and proportion. " This is amateur work," said he to himself; " and yet not without cleverness, and a touch of genius too. Your dilettante scorns anatomy, and will not submit to drudgery; hence, here are muscles incorrectly developed, and their action ill expressed." So saying, he sat down before the model, and taking up one of the tools at his side, began to correct some of the errors in the work. It was exactly the kind of task for which his skill adapted him. Too impatient and too discursive to accomplish anything of his own, he was admirably fitted to correct the faults of another, and so he worked away vigorously, — totally forgetting where he was, how he had come there, and as utterly oblivious of Stubber, whom he had left without. Growing more and more interested as he proceeded, he arose at length to take a better view of what he had done, and, standing some distance off, exclaimed aloud, " *Per Bacco!* I have made a good thing of it — there's life in it now!"

"So indeed is there," cried a gentle voice behind him; and, turning, he beheld a young and very beautiful girl, whose dress was covered by the loose blouse of a sculptor. "How I thank you for this!" said she, blushing deeply, as she courtesied before him. "I have had no teaching, and never till this moment knew how much I needed it."

"And this is your work, then?" said the Duke, who turned again towards the model. "Well, there is promise in it. There is even more. Still, you have hard labor before you, if you would be really an artist. There is a grammar in these things, and he who would speak the tongue must get over the declensions. I know but little myself — "

"Oh, do not say so!" cried she, eagerly; "I feel that I am in a master's presence."

The Duke started, partly struck by the energy of her manner, in part by the words themselves. It is often difficult for men in his station to believe that they are not known and recognized; and so he stood wondering at her, and thinking who she could be that did not know him to be the Prince. "You mistake me," said he, gently, and with that dignity which is the birthright of those born to command. "I am but a very indifferent artist. I have studied a little, it is true; but other pursuits and idleness have swept away the small knowledge I once possessed, and left me, as to art, pretty much as I am in morals, — that is, I know what is right, but very often I can't accomplish it."

" You are from Carrara, I conclude?" said the young girl, timidly, still curious to hear more about him.

" Pardon me," said he, smiling; " I am a native of Massa, and live here."

" And are you not a sculptor by profession?" asked she, still more eagerly.

" No," said he, laughing pleasantly; " I follow a more precarious trade, nor can I mould the clay I work in so deftly."

" At least you love art," said she, with an enthusiasm heightened by the changes he had effected in her group.

" Now it is my turn to question, Signorina," said he, gayly. " Why, with a talent like yours, have you not given yourself to regular study? You live in a land where instruction should not be difficult to obtain. Carrara is one vast studio; there must be many there who would not alone be willing, but even proud, to have such a pupil. Have you never thought of this?"

" I have thought of it," said she, pensively, " but my aunt, with whom I live, desires to see no one, to know no one; — even now," added she, blushing deeply, " I find myself conversing with an utter stranger, in a way — " She stopped, overwhelmed with confusion, and he finished her sentence for her.

" In a way which shows how naturally a love of art establishes a confidence between those who profess it." As he spoke, the curtain was drawn back, and a lady entered, who, though several years older, bore such a likeness to the young girl that she might readily have been taken for her sister.

. " It is at length time I should make my excuses for this intrusion, madame," said he, turning towards her; and then in a few words explained how the accidental passing by the spot, and the temptation of the open wicket, had led him to a trespass, " which," added he, smiling, " I can only say I shall be charmed if you will condescend to retaliate. I, too, have some objects of art, and gardens which are thought worthy of a visit."

" We live here, sir, apart from the world. It is for that reason we have selected this residence," replied she, coldly.

"I shall respect your seclusion, madame," answered he, with a deep bow, "and only beg once more to tender my sincere apologies for the past." He moved towards the door as he spoke, the ladies courtesied deeply, and, with a still lowlier reverence, he passed out.

The Duke lingered in the garden, as though unwilling to leave the spot. For a while some doubt as to whether he had been recognized passed through his mind, but he soon satisfied himself that such was not the case, and the singularity of the situation amused him.

"I am culling a souvenir, madame," said he, plucking a moss-ross as the lady passed.

"I will give you a better one, sir," said she, detaching one from her bouquet, and handing it to him. And so they parted.

"*Per Bacco!* Stubber, I have seen two very charming women. They are evidently persons of condition; find out all about them, and let me hear it to-morrow." And so saying, his Highness rode away, thinking pleasantly over his adventure, and fancying a hundred ways in which it might be amusingly carried out. The life of princes is rarely fertile in surprises; perhaps, therefore, the uncommon and unusual are the pleasantest of all their sensations.

CHAPTER XXVI.

STUBBER knew his master well. There was no need for any "perquisitions" on his part; the ladies, the studio, and the garden were totally forgotten ere nightfall. Some rather alarming intelligence had arrived from Carrara, which had quite obliterated every memory of his late adventure. That little town of artists had long been the resort of an excited class of politicians, and it was more than rumored that the "Carbonari" had established there a lodge of their order. Inflammatory placards had been posted through the town — violent denunciations of the Government — vengeance, even on the head of the sovereign, openly proclaimed, and a speedy day promised when the wrongs of an enslaved people should be avenged in blood. The messenger who brought the alarming tidings to Massa carried with him many of the inflammatory documents, as well as several knives and poniards, discovered by the activity of the police in a ruined building at the sea-shore. No arrests had as yet been made, but the authorities were in possession of information with regard to various suspicious characters, and the police prepared to act at a moment's notice.

It was an hour after midnight when the Council met; and the Duke sat, pale, agitated, and terrified, at the table, with Landelli, the Prime Minister, Caprini, the Secretary for Foreign Affairs, and General Ferrucio, the War Minister; a venerable ecclesiastic, Monsignore Abbati, occupying the lowest place, in virtue of his humble station as confessor of his Highness. He who of all others enjoyed his master's confidence, and whose ready intelligence was most needed in the emergency, was not present; his title of Minister of the Household not qualifying him for a place at the Council.

Whatever the result, the deliberation was a long one. Even while it continued, there was time to despatch a courier to Carrara, and receive the answer he brought back; and when the Duke returned to his room, it was already far advanced in the morning. Fatigued and harassed, he dismissed his valet at once, and desired that Stubber might attend him. When he arrived, however, his Highness had fallen off asleep, and lay, dressed as he was, on his bed.

Stubber sat noiselessly beside his master, his mind deeply pondering over the events which, although he had not been present at the Council, had all been related to him. It was not the first time he had heard of that formidable conspiracy, which, under the title of the Carbonari, had established themselves in every corner of Europe.

In the days of his humbler fortune he had known several of them intimately; he had been often solicited to join their band; but while steadily refusing this, he had detected much which to his keen intelligence savored of treachery to the cause amongst them. This cause was necessarily recruited from those whose lives rejected all honest and patient labor. They were the disappointed men of every station, from the highest to the lowest. The ruined gentleman, the beggared noble, the bankrupt trader, the houseless artisan, the homeless vagabond, were all there; bold, daring, and energetic, fearless as to the present, reckless as to the future. They sought for any change, no matter what, seeing that in the convulsion their own condition must be bettered. Few troubled their heads how these changes were to be accomplished; they cared little for the real grievances they assumed to redress: their work was demolition. It was to the hour of pillage alone they looked for the recompense of their hardihood. Some, unquestionably, took a different view of the agencies and the objects; dreamy, speculative men, with high aspirations, hoped that the cruel wrongs which tyranny inflicted on many a European state might be effectually curbed by a glorious freedom, when each man's actions should be made comformable to the benefit of the community, and the will of all be typified in the conduct of each. There was, however, another class, and to these Stubber had given deep attention. It was a party whose singular activity and energy were always in the ascendant, — ever suggesting bold measures whose results could scarcely be more than menaces, and advocating actions whose greatest effect could not rise above acts of terror and dismay. And thus while the leaders plotted great political convulsions, and the masses dreamed of sack and pillage, these latter dealt in acts of assassination, — the vengeance of the poniard and the poison-cup. These were the men Stubber had studied with no common attention. He fancied he saw in them neither the dupes of their own excited imaginations, nor the reckless followers of rapine, but an order of men equal to the former by intelligence, but far transcending the last in crime and infamy. In his own early experiences he had perceived that more than one of these had expatriated themselves suddenly, carrying away to foreign shores considerable wealth, and, that, too, under circumstances where the acquisition of property seemed scarcely possible. Others he had seen as suddenly, throwing off their political associates, rise into stations of rank and power; and one memorable case he knew where the individual had become the chief adviser of the very state whose destruction he had sworn to accomplish. Such a one he now fancied he had detected among the advisers of his Prince; and deeply ruminating on this theme, he sat at the bedside.

"Is it a dream, Stubber, or have we really heard bad news from Carrara? Has Fraschetti been stabbed, or not?"

"Yes, your Highness, he has been stabbed exactly two inches below where he was wounded in September last, — then, it was his pocket-book saved him; now, it was your Highness's picture, which, like a faithful follower, he always carried about him."

"Which means, that you disbelieve the whole story."

"Every word of it."

"And the poniards found at the Bocca di Magra?"

"Found by those who placed them there."

"And the proclamations?"

"Blundering devices. See, here is one of them, printed on the very paper supplied to the Government offices. There's the water-mark, with the crown and your own cipher on it."

" *Per Bacco!* so it is. Let me show this to Landelli."

" Wait awhile, your Highness; let us trace this a little farther. No arrests have been made?"

" None."

" Nor will any. The object in view is already gained; they have terrified you, and secured the next move."

" What do you mean?"

" Simply, that they have persuaded you that this state is the hotbed of revolutionists; that your own means of security and repression are unequal to the emergency; that disaffection exists in the army; and that, whether for the maintenance of the Government or your safety, you have only one course remaining."

" Which is —"

" To call in the Austrians."

" *Per Bacco!* it is exactly what they have advised. How did you come to know it? Who is the traitor at the Council-board?"

" I wish I could tell you the name of one who was not such. Why, your Highness, these fellows are not *your* Ministers, except in so far as they are paid by you. They are Metternich's people; they receive their appointments from Vienna, and are only accountable to the cabinet held at Schönbrunn. If wise and moderate counsels prevailed here, if our financial measures prospered, if the people were happy and contented, how long, think you, would Lombardy submit to be ruled by the rod and the bayonet? Do you imagine that *you* will be suffered to give an example to the Peninsula of a good administration?"

" But so it is," broke in the Prince; " I defy any man to assert the opposite. The country *is* prosperous, the people *are* contented, the laws justly administered, and, I hesitate not to say, myself as popular as any sovereign of Europe."

" And I tell your Highness, just as distinctly, that the country is ground down with taxation, even to export duties on the few things we have to export; that the people are poor to the very verge of starvation; that if they do not take to the highways as brigands, it is because some traditions as honest men yet survive amongst them; that the laws only exist as an agent of tyranny, arrest and imprisonment being at the mere caprice of the authorities. Nor is there a means by which an innocent man can demand his trial, and insist on being confronted with his accuser. Your jails are full, crowded to a state of pestilence with supposed political offenders, men that, in a free country, would be at large, toiling industriously for their families, and whose opinions could never be dangerous, if not festering in the foul air of a dungeon. And as to *your own* popularity, all I say is, don't walk in the Piazza at Carrara after dusk. No, nor even at noonday."

"And you dare to speak thus to *me*, Stubber!" said the Prince, his face covered with a deadly pallor as he spoke, and his white lips trembling, but less in passion than in fear.

"And why not, sir? Of what value could such a man as I am be to your service, if I were not to tell you what you'll never hear from others, — the plain, simple truth? Is it not clear enough that if I only thought of my own benefit, I'd say whatever you'd like best to hear? — I'd tell you, like Landelli, that the taxes were well paid, or say, as Cerreccio did t' other day, that your army would do credit to any state in Europe, when he well knew at the time that the artillery was in mutiny from arrears of pay, and the cavalry horses dying from short rations!"

"I am well weary of all this," said the Duke, with a sigh. "If the half of what I hear of my kingdom every day be but true, my lot in life is worse than a galley-slave's. One assures me that I am bankrupt; another calls me a vassal of Austria; a third makes me out a Papal spy; and *you* aver that if I venture into the streets of my own town, in the midst of my own people, I am almost sure to be assassinated!"

"Take no man's word, sir, for what, while you can see for yourself, it is your own duty to ascertain," said Stubber, resolutely. "If you really only desire a life of ease and indolence, forgetting what you owe to yourself and those you rule over, send for the Austrians. Ask for a brigade and a general. You'll have them for the asking. They'd come at a word, and try your people at the drum-head, and flog and shoot them with as little disturbance to you as need be. You may pension off the judges; for a court-martial is a far speedier tribunal, and a corporal's guard is quite an economy in criminal justice. Trade will not, perhaps, prosper with martial law, nor is a state of siege thought favorable to commerce. No matter. You'll sleep safe so long as you keep within doors, and the band under your window will rouse the spirit of nationality in your heart, as it plays, 'God preserve the Emperor!'"

"You forget yourself, sir, and you forget *me!*" said the Duke, sternly, as he drew himself up, and threw a look of insolent pride at the speaker.

"Mayhap I do, your Highness," was the ready answer; "and out of that very forgetfulness let your Highness take a warning. I say, once more, I distrust the people about you; and as to this conspiracy at Carrara, I'll wager a round sum on it that it was hatched on t'other side of the Alps, and paid for in good florins of the Holy Roman Empire. At all events, give me time to investigate the matter. Let me have till the end of the week to examine into it, and, if I find nothing to confirm my views, I'll say not one word against all the measures of precaution that your Council are bent on importing from Austria."

"Take your own way; I promise nothing," said the Duke, haughtily; and, with a motion of his hand, dismissed his adviser.

CHAPTER XXVII.

CARRARA.

To all the luxuriant vegetation and cultivated beauty of Massa, glowing in the "golden glories" of its orange-groves, — steeped in the perfume of its thousand gardens, — Carrara offers the very strongest contrast. Built in a little cleft of the Apennines, it is begirt with great mountains, — wild, barren, and desolate. Some, dark and precipitous, have no traces in their sides but those of the torrents which are formed by the melting snows; others show the white caves, as they are called, of that pure marble which has made the name of the spot famous throughout Europe. High in the mountain sides, escarped amidst rocks, and zig-zagging over many a dangerous gorge and deep abyss, are the rough roads trodden by the weary oxen, — trailing along their massive loads and straining their stout chests to drag the great white blocks of glittering stone. Far down below, crossed and recrossed by splashing torrents, sprinkled with the spray of a hundred cataracts, stands Carrara itself, — a little marble city of art, every house a studio, every citizen a sculptor. Hither are sent all the marvellous conceptions of genius, — the models which mighty imaginations have begotten, — to be converted into imperishable stone. Here are the grand conceptions gathered for every land and clime, treasures destined to adorn the great galleries of nations, or the splendid palaces of kings.

Some of these studios are of imposing size and vast proportions, and not devoid of a certain architectural pretension, — a group, a figure, or a bas-relief usually adorning the space over the door, and by its subject giving some indication of the tastes of the proprietor. Thus, Madonnas

and saints are of frequent occurrence; and the majority of
the artists display their faith by an image of the saint whose
patronage they claim. Others exhibit some ideal conception; and a few denote their nationality by the bust of their
sovereign, or some prince of his house.

One of these buildings, a short distance from the town,
and so small as to be little more than a mere crypt, was distinguished by the chaste and simple elegance of its design,
and the tasteful ornament with which its owner had decorated
the most minute details of the building. He was a young
artist who had arrived in Carrara friendless and unknown,
but whose abilities had soon obtained for him consideration
and employment. At first, the tasks intrusted to him were
the humbler ones of friezes and decorative art; but at length,
his skill becoming acknowledged, to his hands were confided
the choicest conceptions of Danneker, the most rare creations of Canova. Little or nothing was known of him; his
habits were of the strictest seclusion, — he went into no
society, he formed no friendships. His solitary life, after a
while, ceased to attract any notice; and men saw him pass,
and come and go, without question, — almost without greeting; and, save when some completed work was about to be
packed off to its destination, the name of Sebastian Greppi
was rarely heard in Carrara.

His strict retirement had not, however, exempted him
from the jealous suspicions of the authorities; on the contrary, the seeming mystery of his life had sharpened their
curiosity and aroused their zeal; and more than once was
he summoned to the Prefecture to answer some frivolous
questions about his passport or his means of subsistence.

It was on one of these errands that he stood one morning
in the antechamber of the Podestà's court, awaiting his turn
to be called and interrogated. The heat of a crowded
chamber, the wearisome delay, — perhaps, too, some vexa-
tion at the frequency of these irritating calls, — had par-
tially excited him; and when he was at length introduced,
his manner was confused, and his replies vague and almost
wandering.

Two strangers, whose formal permission to reside were
then being filled up by a clerk, were accommodated with

seats in the room, and listened with no slight interest to a course of inquiry so strange and novel to their ears.

"Greppi!" cried the harsh voice of the President, "come forward;" and a youth stood up, dressed in the blue blouse of a common workman, and wearing the coarse shoes of the very humblest laborer; but yet, in the calm dignity of his mien and the mild character of his sad but handsome features, already proclaiming that he came of a class whose instincts denote good blood.

"Greppi, you have a servant, it would seem, whose name is not in your passport. How is this?"

"He is an humble friend who shares my fortunes, sir," said the artist. "They asked no passport from him when we crossed the Tuscan frontier; and he has been here some months without any demand for one."

"Does he assist you in your work?"

"He does, sir, by advice and counsel; but he is not a sculptor. Poor fellow! he never dreamed that his presence here could have attracted any remark."

"His tongue and accent betray a foreign origin, Greppi?"

"Be it so, — so do mine, perhaps. Are we the less submissive to the laws?"

"The laws can make themselves respected," said the Podestà, sternly. "Where is this man, — how is he called?"

"He is known as Guglielmo, sir. At this moment he is ill; he has caught the fever of the Campagna, and is confined to bed."

"We shall send to ascertain the fact," was the reply.

"Then my word is doubted!" said the youth, haughtily.

The Podestà started, but more in amazement than anger. There was, indeed, enough to astonish him in the haughty ejaculation of the poorly clad boy.

"I am given to believe that you are not — as your passport would imply — a native of Capri, nor a Neapolitan born," said the Podestà.

"If my passport be regular and my conduct blameless, what have you or any one to do with my birthplace? Is there any charge alleged against me?"

"You are forgetting where you are, boy; but I may take

measures to remind you of it," said the Podestà, whispering to a sergeant of the gendarmes at his side.

" I hope I have said nothing that could offend you," said the boy, eagerly; " I scarcely know what I have said. My wish is to submit myself in all obedience to the laws; to live quietly and follow my trade. If my presence here give displeasure to the authorities, I will, however sorry, take my departure, though I cannot say whither to." The last words were uttered falteringly, and in a kind of soliloquy, and only overheard by the two strangers, who now, having received their papers, arose to withdraw.

" Will you call at our inn and speak with us? That's my card," said one, as he passed out, and gave a visiting-card into the youth's hand.

He took it without a word; indeed, he was too deeply engaged in his own thoughts to pay much attention to the request.

" The sergeant will accompany you, my good youth, to your lodgings, and verify what you have stated as to your companion. To-morrow you will appear here again, to answer certain questions we shall put to you as to your subsistence, and the means by which you live."

" Is it a crime to have wherewithal to subsist upon?" asked the boy.

" He whose means of living are disproportionate to his evident station may well be an object of suspicion," said the other, with a sneer.

" And who is to say what is my station, or what becomes it? Will *you* take upon you to pronounce upon the question?" cried the boy, boldly.

" Mayhap it is what I shall do very soon!" was the calm answer.

" Then let me have done with this. I'll leave the place as soon as my friend be able to bear removal."

" Even that I'll not promise for."

" Why, you'll not detain me here by force?" exclaimed the youth.

A cold, ambiguous smile was the only reply he received to this speech.

" Well, let us see when this restraint is to begin," cried

the boy, passionately, as he moved towards the door; but no impediment was offered to his departure. On the contrary, the servant, at a signal from the Prefect, threw wide the two sides of the folding-doors, and the youth passed out, down the stairs, and into the street.

His mind obscured by passion, his heart bursting with indignation, he threaded his way through many a narrow lane and alley, till he reached a small rustic bridge, crossing over which he ascended a narrow flight of steps cut in the solid rock, and gained a little terrace, on which stood a small cottage of the humblest kind.

As usual in Italy, during the summer-time, the glass sashes of the windows had been removed, and the shutters closed. Opening one of these gently with his hand, he peeped in, and as suddenly a voice cried out, " Are you come back? Oh, how my heart was aching to see you here again! Come in quickly, and let me touch your hand."

The next moment the boy was seated by the bed, where lay a man greatly emaciated by sickness, and bearing in his worn features the traces of a severe tertian.

" It's going off now," said he, " but the fit was a long one. This morning it began at eight o'clock; but I'm throwing it off now, and I'll soon be better."

" My poor fellow," said the boy, caressing the cold fingers within his own hands, " it was in these midnight rambles of mine you caught the terrible malady. As it ever has been, your fidelity is fatal to you. I told you a thousand times that I was born to hard luck, and carried more than enough to swamp all who might try to succor me."

" And don't I say, as the ould heathen philosopher did of fortune, ' Nullum numen habes, si sit prudentia'?" Is it necessary to say that the speaker was Billy Traynor, and the boy his pupil?

"*Prudentia*," said the youth, scoffingly, " may mean anything, from trickery to downright meanness; since, by such acts as these, men grow great in life. *Prudentia* is thrift and self-denial; but it is more too, it is a compromise between a man's dignity and his worldly success:

it is the compact that says, Bear *this*, that *that* may happen; and so I 'll none of it."

" Tell me how you fared with the Prefect," asked Billy.

" You shall hear, and judge for yourself," said the other; and related, as well as his memory would serve him, the circumstances of his late interview.

" Well, well! " said Billy, " it might be worse."

" I knew you'd say so, poor fellow! " said the youth, affectionately; " you accept the rubs of life as cheerfully as I take them with impatience. But, after all, this is matter of temperament too. *You* can forgive, — I love better to resist."

" Mine is the better philosophy, though," said Billy, " since it will last one's lifetime. Forgiveness must dignify old age, when your virtue of resistance be no longer possible."

" I never wish to reach the time when I may be too old for it," said the boy, passionately.

" Hush! don't say that. It's not for you to determine how long you are to live, nor in what frame of mind years are to find you." He paused, and there was a long unbroken silence between them.

" I have been at the post," said the youth, at last, " and found that letter, which, by the Neapolitan postmark, must have been despatched many weeks since."

Billy Traynor took up the letter, whose seal was yet unbroken, and having examined it carefully, returned it to him, saying, " You did n't answer his last, I think?"

" No; and I half hoped he might have felt offended, and given up the correspondence. What have we to do with ambassadors or great ministers, Billy? Ours is not the grand highway in life, but the humble path on the mountain side."

" I'm content if it only lead upwards," said the sick man; and the words were uttered firmly, but with the solemn fervor of prayer.

CHAPTER XXVIII.

As young Massy — for so we like best to call him — sat with the letter in his hand, a card fell to the ground from between his fingers, and, taking it up, he read the name " Lord Selby."

" What does this mean, Billy?" asked he; " whom can it belong to? Oh, I remember now. There were some strangers at the Podestà's office this morning when I was there; and one of them asked me to call at this inn, and speak with them."

" He has seen the ' Alcibiades,' " exclaimed Billy, eagerly. " He has been at the studio?"

" How should he?" rejoined the youth. " I have not been there myself for two days: here is the key!"

" He has heard of it then, — of that I 'm certain; since he could not be in town here an hour without some one telling him of it."

Massy smiled half sadly, and shook his head.

" Go and see him, at all events." said Billy; " and be sure to put on your coat and a hat; for one would n't know what ye were at all, in that cap and dirty blouse."

" I 'll go as I am, or not at all," said the other, rising. " I am Sebastian Greppi, a young sculptor. At least," added he, bitterly. " I have about the same right to that name that I have to any other." He turned abruptly away as he spoke, and gained the open air. There for a few moments he stood seemingly irresolute, and then, wiping away a heavy tear that had fallen on his cheek, he slowly descended the steps towards the bridge.

When he reached the inn, the strangers had just dined, but left word that when he called he should be introduced at once, and Massy followed the waiter into a small garden.

14

where, in a species of summer-house, they were seated at their wine. One of them arose courteously as the youth came forward, and placing a chair for him, and filling out a glass of wine, invited him to join them.

" Give him one of your cigars, Baynton," said the other; " they are better than mine." And Massy accepted, and began smoking without a word.

" That fellow at the police-office gave you no further trouble, I hope," said my lord, in a half-languid tone, and with that amount of difficulty that showed he was no master of Italian.

" No," replied Massy; " for the present, he has done nothing more. I 'm not so certain, however, that to-morrow or next day I shall not be ordered away from this."

" On what grounds? "

" Suspicion, — Heavens knows of what! "

" That 's infamous, I say. Eh, Baynton? "

" Detestable," muttered the other.

" And whereto can you go? "

" I scarcely know as yet, since the police are in communication throughout the whole Peninsula, and they transmit your character from state to state."

" They 'd not credit this in England, Baynton! "

" No, not a word of it! " rejoined the other.

" You 're a Neapolitan, I think I heard him say."

" So my passport states."

" Ah, he won't say that he is one, though," interposed his Lordship, in English. " Do you mind that, Baynton? "

" Yes, I remarked it," was the reply.

" And how came you here originally? " asked Selby, turning towards the youth.

" I came here to study and to work. There is always enough to be had to do in this place, copying the works of great masters; and at one's spare moments there is time to try something of one's own."

" And have you done anything of that kind? "

" Yes, I have begun. I have attempted two or three."

" We should like to see them, — eh, Baynton? "

" Of course, when we 've finished our wine. It 's not far off, is it? "

"A few minutes' walk; but not worth even that, when the place is full of things really worth seeing. There's Danneker's 'Bathing Nymph,' and Canova's 'Dead Cupid,' and Rauch's 'Antigone,' all within reach."

"Mind that, Baynton; we must see all these to-morrow. Could you come about with us, and show us what we ought to see?"

"Who knows if I shall not be on the road to-morrow?" said the youth, smiling faintly.

"Oh, I think not, if there's really nothing against you; if it's only mere suspicion."

"Just so!" said the other, and drank off his wine.

"And you are able to make a good thing of it here, — by copying, I mean?" asked his Lordship, languidly.

"I can live," said the youth; "and as I labor very little and idle a great deal, that is saying enough, perhaps."

"I'm not sure the police are not right about him, after all, Baynton," said his Lordship; "he does n't seem to care much about his trade;" and Massy was unable to repress a smile at the remark.

"You don't understand English, do you?" asked Selby, with a degree of eagerness very unusual to him.

"Yes, I am English by birth," was the answer.

"English! and how came you to call yourself a Neapolitan? What was the object of that?"

"I wished to excite less notice and less observation here, and, if possible, to escape the jealousy with which Englishmen are regarded by the authorities; for this I obtained a passport at Naples."

Baynton eyed him suspiciously as he spoke, and as he sipped his wine continued to regard him with a keen glance.

"And how did you manage to get a Neapolitan passport?"

"Our Minister, Sir Horace Upton, managed that for me."

"Oh, you are known to Sir Horace, then?"

"Yes."

A quick interchange of looks between my lord and his friend showed that they were by no means satisfied that the young sculptor was simply a worker in marble and a fashioner in modelling-clay.

"Have you heard from Sir Horace lately?" asked Lord Selby.

"I received this letter to-day, but I have not read it;" and he showed the unopened letter as he spoke.

"The police may, then, have some reasonable suspicions about your residence here," said his Lordship, slowly.

"My Lord," said Massy, rising. "I have had enough of this kind of examination from the Podestà himself this morning, not to care to pass my evening in a repetition of it. Who I am, what I am, and with what object here, are scarcely matters in which you have any interest, and assuredly were not the subjects on which I expected you should address me. I beg now to take my leave." He moved towards the garden as he spoke, bowing respectfully to each.

"Wait a moment; pray don't go, — sit down again, — I never meant, — of course I couldn't mean so, — eh, Baynton?" said his Lordship, stammering in great confusion.

"Of course not," broke in Baynton; "his Lordship's inquiries were really prompted by a sincere desire to serve you."

"Just so, — a sincere desire to serve you."

"In fact, seeing you, as I may say, in the toils."

"Exactly so, — in the toils."

"He thought very naturally that his influence and his position might, — you understand, — for these fellows know perfectly well what an English peer is, — they take a proper estimate of the power of Great Britain."

His Lordship nodded assentingly, as though any stronger corroboration might not be exactly graceful on his part, and Baynton went on : —

"Now you perfectly comprehend why, — you see at once the whole thing; and I 'm sure, instead of feeling any soreness or irritation at my lord's interference, that in point of fact — "

"Just so," broke in his Lordship, pressing Massy into a seat at his side, — "just so; that 's it!"

It requires no ordinary tact for any man to reseat himself at a table from which he has risen in anger or irritation, and Massy had far too little knowledge of life to overcome this

difficulty gracefully. He tried, indeed, to seem at ease, he
endeavored even to be cheerful; but the efforts were all
unsuccessful. My lord was no very acute observer at any
time; he was, besides, so constitutionally indolent that the
company which exacted least was ever the most palatable to
him. As for Baynton, he was only too happy whenever
least reference was made to his opinion, and so they sat and
sipped their wine with wonderfully little converse between
them.

"You have a statue, or a group, or something or other,
have n't you?" said my lord, after a very long interval.

"I have a half-finished model," said the youth, not without a certain irritation at the indifference of his questioner.

"Scarcely light enough to look at it to-night, — eh,
Baynton?"

"Scarcely!" was the dry answer.

"We can go in the morning though, eh?"

The other nodded a cool assent.

My lord now filled his glass, drank it off, and refilled,
with the air of a man nerving himself for a great undertaking,
— and such was indeed the case. He was about to deliver
himself of a sentiment, and the occasion was one to which
Baynton could not lend his assistance.

"I have been thinking," said he, "that if that same
estate we spoke of, Baynton, — that Welsh property, you
know, and that thing in Ireland, — should fall in, I'd buy
some statues and have a gallery!"

"Devilish costly work you'd find it," muttered Baynton.

"Well, I suppose it is, — not more so than a racing
stable, after all."

"Perhaps not."

"Besides, I look upon that property — if it does ever
come to me — as a kind of windfall; it was one of those
pieces of fortune one could n't have expected, you know."
Then, turning towards the youth, as if to apologize for a
discussion in which he could take no part, he said, "We
were talking of a property which, by the eccentricity of its
owner, may one day become mine."

"And which doubtless some other had calculated on
inheriting," said the youth.

" Well, that may be very true; I never thought about that, — eh, Baynton?"

" Why should you?" was the short response.

" Gain and loss, loss and gain," muttered the youth, moodily, " are the laws of life."

" I say, Baynton, what a jolly moonlight there is out there in the garden! Would n't it be a capital time this to see your model, eh?"

" If you are disposed to take the trouble," said the youth, rising, and blushing modestly; and the others stood up at the same moment.

Nothing passed between them as they followed the young sculptor through many an intricate by-way and narrow lane, and at last reached the little stream on whose bank stood his studio.

" What have we here!" exclaimed Baynton as he saw it; " is this a little temple?"

" It is my workshop," said the boy, proudly, and produced the key to open the door.

Scarcely had he crossed the threshold, however, than his foot struck a roll of papers, and, stooping down, he caught up a large placard, headed, " Morte al Tiranno," in large capitals. Holding the sheet up to the moonlight, he saw that it contained a violent and sanguinary appeal to the wildest passions of the Carbonari, — one of those savage exhortations to bloodshedding which were taken from the terrible annals of the French Revolution. Some of these bore the picture of the guillotine at top, others were headed with cross poniards.

" What are all these about?" asked Baynton, as he took up three or four of them in his hand; but the youth, overcome with terror, could make no answer.

" These are all *sans-culotte* literature, I take it," said his Lordship; but the youth was stupefied and silent.

" Has there been any treachery at work here?" asked Baynton. " Is there a scheme to entrap you?"

The youth nodded a melancholy and slow assent.

" But why should you be obnoxious to these people? Have you any enemies amongst them?"

" I cannot tell," gloomily muttered the youth.

"And this is your statue?" said Baynton, as, opening a large shutter, he suffered a flood of moonlight to fall on the figure.

"Fine! — a work of great merit, Baynton." broke in his Lordship, whose apathy was at last overcome by admiration. But the youth stood regardless of their comments, his eyes bent upon the ground; nor did he heed them as they moved from side to side, examining the statue in all its details, and in words of high praise speaking their approval.

"I'll buy this," muttered his Lordship. "I'll give him an order, too, for another work, — leaving the subject to himself."

"A clever fellow, certainly," replied the other.

"Whom does he mean the figure to represent?"

"It is Alcibiades as he meets his death," broke in the youth; "he is summoned to the door as though to welcome a friend, and he falls pierced by a poisoned arrow, — there is but legend to warrant the fact. I cared little for the incident, — I was full of the man, as he contended with seven chariots in the Olympic games, and proudly rode the course with his glittering shield of ivory and gold, and his waving locks all perfumed. I thought of him in his gorgeous panoply, and his voluptuousness; lion-hearted and danger-seeking, pampering the very flesh he offered to the spears of the enemy. I pictured him to my mind, embellishing life with every charm, and daring death in every shape, — beautiful as Apollo, graceful as the bounding Mercury, bold as Achilles, the lion's whelp, as Æschylus calls him. This," added he, in a tone of depression, — "this is but a sorry version of what my mind had conceived."

"I arrest you, Sebastiano Greppi," said a voice from behind; and suddenly three gendarmes surrounded the youth, who stood still and speechless with terror, while a mean-looking man in shabby black gathered up the printed proclamations that lay about, and commenced a search for others throughout the studio.

"Ask them will they take our bail for his appearance, Baynton," said my lord, eagerly.

" No use. — they 'd only laugh at us," was the reply.

" Can we be of any service to you?　Is there anything we can do?" asked his Lordship of the boy.

" You must not communicate with the prisoner, signore," cried the brigadier, " if you don't wish to share his arrest."

" And this, doubtless," said the man in black, standing, and holding up the lantern to view the statue, — " this is the figure of Liberty we have heard of, pierced by the deadly arrow of Tyranny!"

" You hear them!" cried the boy, in wild indignation, addressing the Englishmen; " you hear how these wretches draw their infamous allegations!　But this shall not serve them as a witness."　And with a spring he seized a large wooden mallet from the floor, and dashed the model in pieces.

A cry of horror and rage burst from the bystanders, and as the Englishmen stooped in sorrow over the broken statue, the gendarmes secured the boy's wrists with a stout cord, and led him away.

" Go after them, Baynton; tell them he is an Englishman, and that if he comes to harm they 'll hear of it!" cried my lord, eagerly; while he muttered in a lower tone, " I think we might knock these fellows over and liberate him at once, eh, Baynton?"

" No use if we did," replied the other; " they 'd over-power us afterwards.　Come along to the inn; we 'll see about it in the morning."

CHAPTER XXIX.

A COUNCIL OF STATE.

IT was a fine mellow evening of the late autumn as two men sat in a large and handsomely furnished chamber opening upon a vast garden. There was something in the dim half-light, the heavily perfumed air, rich with the odor of the orange and the lime, and the stillness, that imparted a sense of solemnity to the scene, where, indeed, few words were interchanged, and each seemed to ponder long after every syllable of the other.

We have no mysteries with our reader, and we hasten to say that one of these personages was the Chevalier Stubber, — confidential minister of the Duke of Massa; the other was our old acquaintance Billy Traynor. If there was some faint resemblance in the fortunes of these two men, who, sprung from the humblest walks of life, had elevated themselves by their talents to a more exalted station, there all likeness between them ended. Each represented, in some of the very strongest characteristics, a nationality totally unlike that of the other: the Saxon, blunt, imperious, and decided; the Celt, subtle, quick-sighted, and suspicious, distrustful of all, save his own skill in a moment of difficulty.

"But you have not told me his real name yet," said the Chevalier, as he slowly smoked his cigar, and spoke with the half-listlessness of a careless inquirer.

"I know that, sir," said Billy, cautiously; "I don't see any need of it."

"Nor your own, either," remarked the other.

"Nor even that, sir," responded Billy, calmly.

"It comes to this, then, my good friend," rejoined Stubber, "that, having got yourself into trouble, and having discovered, by the aid of a countryman, that a little frankness would serve you greatly, you prefer to preserve a mystery that I could easily penetrate if I cared for it, to speaking openly and freely, as a man might with one of his own."

"We have no mysteries, sir. We have family secrets that don't regard any one but ourselves. My young ward, or pupil, whichever I ought to call him, has, maybe, his own reasons for leading a life of unobtrusive obscurity, and what one may term an umbrageous existence. It's enough for me to know that, to respect it."

"Come, come, all this is very well if you were at liberty, or if you stood on the soil of your own country; but remember where you are now, and what accusations are hanging over you. I have here beside me very grave charges indeed, — constant and familiar intercourse with leaders of the Carbonari — "

"We don't know one of them," broke in Billy.

"Correspondence with others beyond the frontier," continued the Chevalier.

"Nor that either," interrupted Billy.

"Treasonable placards found by the police in the very hands of the accused; insolent conduct to the authorities when arrested; attempted escape: all these duly certified on oath."

"Devil may care for that; oaths are as plenty with these blaguards as clasp-knives, and for the same purpose too. Here's what it is, now," said he, crossing his arms on the table, and staring steadfastly at the other: "we came here to study and work, to perfect ourselves in the art of modellin', with good studies around us; and, more than all, a quiet, secluded little spot, with nothing to distract our attention, or take us out of a mind for daily labor. That we made a mistake, is clear enough. Like everywhere else in this fine country, there's nothing but tyrants on one side, and assassins on the other; and meek and humble as we lived, we could n't escape the thievin' blaguards of spies."

"Do you know the handwriting of this address?" said the Chevalier, showing a sealed letter directed to Sebastiano Greppi, Sculptore, Carrara.

"Maybe I do, maybe I don't," was the gruff reply. "Won't you let me finish what I was sayin'?"

"This letter was found in the possession of the young prisoner, and is of some consequence," continued the other, totally inattentive to the question.

"I suppose a letter is always of consequence to him it's meant for," was the half-sulky reply. "Sure you're not goin' to break the seal — sure you don't mean to read it!" exclaimed he, almost springing from his seat as he spoke.

"I don't think I'd ask your permission for anything I think fit to do, my worthy fellow," said the other, sternly; and then, passing across the room, he summoned a gendarme, who waited at the door, to enter.

"Take this man back to the Fortezza," said he, calmly; and while Billy Traynor slowly followed the guard, the other seated himself leisurely at the table, lighted his candles, and perused the letter. Whether disappointed by the contents, or puzzled by the meaning, he sat long pondering with the document before him.

It was late in the night when a messenger came to say that his Highness desired to see him; and Stubber arose at once, and hastened to the Duke's chamber.

In a room studiously plain and simple in all its furniture, and on a low, uncurtained bed, lay the Prince, half dressed, a variety of books and papers littering the table, and even the floor at his side. Maps, prints, colored drawings, — some representing views of Swiss scenery, others being portraits of opera celebrities, — were mingled with illuminated missals and richly-embossed rosaries; while police reports, petitions, rose-colored billets and bon-bons, made up a mass of confusion wonderfully typical of the illustrious individual himself.

Stubber had scarcely crossed the threshold of the room when he appeared to appreciate the exact frame of his master's mind. It was the very essence of his tact to catch in a moment the ruling impulse which swayed for a time that strange and vacillating nature, and he had but to glance at him to divine what was passing within.

"So then," broke out the Prince, "here we are actually in the very midst of revolution. Marocchi has been stabbed in the Piazza of Carrara. Is it a thing to laugh at, sir?"

"The wound has only been fatal to the breast of his

surtout, your Highness; and so adroitly given, besides, that it does not correspond with the incision in his waistcoat."

"You distrust every one and everything, Stubber; and, of course, you attribute all that is going forward to the police."

"Of course I do, your Highness. They predict events with too much accuracy not to have a hand in their fulfilment. I knew three weeks ago when this outbreak was to occur, who was to be assassinated, — since that is the phrase for Marocchi's mock wound, who was to be arrested, and the exact nature of the demand the Council would make of your Royal Highness to suppress the troubles."

"And what was that?" asked the Duke, grasping a paper in his hand as he spoke.

"An Austrian division, with a half-battery of field-artillery, a judge-advocate to try the prisoners, and a provost-marshal to shoot them."

"And you'd have me believe that all these disturbances are deliberate plots of a party who desire Austrian influence in the Duchy?" cried the Duke, eagerly. "There may be really something in what you suspect. Here's a letter I have just received from La Sabloukoff, — she's always keen-sighted; and *she* thinks that the Court at Vienna is playing out here the game that they have not courage to attempt in Lombardy. What if this Wahnsdorf was a secret agent in the scheme, eh, Stubber?"

Stubber started with well-affected astonishment, and appeared as if astounded at the keen acuteness of the Duke's suggestion.

"Eh!" cried his Highness, in evident delight. "That never occurred to *you*, Stubber? I'd wager there's not a man in the Duchy could have hit that plot but myself."

Stubber nodded sententiously, without a word.

"I never liked that fellow," resumed the Duke. "I always had my suspicion about that half-reckless, wasteful manner he had. I know that I was alone in this opinion, eh, Stubber? It never struck *you*?"

"Never! your Highness, never!" replied Stubber, frankly.

"I can't show you the Sabloukoff's letter, Stubber, there are certain private details for my own eye alone; but she speaks of a young sculptor at Carrara, a certain — Let me find his name. Ah! here it is, Sebastian Greppi, a young artist of promise, for whom she bespeaks our protection. Can you make him out, and let us see him?"

Stubber bowed in silence.

" I will give him an order for something. There's a pedestal in the flower-garden where the Psyche stood. You remember. I smashed the Psyche, because it reminded me of Camilla Monti. He shall design a figure for that place. I'd like a youthful Bacchus. I have a clever sketch of one somewhere; and it shall be tinted, — slightly tinted. The Greeks always colored their statues. Strange enough, too; for, do you remark, Stubber. they never represented the iris of the eye, which the Romans invariably did. And yet. if you observe closely, you'll see that the eyelid implies the direction of the eye more accurately than in the Roman heads. I'm certain you never detected what I'm speaking of. eh, Stubber?"

Stubber candidly confessed that he had not, and listened patiently while his master descanted critically on the different styles of art. and his own especial tact and skill in discriminating between them.

" You'll look after these police returns, then, Stubber." said he, at last. " You'll let these people understand that we can suffice for the administration of our own duchy. We neither want advice from Metternich, nor battalions from Radetzky. The laws here are open to every man; and if we have any claim to the gratitude of our people. it rests on our character for justice."

While he spoke with a degree of earnestness that indicated sincerity. there was something in the expression of his eye — a half-malicious drollery in its twinkle — that made it exceedingly difficult to say whether his words were uttered in honesty of purpose. or in mere mockery and derision. Whether Stubber rightly understood their import is more than we are able to say; but it is very probable that he was. with all his shrewdness. mystified by one whose nature was a puzzle to himself.

" Let Marocchi return to Carrara. Say we have taken the matter into our own hands. Change the brigadier in command of the gendarmerie there. Tell the *canonico* Baldetti that we look to *him* and his deacons for true reports of any movement that is plotting in the town. I take no steps with regard to Wahnsdorf for the present, but let him be closely watched. And then, Stubber, send off an *estafetta* to Pietra Santa for the ortolans, for I think we have earned our breakfast by all this attention to state affairs." And then, with a laugh whose accents gave not the very faintest clew to its meaning, he lay back on his pillow again.

" And these two prisoners, your Highness, what is to be done with them?"

" Whatever you please, Stubber. Give them the third-class cross of Massa, or a month's imprisonment, at your own good pleasure. Only, no more business, — no papers to sign, no schemes to unravel; and so good night." And the Chevalier retired at once from a presence which he well knew resented no injury so unmercifully as any invasion of his personal comfort.

CHAPTER XXX.

THE LIFE THEY LED AT MASSA.

It was with no small astonishment young Massy heard that he and his faithful follower were not alone restored to liberty, but that an order of his Highness had assigned them a residence in a portion of the palace, and a promise of future employment.

"This smacks of Turkish rather than of European rule," said the youth. "In prison yesterday, — in a palace to-day. My own fortunes are wayward enough, Heaven knows, not to require any additional ingredient of uncertainty. What think you, Traynor?"

"I 'm thinkin'," said Billy, gravely, "that as the bastes of the field are guided by their instincts to objects that suit their natures, so man ought, by his reason, to be able to pilot himself in difficulties, - choosin' this, avoidin' that; seein' by the eye of prophecy where a road would lead him, and makin' of what seem the accidents of life, steppin'-stones to fortune."

"In what way does your theory apply here?" cried the other. "How am I to guess whither this current may carry me?"

"At all events, there 's no use wastin' your strength by swimmin' against it," rejoined Billy.

"To be the slave of some despot's whim, — the tool of a caprice that may elevate me to-day, and to-morrow sentence me to the gallows. The object I have set before myself in life is to be independent. Is this, then, the road to it?"

"You 're tryin' to be what no man ever was, or will be, to the world's end, then," said Billy. "Sure it 's the very nature and essence of our life here below that we are dependent one on the other for kindness, for affection, for material help in time of difficulty, for counsel in time of doubt. The rich man and the poor one have their mutual dependencies; and if it was n't so, cowld-hearted and selfish as the world is, it would be five hundred times worse."

"You mistake my meaning," said Massy, sternly, "as you often do, to read me a lesson on a text of your own. When I spoke of independence, I meant freedom from the serfdom of another's charity. I would that my life here, at least, should be of my own procuring."

"*I* get mine from *you*," said Traynor, calmly, "and never felt myself a slave on that account."

"Forgive me, my dear, kind friend. I could hate myself if I gave you a moment's pain. This temper of mine does not improve by time."

"There's one way to conquer it. Don't be broodin' on what's within. Don't be magnifyin' your evil fortunes to your own heart till you come to think the world all little, and yourself all great. Go out to your daily labor, whatever it be, with a stout spirit to do your best, and a thankful, grateful heart that you are able to do it. Never let it out of your mind that if there's many a one your inferior, winnin' his way up to fame and fortune before you, there's just as many better than you toilin' away unseen and unnoticed, wearin' out genius in a garret, and carryin' off a Godlike intellect to an obscure grave!"

"You talk to me as though my crying sin were an overweening vanity," said the youth, half angrily.

"Well, it's one of them," said Billy; and the blunt frankness of the avowal threw the boy into a fit of laughing.

"You certainly do not intend to spoil me, Billy," said he, still laughing.

"Why would I do what so many is ready to do for nothing? What does the crowd that praise the work of a young man of genius care where they're leading him to? It's like people callin' out to a strong swimmer, 'Go out farther and farther, — out to the open say, where the waves is rollin' big, and the billows is roughest; that's worthy of you, in your strong might and your stout limbs. Lave the still water and the shallows to the weak and the puny. *Your*

course is on the mountain wave, over the bottomless ocean.'
It's little they think if he's ever to get back again.   'T is
their boast and their pride that they said, 'Go on;' and
when his cold corpse comes washed to shore, all they have
is a word of derision and scorn for one who ventured beyond
his powers."

"How you cool down one's ardor; with what pleasure
you check every impulse that nerves one's heart for high
daring!" said the youth, bitterly. "These eternal warnings — these never-ending forebodings of failure — are sorry
stimulants to energy."

"Is n't it better for you to have all your reverses at the
hands of a crayture as humble as me?" said Billy, while the
tears glistened in his eyes. "What good am I, except for
this?"

In a moment the boy's arms were around him, while he
cried out, —

"There, forgive me once more, and let me try if I cannot amend a temper that any but yourself had grown weary
of correcting.   I 'll work — I 'll labor — I 'll submit — I 'll
accept the daily rubs of life, as others take them, and you
shall be satisfied with me.   We shall go back to all our old
pursuits, my dear Billy.   I 'll join all your ecstasies over
Æschylus, and believe as much as I can of Herodotus, to
please you.   You shall lead me to all the wonders of the
stars, and dazzle me with the brightness of visions that my
intellect is lost in; and in revenge I only ask that you
should sit with me in the studio, and read to me some of
those songs of Horace that move the heart like old wine.
Shall I own to you what it is which sways me thus uncer-
tainly, — jarring every chord of my existence, making life
a sea of stormy conflict?   Shall I tell you?"

He grasped the other's hand with both his own as he
spoke, and, while his lips quivered in strong emotion,
went on:

"It is this, then. I cannot forget, do all that I will, I
cannot root out of my heart what I once believed myself to
be. You know what I mean. Well, there it is still, like
the sense of a wrong or foul injustice, as though I had been
robbed and cheated of what never was mine!   This contrast

15

between the life my earliest hopes had pictured, and that
which I am destined to, never leaves me. All your teachings — and I have seen how devotedly you have addressed
yourself to this lesson — have not eradicated from my nature
the proud instincts that guided my childhood. Often and
often have you warmed my blood by thoughts of a triumph
to be achieved by me hereafter, — how men should recognize
me as a genius, and elevate me to honors and rewards; and
yet would I barter such success, ten thousand times told,
for an hour of that high station that comes by birth alone,
independent of all effort, — the heirloom of deeds chronicled
centuries back, whose actors have been dust for ages. That
is real pride." cried he, enthusiastically, "and has no alloy
of the petty vanity that mingles with the sense of a personal
triumph."

Traynor hung his head heavily as the youth spoke, and
a gloomy melancholy settled on his features; the sad conviction came home to him of all his counsels being fruitless, all his teachings in vain; and as the boy sat wrapped
in a wild, dreamy revery of ancestral greatness, the humble
peasant brooded darkly over the troubles such a temperament might evoke.

"It is agreed, then," cried Massy, suddenly, "that we
are to accept of this great man's bounty, live under his
roof, and eat his bread. Well, I accede, - as well his as
another's. Have you seen the home they destine for us?"

"Yes, it's a real paradise, and in a garden that would
beat Adam's now," exclaimed Traynor; "for there's marble fountains, and statues, and temples, and grottos in it;
and it's as big as a prairie, and as wild as a wilderness.
And, better than all, there's a little pathway leads to a
private stair that goes up into the library of the palace, —
a spot nobody ever enters, and where you may study the
whole day long without hearin' a footstep. All the books
is there that ever was written, and manuscripts without end
besides; and the Minister says I'm to have my own kay,
and go in and out whenever I plaze. 'And if there's anything wantin',' says he, 'just order it on a slip of paper and
send it to me, and you'll have it at once.' When I asked
if I ought to spake to the librarian himself, he only laughed,

and said, 'That's me; but I'm never there. Take my word for it, Doctor, you'll have the place to yourself.'"

He spoke truly. Billy Traynor had it, indeed, to himself. There, the gray dawn of morning, and the last shadows of evening, ever found him, seated in one of those deep, cell-like recesses of the windows; the table, the seats, the very floor littered with volumes which, revelling in the luxury of wealth, he had accumulated around him. His greedy avidity for knowledge knew no bounds. The miser's thirst for gold was weak in comparison with that intense craving that seized upon him. Historians, critics, satirists, poets, dramatists, metaphysicians, never came amiss to a mind bent on acquiring. The life he led was like the realization of a glorious dream, — the calm repose, the perfect stillness of the spot, the boundless stores that lay about him; the growing sense of power, as day by day his intellect expanded; new vistas opened themselves before him, and new and unproved sources of pleasure sprang up in his nature. The never-ending variety gave a zest, too, to his labors that averted all weariness; and at last he divided his time ingeniously, alternating grave and difficult subjects with lighter topics, — making, as he said himself, "Aristophanes digest Plato."

And what of young Massy all this while? His life was a dream, too, but of another and very different kind. Visions of a glorious future alternated with sad and depressing thoughts; high darings, and hopeless views of what lay before him, came and went, and went and came again. The Duke, who had just taken his departure for some watering-place in Germany, gave him an order for certain statues, the models for which were to be ready by his return, — at least, in that sketchy state of which clay is even more susceptible than canvas. The young artist chafed and fretted under the restraint of an assigned task. It was gall to his haughty nature to be told that his genius should accept dictation, and his fancy be fettered by the suggestions of another. If he tried to combat this rebellious spirit, and addressed himself steadily to labor, he found that his imagination grew sluggish, and his mind uncreative. The sense of servitude oppressed him; and though he essayed to

subdue himself to the condition of an humble artist, the old
pride still rankled in his heart, and spirited him to a haughty
resistance. His days thus passed over in vain attempts to
work, or still more unprofitable lethargy. He lounged
through the deserted garden, or lay, half-dreamily, in the
long, deep grass, listening to the cicala, or watching the
emerald-backed lizards as they lay basking in the sun.
He drank in all the soft voluptuous influences of a climate
which steeps the senses in a luxurious stupor, making the
commonest existence a toil, but giving to mere indolence all
the zest of a rich enjoyment. Sometimes he wandered into
the library, and noiselessly drew nigh the spot where Billy
sat deeply busied in his books. He would gaze silently,
half curiously, at the poor fellow, and then steal noiselessly
away, pondering on the blessings of that poor peasant's
nature, and wondering what in his own organization had
denied him the calm happiness of this humble man's life.

CHAPTER XXXI.

AT MASSA.

BILLY TRAYNOR sat, deeply sunk in study, in the old recess of the palace library. A passage in the "Antigone" had puzzled him, and the table was littered with critics and commentators, while manuscript notes, scrawled in the most rude hand, lay on every side. He did not perceive, in his intense preoccupation, that Massy had entered and taken the place directly in front of him. There the youth sat gazing steadfastly at the patient and studious features before him. It was only when Traynor, mastering the difficulty that had so long opposed him, broke out into an enthusiastic declamation of the text that Massy, unable to control the impulse, laughed aloud.

"How long are you there? I never noticed you comin' in," said Billy, half-shamed at his detected ardor.

"But a short time; I was wondering at — ay, Billy, and was envying, too — the concentrated power in which you address yourself to your task. It is the real secret of all success, and somehow it is a frame of mind I cannot achieve."

"How is the boy Bacchus goin' on?" asked Billy, eagerly.

"I broke him up yesterday, and it is like a weight off my heart that his curly bullet head and sensual lips are not waiting for me as I enter the studio."

"And the Cleopatra?" asked Traynor, still more anxiously.

"Smashed, — destroyed. Shall I own to you, Billy, I see at last myself what you have so often hinted to me, — I have no genius for the work?"

"I never said, — I never thought so," cried the other; "I only insisted that nothing was to be done without labor, — hard, unflinching labor; that easy successes were poor triumphs, and bore no results."

"There, — there, I 'll hear that sermon no more. I 'd not barter the freedom of my own unfettered thoughts, as they come and go, in hours of listless idleness, for all the success you ever promised me. There are men toil elevates, — me it wearies to depression, and brings no compensation in the shape of increased power. Mine is an unrewarding clay, — that 's the whole of it. Cultivation only develops the rank weeds which are deep sown in the soil. I 'd like to travel, — to visit some new land, some scene where all association with the past shall be broken. What say you?"

"I 'm ready, and at your orders," said Traynor, closing his book.

"East or west, then, which shall it be? If sometimes my heart yearns for the glorious scenes of Palestine, full of memories that alone satisfy the soul's longings, there are days when I pant for the solitude of the vast savannas of the New World. I feel as if to know one's self thoroughly, one's nature should be tested by the perils and exigencies of a life hourly making some demand on courage and ingenuity. The hunter's life does this. What say you, — shall we try it?"

"I 'm ready," was the calm reply.

"We have means for such an enterprise, have we not? You told me, some short time past, that nearly the whole of our last year's allowance was untouched."

"Yes, it 's all there to the good," said Billy; "a good round sum too."

"Let us get rid of all needless equipment, then," cried Massy, "and only retain what beseems a prairie life. Sell everything, or give it away at once."

"Leave all that to me, — I 'll manage everything; only say when you make up your mind."

"But it is made up. I have resolved on the step. Few can decide so readily; for I leave neither home nor country behind."

"Don't say that," burst in Billy; "here 's myself, the poorest crayture that walks the earth, that never knew where he was born or who nursed him, yet even to me there 's the tie of a native land, — there 's the soil that reared warriors and poets and orators that I heard of when a child, and

gloried in as a man; and, better than that, there's the green
meadows and the leafy valleys where kind-hearted men and
women live and labor, spakin' our own tongue and feelin'
our own feelin's, and that, if we saw to-morrow, we'd know
were our own, — heart and hand our own. The smell of the
yellow furze, under a griddle of oaten bread, would be
sweeter to me than all the gales of Araby the Blest; for it
would remind me of the hearth I had my share of, and the
roof that covered me when I was alone in the world."

The boy buried his face in his hands and made no answer.
At last, raising up his head, he said, —

"Let us try this life; let us see if action be not better
than mere thought. The efforts of intellect seem to inspire
a thirst there is no slaking. Sleep brings no rest after
them. I long for the sense of some strong peril which,
over, gives the proud feeling of a goal reached, — a feat
accomplished."

"I'll go wherever you like; I'll be whatever you want
me," said Billy, affectionately.

"Let us lose no time, then. I would not that my present
ardor should cool ere we have begun our plan. What day
is this? The seventh. Well, on the eighteenth there is a
ship sails from Genoa for Porto Rico. It was the announcement set my heart a-thinking of the project. I dreamed of
it two entire nights. I fancied myself walking the deck on
a starlit night, and framing all my projects for the future.
The first thing I saw next morning was the same placard,
'The "Colombo" will sail for Porto Rico on Friday, the
eighteenth.'"

"An unlucky day," muttered Billy, interrupting.

"I have fallen upon few that were otherwise," said Massy,
gloomily; "besides," he added, after a pause, "I have no
faith in omens, or any care for superstitions. Come, let us
set about our preparations. Do *you* bethink you how to rid
ourselves of all useless encumbrances here. Be it *my* care
to jot down the list of all we shall need for the voyage and
the life to follow it. Let us see which displays most zeal
for the new enterprise."

Billy Traynor addressed himself with a will to the duty
allotted him. He rummaged through drawers and desks,

destroyed papers and letters, laid aside all the articles which he judged suitable for preservation, and then hastened off to the studio to arrange for the disposal of the few "studies," for they were scarcely more, which remained of Massy's labors.

A nearly finished Faun, the head of a Niobe, the arm and hand of a Jove launching a thunderbolt, the torso of a dead sailor after shipwreck, lay amid fragments of shattered figures, grotesque images, some caricatures of his own works, and crude models of anatomy. The walls were scrawled with charcoal drawings of groups, — one day to be fashioned in sculpture, — with verses from Dante, or lines from Tasso, inscribed beneath; proud resolves to a life of labor figured beside stanzas in praise of indolence and dreamy abandonment. There were passages of Scripture, too, glorious bursts of the poetic rapture of the Psalms, intermingled with quaint remarks on life from Jean Paul or Herder. All that a discordant, incoherent nature consisted of was there in some shape or other depicted; and as Billy ran his eye over this curious journal, — for such it was, — he grieved over the spirit which had dictated it.

The whole object of all his teaching had been to give a purpose to this uncertain and wavering nature, and yet everything showed him now that he had failed. The blight which had destroyed the boy's early fortunes still worked its evil influences, poisoning every healthful effort, and dashing with a sense of shame every successful step towards fame and honor.

" Maybe he's right after all," muttered Billy to himself. " The New World is the only place for those who have not the roots of an ancient stock to hold them in the Old. Men can be there whatever is in them, and they can be judged without the prejudices of a class."

Having summed up, as it were, his own doubts in this remark, he proceeded with his task. While he was thus occupied, Massy entered, and threw himself into a chair.

" There, you may give it up, Traynor. Fate is ever against us, do and decide on what we will. Your confounded omen of a Friday was right this time."

" What do you mean? Have you altered your mind?"

"I expected you to say so," said the other, bitterly. "I knew that I should meet with this mockery of my resolution, but it is uncalled for. It is not I that have changed!"

"What is it, then, has happened, — do they refuse your passport?"

"Not that either; I never got so far as to ask for it. The misfortune is in this wise: on going to the bank to learn the sum that lay to my credit and draw for it, I was met by the reply that I had nothing there, — not a shilling. Before I could demand how this could be the case, the whole truth suddenly flashed across my memory, and I recalled to mind how one night, as I lay awake, the thought occurred to me that it was base and dishonorable in me, now that I was come to manhood, to accept of the means of life from one who felt shame in my connection with him. 'Why,' thought I, 'is there to be the bond of dependence where there is no tie of affection to soften its severity?' And so I arose from my bed, and wrote to Sir Horace, saying that by the same post I should remit to his banker at Naples whatever remained of my last year's allowance, and declined in future to accept of any further assistance. This I did the same day, and never told you of it, — partly, lest you should try to oppose me in my resolve; partly," and here his voice faltered. "to spare myself the pain of revealing my motives. And now that I have buoyed my heart up with this project, I find myself without means to attempt it. Not that I regret my act, or would recall it," cried he, proudly, "but that the sudden disappointment is hard to bear. I was feeding my hopes with such projects for the future when this stunning news met me, and the thought that I am now chained here by necessity has become a torture."

"What answer did Sir Horace give to your letter?" asked Billy.

"I forget; I believe he never replied to it, or if he did, I have no memory of what he said. Stay, — there was a letter of his taken from me when I was arrested at Carrara. The seal was unbroken at the time."

"I remember the letter was given to the Minister, who has it still in his keeping."

"What care I," cried Massy, angrily, "in whose hands it may be?"

" The Minister is not here now," said Billy, half speaking to himself. " he is travelling with the Duke; but when he comes back — "

" When he comes back! " burst in Massy, impatiently; " with what calm philosophy you look forward to a remote future. I tell you that this scheme is now a part and parcel of my very existence. I can turn to no other project, or journey no other road in life, till at least I shall have tried it! "

" Well, it is going to work in a more humble fashion," said Billy, calmly. " Leave me to dispose of all these odds and ends here — "

" This trash! " cried the youth, fiercely. " Who would accept it as a gift?"

" Don't disparage it; there are signs of genius even in these things; but, above all, don't meddle with me, but just leave me free to follow my own way. There now, go back and employ yourself preparing for the road; trust the rest to me."

Massy obeyed without speaking. It was not, indeed, that he ventured to believe in Traynor's resources, but he was indisposed to further discussion, and longed to be in solitude once more.

It was late at night when they met again. Charles Massy was seated at a window of his room, looking out into the starry blue of a cloudless sky, when Traynor sat down beside him. " Well," said he, gently, " it's all done and finished. I have sold off everything, and if you will only repair the hand of the Faun, which I broke in removing, there's nothing more wanting."

" That much can be done by any one," said Massy, haughtily. " I hope never to set eyes on the trumpery things again."

" But I have promised you would do it," said Traynor, eagerly.

" And how — by what right could you pledge yourself for my labor? Nay," cried he, suddenly changing the tone in which he spoke, " knowing my wilful nature, how could you answer for what I might or might not do?"

" I knew," said Billy, slowly, " that you had a great project in your head, and that to enable you to attempt it, you would scorn to throw all the toil upon another."

" I never said I was ashamed of labor," said the youth, reddening with shame.

" If you had, I would despair of you altogether," rejoined the other.

" Well, what is it that I have to do?" said Massy, bluntly.

" It is to remodel the arm, for I don't think you can mend it; but you 'll see it yourself."

" Where is the figure, — in the studio?"

" No; it is in a small pavilion of a villa just outside the gates. It was while I was conveying it there it met this misfortune. There 's the name of the villa on that card. You 'll find the garden gate open, and by taking the path through the olive wood you 'll be there in a few minutes; for I must go over to-morrow to Carrara with the Niobe; the Academy has bought it for a model."

A slight start of surprise and a faint flush bespoke the proud astonishment with which he heard of this triumph; but he never spoke a word.

" If you had any pride in your works, you 'd be delighted to see where the Faun is to be placed. It is in a garden, handsomer even than this here, with terraces rising one over the other, and looking out on the blue sea, from the golden strand of Via Reggio down to the headlands above Spezia. The great olive wood in the vast plain lies at your feet, and the white cliffs of Serravezza behind you."

" What care I for all this?" said Massy, gloomily. " Benvenuto could afford to be in love with his own works. — *I* cannot ! "

Traynor saw at once the mood of mind he was in, and stole noiselessly away to his room.

CHAPTER XXXII.

CHARLES MASSY, dressed in the blouse of his daily labor, and with the tools of his craft in his hand, set out early in search of the garden indicated by Billy Traynor. A sense of hope that it was for the last time he was to exercise his art, that a new and more stirring existence was now about to open before him, made his step lighter and his spirits higher as he went. "Once amid the deep woods, and on the wide plains of the New World, I shall dream no more of what judgment men may pass upon my efforts. There, if I suffice to myself, I have no other ordeal to meet. Perils may try me, but not the whims and tastes of other men."

Thus, fancying an existence of unbounded freedom and unfettered action, he speedily traversed the olive wood, and almost ere he knew it found himself within the garden. The gorgeous profusion of beautiful flowers, the graceful grouping of shrubs, the richly perfumed air, laden with a thousand odors, first awoke him from his day dream, and he stood amazed in the midst of a scene surpassing all that he had ever conceived of loveliness. From the terrace, where under a vine trellis he was standing, he could perceive others above him rising on the mountain side, while some beneath descended towards the sea, which, blue as a turquoise, lay basking and glittering below. A stray white sail or so was to be seen, but there was barely wind to shake the olive leaves, and waft the odors of the orange and the oleander. It was yet too early for the hum of insect life, and the tricklings of the tiny fountains that sprinkled the flower-beds were the only sounds in the stillness. It was in color, outline, effect, and shadow, a scene such as only Italy can present, and Massy drank in all its influences with an eager delight.

"Were I a rich man," said he, "I would buy this paradise. What in all the splendor of man's invention can compare with the gorgeous glory of this flowery carpet? What frescoed ceiling could vie with these wide-leaved palms, interlaced with these twining acacias, glimpses of the blue sky breaking through? And for a mirror, there lies Nature's own, — the great blue ocean! What a life were it, to linger days and hours here, amid such objects of beauty, having one's thoughts ever upwards, and making in imagination a world of which these should be the types. The faintest fancies that could float across the mind in such an existence would be pleasures more real, more tangible, than ever were felt in the tamer life of the actual world."

Loitering along, he at length came upon the little temple which served as a studio, on entering which, he found his own statue enshrined in the place of honor. Whether it was the frame of mind in which he chanced to be, or that place and light had some share in the result, for the first time the figure struck him as good, and he stood long gazing at his own work with the calm eye of a critic. At length, detecting, as he deemed, some defects in design, he drew nigh, and began to correct them. There are moments in which the mind attains the highest and clearest perception, — seasons in which, whatever the nature of the mental operation, the faculties address themselves readily to the task, and labor becomes less a toil than an actual pleasure. This was such. Massy worked on for hours; his conceptions grew rapidly under his hand into bold realities, and he saw that he was succeeding. It was not alone that he had imparted a more graceful and lighter beauty to his statue, but he felt within himself the promptings of a spirit that grew with each new suggestion of its own. Efforts that before had seemed above him he now essayed boldly; difficulties that once had appeared insurmountable he now encountered with courageous daring. Thus striving, he lost all sense of fatigue. Hunger and exhaustion were alike unremembered, and it was already late in the afternoon, as, overcome by continued toil, he threw himself heavily down, and sank off into a deep sleep.

It was nigh sunset as he awoke. The distant bell of a

monastery was ringing the hour of evening prayer, the
solemn chime of the "Venti quattro," as he leaned on his
arm and gazed in astonishment around him. The whole
seemed like a dream. On every side were objects new and
strange to his eyes, — casts and models he had never seen
before; busts and statues and studies all unknown to him.
At last his eyes rested on the Faun, and he remembered at
once where he was. The languor of excessive fatigue, however, still oppressed him, and he was about to lie back
again in sleep, when, bending gently over him, a young girl,
with a low, soft accent, asked if he felt ill, or only tired.

Massy gazed, without speaking, at features regular as the
most classic model, and whose paleness almost gave them
the calm beauty of the marble. His steady stare slightly
colored her cheek, and made her voice falter a little as she
repeated her question.

"I scarcely know," said he, sighing heavily. "I feel as
though this were a dream, and I am afraid to awaken from
it."

"Let me give you some wine," said she, bending down
to hand him the glass; "you have over-fatigued yourself.
The Faun is by your hand, is it not?"

He nodded a slow assent.

"Whence did you derive that knowledge of ancient art?"
said she, eagerly. "Your figure has the light elasticity of
the classic models, and yet nothing strained or exaggerated
in attitude. Have you studied at Rome?"

"I could do better now," said the youth, as, rising on his
elbow, he strained his eyes to examine her. "I could
achieve a real success."

A deep flush covered her face at these words, so palpably
alluding to herself, and she tried to repeat her question.

"No," said he. "I cannot say I have ever studied: all
that I have done is full of faults; but I feel the spring of
better things within me. Tell me, is this *your* home?"

"Yes," said she, smiling faintly. "I live in the villa
here with my aunt. She has purchased your statue, and
wishes you to repair it, and then to engage in some other
work for her. Let me assist you to rise; you seem very
weak."

"I *am* weak, and weary too," said he, staggering to a seat. "I have overworked myself, perhaps, — I scarcely know. Do not take away your hand."

"And you are, then, the Sebastian Greppi of whom Carrara is so proud?"

"They call me Sebastian Greppi; but I never heard that my name was spoken of with any honor."

"You are unjust to your own fame. We have often heard of you. See, here are two models taken from your works. They have been my studies for many a day. I have often wished to see you, and ask if my attempt were rightly begun. Then here is a hand."

"Let me model yours," said the youth, gazing steadfastly at the beautifully shaped one which rested on the chair beside him.

"Come with me to the villa, and I will present you to my aunt; she will be pleased to know you. There, lean on my arm, for I see you are very weak."

"Why are you so kind, so good to me?" said he, faintly, while a tear rose slowly to his eye.

He arose totteringly, and, taking her arm, walked slowly along at her side. As they went, she spoke kindly and encouragingly to him, praised what she had seen of his works, and said how frequently she had wished to know him, and enjoy the benefit of his counsels in art. "For I, too," said she, laughing, "would be a sculptor."

The youth stopped to gaze at her with a rapture he could not control. That one of such a station, surrounded by all the appliances of a luxurious existence, could devote herself to the toil and labor of art, implied an amount of devotion and energy that at once elevated her in his esteem. She blushed deeply at his continued stare, and turned at last away.

"Oh, do not feel offended with me," cried he, passionately. "If you but knew how your words have relighted within me the dying-out embers of an almost exhausted ambition, — if you but knew how my heart has gained courage and hope, — how light and brightness have shone in upon me after hours and days of gloom! It was but yesterday I had resolved to abandon this career forever. I was bent on a new life, in a new world beyond the seas. These few things that a faithful companion of mine had charged himself to dispose of, were to supply the means of the journey; and now I think of it no more. I shall remain here to work hard and study, and try to achieve what may one day be called good. You will sometimes deign to see what I am doing, to tell me if my efforts are on the road to success, to give me hope when I am weak-hearted, and courage when I am faint. I know and feel," said he, proudly, " that I am not devoid of what accomplishes success, for I can toil and toil, and throw my whole soul into my work; but for this I need, at least, one who shall watch me with an eye of interest, glorying when I win, sorrowing when I am defeated. — Where are we? What palace is this?" cried he, as they crossed a spacious hall paved with porphyry and Sienna marble.

"This is my home," said the girl, "and this is its mistress."

Just as she spoke, she presented the youth to a lady, who, reclining on a sofa beside a window, gazed out towards the sea. She turned suddenly, and fixed her eyes on the stranger. With a wild start, she sprang up, and, staring eagerly at him, cried, " Who is this? Where does he come from?"

The young girl told his name and what he was; but the words did not fall on listening ears, and the lady sat like one spell-bound, with eyes riveted on the youth's face.

" Am I like any one you have known, signora?" asked he, as he read the effect his presence had produced on her. " Do I recall some other features?"

" You do," said she, reddening painfully.

" And the memory is not of pleasure?" added the youth.

" Far, far from it; it is the saddest and cruelest of all my life," muttered she, half to herself. " What part of Italy are you from? Your accent is Southern."

" It is the accent of Naples, signora," said he, evading her question.

" And your mother, was she Neapolitan?"

" I know little of my birth, signora. It is a theme I would not be questioned on."

"And you are a sculptor?"

"The artist of the Faun, dearest aunt," broke in the girl, who watched with intense anxiety the changing expressions of the youth's features.

" Your voice even more than your features brings up the past," said the lady, as a deadly pallor spread over her own face, and her lips trembled as she spoke. "Will you not tell me something of your history?"

" When you have told me the reason for which you ask it, perhaps I may," said the youth, half sternly.

"There, there!" cried she, wildly, "in every tone, in every gesture, I trace this resemblance. Come nearer to me; let me see your hands."

"They are seamed and hardened with toil, lady," said the youth, as he showed them.

"And yet they look as if there was a time when they did not know labor," said she, eagerly.

An impatient gesture, as if he would not endure a continuance of this questioning, stopped her, and she said in a faint tone.

" I ask your pardon for all this. My excuse and my apology are that your features have recalled a time of sorrow more vividly than any words could. Your voice, too, strengthens the illusion. It may be a mere passing impression; I hope and pray it is. Come, Ida, come with me. Do not leave this, sir, till we speak with you again." So saying, she took her niece's arm and left the room.

16

CHAPTER XXXIII.

It was with a proud consciousness of having well fulfilled
his mission that Billy Traynor once more bent his steps
towards Massa. Besides providing himself with books of
travel and maps of the regions they were about to visit, he
had ransacked Genoa for weapons, and accoutrements, and
horse-gear. Well knowing the youth's taste for the costly
and the splendid, he had suffered himself to be seduced into
the purchase of a gorgeously embroidered saddle mounting,
and a rich bridle, in Mexican taste; a pair of splendidly
mounted pistols, chased in gold and studded with large
turquoises, with a Damascus sabre, the hilt of which was
a miracle of fine workmanship, were also amongst his acqui-
sitions; and poor Billy fed his imagination with the thought
of all the delight these objects were certain to produce.
In this way he never wearied admiring them; and a dozen
times a day would he unpack them, just to gratify his mind
by picturing the enjoyment they were to afford.

"How well you are lookin', my dear boy!" cried he, as
he burst into the youth's room, and threw his arms around
him; "'t is like ten years off my life to see you so fresh and
so hearty. Is it the prospect of the glorious time before us
that has given this new spring to your existence?"

"More likely it is the pleasure I feel in seeing you back
again," said Massy; and his cheek grew crimson as he
spoke.

"'T is too good you are to me, — too good," said Billy,
and his eyes ran over in tears, while he turned away his
head to hide his emotion; "but sure it is part of yourself
I do be growing every day I live. At first I could n't bear
the thought of going away to live in exile, in a wilderness,

as one may say; but now that I see your heart set upon it, and that your vigor and strength comes back just by the mere anticipation of it, I'm downright delighted with the plan."

"Indeed!" said the youth, dreamily.

"To be sure I am," resumed Billy; "and I do be thinking there's a kind of poethry in carrying away into the solitary pine forest minds stored with classic lore, to be able to read one's Horace beside the gushing stream that flows on nameless and unknown, and con over ould Herodotus amidst adventures stranger than ever he told himself."

"It might be a happy life," said the other, slowly, almost moodily.

"Ay, and it will be," said Billy, confidently. "Think of yourself, mounted on that saddle on a wild prairie horse, galloping free as the wind itself over the wide savannas, with a drove of rushing buffaloes in career before you, and so eager in pursuit that you won't stop to bring down the scarlet-winged bustard that swings on the branch above you. There they go, plungin' and snortin', the mad devils, with a force that would sweep a fortress before them; and here are we after them, makin' the dark woods echo again with our wild yells. That's what will warm up our blood, till we'll not be afeard to meet an army of dragoons themselves. Them pistols once belonged to Cariatoké, a chief from Scio; and that blade — a real Damascus — was worn by an Aga of the Janissaries. Isn't it a picture?"

The youth poised the sword in his hand, and laid it down without a word; while Billy continued to stare at him with an expression of intensest amazement.

"Is it that you don't care for it all now, that your mind is changed, and that you don't wish for the life we were talkin' over these three weeks? Say so at once, my own darlin', and here I am, ready and willin' never to think more of it. Only tell me what's passin' in your heart; I ask no more."

"I scarcely know it myself," said the youth. "I feel as though in a dream, and know not what is real and what fiction."

"How have you passed your time? What were you doin' while I was away?"

"Dreaming, I believe," said the other, with a sigh. "Some embers of my old ambition warmed up into a flame once more, and I fancied that there was that in me that by toil and labor might yet win upwards; and that, if so, this mere life of action would but bring repining and regret, and that I should feel as one who chose the meaner casket of fate, when both were within my reach."

"So you were at work again in the studio?"

"I have been finishing the arm of the Faun in that pavilion outside the town." A flush of crimson covered his face as he spoke, which Billy as quickly noticed, but misinterpreted.

"Ay, and they praised you, I'll be bound. They said it was the work of one whose genius would place him with the great ones of art, and that he who could do this while scarcely more than a boy, might, in riper years, be the great name of his century. Did they not tell you so?"

"No; not that, not that," said the other, slowly.

"Then they bade you go on, and strive and labor hard to develop into life the seeds of that glorious gift that was in you?"

"Nor that," sighed the youth, heavily, while a faint spot of crimson burned on one cheek, and a feverish lustre lit up his eye.

"They didn't dispraise what you done, did they?" broke in Billy. "They could not, if they wanted to do it; but sure there's nobody would have the cruel heart to blight the ripenin' bud of genius, — to throw gloom over a spirit that has to struggle against its own misgivin's?"

"You wrong them, my dear friend; their words were all kindness and affection. They gave me hope, and encouragement too. They fancy that I have in me what will one day grow into fame itself; and even you, Billy, in your most sanguine hopes, have never dreamed of greater success for me than they have predicted in the calm of a moonlit saunter."

"May the saints in heaven reward them for it!" said Billy, and in his clasped hands and uplifted eyes was all the fervor of a prayer. "They have my best blessin' for their goodness," muttered he to himself.

"And so I am again a sculptor!" said Massy, rising and

walking the room. "Upon this career my whole heart and soul are henceforth to be concentrated; my fame, my happiness are to be those of the artist. From this day and this hour let every thought of what — not what I once was, but what I had hoped to be, be banished from my heart. I am Sebastian Greppi. Never let another name escape your lips to me. I will not, even for a second, turn from the path in which my own exertions are to win the goal. Let the faraway land of my infancy, its traditions, its associations, be but dreams for evermore. Forwards! forwards!" cried he, passionately; "not a glance, not a look, towards the past."

Billy stared with admiration at the youth, over whose features a glow of enthusiasm was now diffused, and in broken, unconnected words spoke encouragement and good cheer.

"I know well," said the youth, "how this same stubborn pride must be rooted out, how these false, deceitful visions of a stand and a station that I am never to attain must give place to nobler and higher aspirations; and you, my dearest friend, must aid me in all this, — unceasingly, unwearyingly reminding me that to myself alone must I look for anything; and that if I would have a country, a name, or a home, it is by the toil of this head and these hands they are to be won. My plan is this," said he, eagerly seizing the other's arm, and speaking with immense rapidity: "A life not alone of labor, but of the simplest; not a luxury, not an indulgence; our daily meals the humblest, our dress the commonest, nothing that to provide shall demand a moment's forethought or care; no wants that shall turn our thoughts from this great object, no care for the requirements that others need. Thus mastering small ambitions and petty desires, we shall concentrate all our faculties on our art; and even the humblest may thus outstrip those whose higher gifts reject such discipline."

"You'll not live longer under the Duke's patronage, then?" said Traynor.

"Not an hour. I return to that garden no more. There's a cottage on the mountain road to Serravezza will suit us well: it stands alone and on an eminence, with a view over the plain and the sea beyond. You can see it from the door, — there, to the left of the olive wood, lower down than the old ruin. We 'll live there, Billy, and we 'll make of that mean spot a hallowed one, where young enthusiasts in art will come, years hence, when we have passed away, to see the humble home Sebastian lived in, — to sit upon the grassy seat where he once sat, when dreaming of the mighty triumphs that have made him glorious." A wild burst of mocking laughter rung from the boy's lips as he said this; but its accents were less in derision of the boast than a species of hysterical ecstasy at the vision he had conjured up.

" And why would n't it be so?" exclaimed Billy, ardently, — " why would n't you be great and illustrious?"

The moment of excitement was now over, and the youth stood pale, silent, and almost sickly in appearance; great drops of perspiration, too, stood on his forehead, and his quivering lips were bloodless.

" These visions are like meteor streaks," said he, falteringly; " they leave the sky blacker than they found it! But come along, let us to work, and we 'll soon forget mere speculation."

Of the life they now led each day exactly resembled the other. Rising early, the youth was in his studio at dawn; the faithful Billy, seated near, read for him while he worked. Watching, with a tact that only affection ever bestows, each changeful mood of the youth's mind, Traynor varied the topics with the varying humors of the other, and thus little of actual conversation took place between them, though their minds journeyed along together. To eke out subsistence, even humble as theirs, the young sculptor was obliged to make small busts and figures for sale, and Billy disposed of them at Lucca and Pisa, making short excursions to these cities as need required.

The toil of the day over, they wandered out towards the seashore, taking the path which led through the olive road by the garden of the villa. At times the youth would steal away a moment from his companion, and enter the little park, with every avenue of which he was familiar; and although Billy noticed his absence, he strictly abstained from the slightest allusion to it. As he delayed longer and longer to return, Traynor maintained the same reserve, and thus there grew up gradually a secret between them, —a mystery that neither ventured to approach. With a delicacy that seemed an instinct in his humble nature, Billy would now and then feign occupation or fatigue to excuse himself from the evening stroll, and thus leave the youth free to wander as he wished; till at length it became a settled habit between them to separate at nightfall, to meet only on the morrow. These nights were spent in walking the garden around the villa, lingering stealthily amid the trees to watch the room where she was sitting, to catch a momentary glimpse of her figure as it passed the window, to hear perchance a few faint accents of her voice. Hours long would he so watch in the silent night, his whole soul steeped in a delicious dream wherein her image moved, and came and went, with every passing fancy. In the calm moonlight he would try to trace her footsteps in the gravel walk that led to the studio, and, lingering near them, whisper to her words of love.

One night, as he loitered thus, he thought he was perceived, for as he suddenly emerged from a dark alley into a broad space where the moonlight fell strongly, he saw a figure on a terrace above him, but without being able to recognize to whom it belonged. Timidly and fearfully he retired within the shade, and crept noiselessly away, shocked at the very thought of discovery. The next day he found a small bouquet of fresh flowers on the rustic seat beneath the window. At first he scarcely dared to touch it; but with a sudden flash of hope that it had been destined for himself, he pressed the flowers to his lips, and hid them in his bosom. Each night now the same present attracted him to the same place, and thus at once within his heart was lighted a flame of hope that illuminated all his being, making his whole life a glorious episode, and filling all the long hours of the day with thoughts of her who thus could think of him.

Life has its triumphant moments, its dream of entrancing, ecstatic delight, when success has crowned a hard-fought struggle, or when the meed of other men's praise comes showered on us. The triumphs of heroism, of intellect, of

noble endurance; the trials of temptation met and conquered; the glorious victory over self-interest, — are all
great and ennobling sensations; but what are they all compared with the first consciousness of being loved, of being
to another the ideal we have made of her?   To this, nothing
the world can give is equal.   From the moment we have
felt it, life changes around us.   Its crosses are but barriers
opposed to our strong will, that to assail and storm is a duty.
Then comes a heroism in meeting the every-day troubles of
existence, as though we were soldiers in a good and holy
cause.   No longer unseen or unmarked in the great ocean
of life, we feel that there is an eye ever turned towards us,
a heart ever throbbing with our own: that our triumphs
are its triumphs, — our sorrows its sorrows.   Apart from all
the intercourse with the world, with its changeful good and
evil, we feel that we have a treasure that dangers cannot
approach; we know that in our heart of hearts a blessed
mystery is locked up, — a well of pure thoughts that can
calm down the most fevered hour of life's anxieties.   So the
youth felt, and, feeling so, was happy.

CHAPTER XXXIV.

A MINISTER'S LETTER.

BRITISH LEGATION, NAPLES,
Nov. ——, 18—.

MY DEAR HARCOURT, — Not mine the fault that your letter has lain six weeks unanswered; but having given up penwork myself for the last eight months, and Crawley, my private sec., being ill, the delay was unavoidable. The present communication you owe to the fortunate arrival here of Captain Mellish, who has kindly volunteered to be my amanuensis. I am indeed sorely grieved at this delay. I shall be *désolé* if it occasion you anything beyond inconvenience. How a private sec. should permit himself the luxury of an attack of influenza I cannot conceive. We shall hear of one's hairdresser having the impertinence to catch cold, to-morrow or next day!

If I don't mistake, it was you yourself recommended Crawley to me, and I am only half grateful for the service. He is a man of small prejudices: fancies that he ought to have a regular hour for dinner: thinks that he should have acquaintances: and will persist in imagining himself an existent something, appertaining to the Legation, — while, in reality, he is only a shadowy excrescence of my own indolent habits, the recipient of the trashy superfluities one commits to paper and calls despatches. Latterly, in my increasing laziness, I have used him for more intimate correspondence: and, as Doctor Allitore has now denied me all manual exertion whatever, I am actually wholly dependent on such aid. I'm sure I long for the discovery of some other mode of transmitting one's brain-efforts than by the slow process of manuscript, — some photographic process that, by a series of bright pictures, might display *en tableau* what one is now reduced to accomplish by narrative. As it ever did and ever will happen too, they have deluged me with work when I crave rest. Every session of Parliament must have its blue-book: and by the devil's luck they have decided that Italy is to furnish the present one.

You have always been a soldier, and whenever your inspecting general came his round, your whole care has been to make the troop horses look as fat, the men's whiskers as trim, their overalls as clean, and their curb-chains as bright, as possible. You never imagined or dreamed of a contingency when it would be desirable that the animals should be all sore-backed, the whole regiment under stoppages, and the trumpeter in a quinsy. Had you been a diplomatist instead of a dragoon, this view of things might, perhaps, have presented itself, and the chief object of your desire have been to show that the system under which you functionated worked as ill as need be; that the court to which you were accredited abhorred you; its Ministers snubbed, its small officials slighted you; that all your communications were ill received, your counsels ill taken: that what you reprobated was adopted, what you advised rejected: in fact, that the only result of your presence was the maintenance of a perpetual ill-will and bad feeling; and that without the aid of a line-of-battle ship, or at least a frigate, your position was no longer tenable. From the moment, my dear H——, that you can establish this fact, you start into life as an able and active Minister, imbued with thoroughly British principles — an active asserter of what is due to his country's rights and dignity, not truckling to court favor, or tamely submitting to royal impertinences: not like the noble lord at this place, or the more subservient viscount at that, but, in plain words, an admirable public servant, whose reward, whatever courts and cabinets may do, will always be willingly accorded by a grateful nation.

I am afraid this sketch of a special envoy's career will scarcely tempt you to exchange for a mission abroad! And you are quite right, my dear friend. It is a very unrewarding profession. I often wish myself that I had taken something in the colonies, or gone into the Church, or some other career which had given me time and opportunity to look after my health, — of which, by the way, I have but an indifferent account to render you. These people here can't hit it off at all, Harcourt; they keep muddling away about indigestion, deranged functions, and the rest of it. The mischief is in the blood, — I mean, in the undue distribution of the blood. So Treysenac, the man of Bagnères, proved to me. There is a flux and reflux in us, as in the tides, and when, from deficient energy or lax muscular power, that ceases, we are all driven by artificial means to remedy the defect. Treysenac's theory is position. By a number of ingeniously contrived positions he accomplishes an artificial congestion of any part he pleases; and in his establishment at Bagnères you may see some fifty people strung up by the arms and legs, by the waists or the ankles, in the most marvellous manner, and with truly fabulous success. I myself passed three mornings suspended by the middle, like the sheep in the decoration of the Golden Fleece, and was amazed at the strange sensations I experienced before I was cut down.

You know the obstinacy with which the medical people reject every discovery in the art, and only sanction its employment when the world has decreed in its favor. You will, therefore, not be surprised to hear that Larrey and Cooper, to whom I wrote about Treysenac's theory, sent me very unsatisfactory, indeed very unseemly, replies. I have resolved, however, not to let the thing drop, and am determined to originate a Suspensorium in England, when I can chance upon a man of intelligence and scientific knowledge to conduct it. Like mesmerism, the system has its antipathies; and thus yesterday Crawley fainted twice after a few minutes' suspension by the arms. But he is a bigot about anything he hears for the first time, and I was not sorry at his punishment.

I wish you would talk over this matter with any clever medical man in your neighborhood, and let me hear the result.

And so you are surprised, you say, how little influence English representations exercise over the determinations of foreign cabinets. I go farther, and confess no astonishment at all at the no-influence! My dear dragoon, have you not, some hundred and fifty times in this life, endured a small martyrdom in seeing a very indifferent rider torment almost to madness the animal he bestrode, just by sheer ignorance and awkwardness, — now worrying the flank with incautious heel, now irritating the soft side of the mouth with incessant jerkings; always counteracting the good impulses, ever prompting the bad ones of his beast? And have you not, while heartily wishing yourself in the saddle, felt the utter inutility of administering any counsels to the rider? You saw, and rightly saw, that even if he attempted to follow your suggestions, he would do so awkwardly and inaptly, acting at wrong moments and without that continuity of purpose which must ever accompany an act of address; and that for his safety, and even for the welfare of the animal, it were as well they should jog on together as they had done, trusting that after a time they might establish a sort of compromise, endurable, if not beneficial, to both.

Such, my dear friend, in brief, is the state of many of those foreign governments to whom we are so profuse of our wise counsels. It were doubtless much better if they ruled well: but let us see if the road to this knotty consummation be by the adoption of methods totally new to them, estranged from all their instincts and habits, and full of perils which their very fears will exaggerate. Constitutional governments, like underdone roast beef, suit our natures and our latitude; but they would seem lamentable

experiments when tried south of the Alps. Liberty with us means
the right to break heads at a county election, and to print impertinences in newspapers. With the Spaniard or the Italian
it would be to carry a poniard more openly, and use it more
frequently than at present.

At all events, if it be any satisfaction to you, you may be
assured that the rulers in all these cases are not much better off
than those they rule over. They lead lives of incessant terror,
distrust, and anxiety. Their existence is poisoned by ceaseless
fears of treachery, — they know not where. They change ministers as travellers change the direction of their journey, to disconcert the supposed plans of their enemies; and they vacillate
between cruelty and mercy, really not knowing in which lies
their safety. Don't fancy that they have any innate pleasure in
harsh measures. The likelihood is, they hate them as much as
you do yourself; but they know no other system; and, to come
back to my cavalry illustration, the only time they tried a snaffle,
they were run away with.

I trust these prosings will be a warning to you how you touch
upon politics again in a letter to me; but I really did not wish to
be a bore, and now here I am, ready to answer, as far as in me
lies, all your interrogatories; first premising that I am not at
liberty to enter upon the question of Glencore himself, and for the
simple reason that he has made me his confidant. And now, as
to the boy, I could make nothing of him, Harcourt; and for this
reason, — he had not what sailors call "steerage way" on him. He
went wherever you bade, but without an impulse. I tried to make
him care for his career; for the gay world; for the butterfly
life of young diplomacy; for certain dissipations, — excellent
things occasionally to develop nascent faculties. I endeavored
to interest him by literary society and savans, but unsuccessfully.
For art indeed he showed some disposition, and modelled prettily;
but it never rose above "amateurship." Now, enthusiasm, although
a very excellent ingredient, will no more make an artist than a
brisk kitchen fire will provide a dinner where all the materials are
wanting.

I began to despair of him, Harcourt, when I saw that there
were no features about him. He could do everything reasonably
well, because there was no hope of his doing anything with real
excellence. He wandered away from me to Carrara, with his
quaint companion the Doctor; and after some months wrote me
rather a sturdy letter, rejecting all moneyed advances, past and
future, and saying something very haughty, and of course very
stupid, about the "glorious sense of independence." I replied,
but he never answered me; and here might have ended all my

knowledge of his history, had not a letter, of which I send you an extract, resumed the narrative. The writer is the Princess Sabloukoff, a lady of whose attractions and fascinations you have often heard me speak. When you have read and thought over the enclosed, let me have your opinion. I do not, I cannot, believe in the rumor you allude to. Glencore is not the man to marry at his time of life, and in his circumstances. Send me, however, all the particulars you are in possession of. I hope they don't mean to send you to India, because you seem to dislike it. For my own part, I suspect I should enjoy that country immensely. Heat is the first element of daily comfort, and all the appliances to moderate it are *ex-officio* luxuries; besides that in India there is a splendid and enlarged selfishness in the mode of life very different from the petty egotisms of our rude Northland.

If you do go, pray take Naples in the way. The route by Alexandria and Suez, they all tell me, is the best and most expeditious.

Mellish desires me to add his remembrances, hoping you have not forgotten him. He served in the "Fifth" with you in Canada. — that is, if you be the same George Harcourt who played Tony Lumpkin so execrably at Montreal. I have told him it is probable, and am yours ever,

H. U.

CHAPTER XXXV.

WHEN Harcourt had finished the reading of that letter we have presented in our last chapter, he naturally turned for information on the subject which principally interested him to the enclosure. It was a somewhat bulky packet, and, from its size, at once promised very full and ample details. As he opened it, however, he discovered it was in various handwritings; but his surprise was further increased by the following heading, in large letters, in the top of a page: "Sulphur Question," and beginning, "My Lord, by a reference to my despatch, No. 478, you will perceive that the difficulties which the Neapolitan Government — " Harcourt turned over the page. It was all in the same strain. Tariffs, treaties, dues, and duties occurred in every line. Three other documents of like nature accompanied this; after which came a very ill-written scrawl on coarse paper, entitled, "Hints as to diet and daily exercise for his Excellency's use."

The honest Colonel, who was not the quickest of men, was some time before he succeeded in unravelling to his satisfaction the mystery before him, and recognizing that the papers on his table had been destined for a different address, while the letter of the Princess had, in all probability, been despatched to the Foreign Office, and was now either confounding or amusing the authorities in Downing Street. While Harcourt laughed over the blunder, he derived no small gratification from thinking that nothing but great geniuses ever fell into these mistakes, and was about to write off in this very spirit to Upton, when he suddenly bethought him that, before an answer could arrive, he himself would be far away on his journey to India.

"I asked nothing," said he, "that could be difficult to reply to. It was plain enough, too, that I only wanted such information as he could have given me off-hand. If I could but assure Glencore that the boy was worthy of him, — that there was stuff to give good promise of future excellence, that he was honorable and manly in all his dealings, —who knows what effect such assurance might have had? There are days when it strikes me Glencore would give half his fortune to have the youth beside him, and be able to call him his own. Why he cannot, does not do it, is a mystery which I am unable to fathom. He never gave me his confidence on this head; indeed, he gave me something like a rebuff one evening, when he erroneously fancied that I wanted to probe the mysterious secret. It shows how much he knows of my nature," added he, laughing. "Why, I'd rather carry a man's trunk or his portmanteau on my back than his family secrets in my heart. I could rest and lay down my burden in the one case, — in the other, there's never a moment of repose! And now Glencore is to be here this very day — the ninth — to learn my news. The poor fellow comes up from Wales, just to talk over these matters, and I have nothing to offer him but this blundering epistle. Ay, here's the letter: —

"DEAR HARCOURT, — Let me have a mutton-chop with you on the ninth, and give me, if you can, the evening after it.

"Yours,
"GLENCORE.

"A man must be ill off for counsel and advice when he thinks of such aid as mine. Heaven knows, I never was such a brilliant manager of my own fortunes that any one should trust his destinies in my hands. Well, he shall have the mutton-chop, and a good glass of old port after it; and the evening, or, if he likes it, the night shall be at his disposal." And with this resolve, Harcourt, having given orders for dinner at six, issued forth to stroll down to his club, and drop in at the Horse Guards, and learn as much as he could of the passing events of the day, — meaning, thereby, the details of whatever regarded the army-list, and those who walk in scarlet attire.

It was about five o'clock of a dreary November afternoon that a hackney-coach drew up at Harcourt's lodgings in Dover Street, and a tall and very sickly looking man, carrying his carpet-bag in one hand and a dressing-case in the other, descended and entered the house.

" Mr. Massy, sir?" said the Colonel's servant, as he ushered him in; for such was the name Glencore desired to be known by. And the stranger nodded, and throwing himself wearily down on a sofa, seemed overcome with fatigue.

" Is your master out?" asked he, at length.

" Yes, sir; but I expect him immediately. Dinner was ordered for six, and he'll be back to dress half an hour before that time."

" Dinner for two?" half impatiently asked the other.

" Yes, sir, for two."

" And all visitors in the evening denied admittance? Did your master say so?"

" Yes, sir; out for every one."

Glencore now covered his face with his hands, and relapsed into silence. At length he lifted his eyes till they fell upon a colored drawing over the chimney. It was an officer in hussar uniform, mounted on a splendid charger, and seated with all the graceful ease of a consummate horseman. This much alone he could perceive from where he lay, and indolently raising himself on one arm, he asked if it were " a portrait of his master"?

" No, sir; of my master's colonel, Lord Glencore, when he commanded the Eighth, and was said to be the handsomest man in the service."

" Show it to me!" cried he, eagerly, and almost snatched the drawing from the other's hands. He gazed at it intently and fixedly, and his sallow cheek once reddened slightly as he continued to look.

" That never was a likeness!" said he, bitterly.

" My master thinks it a wonderful resemblance, sir, — not of what he is now, of course; but that was taken fifteen years ago or more."

" And is he so changed since that?" asked the sick man, plaintively.

"So I hear, sir. He had a stroke of some kind, or fit of one sort or another, brought on by fretting. They took away his title, I'm told. They made out that he had no right to it, that he wasn't the real lord. But here's the Colonel, sir;" and almost as he spoke, Harcourt's step was on the stair. The next moment his hand was cordially clasped in that of his guest.

"I scarcely expected you before six; and how have you borne the journey?" cried he, taking a seat beside the sofa. A gentle motion of the eyebrows gave the reply.

"Well, well, you'll be all right after the soup. Marcom, serve the dinner at once. I'll not dress. And mind, no admittance to any one."

"You have heard from Upton?" asked Glencore.

"Yes."

"And satisfactorily?" asked he, more anxiously.

"Quite so; but you shall know all by and by. I have got mackerel for you. It was a favorite dish of yours long ago, and you shall taste such mutton as your Welsh mountains can't equal. I got the haunch from the Ardennes a week ago, and kept it for you."

"I wish I deserved such generous fare; but I have only an invalid's stomach," said Glencore, smiling faintly.

"You shall be reported well, and fit for duty to-day, or my name is not George Harcourt. The strongest and toughest fellow that ever lived couldn't stand up against the united effects of low diet and low spirits. To act generously and think generously, you must live generously, take plenty of exercise, breathe fresh air, and know what it is to be downright weary when you go to bed, — not bored, mark you, for that's another thing. Now, here comes the soup, and you shall tell me whether turtle be not the best restorative a man ever took after twelve hours of the road."

Whether tempted by the fare, or anxious to gratify the hospitable wishes of his host, Glencore ate heartily, and drank what for his abstemious habit was freely, and, so far as a more genial air and a more ready smile went, fully justified Harcourt's anticipations.

"By Jove! you're more like yourself than I have seen you this many a day," said the Colonel, as they drew their

17

chairs towards the fire, and sat with that now banished, but ever to be regretted, little spider-table, that once emblematized after-dinner blessedness, between them. "This reminds one of long ago, Glencore, and I don't see why we cannot bring to the hour some of the cheerfulness that we once boasted."

A faint, very faint smile, with more of sorrow than joy in it, was the other's only reply.

"Look at the thing this way, Glencore," said Harcourt, eagerly. "So long as a man has, either by his fortune or by his personal qualities, the means of benefiting others, there is a downright selfishness in shutting himself up in his sorrow, and saying to the world, 'My own griefs are enough for me; I'll take no care or share in yours.' Now, there never was a fellow with less of this selfishness than you —"

"Do not speak to me of what I was, my dear friend. There's not a plank of the old craft remaining. The name alone lingers, and even that will soon be extinct."

"So, then, you still hold to this stern resolution? Shall I tell you what I think of it?"

"Perhaps you had better not do so," said Glencore, sternly.

"By Jove! then, I will, just for that menace," said Harcourt. "I said, 'This is vengeance on Glencore's part.'"

"To whom, sir, did you make this remark?"

"To myself, of course. I never alluded to the matter to any other; never."

"So far, well," said Glencore, solemnly; "for had you done so, we had never exchanged words again!"

"My dear fellow," said Harcourt, laying his hand affectionately on the other's. "I can well imagine the price a sensitive nature like yours must pay for the friendship of one so little gifted with tact as I am. But remember always that there's this advantage in the intercourse: you can afford to hear and bear things from a man of *my* stamp, that would be outrages from perhaps the lips of a brother. As Upton, in one of his bland moments, once said to me, 'Fellows like you, Harcourt, are the bitters of the human pharmacopœia, — somewhat hard to take, but very wholesome when you're once swallowed.'"

"You are the best of the triad, and no great praise that, either," muttered Glencore to himself. After a pause, he continued: "It has not been from any distrust in your friendship, Harcourt, that I have not spoken to you before on this gloomy subject. I know well that you bear me more affection than any one of all those who call themselves my friends; but when a man is about to do that which never can meet approval from those who love him, he seeks no counsel, he invites no confidence. Like the gambler, who risks all on a single throw, he makes his venture from the impulse of a secret mysterious prompting within, that whispers, 'With this you are rescued or ruined!' Advice, counsel!" cried he, in bitter mockery, "tell me, when have such ever alleviated the tortures of a painful malady? Have you ever heard that the writhings of the sick man were calmed by the honeyed words of his friends at the bedside? I" — here his voice became full and loud — "I was burdened with a load too great for me to bear. It had bowed me to the earth, and all but crushed me! The sense of an unaccomplished vengeance was like a debt which, unrequited ere I died, sent me to my grave dishonored. Which of you all could tell me how to endure this? What shape could your philosophy assume?"

"Then I guessed aright," broke in Harcourt. "This was done in vengeance."

"I have no reckoning to render you, sir," said Glencore, haughtily; "for any confidence of mine, you are more indebted to my passion than to my inclination. I came up here to speak and confer with you about this boy, whose guardianship you are unable to continue longer. Let us speak of that."

"Yes," said Harcourt, in his habitual tone of easy good humor, "they are going to send me out to India again. I have had eighteen years of it already; but I have no Parliamentary influence, nor could I trace a fortieth cousinship with the House of Lords; but, after all, it might be worse. Now, as to this lad, what if I were to take him out with me?

This artist life that he seems to have adopted scarcely promises much."

" Let me see Upton's letter," said Glencore, gravely.

" There it is. But I must warn you that the really important part is wanting; for instead of sending us, as he promised, the communication of his Russian Princess, he has stuffed in a mass of papers intended for Downing Street, and a lot of doctor's prescriptions, for whose loss he is doubtless suffering martyrdom."

" Is this credible?" cried Glencore.

" There they are, very eloquent about sulphur, and certain refugees with long names, and with some curious hints about Spanish flies and the flesh-brush."

Glencore flung down the papers in indignation, and walked up and down the room without speaking.

" I'd wager a trifle," cried Harcourt, " that Madame — What's-her-name's letter has gone to the Foreign Office in lieu of the despatches; and, if so, they have certainly gained most by the whole transaction."

" You have scarcely considered, perhaps, what publicity may thus be given to my private affairs," said Glencore. " Who knows what this woman may have said; what allusions her letter may contain?"

" Very true; I never did think of that," muttered Harcourt.

" Who knows what circumstances of my private history are now bandied about from desk to desk by flippant fools, to be disseminated afterwards over Europe by every courier?" cried he, with increasing passion.

Before Harcourt could reply, the servant entered, and whispered a few words in his ear. " But you already denied me," said Harcourt. " You told him that I was from home?"

" Yes, sir; but he said that his business was so important that he'd wait for your return, if I could not say where he might find you. This is his card."

Harcourt took it, and read, " Major Scaresby, from Naples." " What think you, Glencore? Ought we to admit this gentleman? It may be that his visit relates to what we have been speaking about."

"Scaresby — Scaresby — I know the name," muttered Glencore. "To be sure! There was a fellow that hung about Florence and Rome long ago, and called himself Scaresby; an ill-tongued old scandal-monger people encouraged in a land where newspapers are not permitted."

"He affects to have something very pressing to communicate. Perhaps it were better to have him up."

"Don't make me known to him, then, or let me have to talk to him," said Glencore, throwing himself down on a sofa; "and let his visit be as brief as you can manage."

Harcourt made a significant sign to his servant, and the moment after the Major was heard ascending the stairs.

"Very persistent of me, you'll say, Colonel Harcourt. Devilish tenacious of my intentions, to force myself thus upon you!" said the Major, as he bustled into the room, with a white leather bag in his hand; "but I promised Upton I'd not lie down on a bed till I saw you."

"All the apologies should come from my side, Major," said Harcourt, as he handed him to a chair; "but the fact was, that having an invalid friend with me, quite incapable of seeing company, and having matters of some importance to discuss with him —"

"Just so," broke in Scaresby; "and if it were not that I had given a very strong pledge to Upton, I'd have given my message to your servant, and gone off to my hotel. But he laid great stress on my seeing you, and obtaining certain papers which, if I understand aright, have reached you in mistake, being meant for the Minister at Downing Street. Here's his own note, however, which will explain all."

It ran thus : —

DEAR H——. So I find that some of the despatches have got into your enclosure instead of that "on his Majesty's service." I therefore send off the insupportable old bore who will deliver this, to rescue them, and convey them to their fitting destination. "The extraordinaries" will be burdened to some fifty or sixty pounds for it; but they very rarely are expended so profitably as in getting rid of an intolerable nuisance. Give him all the things, therefore, and pack him off to Downing Street. I'm far more uneasy, however, about some prescriptions which I suspect are along with them. One, a lotion for the cervical vertebræ, of invaluable activity, which you may take a copy of, but strictly, on honor, for your own use only. Scaresby will obtain the Princess's letter, and hand it to you. It is certain not to have been opened at F. O., as they never read anything not alluded to in the private correspondence.

This blunder has done me a deal of harm. My nerves are not in a state to stand such shocks; and though, in fact, you are not the culpable party, I cannot entirely acquit you for having in part occasioned it. [Harcourt laughed good-humoredly at this, and continued:] If you care for it, old S. will give you all the last gossip from these parts, and be the channel of yours to me. But don't dine him; he's not worth a dinner. He'll only repay sherry and soda-water, and one of those execrable cheroots you used to be famed for. Amongst the recipes, let me recommend you an admirable tonic, the principal ingredient in which is the oil of the star-fish. It will probably produce nausea, vertigo, and even fainting for a week or two, but these symptoms decline at last, and, except violent hiccup, no other inconvenience remains. Try it, at all events.

Yours ever,
H. U.

While Harcourt perused this short epistle, Scaresby, on the invitation of his host, had helped himself freely to the Madeira, and a plate of devilled biscuits beside it, giving, from time to time, oblique glances towards the dark corner of the room, where Glencore lay, apparently asleep.

"I hope Upton's letter justifies my insistence, Colonel. He certainly gave me to understand that the case was a pressing one," said Scaresby.

"Quite so, Major Scaresby; and I have only to reiterate my excuses for having denied myself to you. But you are aware of the reason;" and he glanced towards where Glencore was lying.

"Very excellent fellow, Upton," said the Major, sipping his wine, "but very — what shall I call it? — eccentric; very odd; not like any one else, you know, in the way he does things. I happened to be one of his guests t'other day. He had detained us above an hour waiting dinner, when he came in all flurried and excited, and, turning to me, said, 'Scaresby, have you any objection to a trip to England at his Majesty's expense?' and as I replied, 'None whatever; indeed, it would suit my book to perfection just now,'

'Well, then,' said he. 'get your traps together, and be here within an hour. I'll have all in readiness for you.' I did not much fancy starting off in this fashion, and without my dinner, too; but egad! he's one of those fellows that don't stand parleying, and so I just took him at his word, and here I am. I take it the matter must be a very emergent one, eh?"

"It is clear Sir Horace Upton thought so," said Harcourt, rather amused than offended by the other's curiosity.

"There's a woman in it, somehow, I'll be bound, eh?"

Harcourt laughed heartily at this sally, and pushed the decanter towards his guest.

"Not that I'd give sixpence to know every syllable of the whole transaction," said Scaresby. "A man that has passed, as I have, the last twenty-five years of his life between Rome, Florence, and Naples, has devilish little to learn of what the world calls scandal."

"I suppose you must indeed possess a wide experience," said Harcourt.

"Not a man in Europe, sir, could tell you as many dark passages of good society! I kept a kind of book once, — a record of fashionable delinquencies; but I had to give it up. It took me half my day to chronicle even the passing events; and then my memory grew so retentive by practice, I didn't want the reference, but could give you date, and name, and place for every incident that has scandalized the world for the last quarter of the century."

"And do you still possess this wonderful gift, Major?"

"Pretty well; not, perhaps, to the same extent I once did. You see, Colonel Harcourt," — here his voice became low and confidential, — "some twenty, or indeed fifteen years back, it was only persons of actual condition that permitted themselves the liberty to do these things; but, hang it, sir! now you have your middle-class folk as profligate as their betters. Jones, or Smith, or Thompson runs away with his neighbor's wife, cheats at cards, and forges his friend's name, just as if he had the best blood in his veins, and fourteen quarterings on his escutcheon. What memory, then, I ask you, could retain all the shortcomings of these people?"

"But I'd really not trouble my head with such ignoble delinquents," said Harcourt.

"Nor do I, sir, save when, as will sometimes happen, they have a footing, with one leg at least, in good society. For, in the present state of the world, a woman with a pretty face, and a man with a knowledge of horseflesh, may move in any circle they please."

"You're a severe censor of the age we live in, I see," said Harcourt, smiling. "At the same time, the offences could scarcely give you much uneasiness, or you'd not take up your residence where they most abound."

"If you want to destroy tigers, you must frequent the jungle," said Scaresby, with one of his heartiest laughs.

"Say, rather, if you have the vulture's appetite, you must go where there is carrion!" cried Glencore, with a voice to which passion lent a savage vehemence.

"Eh? ha! very good! devilish smart of your sick friend. Pray present me to him," said Scaresby, rising.

"No, no, never mind him," whispered Harcourt, pressing him down into his seat. "At some other time, perhaps. He is nervous and irritable. Conversation fatigues him, too."

"Egad! that was neatly said, though; I hope I shall not forget it. One envies these sick fellows, sometimes, the venom they get from bad health. But I am forgetting myself in the pleasure of your society," added he, rising from the table, as he finished off the last glass in the decanter. "I shall call at Downing Street to-morrow for that letter of Upton's, and, with your permission, will deposit it in your hands afterwards."

Harcourt accompanied him to the door with thanks. Profuse, indeed, was he in his recognitions, desiring to get him clear off the ground before any further allusions on his part, or rejoinders from Glencore, might involve them all in new complications.

"I know that fellow well," cried Glencore, almost ere the door closed on him. "He is just what I remember him some twenty years ago. Dressed up in the cast-off vices of his betters, he has passed for a man of fashion amongst his own set, while he is regarded as a wit by those who mistake malevolence for humor. I ask no other test of a society than that such a man is endured in it."

" I sometimes suspect," said Harcourt, " that the world never believes these fellows to be as ill-natured as their tongues bespeak them."

" You are wrong, George; the world knows them well. The estimation they are held in is, for the reflective flattery by which each listener to their sarcasms soothes his own conscience as he says, ' I could be just as bitter, if I consented to be as bad.' "

" I cannot at all account for Upton's endurance of such a man." said Harcourt.

" As there are men who fancy that they strengthen their animal system by braving every extreme of climate, so Upton imagines that he invigorates his *morale* by associating with all kinds and descriptions of people; and there is no doubt that in doing so he extends the sphere of his knowledge of mankind. After all," muttered he, with a sigh, " it 's only learning the geography of a land too unhealthy to live in."

Glencore arose as he said this, and, with a nod of leave-taking, retired to his room.

CHAPTER XXXVI.

A FEVERED MIND.

Harcourt passed the morning of the following day in watching the street for Scaresby's arrival. Glencore's impatience had grown into absolute fever to obtain the missing letter, and he kept asking every moment at what hour he had promised to be there, and wondering at his delay.

Noon passed over, — one o'clock; it was now nearly half-past, as a carriage drove hastily to the door.

" At last," cried Glencore, with a deep sigh.

" Sir Gilbert Bruce, sir, requests to know if you can receive him," said the servant to Harcourt.

" Another disappointment!" muttered Glencore, as he left the room, when Harcourt motioned to the servant to introduce the visitor.

" My dear Colonel Harcourt," cried the other, entering, " excuse a very abrupt call; but I have a most pressing need of your assistance. I hear you can inform me of Lord Glencore's address."

" He is residing in North Wales at present. I can give you his post town."

" Yes, but can I be certain that he will admit me if I should go down there? He is living, I hear, in strict retirement, and I am anxious for a personal interview."

" I cannot insure you that," said Harcourt. " He does live, as you have heard, entirely estranged from all society. But if you write to him "

" Ah! there's the difficulty. A letter and its reply takes some days."

" And is the matter, then, so very imminent?"

"It is so; at least it is thought to be so by an authority that neither you nor I will be likely to dispute. You know his Lordship intimately, I fancy?"

"Perhaps I may call myself as much his friend as any man living."

"Well, then, I may confide to you my business with him. It happened that, a few days back, Lord Adderley was on a visit with the King at Brighton, when a foreign messenger arrived with despatches. They were, of course, forwarded to him there; and as the King has a passion for that species of literature, he opened them all himself. Now, I suspect that his Majesty cares more for the amusing incidents which occasionally diversify the life of foreign courts than for the great events of politics. At all events, he devours them with avidity, and seems conversant with the characters and private affairs of some hundreds of people he has never seen, nor in all likelihood will ever see! In turning over the loose pages of one of the despatches from Naples, I think, he came upon what appeared to be a fragment of a letter. Of what it was, or what it contained, I have not the slightest knowledge. Adderley himself has not seen it, nor any one but the King. All I know is that it concerns in some way Lord Glencore; for immediately on reading it he gave me instructions to find him out, and send him down to Brighton."

"I am afraid, were you to see Glencore, your mission would prove a failure. He has given up the world altogether, and even a royal command would scarcely withdraw him from his retirement."

"At all events, I must make the trial. You can let me have his address, and perhaps you would do more, and give me some sort of introduction to him, — something that might smooth down the difficulty of a first visit."

Harcourt was silent, and stood for some seconds in deep thought; which the other, mistaking for a sign of unwillingness to comply with his request, quickly added, "If my demand occasion you any inconvenience, or if there be the slightest difficulty — "

"Nay, nay, I was not thinking of that," said Harcourt. "Pray excuse me for a moment. I will fetch you the address you spoke of;" and without waiting for more, he left the room. The next minute he was in Glencore's room, hurriedly narrating to him all that had passed, and asking him what course he should pursue. Glencore heard the story with a greater calm than Harcourt dared to hope for; and seemed pleased at the reiterated assurance that the King alone had seen the letter referred to; and when Harcourt abruptly asked what was to be done, he slowly replied, "I must obey his Majesty's commands. I must go to Brighton."

"But are you equal to all this? Have you strength for it?"

"I think so; at all events, I am determined to make the effort. I was a favorite with his Majesty long ago. He will say nothing to hurt me needlessly; nor is it in his nature to do so. Tell Bruce that you will arrange everything, and that I shall present myself to-morrow at the palace."

"Remember, Glencore, that if you say so — "

"I must be sure and keep my word. Well, so I mean, George. I was a courtier once upon a time, and have not outlived my deference to a sovereign. I'll be there; you may answer for me."

From the moment that Glencore had come to this resolve, a complete change seemed to pass over the nature of the man. It was as though a new spring had been given to his existence. The reformation that all the blandishments of friendship, all the soft influences of kindness, could never accomplish, was more than half effected by the mere thought of an interview with a king, and the possible chance of a little royal sympathy!

If Harcourt was astonished, he was not the less pleased at all this. He encouraged Glencore's sense of gratification by every means in his power, and gladly lent himself to all the petty anxieties about dress and appearance in which he seemed now immersed. Nothing could exceed, indeed, the care he bestowed on these small details; ever insisting as he did that, his Majesty being the best-dressed gentleman in Europe, these matters assumed a greater importance in his eyes.

"I must try to recover somewhat of my former self," said he. "There was a time when I came and went freely to Carlton House, when I was somewhat more than a mere frequenter of the Prince's society. They tell me that of late he is glad to see any of those who partook of his intimacy of those times; who can remember the genial spirits who made his table the most brilliant circle of the world; who can talk to him of Hanger, and Kelly, and Sheridan, and the rest of them. I spent my days and nights with them."

Warming with the recollection of a period which, dissolute and dissipated as it was, yet redeemed by its brilliancy many of its least valuable features, Glencore poured forth story after story of a time when statesmen had the sportiveness of schoolboys, and the greatest intellects loved to indulge in the wildest excesses of folly. A good jest upon Eldon, a smart epigram on Sidmouth, a quiz against Vansittart, was a fortune at Court; and there grew up thus around the Prince a class who cultivated ridicule so assiduously that nothing was too high or too venerable to escape their sarcasms.

Though Glencore was only emerging out of boyhood, — a young subaltern in the Prince's own regiment, — when he first entered this society, the impression it had made upon his mind was not the less permanent. Independently of the charm of being thus admitted to the most choice circle of the land, there was the fascination of intimacy with names that even amongst contemporaries were illustrious.

"I feel in such spirits to-day, George," cried Glencore at length, "that I vote we go and pass the day at Richmond. We shall escape the possibility of being bored by your acquaintance. We shall have a glorious stroll through the fields, and a pleasant dinner afterwards at the Star and Garter."

Only too well pleased at this sudden change in his friend's humor, Harcourt assented.

The day was a bright and clear one, with a sharp, frosty air and that elasticity of atmosphere that invigorates and stimulates. They both soon felt its influence, and as the hours wore on, pleasant memories of the past were related, and old friends remembered and talked over in a spirit that brought back to each much of the youthful sentiments they recorded.

"If one could only go over it all again, George," said Glencore, as they sat after dinner, "up to three-and-twenty, or even a year or two later, I'd not ask to change a day, — scarcely an hour. Whatever was deficient in fact, was supplied by hope. It was a joyous, brilliant time, when we all made partnership of our good spirits, and traded freely on the capital. Even Upton was frank and free-hearted then. There were some six or eight of us, with just fortune enough never to care about money, and none of us so rich as to be immersed in dreams of gold, as ever happens with your millionnaire. Why could we not have continued so to the end?"

Harcourt adroitly turned him from the theme which he saw impending, — his departure for the Continent, his residence there, and his marriage, — and once more occupied him in stories of his youthful life in London, when Glencore suddenly came to a stop, and said, "I might have married the greatest beauty of the time, — of a family, too, second to none in all England. You know to whom I allude. Well, she would have accepted me; her father was not averse to the match; a stupid altercation with her brother, Lord Hervey, at Brookes's one night — an absurd dispute about some etiquette of the play-table — estranged me from their house. I was offended at what I deemed their want of courtesy in not seeking me, — for I was in the right; every one said so. I determined not to call first. They gave a great entertainment, and omitted me; and rather than stay in town to publish this affront, I started for the Continent; and out of that petty incident, a discussion of the veriest trifle imaginable, there came the whole course of my destiny."

"To be sure," said Harcourt, with assumed calm, "every man's fortune in life is at the sport of some petty incident or other, which at the time he undervalues."

"And then we scoff at those men who scrutinize each move, and hesitate over every step in life, as triflers and little-minded; while, if your remark be just, it is exactly they who are the wise and prudent," cried Glencore, with warmth. "Had I, for instance, seen this occurrence, trivial as it was, in its true light, what and where might I not have been to-day?"

"My dear Glencore, the luckiest fellow that ever lived, were he only to cast a look back on opportunities neglected, and conjunctures unprofited by, would be sure to be miserable. I am far from saying that some have not more than their share of the world's sorrows; but, take my word for it, every one has his load, be it greater or less; and, what is worse, we all of us carry our burdens with as much inconvenience to ourselves as we can."

"I know what you would say, Harcourt. It is the old story about giving way to passion, and suffering temper to get the better of one; but let me tell you that there are trials where passion is an instinct, and reason works too slowly. I have experienced such as this."

"Give yourself but fair play, Glencore, and you will surmount all your troubles. Come back into the world again, — I don't mean this world of balls and dinner-parties, of morning calls and afternoons in the Park; but a really active, stirring life. Come with me to India, and let us have a raid amongst the jaguars; mix with the pleasant, light-hearted fellows you'll meet at every mess, who ask for nothing better than their own good spirits and good health, to content them with the world; just look out upon life, and see what numbers are struggling and swimming for existence, while you, at least, have competence and wealth for all you wish; and bear in mind that round the table where wit is flashing and the merriest laughter rings, there is not a man — no, not one — who hasn't a something heavy in his heart, but yet who'd feel himself a coward if his face confessed it."

"And why am I to put this mask upon me? For what and for whom have I to wear this disguise?" cried Glencore, angrily.

"For yourself! It is in bearing up manfully before the world you'll gain the courage to sustain your own heart. Ay, Glencore, you'll do it to-morrow. In the presence of royalty you'll comport yourself with dignity and reserve, and you'll come out from the interview higher and stronger in self-esteem."

"You talk as if I were some country squire who would stand abashed and awe-struck before his King; but re-

member, my worthy Colonel, I have lived a good deal
inside the tabernacle, and its mysteries are no secrets to
me."

"Reason the more for what I say!" broke in Harcourt;
"your deference will not obliterate your judgment; your
just respect will not alloy your reason."

"I'll talk to the King, sir, as I talk to you," said
Glencore, passionately; "nor is the visit of my seeking. I
have long since done with courts and those who frequent
them. What can royalty do for *me?* Upton and yourself
may play the courtier, and fawn at levées; you have your
petitions to present, your favors to beg for; you want to
get this, or be excused from that: but I am no supplicant;
I ask for no place, no ribbon. If the King speak to me
about my private affairs, he shall be answered as I would
answer any one who obtrudes his rank into the place that
should only be occupied by friendship."

"It may be that he has some good counsel to offer."

"Counsel to offer me!" burst in Glencore, with increased
warmth. "I would no more permit any man to give me
advice unasked than I would suffer him to go to my tradespeople and pay my debts for me. A man's private sorrows
are his debts, — obligations between himself and his own
heart. Don't tell me, sir, that even a king's prerogative
absolves him from the duties of a gentleman."

While he uttered these words, he continued to fill and
empty his wine-glass several times, as if passion had
stimulated his thirst; and now his flashing eyes and his
heightened color betrayed the effect of wine.

"Let us stroll out into the cool air," said Harcourt.
"See what a gorgeous night of stars it is!"

"That you may resume your discourse on patience and
resignation!" said Glencore, scoffingly. "No, sir. If I
must listen to you, let me have at least the aid of the decanter. Your bitter maxims are a bad substitute for olives, but
I must have wine to swallow them."

"I never meant them to be so distasteful to you," said
Harcourt, good-humoredly.

"Say, rather, you troubled your head little whether they
were or not," replied Glencore, whose voice was now thick

from passion and drink together. "You and Upton, and two or three others, presume to lecture *me* — who, because gifted, if you call it gifted — I'd say cursed — ay, sir, cursed with coarser natures — temperaments where higher sentiments have no place — fellows that can make what they feel subordinate to what they want — you appreciate *that*, I hope — *that* stings you, does it? Well, sir, you'll find me as ready to act as to speak. There's not a word I utter here I mean to retract to-morrow."

"My dear Glencore, we have both taken too much wine."

"Speak for yourself, sir. If you desire to make the claret the excuse for your language, I can only say it's like everything else in your conduct, — always a subterfuge, always a scapegoat. Oh, George, George, I never suspected this in you;" and burying his head between his hands, he burst into tears.

He never spoke a word as Harcourt assisted him to the carriage, nor did he open his lips on the road homewards.

18

CHAPTER XXXVII.

In one of the most sequestered nooks of Sorrento, almost escarped out of the rocky cliff, and half hid in the foliage of orange and oleander trees, stood the little villa of the Princess Sabloukoff. The blue sea washed the white marble terrace before the windows, and the arbutus, whose odor scented the drawing-room, dipped its red berries in the glassy water. The wildest and richest vegetation abounded on every side. Plants and shrubs of tropical climes mingled with the hardier races of Northern lands; and the cedar and the plantain blended their leaves with the sycamore and the ilex; while, as if to complete the admixture, birds and beasts of remote countries were gathered together; and the bustard, the ape, and the antelope mixed with the peacock, the chamois, and the golden pheasant. The whole represented one of those capricious exhibitions by which wealth so often associates itself with the beautiful, and, despite all errors in taste, succeeds in making a spot eminently lovely. So was it. There was often light where a painter would have wished shadow. There were gorgeous flowers where a poet would have desired nothing beyond the blue heather-bell. There were startling effects of view, managed where chance glimpses through the trees had been infinitely more picturesque. There was, in fact, the obtrusive sense of riches in a thousand ways and places where mere unadorned nature had been far preferable; and yet, with all these faults, sea and sky, rock and foliage, the scented air, the silence, only broken by the tuneful birds, the rich profusion of color upon a sward strewn with flowers, made of the spot a perfect paradise.

In a richly decorated room, whose three windows opened on a marble terrace, sat the Princess. It was December;

but the sky was cloudless, the sea a perfect mirror, and the light air that stirred the leaves soft and balmy as the breath of May. Her dress was in keeping with the splendor around her: a rich robe of yellow silk fastened up the front with large carbuncle buttons; sleeves of deep Valenciennes lace fell far over her jewelled fingers; and a scarf of golden embroidery, negligently thrown over an arm of her chair, gave what a painter would call the warm color to a very striking picture. Farther from the window, and carefully protected from the air by a screen, sat a gentleman whose fur-lined pelisse and velvet skull-cap showed that he placed more faith in the almanac than in the atmosphere. From his cork-soled boots to his shawl muffled about the throat, all proclaimed that distrust of the weather that characterizes the invalid. No treachery of a hot sun, no seductions of that inveterate cheat, a fine day in winter, could inveigle Sir Horace Upton into any forgetfulness of his precautions. He would have regarded such as a palpable weakness on his part, — a piece of folly perfectly unbecoming in a man of his diplomatic standing and ability.

He was writing, and smoking, and talking by turns, the table before him being littered with papers, and even the carpet at his feet strewn with the loose sheets of his composition. There was not in his air any of the concentration, or even seriousness, of a man engaged in an important labor; and yet the work before him employed all his faculties, and he gave to it the deepest attention of abilities of which very few possessed the equal. To great powers of reasoning and a very strong judgment he united a most acute knowledge of men; not exactly of mankind in the mass, but of that especial order with whom he had habitually to deal. Stolid, commonplace stupidity might puzzle or embarrass him; while for any amount of craft, for any degree of subtlety, he was an over-match. The plain matter-of-fact intelligence occasionally gained a slight advantage over him at first; the trained and polished mind of the most astute negotiator was a book he could read at sight. It was his especial tact to catch up all this knowledge at once, — very often in a first interview, — and thus, while others were interchanging the customary platitudes of every-day courtesy, he was gleaning and recording within himself the traits and characteristics of all around him.

"A clever fellow, very clever fellow, Cineselli," said he, as he continued to write. "His proposition is — certain commercial advantages, and that we, on our side, leave him alone to deal his own way with his own rabble. I see nothing against it, so long as they continue to be rabble; but grubs grow into butterflies, and very vulgar populace have now and then emerged into what are called liberal politicians."

"Only where you have the blessing of a free press," said the Princess, in a tone of insolent mockery.

"Quite true, Princess; a free press is a tonic that with an increased dose becomes a stimulant, and occasionally over-excites."

"It makes your people drunk now and then!" said she, angrily.

"They always sleep it off over-night," said he, softly. "They very rarely pay even the penalty of the morning headache for the excess, which is exactly why it will not answer in warmer latitudes."

"Ours is a cold one, and I'm sure it would not suit us."

"I'm not so certain of that," said he, languidly. "I think it is eminently calculated for a people who don't know how to read."

She would have smiled at the remark, if the sarcasm had not offended her.

"Your Lordship will therefore see," muttered he, reading to himself as he wrote, "that in yielding this point we are, while apparently making a concession, in reality obtaining a very considerable advantage —"

"Rather an English habit, I suspect," said she, smiling.

"Picked up in the course of our Baltic trade, Princess. In sending us your skins, you smuggled in some of your sentiments; and Russian tallow has enlightened the nation in more ways than one!"

"You need it all, my dear chevalier," said she, with a saucy smile. "Harzewitch told me that your diplomatic people were inferior to those of the third-rate German States; that, in fact, they never had any 'information.'"

" I know what he calls ' information,' Princess; and his remark is just. Our Government is shockingly mean, and never would keep up a good system of spies."

" Spies! If you mean by an odious word to inculpate the honor of a high calling — "

" Pray forgive my interruption, but I am speaking in all good faith. When I said ' spy,' it was in the bankrupt misery of a man who had nothing else to offer. I wanted to imply that pure but small stream which conveys intelligence from a fountain to a river it was not meant to feed. Was n't that a carriage I heard in the ' cour'? Oh, pray don't open the window; there 's an odious *libeccio* blowing to-day, and there 's nothing so injurious to the nervous system."

" A cabinet messenger, your Excellency," said a servant, entering.

" What a bore! I hoped I was safe from a despatch for at least a month to come. I really believe they have no veneration for old institutions in England. They don't even celebrate Christmas ! "

" I'm charmed at the prospect of a bag," cried the Princess.

" May I have the messenger shown in here, Princess? "

" Certainly; by all means."

" Happy to see your Excellency; hope your Ladyship is in good health," said a smart-looking young fellow, who wore a much-frogged pelisse, and sported a very well-trimmed moustache.

" Ah, Stevins, how d'ye do?" said Upton. " You 've had a cold journey over the Cenis."

" Came by the Splugen, your Excellency. I went round by Vienna, and Maurice Esterhazy took me as far as Milan."

The Princess stared with some astonishment. That the messenger should thus familiarly style one of that great family was indeed matter of wonderment to her; nor was it lessened as Upton whispered her, " Ask him to dine."

" And London, how is it? Very empty, Stevins?" continued he.

" A desert," was the answer.

"Where's Lord Adderley?"

"At Brighton. The King can't do without him, — greatly to Adderley's disgust; for he is dying to have a week's shooting in the Highlands."

"And Cantworth, where is he?"

"He's off for Vienna, and a short trip to Hungary. I met him at dinner at the mess while waiting for the Dover packet. By the way, I saw a friend of your Excellency's, — Harcourt."

"Not gone to India?"

"No. They've made him a governor or commander-in-chief of something in the Mediterranean; I forget exactly where or what."

"You have brought me a mighty bag, Stevins," said Upton, sighing. "I had hoped for a little ease and rest now that the House is up."

"They are all blue-books, I believe," replied Stevins. "There's that blacking your Excellency wrote about, and the cricket-bats; the lathe must come out by the frigate, and the down mattress at the same time."

"Just do me the favor to open the bag, my dear Stevins. I am utterly without aid here," said Upton, sighing drearily; and the other proceeded to litter the table and the floor with a variety of strange and incongruous parcels.

"Report of factory commissioners," cried he, throwing down a weighty quarto. "Yarmouth bloaters; Atkinson's cerulean paste for the eyebrows; Worcester sauce; trade returns for Tahiti; a set of shoemaking tools; eight bottles of Darby's pyloric corrector; buffalo flesh-brushes, — devilish hard they seem; Hume's speech on the reduction of foreign legations; novels from Bull's; top-boots for a tiger; and a mass of letters," said Stevins, throwing them broadcast over the sofa.

"No despatches?" cried Upton, eagerly.

"Not one, by Jove!" said Stevins.

"Open one of those Darby's. I'll take a teaspoonful at once. Will you try it, Stevins?"

"Thanks, your Excellency, I never take physic."

"Well, you dine here, then," said he, with a sly look at the Princess.

" Not to-day, your Excellency. I dine with Grammont at eight."

" Then I 'll not detain you. Come back here to-morrow about eleven or a little later. Come to breakfast if you like."

" At what hour?"

" I don't know. — at any hour," sighed Upton, as he opened one of his letters and began to read; and Stevins bowed and withdrew, totally unnoticed and unrecognized as he slipped from the room.

One after another Upton threw down, after reading half a dozen lines, muttering some indistinct syllables over the dreary stupidity of letter-writers in general. Occasionally he came upon some pressing appeal for money, — some urgent request for even a small remittance by the next post; and these he only smiled at, while he refolded them with a studious care and neatness. " Why will you not help me with this chaos, dear Princess?" said he, at last.

" I am only waiting to be asked," said she; " but I feared that there might be secrets — "

" From you?" said he, with a voice of deep tenderness, while his eyes sparkled with an expression far more like raillery than affection. The Princess, however, had either not seen or not heeded it, for she was already deep in the correspondence.

"This is strictly private. Am I to read it?" said she.

"Of course," said he, bowing courteously. And she read : —

"DEAR UPTON, — Let us have a respite from tariffs and trade-talk for a month or two, and tell me rather what the world is doing around you. We have never got the right end of that story about the Princess Celestine as yet. Who was he? Not Labinsky, I 'll be sworn. The K—— insists it was Roseville, and I hope you may be able to assure me that he is mistaken. He is worse tempered than ever. That Glencore business has exasperated him greatly. Could n't your Princess, — the world calls her yours [" How good of the world, and how delicate of your friend!" said she, smiling superciliously. " Let us see who the writer is. Oh! a great man, — the Lord Adderley," and went on with her reading:] could n't your Princess find out something of real consequence to us about the Q—— "

"What queen does he mean?" cried she, stopping.

"The Queen of Sheba, perhaps," said Upton, biting his lips with anger, while he made an attempt to take the letter from her.

"Pardon! this is interesting," said she, and went on:

"We shall want it soon; that is, if the manufacturing districts will not kindly afford us a diversion by some open-air demonstrations and a collision with the troops. We have offered them a most taking bait, by announcing wrongfully the departure of six regiments for India: thus leaving the large towns in the North apparently ungarrisoned. They are such poltroons that the chances are they'll not bite! You were right about Emerson. We have made his brother a Bishop, and he voted with us on the Arms Bill. Cole is a sterling patriot and an old Whig. He says nothing shall seduce him from his party, save a Lordship of the Admiralty. Corruption everywhere, my dear Upton, except on the Treasury benches!

"Holecroft insists on being sent to Petersburg; and having ascertained that the Emperor will not accept him, I have induced the K—— to nominate him to the post. 'Non culpa nostra,' etc. He can scarcely vote against us after such an evidence of our good-will. Find out what will give most umbrage to your Court, and I will tell you why in my next.

"Don't bother yourself about the Greeks. The time is not come yet, nor will it till it suit our policy to loosen the ties with Russia. As to France, there is not, nor will there be, in our time at least, any Government there. We must deal with them as with a public meeting, which may reverse to-morrow the resolutions they have adopted to-day. The French will never be formidable till they are unanimous. They'll never be unanimous till we declare war with them! Remember, I don't want anything serious with Cinoselli. Irritate and worry as much as you can. Send even for a ship or two from Malta; but go no farther. I want this for our radicals at home. Our own friends are in the secret. Write me a short despatch about our good relations with the Two Sicilies: and send me some news in a private letter. Let me have some ortolans in the bag, and believe me yours,

"ADDERLEY."

"There," said she, turning over a number of letters with a mere glance at their contents, "these are all trash, — shooting and fox-hunting news, which one reads in the newspapers better, or at least more briefly, narrated, with all that death and marriage intelligence which you English are so fond of parading before the world. But what is this literary gem here? Where did the paper come from? And that wonderful seal, and still more wonderful address? — 'To his Worshipful Excellency the Truly Worthy and Right Honorable Sir Horace Upton, Plenipotentiary, Negotiator, and Extraordinary Diplomatist, living at Naples.'"

"What can it mean?" said he, languidly.

"You shall hear," said she, breaking the massive seal of green wax, which, to the size of a crown piece, ornamented one side of the epistle. "It is dated Schwats, Tyrol, and begins: 'Venerated and Reverend Excellency, when these unsymmetrically-designed, and not more ingeniously-conceived syllables — ' Let us see his name," said she, stopping suddenly, and turning to the last page, read, "'W. T., *vulgo*, Billy Traynor. — a name cognate to your Worshipful Eminence in times past.'"

"To be sure. I remember him perfectly. — a strange creature that came out here with that boy you heard me speak of. Pray read on."

"I stopped at 'syllables.' Yes — when these curiously-conceived syllables, then, 'come under the visionary apertures of your acute understanding, they will disclose to your much-reflecting and nice-discriminating mind as cruel and murderous a deed as ever a miscreant imagination suggested to a diabolically-constructed and nefariously-fashioned organization, showing that Nature in her bland adaptiveness never imposes a mistaken fruit on a genuine arborescence' — Do you understand him?" asked she.

"Partly, perhaps." continued he. "Let us have the subject."

"'Not to weary your exalted and never-enough-to-be-esteemed intelligence, I will proceed, without further ambiguous or circumgyratory evolutions, to the main body of my allegation. It happened in this way: Charley — your venerated worship knows who I mean — Charley, ever deep in marmorial pursuits, and far progressed in sculptorial excellence, with a genius that Phidias, if he did not envy, would esteem — '

"Really I cannot go on with these interminable parentheses." said she; "you must decipher them yourself."

Upton took the letter, and read it, at first hastily, and then, recommencing, with more of care and attention, occasionally stopping to reflect, and consider the details. "This is likely to be a troublesome business," said he. "This boy has got himself into a serious scrape. Love and a duel are bad enough; but an Austrian state-prison, and a sentence of twenty years in irons, are even worse. So far as I can make out from my not over lucid correspondent, he had conceived a violent affection for a young lady at Massa, to whose favor a young Austrian of high rank at the same time pretended."

"Wahnsdorf, I'm certain," broke in the Princess; "and the girl — that Mademoiselle — "

"Harley," interposed Sir Horace.

"Just so, — Harley. Pray go on," said she, eagerly.

"A very serious altercation and a duel were the consequences of this rivalry, and Wahnsdorf has been dangerously wounded; his life is still in peril. The Harleys have been sent out of the country, and my unlucky *protégé*, handed over to the Austrians, has been tried, condemned, and sentenced to twenty years in Kuffstein, a Tyrol fortress where great severity is practised, — from the neighborhood of which this letter is written, entreating my speedy interference and protection."

"What can you do? It is not even within your jurisdiction," said she, carelessly.

"True; nor was the capture by the Austrians within theirs, Princess. It is a case where assuredly everybody was in the wrong, and, therefore, admirably adapted for nice negotiation."

"Who and what is the youth?"

"I have called him a *protégé*."

"Has he no more tender claim to the affectionate solicitude of Sir Horace Upton?" said she, with an easy air of sarcasm.

"None, on my honor," said he, eagerly; "none, at least, of the kind you infer. His is a very sad story, which I'll tell you about at another time. For the present, I may say that he is English, and as such must be protected by the English authorities. The Government of Massa have clearly committed a great fault in handing him over to the Austrians. Stubber must be ' brought to book ' for this in the first instance. By this we shall obtain a perfect insight into the whole affair."

"The Imperial family will never forgive an insult offered to one of their own blood," said the Princess, haughtily.

"We shall not ask them to forgive anything, my dear Princess. We shall only prevent their natural feelings betraying them into an act of injustice. The boy's offence, whatever it was, occurred outside the frontier, as I apprehend."

"How delighted you English are when you can convert an individual case into an international question! You would at any moment sacrifice an ancient alliance to the trumpery claim of an aggrieved tourist," said she, rising angrily, and swept out of the room ere Sir Horace could arise to open the door for her.

Upton walked slowly to the chimney and rang the bell. "I shall want the calèche and post-horses at eight o'clock, Antoine. Put up some things for me, and get all my furs ready." And with this he measured forty drops from a small phial he carried in his waistcoat pocket, and sat down to pare his nails with a very diminutive penknife.

CHAPTER XXXVIII.

A DIPLOMATIST'S DINNER.

WERE we writing a drama instead of a true history, we might like to linger for a few moments on the leave-taking between the Princess and Sir Horace Upton. They were indeed both consummate "artists," and they played their parts to perfection, — not as we see high comedy performed on the stage, by those who grotesque its refinements and exaggerate its dignity; "lashing to storm" the calm and placid lake, all whose convulsive throes are many a fathom deep, and whose wildest workings never bring a ripple to the surface. No, theirs was the true version of well-bred "performance." A little well-affected grief at separation, brief as it was meant to be; a little half-expressed surprise, on the lady's part, at the suddenness of the departure; a little, just as vaguely conveyed, complaint on the other side, over the severe requirements of duty, and a very little tenderness — for there was no one to witness it — at the thought of parting; and with a kiss upon her hand, whose respectful courtesy no knight-errant of old could have surpassed, Sir Horace backed from the "presence," sighed, and slipped away.

Had our reader been a spectator instead of a peruser of the events we have lately detailed, he might have fancied, from certain small asperities of manner, certain quicknesses of reproof and readiness at rejoinder, that here were two people only waiting for a reasonable and decent pretext to go on their separate roads in life. Yet nothing of this kind was the case; the bond between them was not affection, it was simply convenience. Their partnership gave them a strength and a social solvency which would have been sorely damaged had either retired from "the firm;" and they knew it.

What would the Princess's dinners have been without the polished ease of him who felt himself half the host? What would all Sir Horace Upton's subtlety avail him, if it were not that he had sources of information which always laid open the game of his adversaries? Singly, each would have had a tough struggle with the world; together, they were more than a match for it.

The highest order of diplomatist, in the estimation of Upton, was the man who, at once, knew what was *possible* to be done. It was his own peculiar quality to possess this gift; but great as his natural acuteness was, it would not have availed him, without those secret springs of intelligence we have alluded to. There is no saying to what limit he might not have carried this faculty, had it not been that one deteriorating and detracting feature marred and disfigured the fairest form of his mind.

He could not, do all that he would, disabuse himself of a very low estimate of men and their motives. He did not slide into this philosophy, as certain indolent people do, just to save them the trouble of discriminating; he did not acquire it by the hard teachings of adversity. No; it came upon him slowly and gradually, the fruit, as he believed, of calm judgment and much reflection upon life. As little did he accept it willingly; he even labored against the conviction: but, strive as he might, there it was, and there it would remain.

His fixed impression was, that in every circumstance and event in life there was always a *dessous des cartes*, — a deeper game concealed beneath the surface, — and that it was a mere question of skill and address how much of this penetrated through men's actions. If this theory unravelled many a tangled web of knavery to him, it also served to embarrass and confuse him in situations where inferior minds had never recognized a difficulty! How much ingenuity did he expend to detect what had no existence! How wearily did he try for soundings where there was no bottom!

Through the means of the Princess he had learned — what some very wise heads do not yet like to acknowledge — that the feeling of the despotic governments towards

England was very different from what it had been at the
close of the great war with Napoleon. They had grown
more dominant and exacting, just as we were becoming
every hour more democratic. To maintain our old relations
with them, therefore, on the old footing, would be only to
involve ourselves in continual difficulty, with a certainty of
final failure; and the only policy that remained was to encourage the growth of liberal opinions on the Continent, out
of which new alliances might be formed, to recompense us
for the loss of the old ones. There is a story told of a certain benevolent prince, whose resources were, unhappily,
not commensurate with his good intentions, and whose
ragged retinue wearied him with entreaties for assistance.
" Be of good cheer," said he, one day, " I have ordered a
field of flax to be sown, and you shall all of you have new
shirts." Such were pretty much the position and policy of
England. Out of our crop of Constitutionalism we speculated on a rich harvest, to be afterwards manufactured for
our use and benefit. We leave it to deeper heads to say if
the result has been all that we calculated on, and, asking
pardon for such digression, we join Sir Horace once more.

When Sir Horace Upton ordered post-horses to his carriage, he no more knew where he was going, nor where he
would halt, than he could have anticipated what course any
conversation might take when once started. He had, to be
sure, a certain ideal goal to be reached; but he was one of
those men who liked to think that the casual interruptions
one meets with in life are less obstruction than opportunity;
so that, instead of deeming these subjects for regret or
impatience, he often accepted them as indications that there
was some profit to be derived from them, — a kind of fatalism
more common than is generally believed. When he set out for
Sorrento it was with the intention of going direct to Massa;
not that this state lay within the limits his functions ascribed
to him, — that being probably the very fact which imparted
a zest to the journey. Any other man would have addressed
himself to his colleague in Tuscany, or wherever he might
be; while he, being Sir Horace Upton, took the whole business upon himself in his own way. Young Massy's case
opened to his eyes a great question, viz., what was the posi-

tion the Austrians assumed to take in Italy? For any care about the youth, or any sympathy with his sufferings, he distressed himself little; not that he was, in any respect, heartless or unfeeling, it was simply that greater interests were before him. Here was one of those "grand issues" that he felt worthy of his abilities, — it was a cause where he was proud to hold a brief.

Resolving all his plans of action methodically, yet rapidly; arranging every detail in his own mind, even to the use of certain expressions he was to employ, - he arrived at the palace of the Embassy, where he desired to halt to take up his letters and make a few preparations before his departure. His Maestro di Casa, Signor Franchetti, was in waiting for his arrival, and respectfully assured him "that all was in readiness, and that his Excellency would be perfectly satisfied. We had, it is true," continued he, "a difficulty about the fish, but I sent off an express to Baia, and we have secured a sturgeon."

"What are you raving about, caro Pipo?" said the Minister; "what is all this long story of Baia and the fish?"

"Has your Excellency forgotten that we have a grand dinner to-day, at eight o'clock; that the Prince Maximilian of Bavaria and all the foreign ambassadors are invited?"

"Is this Saturday, Pipo?" said Sir Horace, blandly.

"Yes, your Excellency."

"Send Mr. Brockett to me," said Sir Horace, as he slowly mounted the stairs to his own apartment.

Sir Horace was stretched on a sofa, in all the easy luxury of magnificent dressing-gown and slippers, when Mr. Brockett entered; and without any preliminary of greeting he said, with a quiet laugh, "You have let me forget all about the dinner to-day, Brockett!"

"I thought you knew it; you took great trouble about the persons to be asked, and you canvassed whether the Duc de Borodino, being only a Chargé d'Affaires — "

"There, there; don't you see the — the inappropriateness of what you are doing? Even in England a man is not asked to criminate himself. How many are coming?"

"Nineteen; the 'Nonce' is ill, and has sent an apology."

"Then the party can be eighteen, Brockett; you must tell them that I am ill, — too ill to come to dinner. I know the Prince Max very well, — he'll not take it badly; and as to Cineselli, we shall see what humor he is in!"

"But they'll know that you arrived here this afternoon; they'll naturally suppose — "

"They'll naturally suppose — if people ever do anything so intensely stupid as naturally to suppose anything — that I am the best judge of my own health; and so, Mr. Brockett, you may as well con over the terms by which you may best acquaint the company with the reasons for my absence; and if the Prince proposes a visit to me in the evening, let him come; he'll find me here in my own room. Would you do me the kindness to let Antinori fetch his cupping-glasses, and tell Franchetti also that I'll take my chicken grilled, not roasted. I'll look over the treaty in the evening. One mushroom, only one, he may give me, and the Carlsbad water, at 28 degrees. I'm very troublesome, Brockett, but I'm sure you'll excuse it. Thanks, thanks;" and he pressed the Secretary's hand, and gave him a smile, whose blandishment had often done good service, and would do so again!

To almost any other man in the world this interruption to his journey — this sudden tidings of a formally-arranged dinner which he could not or would not attend — would have proved a source of chagrin and dissatisfaction. Not so with Upton; he liked a "contrariety." Whatever stirred the still waters of life, even though it should be a head-wind, was far more grateful than a calm! He laughed to himself at the various comments his company were sure to pass over his conduct; he pictured to his mind the anger of some and the astonishment of others, and revelled in the thought of the courtier-like indignation such treatment of a Royal Highness was certain to elicit.

"But who can answer for his health?" said he, with an easy laugh to himself. "Who can promise what he may be ten days hence?" The appearance of his dinner — if one may dignify by such a name the half of a chicken, flanked by a roasted apple and a biscuit — cut short his lucubrations; and Sir Horace ate and sipped his Carlsbad with as much enjoyment as many another man has felt over venison and Chambertin.

"Are they arrived, Pipo?" said he, as his servant removed the dessert of two figs and a lime.

"Yes, your Excellency, they are at table."

"How many are there?"

"Seventeen, sir, and Mr. Brockett."

"Did the Prince seem to — to feel my absence, Pipo?"

"I thought he appeared very sorry for your Excellency when Mr. Brockett spoke to him, and he whispered something to the aide-de-camp beside him."

"And the others, how did they take it?"

"Count Tarrocco said he'd retire, sir, that he could not dine where the host was too ill to receive him; but the Duc de Campo Stretto said it was impossible they could leave the room while a 'Royal Highness' continued to remain in it; and they all agreed with him."

"Ha, ha, ha!" laughed Upton, in a low tone. "I hope the dinner is a good one?"

"It is exquisite, sir; the Prince ate some of the caviare soup, and was asking a second time for the 'pain des ortolans' when I left the room."

"And the wine, Pipo? have you given them that rare 'La Rose'?"

"Yes, your Excellency, and the 'Klausthaller cabinet;' his Royal Highness asked for it."

"Go back, then, now. I want for nothing more; only drop in here by and by, and tell me how all goes on. Just light that pastil before you go; there — that will do."

And once more his Excellency was left to himself. In that vast palace, — the once home of a royal prince, — no sounds of the distant revelry could reach the remote quarter where he sat, and all was silent and still around him, and Upton was free to ruminate and reflect at ease. There was a sense of haughty triumph in thinking that beneath his roof, at that very moment, were assembled the great representatives of almost every important state of Europe, to whom he had not deigned to accord the honor of his presence; but though this thought did flit across his mind, far more was he intent on reflecting what might be the consequences — good

19

or evil — of the incident. "And then," said he, aloud, "how will Printing House Square treat us? What a fulminating leader shall we not have, denouncing either our insolence or our incompetence, ending with the words : ‘ If, then, Sir Horace Upton be not incapacitated from illness for the discharge of his high functions, it is full time for his Government to withdraw him from a sphere where his caprice and impertinence have rendered him something worse than useless ; ’ and then will come a flood of petty corroborations, — the tourist tribe who heard of us at Berlin, or called upon as at the Hague, and whose unreturned cards and uninvited wives are counts in the long indictment against us. What a sure road to private friendships is diplomacy ! How certain is one of conciliating the world's good opinion by belonging to it ! I wish I had followed the law, or medicine," muttered he ; " they are both abstruse, both interesting ; or been a gardener, or a shipwright, or a mathematical instrument maker, or —" Whatever the next choice might have been we know not, for he dropped off asleep.

From that pleasant slumber, and a dream of Heaven knows what life of Arcadian simplicity, of rippling streams and soft-eyed shepherdesses, he was destined to be somewhat suddenly, if not rudely, aroused, as Franchetti introduced a stranger who would accept no denial.

" Your people were not for letting me up, Upton," cried a rich, mellow voice ; and Harcourt stood before him, bronzed and weather-beaten, as he came off his journey.

" You, George ? Is it possible !" exclaimed Sir Horace ; " what best of all lucky winds has driven you here ? I 'm not sure I was n't dreaming of you this very moment. I know I have had a vision of angelic innocence and simplicity, which you must have had your part in ; but do tell me when did you arrive, and whence —"

" Not till I have dined, by Jove ! I have tasted nothing since daybreak, and then it was only a mere apology for a breakfast."

" Franchetti, get something, will you ?" said Upton, languidly, — " a cutlet, a fowl ; anything that can be had at once."

" Nothing of the kind, Signor Franchetti," interposed

Harcourt; "if I have a wolf's appetite, I have a man's
patience. Let me have a real dinner, — soup, fish, an entrée,
— two if you like, — roast beef; and I leave the wind-up
to your own discretion, only premising that I like game, and
have a weakness for woodcocks. By the way, does this
climate suit Bordeaux, Upton?"

"They tell me so, and mine has a good reputation."

"Then claret be it, and no other wine. Don't I make myself at home, old fellow, eh?" said he, clapping Upton on
the shoulder. "Have I not taken his Majesty's Embassy
by storm, eh?"

"We surrender at discretion, only too glad to receive our
vanquisher. Well, and how do you find me looking? Be
candid: how do I seem to your eyes?"

"Pretty much as I have seen you these last fifteen years.
— not an hour older, at all events. That same delicacy of
constitution is a confounded deal better than most men's
strong health, for it never wears out; but I have always said
it, Upton will see us all down!"

Sir Horace sighed, as though this were too pleasant to be
true.

"Well," said he, at last. "but you have not told me
what good chance has brought you here. Is it the first post-
station on the way to India?"

"No; they've taken me off the saddle, and given me a
staff appointment at Corfu. I'm going out second in command there; and whether it was to prevent my teasing them
for something else, or that there was really some urgency in
the matter, they ordered me off at once."

"Are they reinforcing the garrison there?" asked
Upton.

"No; not so far as I have heard."

"It were better policy to do so than to send out a 'commander-in-chief and a drummer of great experience,'" muttered Upton to himself; but Harcourt could not catch the
remark. "Have you any news stirring in England? What
do the clubs talk about?" asked Sir Horace.

"Glencore's business occupied them for the last week or
so; now. I think, it is yourself furnishes the chief topic for
speculation."

"What of me?" asked Upton, eagerly.

"Why, the rumor goes that you are to have the Foreign Office; Adderley, they say, goes out, and Conway and yourself are the favorites, the odds being slightly on his side."

"This is all news to me, George," said Upton, with a degree of animation that had nothing fictitious about it; "I have had a note from Adderley in the last bag, and there's not a word about these changes."

"Possibly; but perhaps my news is later. What I allude to is said to have occurred the day I started."

"Ah, very true; and now I remember that the messenger came round by Vienna, sent there by Adderley, doubtless," muttered he. "to consult Conway before seeing *me*; and, I have little doubt, with a letter for *me* in the event of Conway declining."

"Well, have you hit upon the solution of it?" said Harcourt, who had not followed him through his half-uttered observation.

"Perhaps so," said Upton, slowly, while he leaned his head upon his hand, and fell into a fit of meditation. Meanwhile, Harcourt's dinner made its appearance, and the Colonel seated himself at the table with a traveller's appetite.

"Whenever any one has called you a selfish fellow, Upton," said he, as he helped himself twice from the same dish, "I have always denied it, and on this good ground, that, had you been so, you had never kept the best cook in Europe, while unable to enjoy his talents. What a rare artist must this be! What's his name?"

"Pipo, how is he called?" said Upton, languidly.

"Monsieur Carmael, your Excellency."

"Ah, to be sure; a person of excellent family. I've been told he's from Provence," said Upton, in the same weary voice.

"I could have sworn to his birthplace." cried Harcourt; "no man can manage cheese and olives in cookery but a Provençal. Ah, what a glass of Bordeaux! To your good health. Upton, and to the day that you may be able to enjoy this as I do," said he, as he tossed off a bumper.

"It does me good even to witness the pleasure it yields," said Upton, blandly.

"By Jove! then, I'll be worth a whole course of tonics to you, for I most thoroughly appreciate all the good things you have given me. By the way, how are you off for dinner company here, — any pleasant people?"

"I have no health for pleasant people, my dear Harcourt; like horse exercise, they only agree with you when you are strong enough not to require them."

"Then what have you got?" asked the Colonel, somewhat abashed.

"Princes, generals, envoys, and heads of departments."

"Good heavens! legions of honor and golden fleeces!"

"Just so," said Upton, smiling at the dismay in the other's countenance; "I have had such a party as you describe to-day. Are they gone yet, Franchetti?"

"They're at coffee, your Excellency, but the Prince has ordered his carriage."

"And you did not go near them?" asked Harcourt, in amazement.

"No; I was poorly, as you see me," said Upton, smiling. "Pipo tells me, however, that the dinner was a good one, and I am sure they pardon my absence."

"Foreign ease, I've no doubt; though I can't say I like it," muttered Harcourt. "At all events, it is not for _me_ to complain, since the accident has given me the pleasure of your society."

"You are about the only man I could have admitted," said Upton, with a certain graciousness of look and manner that, perhaps, detracted a little from its sincerity.

Fortunately, not so to Harcourt's eyes, for he accepted the speech in all honesty and good faith, as he said, "Thank you heartily, my boy. The welcome is better even than the dinner, and that is saying a good deal. No more wine, thank you; I'm going to have a cigar, and, with your leave, I'll ask for some brandy and water."

This was addressed to Franchetti, who speedily reappeared with a liqueur stand and an ebony cigar-case.

"Try these, George; they're better than your own," said Upton, dryly.

"That I will," cried Harcourt, laughing; "I'm determined to draw all my resources from the country in occupation, especially as they are superior to what I can obtain

from home. This same career of yours, Upton, strikes me
as rather a good thing. You have all these things duty
free?"

" Yes, we have that privilege," said Upton, sighing.

"And the privilege of drawing some few thousand pounds
per annum, paid messengers to and from England, secret-
service money, and the rest of it, eh?"

Upton smiled, and sighed again.

"And what do you do for all that, — I mean, what are
you expected to do?"

"Keep your party in when they are in; disconcert the
enemy when your friends are out."

"And is that always a safe game?" asked Harcourt,
eagerly.

"Not when played by unskilful players, my dear George.
They occasionally make sad work, and get bowled out
themselves for their pains; but there's no great harm in
that neither."

"How do you mean there's no harm in it?"

"Simply, that if a man can't keep his saddle, he ought n't
to try to ride foremost; but these speculations will only
puzzle you, my dear Harcourt. What of Glencore? You
said awhile ago that the town was talking of him — how
and wherefore was it?"

"Have n't you heard the story, then?"

"Not a word of it."

"Well, I'm a bad narrator; besides, I don't know where
to begin; and even if I did, I have nothing to tell but the
odds and ends of club gossip, for I conclude nobody knows
all the facts but the King himself."

"If I were given to impatience, George, you would be a
most consummate plague to me," said Upton; "but I am
not. Go on, however, in your own blundering way, and
leave me to glean what I can *in mine.*"

Cheered and encouraged by this flattering speech, Harcourt did begin; but, more courteous to him than Sir
Horace, we mean to accord him a new chapter for his
revelations; promising the while to our reader that the
Colonel, like the knife-grinder, had really "no story to
tell."

CHAPTER XXXIX

A VERY BROKEN NARRATIVE.

"You want to hear all about Glencore?" said Harcourt, as, seated in the easiest of attitudes in an easy-chair, he puffed his cigar luxuriously; "and when I have told you all I know, the chances are you'll be little the wiser." Upton smiled a bland assent to this exordium, but in such a way as to make Harcourt feel less at ease than before.

"I mean," said the Colonel, "that I have little to offer you beyond the guesses and surmises of club talk. It will be for your own intelligence to penetrate through the obscurity afterwards. You understand me?"

"I believe I understand you," said Upton, slowly, and with the same quiet smile. Now, this cold, semi-sarcastic manner of Upton was the one sole thing in the world which the honest Colonel could not stand up against; he always felt as though it were the prelude to something cutting or offensive, — some sly impertinence that he could not detect till too late to resent, — some insinuation that might give the point to a whole conversation, and yet be undiscovered by him till the day following. Little as Harcourt was given to wronging his neighbor, he in this instance was palpably unjust; Upton's manner being nothing more than the impress made upon a very subtle man by qualities very unlike any of his own, and which in their newness amused him. The very look of satire was as often an expression of sorrow and regret that he could not be as susceptible — as easy of deception — as those about him. Let us pardon our worthy Colonel if he did not comprehend this; shrewder heads than his own had made the same mistake. Half to resent this covert slyness, half to arouse himself to any conflict before him, he said, in a tone of determination, "It is only fair to tell you that you are yourself to blame for anything that may have befallen poor Glencore."

"I to blame! Why, my dear Harcourt, you are surely dreaming."

"As wide awake as ever I was. If it had not been for a blunder of yours, — an unpardonable blunder, seeing what has come of it, — sending a pack of trash to me about salt and sulphur, while you forwarded a private letter about Glencore to the Foreign Office, all this might not have happened."

"I remember that it was a most disagreeable mistake. I have paid heavily for it, too. That lotion for the cervical vertebræ has come back all torn, and we cannot make out whether it be a phosphate or a prot'-oxide of bismuth. You don't happen to remember?"

"I? — of course I know nothing about it. I'd as soon have taken a porcupine for a pillow as I'd have adventured on the confounded mixture. But, as I was saying, that blessed letter, written by some Princess or other, as I understand, fell into the King's hands, and the consequence was that he sent off immediately to Glencore an order to go down to him at Brighton. Naturally enough, I thought he'd not go; he had the good and sufficient pretext of his bad health to excuse him. Nobody had seen him abroad in the world for years back, and it was easy enough to say that he could not bear the journey. Nothing of the kind; he received the command as willingly as he might have done an invitation to dinner fifteen years ago, and talked of nothing else for the whole evening after but of his old days and nights in Carlton House; how gracious the Prince used to be to him formerly; how constantly he was a guest at his table; what a brilliant society it was; how full of wit and the rest of it; till, by Jove, what between drinking more wine than he was accustomed to take, and the excitement of his own talking, he became quite wild and unmanageable. He was not drunk, nor anything like it, it was rather the state of a man whose mind had got some sudden shock; for in the midst of perfectly rational conversation, he would fall into paroxysms of violent passion, inveighing against every one, and declaring that he never had possessed one true-hearted, honest friend in his life.

"It was not without great difficulty that I got him back

to my lodgings, for we had gone to dine at Richmond. Then we put him to bed, and I sent for Hunter, who came on the instant. Though by this time Glencore was much more calm and composed, Hunter called the case brain fever; had his hair cut quite close, and ice applied to the head. Without any knowledge of his history or even of his name, Hunter pronounced him to be a man whose intellect had received some terrible shock, and that the present was simply an acute attack of a long-existent malady."

" Did he use any irritants?" asked Upton, anxiously.

" No; he advised nothing but the cold during the night."

" Ah! what a mistake," sighed Upton, heavily. " It was precisely the case for the cervical lotion I was speaking of. Of course he was much worse next morning?"

" That he was; not as regarded his reason, however, for he could talk collectedly enough, but he was irritable and passionate to a degree scarcely credible: would not endure the slightest opposition, and so suspectful of everything and everybody that if he overheard a whisper it threw him into a convulsion of anger. Hunter's opinion was evidently a gloomy one, and he said to me as we went downstairs, ' He may come through it with life, but scarcely with a sound intellect.' This was a heavy blow to *me*, for I could not entirely acquit myself of the fault of having counselled this visit to Brighton, which I now perceived had made such a deep impression upon him. I roused myself, however, to meet the emergency, and walked down to St. James's to obtain some means of letting the King know that Glencore was too ill to keep his appointment. Fortunately, I met Knighton, who was just setting off to Brighton, and who promised to take charge of the commission. I then strolled over to Brookes's to see the morning papers, and lounged till about four o'clock, when I turned homeward.

" Gloomy and sad I was as I reached my door, and rang the bell with a cautious hand. They did not hear the summons, and I was forced to ring again, when the door was opened by my servant, who stood pale and trembling before me. ' He's gone, sir, — he's gone,' cried he, almost sobbing.

" ' Good Heaven!' cried I. ' Dead?'

" ' No, sir, gone away, — driven off, no one knows where. I had just gone out to the chemist's, and was obliged to call round at Doctor Hunter's about a word in the prescription they couldn't read, and when I came back he was away.'

" I then ascertained that the carriage which had been ordered the day before at a particular hour, and which we had forgotten to countermand, had arrived during my servant's absence. Glencore, hearing it stop at the door, inquired whose it was, and as suddenly springing out of bed, proceeded to dress himself, which he did, in the suit he had ordered to wait on the King. So apparently reasonable was he in all he said, and such an air of purpose did he assume, that the nurse-tender averred she could not dare to interpose, believing that his attack might possibly be some sort of passing access that he was accustomed to, and knew best how to deal with.

" I did not lose a moment, but, ordering post-horses, pursued him with all speed. On reaching Croydon, I heard he had passed about two hours before; but though I did my best, it was in vain. I arrived at Brighton late at night, only to learn that a gentleman had got out at the Pavilion, and had not left it since.

" I do not believe that all I have ever suffered in my life equalled what I went through in the two weary hours that I passed walking up and down outside that low paling that skirts the Palace garden. The poor fellow, in all his misery, came before me in so many shapes; sometimes wandering in intellect — sometimes awake and conscious of his sufferings — now trying to comport himself as became the presence he was in — now reckless of all the world and everything. What could have happened to detain him so long? What had been the course of events since he passed that threshold? were questions that again and again crossed me.

" I tried to make my way in, — I know not exactly what I meant to do afterwards; but the sentries refused me admittance. I thought of scaling the enclosure, and reaching the Palace through the garden; but the police kept strict watch on every side. At last, it was nigh twelve o'clock, that I heard a sentry challenge some one, and shortly after a figure passed out and walked towards the pier. I followed, determined to make inquiry, no matter of whom. He walked so rapidly, however, that I was forced to run to overtake him. This attracted his notice; he turned hastily, and by the straggling moonlight I recognized Glencore.

"He stood for a moment still, and beckoning me towards him, he took my arm in silence, and we walked onward in the direction of the sea-shore. It was now a wild and gusty night. The clouds drifted fast, shutting out the moon at intervals, and the sea broke harshly along the strand.

"I cannot tell you the rush of strange and painful emotions which came upon me as I thus walked along, while not a word passed between us. As for myself, I felt that the slightest word from me might, perhaps, change the whole current of his thoughts, and thus destroy my only chance of any clew to what was passing within him. ' Are you cold?' said he, at length, feeling possibly a slight tremor in my arm. ' Not cold, exactly,' said I, ' but the night is fresh, and I half suspect too fresh for *you*.' ' Feel that,' said he, placing his hand in mine; and it was burning. ' The breeze that comes off the sea is grateful to me, for I am like one on fire.' ' Then I am certain, my dear Glencore,' said I, ' that this is a great imprudence. Let us turn back, towards the inn.'

"He made no reply, but with a rough motion of his arm moved forward as before. ' Three hours and more,' said he, with a full and stern utterance, ' they kept me waiting. There were Ministers with the King; there was some foreign envoy, too, to be presented; and if I had not gone in alone and unannounced, I might still be in the ante-chamber. How he stared at me, Harcourt, and my close-cropped hair. It was *that* seemed first to strike him, as he said, " Have you had an illness lately?" He looked poorly, too, bloated and pale, and like one who fretted, and I told him so. " We are both changed, sir," said I. — " sadly changed since we met last. We might almost begin to hope that another change is not far off, — the last and the best one." I don't remember what he answered. It was, I think, something about who came along with me from town, and who was with me at Brighton. — I forget exactly; but I know that he sent for Knighton, and made him feel my pulse. " You'll

find it rapid enough, I've no doubt, Sir William," said I.
"I rose from a sick bed to come here; his Majesty had
deigned to wish to see me." Then the King stopped me,
and made a sign to Knighton to withdraw.

"'Was n't it a strange situation, Harcourt, to be seated
there beside the King, alone? None other present, -- all to
ourselves, — talking as you and I might talk of what interested us most of all the world; and *he* showing me that
letter. — the letter that ought to have come to *me*. How he
could do it I know not. Neither you nor I, George, could
have done so; for, after all, she was, ay, and she *is*, his
wife. He could not avail himself of *my* stratagem. I said
so too, and he answered, " Ay, but I can divorce her if one
half of that be true;" and he pointed to the letter. "The
Lady Glencore," said he, " must know everything, and be
willing to tell it too. She has paid the heaviest penalty
ever woman paid for another. Read that." And I read it,
— ay, I read it four times, five times over; and then my
brain began to burn, and a thousand fancies flitted across
me, and though he talked on. I heard not a word.

"'"But that lady is my wife, sir," broke I in; "and
what a part do you assign her! She is to be a spy. a witness, perhaps, in some infamous cause. How shall I, a
peer of the realm, endure to see my name thus degraded?
Is it Court favor can recompense me for lost or tarnished
honor?" "But it will be her own vindication," said he.
Her own vindication, — these were the words, George; *she*
should be clear of all reproach. By Heaven, he said so,
that I might declare it before the world. And then it
should be proved! — be proved! How base a man can be,
even though he wear a crown! Just fancy his proposition!
But I spurned it, and said, "You must seek for some one
with a longer chance of life, sir, to do this; my days are too
brief for such dishonor;" and he was angry with me, and
said I had forgotten the presence in which I stood. It was
true, I had forgotten it.

"'He called me a wretched fool, too, as I tore up that
letter. That was wrong in me, Harcourt, was it not? I
did not see him go, but I found myself alone in the room,
and I was picking up the fragments of the letter as they

entered. They were less than courteous to me, though I
told them who I was,   an ancient barony better than half
the modern marquisates.   I gave them date and place for a
creation that smacked of other services than theirs.   Knighton would come with me, but I shook him off.   Your Court
physician can carry his complaisance even to poison.   By
George! it is their chief office, and I know well what snares
are now in store for me.'

"And thence he went on to say that he would hasten back
to his Irish solitude, where none could trace him out.   That
there his life, at least, would be secure, and no emissaries of
the King dare follow him.   It was in vain I tried to induce
him to return, even for one night, to the hotel; and I saw
that to persist in my endeavors would be to hazard the little
influence I still possessed over him.   I could not, however,
leave the poor fellow to his fate without at least the assurance of a home somewhere, and so I accompanied him to
Ireland, and left him in that strange old ruin where we once
sojourned together.   His mind had gradually calmed down,
but a deep melancholy had gained entire possession of him,
and he passed whole days without a word.   I saw that he
often labored to recall some of the events of the interview
with the King; but his memory had not retained them, and
he seemed like one eternally engaged in some problem which
his faculties could not solve.

"When I left him and arrived in town, I found the clubs
full of the incident, but evidently without any real knowledge of what had occurred; since the version was that
Glencore had asked an audience of the King, and gone down
to the Pavilion to read to his Majesty a most atrocious
narrative of the Queen's life in Italy, offering to substantiate
— through his Italian connection — every allegation it contained, — a proposal that, of course, was only received by
the King in the light of an insult; and that this reception,
so different from all his expectations, had turned his head
and driven him completely insane!

"I believe now I have told you everything as I heard it;
indeed, I have given you Glencore's own words, since, without them, I could not convey to you what he intended to say.
The whole affair is a puzzle to me, for I am unable to tell

when the poor fellow's brain was wandering, and when he spoke under the guidance of right reason. You, of course, have the clew to it all."

" I! How so?" cried Upton.

" You have seen the letter which caused all the trouble; you know its contents, and what it treats of."

" Very true; I must have read it; but I have not the slightest recollection of what it was about. There was something, I know, about Glencore's boy, — he was called Greppi, though, and might not have been recognized; and there was some gossip about the Princess of Wales — the Queen, as they call her now — and her ladies; but I must frankly confess it did not interest me, and I have forgotten it all."

" Is the writer of the letter to be come at?"

" Nothing easier. I'll take you over to breakfast with her to-morrow morning; you shall catechise her yourself."

" Oh! she is then — "

" She is the Princess Sabloukoff, my dear George, and a very charming person, as you will be the first to acknowledge. But as to this interview at Brighton, I fancy — even from the disjointed narrative of Glencore — one can make a guess of what it portended. The King saw that my Lady Glencore — for so we must call her — knew some very important facts about the Queen, and wished to obtain them; and saw, too, that certain scandals, as the phrase goes, which attached to her ladyship, lay at another door. He fancied, not unreasonably, perhaps, that Glencore would be glad to hear this exculpation of his wife; and he calculated that by the boon of this intelligence he could gain over Glencore to assist him in his project for a divorce. Don't you perceive, Harcourt, of what an inestimable value it would prove, to possess one single gentleman, one man or one woman of station, amid all this rabble that they are summoning throughout the world to bring shame upon England?"

" Then you incline to believe Lady Glencore blameless?" asked Harcourt, anxiously.

" I think well of every one, my charming Colonel. It is the only true philosophy in life. Be as severe as you please

on all who injure yourself, but always be lenient to the
faults that only damage your friends. You have no idea
how much practical wisdom the maxim contains, nor what a
fund of charity it provides."

   " I 'm ashamed to be so stupid, but I must come back to
my old question. Is all this story against Glencore's wife
only a calumny?"

   " And I must fall back upon my old remark, that all the
rogues in the world are in jail; the people you see walking about and at large are unexceptionably honest, — every
man of them. Ah. my dear deputy-assistant. adjutant.
or commissary, or whatever it be, can you not perceive
the more than folly of these perquisitions into character?
You don't require that the ice should be strong enough to
sustain a twenty-four pounder before you venture to put
foot on it, — enough that it is quite equal to your own weight ;
and so of the world at large, — everybody, or nearly everybody, has virtue enough for all we want with him. This
English habit — for it is essentially English — of eternally
investigating everything, is like the policy of a man who
would fire a round-shot every morning at his house, to see if
it were well and securely built."

   " I don't, I can't agree with you," cried Harcourt.

   " Be it so, my dear fellow ; only don't give me your
reasons, and at least I shall respect your motives."

   " What would you do, then, in Glencore's place? Let me
ask you that."

   " You may as well inquire how I should behave if I were
a quadruped. Don't you perceive that I never could,
by any possibility, place myself in such a false position?
The man who, in a case of difficulty, takes counsel from his
passions. is exactly like one, who being thirsty, fills himself
out a bumper of aquafortis and drinks it off."

   " I wish with all my heart you 'd give up aphorisms, and
just tell me how we could serve this poor fellow ; for I feel
that there is a gleam of light breaking through his dark
fortunes."

   " When a man is in the state Glencore is now in, the best
policy is to let him alone. They tell us that when Murat's
blood was up, the Emperor always left him to his own guid-

ance, since he either did something excessively brilliant, or made such a blunder as recalled him to subjection again. Let us treat our friend in this fashion, and wait. Oh, my worthy Colonel, if you but knew what a secret there is in that same waiting policy. Many a game is won by letting the adversary move out of his turn."

"If all this subtlety be needed to guide a man in the plain road of life, what is to become of poor simple fellows like myself?"

"Let them never go far from home, Harcourt, and they'll always find their way back," said Upton; and his eyes twinkled with quiet drollery. "Come, now," said he, with perfect good-nature of look and voice, "If I won't tell you what I should counsel Glencore in this emergency, I'll do the next best thing, I'll tell you what advice you'd give him."

"Let us hear it, then," said the other.

"You'd send him abroad to search out his wife; ask her forgiveness for all the wrong he has done her; call out any man that whispered the shadow of a reproach against her; and go back to such domesticity as it might please Heaven to accord him."

"Certainly, if the woman has been unjustly dealt with —"

"There's the rock you always split on: you are everlastingly in search of a character. Be satisfied when you have eaten a hearty breakfast, and don't ask for a bill of health. Researches are always dangerous. My great grandfather, who had a passion for genealogy, was cured of it by discovering that the first of the family was a staymaker! Let the lesson not be lost on us."

"From all which I am to deduce that you'd ask no questions, — take her home again, and say nothing."

"You forget, Harcourt, we are now discussing the line of action *you* would recommend; I am only hinting at the best mode of carrying out *your* ideas."

"Just for the pleasure of showing me that I didn't know how to walk in the road I made myself," said Harcourt, laughing.

"What a happy laugh that was, Harcourt! How plainly, too, it said, 'Thank Heaven I'm not like that fellow, with all his craft!' And you are right too, my dear friend; if the devil were to walk the world now, he'd be bored beyond endurance, seeing nothing but the old vices played over again and again. And so it is with all of us who have a spice of his nature; we'd give anything to see one new trick on the cards. Good night, and pleasant dreams to you!" And with a sigh that had in its cadence something almost painful, he gave his two fingers to the honest grasp of the other, and withdrew.

"You're a better fellow than you think yourself, or wish any one else to believe you," muttered Harcourt, as he puffed his cigar; and he ruminated over this reflection till it was bedtime.

And Harcourt was right.

20

ABOUT noon on the following day, Sir Horace Upton and the Colonel drove up to the gate of the villa at Sorrento, and learned, to their no small astonishment, that the Princess had taken her departure that morning for Como. If Upton heard these tidings with a sense of pain, nothing in his manner betrayed the sentiment; on the contrary, he proceeded to do the honors of the place like its owner. He showed Harcourt the grounds and the gardens, pointed out all the choice points of view, directed his attention to rare plants and curious animals; and then led him within doors to admire the objects of art and luxury which abounded there.

"And that, I conclude, is a portrait of the Princess," said Harcourt, as he stood before what had been a flattering likeness twenty years back.

"Yes, and a wonderful resemblance," said Upton, eying it through his glass. "Fatter and fuller now, perhaps; but it was done after an illness."

"By Jove!" muttered Harcourt, "she must be beautiful; I don't think I ever saw a handsomer woman!"

"You are only repeating a European verdict. She is the most perfectly beautiful woman of the Continent."

"So there is no flattery in that picture?"

"Flattery! Why, my dear fellow, these people, the very cleverest of them, can't imagine anything as lovely as that. They can imitate, — they never invent real beauty."

"And clever, you say, too?"

"*Esprit* enough for a dozen reviewers and fifty fashionable novelists." And as he spoke he smiled and coquetted with the portrait, as though to say, "Don't mind my saying all this to your face."

" I suppose her history is a very interesting one."

" Her history, my worthy Harcourt! She has a dozen histories. Such women have a life of politics, a life of literature, a life of the *salons*, a life of the affections, not to speak of the episodes of jealousy, ambition, triumph, and sometimes defeat, that make up the brilliant web of their existence. Some three or four such people give the whole character and tone to the age they live in. They mould its interests, sway its fashions, suggest its tastes, and they finally rule those who fancy that they rule mankind."

" Egad, then, it makes one very sorry for poor mankind," muttered Harcourt, with a most honest sincerity of voice.

" Why should it do so, my good Harcourt? Is the refinement of a woman's intellect a worse guide than the coarser instincts of a man's nature? Would you not yourself rather trust your destinies to the fair creature yonder than be left to the legislative mercies of that old gentleman there, Hardenberg, or his fellow on the other side, Metternich?"

" Grim-looking fellow the Prussian; the other is much better," said Harcourt, rather evading the question.

" I confess I prefer the Princess," said Upton, as he bowed before the portrait in deepest courtesy. " But here comes breakfast. I have ordered them to give it to us here, that we may enjoy that glorious sea view while we eat."

" I thought your cook a man of genius, Upton, but this fellow is his master," said Harcourt, as he tasted his soup.

" They are brothers, — twins, too; and they have their separate gifts," said Upton, affectedly. " My fellow, they tell me, has the finer intelligence; but he plays deeply, speculates on the Bourse, and it spoils his nerve."

Harcourt watched the delivery of this speech to catch if there were any signs of raillery in the speaker; he felt that there was a kind of mockery in the words; but there was none in the manner, for there was not any in the mind of him who uttered them.

" My *chef*," resumed Upton, " is a great essayist, who must have time for his efforts. This fellow is a *feuilleton* writer, who is required to be new and sparkling every day of the year, — always varied, never profound."

" And is this your life of every day?" said Harcourt, as he surveyed the splendid room, and carried his glance towards the terraced gardens that flanked the sea.

" Pretty much this kind of thing," sighed Upton, wearily.

" And no great hardship either, I should call it."

" No, certainly not," said the other, hesitatingly. " To one like myself, for instance, who has no health for the wear and tear of public life, and no heart for its ambitions, there is a great deal to like in the quiet retirement of a first-class mission."

" Is there really, then, nothing to do?" asked Harcourt, innocently.

" Nothing, if you don't make it for yourself. You can have a harvest if you like to sow. Otherwise, you may lie in fallow the year long. The subordinates take the petty miseries of diplomacy for *their* share, — the sorrows of insulted Englishmen, the passport difficulties, the custom-house troubles, the police insults. The Secretary calls at the offices of the Government, carries messages and the answers; and *I*, when I have health for it, make my compliments to the King in a cocked hat on his birthday, and have twelve grease-pots illuminated over my door to honor the same festival."

" And is that all?"

" Very nearly. In fact, when one does anything more, they generally do wrong; and by a steady persistence in this kind of thing for thirty years, you are called ' a safe man, who never compromised his Government,' and are certain to be employed by any party in power."

" I begin to think I might be an envoy myself," said Harcourt.

" No doubt of it; we have two or three of your calibre in Germany this moment, — men liked and respected; and, what is of more consequence, well looked upon at ' the Office.' "

" I don't exactly follow you in that last remark."

" I scarcely expected you should; and as little can I make it clear to you. Know, however, that in that vener-

able pile in Downing Street called the Foreign Office, there
is a strange, mysterious sentiment, — partly tradition, partly
prejudice, partly toadyism, — which bands together all within
its walls, from the whiskered porter at the door to the essenced Minister in his bureau, into one intellectual con-
glomerate, that judges of every man in ' the Line ' — as they
call diplomacy — with one accord. By that curious tribunal,
which hears no evidence, nor ever utters a sentence, each
man's merits are weighed ; and to stand well in the Office
is better than all the favors of the Court, or the force of
great abilities."

" But I cannot comprehend how mere subordinates, the
underlings of official life, can possibly influence the fortunes
of men so much above them."

" Picture to yourself the position of an humble guest at
a great man's table ; imagine one to whose pretensions the
sentiments of the servants' hall are hostile : he is served
to all appearance like the rest of the company ; he gets his
soup and his fish like those about him, and his wine-glass
is duly replenished, — yet what a series of petty mortifications is he the victim of ; how constantly is he made to feel
that he is not in public favor ; how certain, too, if he incur
an awkwardness, to find that his distresses are exposed.
The servants' hall is the Office, my dear Harcourt, and its
persecutions are equally polished."

" Are you a favorite there yourself?" asked the other,
slyly.

" A prime favorite ; they all like *me!*" said he, throwing himself back in his chair, with an air of easy self-satis-
faction ; and Harcourt stared at him, curious to know
whether so astute a man was the dupe of his own self-esteem,
or merely amusing himself with the simplicity of another.
Ah, my good Colonel, give up the problem ; it is an enigma
far above your powers to solve. That nature is too complex for *your* elucidation ; in its intricate web no one
thread holds the clew, but all is complicated, crossed, and
entangled.

" Here comes a cabinet messenger again," said Upton,
as a courier's *calèche* drove up, and a well-dressed and
well-looking fellow leaped out.

" Ah, Stanhope, how are you?" said Sir Horace, shaking his hand with what from him was warmth. "Do you know Colonel Harcourt? Well, Frank, what news do you bring me?"

"The best of news."

"From F. O., I suppose," said Upton, sighing.

"Just so. Adderley has told the King you are the only man capable to succeed him. The Press says the same, and the clubs are all with you."

"Not one of them all, I'd venture to say, has asked whether I have the strength or health for it," said Sir Horace, with a voice of pathetic intonation.

"Why, as we never knew you want energy for whatever fell to your lot to do, we have the same hope still," said Stanhope.

"So say I too," cried Harcourt. "Like many a good hunter, he'll do his work best when he is properly weighted."

"It is quite refreshing to listen to you both — creatures with crocodile digestion — talk to a man who suffers nightmare if he over-eat a dry biscuit at supper. I tell you frankly, it would be the death of me to take the Foreign Office. I'd not live through the season, — the very dinners would kill me; and then, the House, the heat, the turmoil, the worry of opposition, and the jaunting back and forward to Brighton or to Windsor!"

While he muttered these complaints, he continued to read with great rapidity the letters which Stanhope had brought him, and which, despite all his practised coolness, had evidently afforded him pleasure in the perusal.

"Adderley bore it," continued he, "just because he was a mere machine, wound up to play off so many despatches, like so many tunes; and then, he permitted a degree of interference on the King's part I never could have suffered; and he liked to be addressed by the King of Prussia as 'Dear Adderley.' But what do I care for all these vanities? Have I not seen enough of the thing they call the great world? Is not this retreat better and dearer to me than all the glare and crash of London, or all the pomp and splendor of Windsor?"

"By Jove! I suspect you are right, after all," said Harcourt, with an honest energy of voice.

"Were I younger, and stronger in health, perhaps," said Upton, "this might have tempted me. Perhaps I can picture to myself what I might have made of it; for you may perceive, George, these people have done nothing: they have been pouring hot water on the tea-leaves Pitt left them, — no more."

"And you'd have a brewing of your own, I've no doubt," responded the other.

"I'd at least have foreseen the time when this compact, this Holy Alliance, should become impossible; when the developed intelligence of Europe would seek something else from their rulers than a well-concocted scheme of repression. I'd have provided for the hour when England must either break with her own people or her allies; and I'd have inaugurated a new policy, based upon the enlarged views and extended intelligence of mankind."

"I'm not certain that I quite apprehend you," muttered Harcourt.

"No matter; but you can surely understand that if a set of mere mediocrities have saved England, a batch of clever men might have done something more. She came out of the last war the acknowledged head of Europe: does she now hold that place, and what will she be at the next great struggle?"

"England is as great as ever she was," cried Harcourt, boldly.

"Greater in nothing is she than in the implicit credulity of her people!" sighed Upton. "I only wish I could have the same faith in my physicians that she has in hers! By the way, Stanhope, what of that new fellow they have got at St. Leonard's? They tell me he builds you up in some preparation of gypsum, so that you can't move or stir, and that the perfect repose thus imparted to the system is the highest order of restorative."

"They were just about to try him for manslaughter when I left England," said Stanhope, laughing.

"As often the fate of genius in these days as in more barbarous times," said Upton. "I read his pamphlet with much interest. If you were going back, Harcourt, I'd have begged of you to try him."

"And I'm forced to say, I'd have refused you flatly."

" Yet it is precisely creatures of robust constitution, like you, that should submit themselves to these trials, for the sake of humanity. Frail organizations, like mine, cannot brave these ordeals. What are they talking of in town? Any gossip afloat?"

"The change of ministry is the only topic. Glencore's affair has worn itself out."

"What was that about Glencore?"·asked Upton, half indolently.

" A strange story; one can scarcely believe it. They say that Glencore, hearing of the King's great anxiety to be rid of the Queen, asked an audience of his Majesty, and actually suggested, as the best possible expedient, that his Majesty should deny the marriage. They add that he reasoned the case so cleverly, and with such consummate craft and skill, it was with the greatest difficulty that the King could be persuaded that he was deranged. Some say his Majesty was outraged beyond endurance; others, that he was vastly amused, and laughed immoderately over it."

" And the world, how do they pronounce upon it?"

" There are two great parties, — one for Glencore's sanity, the other against; but, as I said before, the cabinet changes have absorbed all interest latterly, and the Viscount and his case are forgotten; and when I started, the great question was, who was to have the Foreign Office."

" I believe I could tell them one who will not," said Upton, with a melancholy smile. "Dine with me, both of you, to-day, at seven; no company, you know. There is an opera in the evening, and my box is at your service, if you like to go; and so, till then;" and with a little gesture of the hand he waved an adieu, and glided from the room.

" I'm sorry he's not up to the work of office," said Harcourt; "there's plenty of ability in him."

"The best man we have," said Stanhope; "so they say at the Office."

" He's gone to lie down, I take it; he seemed much exhausted. What say you to a walk back to town?"

" I ask nothing better," said Stanhope; and they started for Naples.

CHAPTER XLI.

THAT happy valley of the Val d'Arno, in which fair Florence stands, possesses, amidst all its virtues, none more conspicuous than the blessed forgetfulness of the past, so eminently the gift of those who dwell there. Faults and follies of a few years back have so faded by time as to be already historical; and as, in certain climates, rocks and stones become shrined by lichens, and moss-covered in a year or two, so here, in equally brief space, bygones are shrouded and shadowed in a way that nothing short of cruelty and violence could once more expose to view.

The palace where Lady Glencore once displayed all her attractions of beauty and toilette, and dispensed a hospitality of princely splendor, had remained for a course of time close barred and shut up. The massive gate was locked, the windows shuttered, and curious tourists were told that there were objects of interest within, but it was impossible to obtain sight of them. The crowds who once flocked there at nightfall, and whose equipages filled the court, now drove on to other haunts, scarcely glancing as they passed at the darkened casements of the grim old edifice; when at length the rumor ran that "some one" had arrived there. Lights were seen in the porter's lodge, the iron *grille* was observed to open and shut, and tradespeople came and went within the building; and, finally, the assurance gained ground that its former owner had returned.

"Only think who has come back to us," said one of the idlers of the Cascine, as he lounged on the steps of a fashionable carriage,—"La Nina!" And at once the story went far and near, repeated at every corner, and discussed in every circle; so that had a stranger to the place but caught the passing sounds, he would have heard that one name uttered in every group he encountered. La Nina! and why not the Countess of Glencore, or, at least, the Countess de la Torre? As when exiled royalists assume titles in accordance with fallen fortunes, so, in Italy, injured fame seeks sympathy in the familiarity of the Christian name, and "Society" at once accepts the designation as that of those who throw themselves upon the affectionate kindness of the world, rather than insist upon its reverence and respect.

Many of her former friends were still there; but there was also a numerous class, principally foreigners, who only knew of her by repute. The traditions of her beauty, her gracefulness, the charms of her demeanor, and the brilliancy of her diamonds, abounded. Her admirers were of all ages, from those who worshipped her loveliness to that not less enthusiastic section who swore by her cook; and it was indeed "great tidings" to hear that she had returned.

Some statistician has asserted that no less than a hundred thousand people awake every day in London, not one of whom knows where he will pass the night. Now, Florence is but a small city, and the lacquered-boot class bear but a slight proportion to the shoeless herd of humanity. Yet there is a very tolerable sprinkling of well-dressed, well-got-up individuals, who daily arise without the very vaguest conception of who is to house them, fire them, light them, and cigar them for the evening. They are an interesting class, and have this strong appeal to human sympathy, that not one of them, by any possible effort, could contribute to his own support.

They toil not, neither do they spin. They have the very fewest of social qualities; they possess no conversational gifts; they are not even moderately good reporters of the passing events of the day. And yet, strange to say, the world they live in seems to have some need of them. Are they the last relics of a once gifted class, — worn out, effete, and exhausted, degenerated like modern Greeks from those who once shook the Parthenon? Or are they what anatomists call "rudimentary structures," — the first abortive attempts of nature to fashion something profitable and good? Who knows?

Amidst this class the Nina's arrival was announced as the happiest of all tidings; and speculation immediately set to work to imagine who would be the favorites of the house; what would be its habits and hours; would she again enter the great world of society, or would she, as her quiet, unannounced arrival portended, seek a less conspicuous position? Nor was this the mere talk of the cafés and the Cascine. The *salons* were eagerly discussing the very same theme.

In certain social conditions a degree of astuteness is acquired as to who may and who may not be visited, that, in its tortuous intricacy of reasons, would puzzle the craftiest head that ever wagged in Equity. Not that the code is a severe one; it is exactly in its lenity lies its difficulty, — so much may be done, but so little may be fatal! The Countess in the present case enjoyed what in England is reckoned a great privilege, — she was tried by her peers — or " something more." They were, however, all nice discriminators as to the class of case before them, and they knew well what danger there was in admitting to their " guild " any with a little more disgrace than their neighbors. It was curious enough that she, in whose behalf all this solicitude was excited, should have been less than indifferent as to the result; and when, on the third day of the trial, a verdict was deliverd in her favor, and a shower of visiting-cards at the porter's lodge declared that the act of her recognition had passed, her orders were that the cards should be sent back to their owners, as the Countess had not the honor of their acquaintance.

" Les grands coups se font respecter toujours," was the maxim of a great tactician in war and politics; and the adage is no less true in questions of social life. We are so apt to compute the strength of resources by the amount of pretension that we often yield the victory to the mere declaration of force. We are not, however, about to dwell on this theme, — our business being less with those who discussed her, than with the Countess of Glencore herself.

In a large *salon*, hung with costly tapestries, and furnished in the most expensive style, sat two ladies at opposite sides of the fire. They were both richly dressed, and one of them (it was Lady Glencore), as she held a screen before her face, displayed a number of valuable rings on her fingers, and a massive bracelet of enamel with a large emerald pendant. The other, not less magnificently attired, wore an imperial portrait suspended by a chain around her neck, and a small knot of white and green ribbon on her shoulder, to denote her quality of a lady in waiting at Court. There was something almost queenly in the haughty dignity of her manner, and an air of command in the tone with which she addressed her companion. It was our acquaintance the Princess Sabloukoff, just escaped from a dinner and reception at the Pitti Palace, and carrying with her some of the proud traditions of the society she had quitted.

" What hour did you tell them they might come, Nina?" asked she.

" Not before midnight, my dear Princess; I wanted to have a talk with you first. It is long since we have met, and I have so much to tell you."

" *Cara mia*," said the other, carelessly, " I know everything already. There is nothing you have done, nothing that has happened to you, that I am not aware of. I might go further, and say that I have looked with secret pleasure at the course of events which to your short-sightedness seemed disastrous."

" I can scarce conceive that possible," said the Countess, sighing.

" Naturally enough, perhaps, because you never knew the greatest of all blessings in this life, which is — liberty. Separation from your husband, my dear Nina, did not emancipate you from the tiresome requirements of the world. You got rid of *him*, to be sure, but not of those who regarded you as his wife. It required the act of courage by which you cut with these people forever, to assert the freedom I speak of."

" I almost shudder at the contest I have provoked, and had you not insisted on it — "

" You had gone back again to the old slavery, to be pitied and compassionated, and condoled with, instead of being feared and envied," said the other; and as she spoke, her flashing eyes and quivering brows gave an expression almost tiger-like to her features. "What was there about your house and its habits distinctive before? What gave you any pre-eminence above those that surround you? You were better looking, yourself; better dressed; your *salons* better lighted; your dinners more choice, — there was the end of it. *Your* company was *their* company, — *your* associates were *theirs*. The homage *you* received to-day had been yesterday the incense of another. There was not a bouquet nor a flattery offered to *you* that had not its *fac-simile*, doing service in some other quarter. You were 'one of them,' Nina, obliged to follow their laws and subscribe to their ideas; and while *they* traded on the wealth of your attractions, *you* derived nothing from the partnership but the same share as those about you."

"And how will it be now?" asked the Countess, half in fear, half in hope.

"How will it be now? I'll tell you. This house will be the resort of every distinguished man, not of Italy, but of the world at large. Here will come the highest of every nation, as to a circle where they can say, and hear, and suggest a thousand things in the freedom of unauthorized intercourse. You will not drain Florence alone, but all the great cities of Europe, of its best talkers and deepest thinkers. The statesman and the author, and the sculptor and the musician, will hasten to a neutral territory, where for the time a kind of equality will prevail. The weary minister, escaping from a Court festival, will come here to unbend; the witty converser will store himself with his best resources for your *salons*. There will be all the freedom of a club to these men, with the added charm of that fascination your presence will confer; and thus, through all their intercourse, will be felt that '*parfum de femme*,' as Balzac calls it, which both elevates and entrances."

"But will not society revenge itself on all this?"

"It will invent a hundred calumnious reports and shocking stories; but these, like the criticisms on an immoral play, will only serve to fill the house. Men — even the quiet ones — will be eager to see what it is that constitutes the charm of these gatherings; and one charm there is that never misses its success. Have you ever experienced, in visiting some

great gallery, or, still more, some choice collection of works
of art, a strange, mysterious sense of awe for objects which
you rather knew to be great by the testimony of others, than
felt able personally to appreciate? You were conscious that
the picture was painted by Raphael, or the cup carved by
Cellini, and, independently of all the pleasure it yielded you,
arose a sense of homage to its actual worth. The same is
the case in society with illustrious men. They may seem
slower of apprehension, less ready at reply, less apt to understand; but there they are, Originals, not Copies of greatness.
They represent value."

Have we said enough to show our reader the kind of
persuasion by which Madame de Sabloukoff led her friend
into this new path? The flattery of the argument was,
after all, its success; and the Countess was fascinated by
fancying herself something more than the handsomest and
the best-dressed woman in Florence. They who constitute
a free port of their house will have certainly abundance of
trade, and also invite no small amount of enterprise.

A little after midnight the *salons* began to fill, and from
the Opera and the other theatres flocked in all that was
pleasant, fashionable, and idle of Florence. The old beau,
painted, padded, and essenced, came with the younger
and not less elaborately dressed "fashionable," great in
watch-chains and splendid in waistcoat buttons; long-haired
artists and moustached hussars mingled with close-shaven
actors and pale-faced authors; men of the world, of politics,
of finance, of letters, of the turf, — all were there. There was
the gossip of the Bourse and the cabinet, the green-room
and the stable. The scandal of society, the events of club
life, the world's doings in dinners, divorces, and duels, were
all revealed and discussed, amidst the most profuse gratitude to the Countess for coming back again to that society
which scarcely survived her desertion.

They were not, it is but fair to say, all that the Princess
Sabloukoff had depicted them; but there was still a very
fair sprinkling of witty, pleasant talkers. The ease of
admission permitted any former intimate to present his
friend, and thus at once, on the very first night of receiving,
the Countess saw her *salons* crowded. They smoked, and

sang, and laughed, and played écarté, and told good stories.
They drew caricatures, imitated well-known actors, and
even preachers, talking away with a volubility that left few
listeners; and then there was a supper laid out on a table
too small to accommodate even by standing, so that each
carried away his plate, and bivouacked with others of his
friends, here and there, through the rooms.

All was contrived to impart a sense of independence and
freedom; all, to convey an impression of "license" special
to the place, that made the most rigid unbend, and relaxed
the gravity of many who seldom laughed.

As in certain chemical compounds a mere drop of some
one powerful ingredient will change the whole property of
the mass, eliciting new elements, correcting this, developing that, and, even to the eye, announcing by altered color
the wondrous change accomplished, so here the element of
womanhood, infinitely small in proportion as it was, imparted
a tone and a refinement to this orgie which, without it, had
degenerated into coarseness. The Countess's beautiful niece,
Ida Della Torre, was also there, singing at times with all
an artist's excellence the triumphs of operatic music; at
others, warbling over those "canzonettes" which to Italian
ears embody all that they know of love of country. How
could such a reception be other than successful; or how
could the guests, as they poured forth into the silent street
at daybreak, do aught but exult that such a house was
added to the haunts of Florence, — so lovely a group had
returned to adorn their fair city?

In a burst of this enthusiastic gratitude they sang a
serenade before they separated; and then, as the closed
curtains showed them that the inmates had left the windows,
they uttered the last "felice Notte," and departed.

"And so Wahnsdorf never made his appearance?" said
the Princess, as she was once more alone with the Countess.

"I scarcely expected him. He knows the ill-feeling
towards his countrymen amongst Italians, and he rarely
enters society where he may meet them."

"It is strange that he should marry one!" said she, half
musingly.

"He fell in love, — there's the whole secret of it," said

the Countess. "He fell in love, and his passion encountered certain difficulties. His rank was one of them, Ida's indifference another."

"And how have they been got over?"

"Evaded rather than surmounted. He has only his own consent after all."

"And Ida, does she care for him?"

"I suspect not; but she will marry him. Pique will often do what affection would fail in. The secret history of the affair is this: There was a youth at Massa, who, while he lived there, made our acquaintance and became even intimate at the Villa: he was a sculptor of some talent, and, as many thought, of considerable promise. I engaged him to give Ida lessons in modelling, and, in this way, they were constantly together. Whether Ida liked him or not I cannot say; but it is beyond a doubt that he loved her. In fact, everything he produced in his art only showed what his mind was full of. — her image was everywhere. This aroused Wahnsdorf's jealousy, and he urged me strongly to dismiss Greppi, and shut my doors to him. At first I consented, for I had a strange sense, not exactly of dislike, but misgiving, of the youth. I had a feeling towards him that if I attempted to convey to you, it would seem as though in all this affair I had suffered myself to be blinded by passion, not guided by reason. There were times that I felt a deep interest in the youth: his genius, his ardor, his very poverty engaged my sympathy; and then, stronger than all these, was a strange, mysterious sense of terror at sight of him, for he was the very image of one who has worked all the evil of my life."

"Was not this a mere fancy?" said the Princess, compassionately, for she saw the shuddering emotion these words had cost her.

"It was not alone his look," continued the Countess, speaking now with impetuous eagerness, "it was not merely his features, but their every play and movement; his gestures when excited; the very voice was *his*. I saw him once excited to violent passion; it was some taunt that Wahnsdorf uttered about men of unknown or ignoble origin; and then He — he himself seemed to stand before me as I have so often seen him, in his terrible outbursts of rage. The sight brought back to me the dreadful recollection of those scenes, — scenes," said she, looking wildly around her, ·· that if these old walls could speak, might freeze your heart where you are sitting.

·· You have heard, but you cannot know, the miserable life we led together; the frantic jealousy that maddened every hour of his existence; how, in all the harmless freedom of our Italian life, he saw causes of suspicion and distrust; how, by his rudeness to this one, his coldness to that, he estranged me from all who have been my dearest intimates and friends, dictating to me the while the custom of a land and a people I had never seen nor wished to see; till at last I was left a mockery to some, an object of pity to others, amidst a society where once I reigned supreme, — and all for a man that I had ceased to love! It was from this same life of misery, unrewarded by the affection by which jealousy sometimes compensates for its tyranny, that I escaped, to attach myself to the fortunes of that unhappy Princess whose lot bore some resemblance to my own.

·· I know well that he ascribed my desertion to another cause, and — shall I own it to you? — I had a savage pleasure in leaving him to the delusion. It was the only vengeance within my reach, and I grasped it with eagerness. Nothing was easier for me than to disprove it, — a mere word would have shown the falsehood of the charge; but I would not utter it. I knew his nature well, and that the insult to his name and the stain to his honor would be the heaviest of all injuries to him; and they were so. He drove *me* from my home, — I banished *him* from the world. It is true, I never reckoned on the cruel blow he had yet in store for me, and when it fell I was crushed and stunned. There was now a declared war between us, — each to do their worst to the other. It was less succumbing before him, than to meditate and determine on the future, that I fled from Florence. It was not here and in such a society I should have to blush for any imputation. But I had always held my place proudly, perhaps too proudly, here, and I did not care to enter upon that campaign of defence — that stooping to cultivate alliances, that humble game of conciliation — that must ensue.

21

"I went away into banishment. I went to Corsica, and thence to Massa. I was meditating a journey to the East. I was even speculating on establishing myself there for the rest of my life, when your letters changed my plans. You once more kindled in my heart a love of life by instilling a love of vengeance. You suggested to me the idea of coming back here boldly, and confronting the world proudly."

"Do not mistake me, Nina," said the Princess, "the 'Vendetta' was the last thing in my thoughts. I was too deeply concerned for you to be turned away from my object by any distracting influence. It was that you should give a bold denial — the boldest — to your husband's calumny, I counselled your return. My advice was: Disregard, and, by disregarding, deny the foul slander he has invented. Go back to the world in the rank that is yours and that you never forfeited, and then challenge him to oppose your claim to it."

"And do you think that for such a consideration as this — the honor to bear the name of a man I loathe — that I'd face that world I know so well? No, no; believe me, I had very different reasons. I was resolved that my future life, *my* name, *his* name, should gain a European notoriety. I am well aware that when a woman is made a public talk, when once her name comes sufficiently often before the world, let it be for what you will, — her beauty, her will, her extravagance, her dress, — from that hour her fame is perilled, and the society she has overtopped take their vengeance in slandering her character. To be before the world as a woman is to be arraigned. If ever there was a man who dreaded such a destiny for his wife, it was *he*. The impertinences of the Press had greater terrors for his heart than aught else in life, and I resolved that he should taste them."

"How have you mistaken, how have you misunderstood me, Nina!" said the Princess, sorrowfully.

"Not so," cried she, eagerly. "You only saw one advantage in the plan you counselled. *I* perceived that it contained a double benefit."

"But remember, dearest Nina, revenge is the most costly of all pleasures, if one pays for it with all that they possess — their tranquillity. I myself might have indulged such thoughts as yours; there were many points alike in our fortunes: but to have followed such a course would be like the wisdom of one who inoculates himself with a deadly malady that he may impart the poison to another."

"Must I again tell you that in all I have done I cared less how it might serve *me* than how it might wound *him?* I know you cannot understand this sentiment; I do not ask of you to sympathize with it. *Your* talents enabled you to shape out a high and ambitious career for yourself. You loved the great intrigues of state, and were well fitted to conduct or control them. None such gifts were mine. I was and I am still a mere creature of society. I never soared, even in fancy, beyond the triumphs which the world of fashion decrees. A cruel destiny excluded me from the pleasures of a life that would have amply satisfied me, and there is nothing left but to avenge myself on the cause."

"My dearest Nina, with all your self-stimulation you cannot make yourself the vindictive creature you would appear," said the Princess, smiling.

"How little do you know my Italian blood!" said the other, passionately. "That boy — he was not much more than boy — that Greppi was, as I told you, the very image of Glencore. The same dark skin, the same heavy brow, the same cold, stern look, which even a smile did not enliven; even to the impassive air with which he listened to a provocation, — all were alike. Well, the resemblance has cost him dearly. I consented at last to Wahnsdorf's continual entreaty to exclude him from the Villa, and charged the Count with the commission. I am not sure that he expended an excess of delicacy on the task; I half fear me that he did the act more rudely than was needed. At all events, a quarrel was the result, and a challenge to a duel. I only knew of this when all was over; believe me, I should never have permitted it. However, the result was as safe in the hands of Fate. The youth fled from Massa; and though Wahnsdorf followed him, they never met."

"There was no duel, you say?" cried the Princess, eagerly.

"How could there be? This Greppi never went to the rendezvous. He quitted Massa during the night, and has

never since been heard of. In this, I own to you, he was
not like *him*." And, as she said the words, the tears swam
in her eyes, and rolled down her cheeks.

" May I ask you how you learned all this? "

" From Wahnsdorf; on his return, in a week or two, he
told me all. Ida, at first, would not believe it; but how
could she discredit what was plain and palpable? Greppi
was gone. All the inquiries of the police were in vain as to
his route; none could guess how he had escaped."

" And this account was given you — you yourself — by
Wahnsdorf?" repeated the Princess.

" Yes, to myself. Why should he have concealed it? "

" And now he is to marry Ida? " said the Princess, half
musingly, to herself.

" We hope, with *your* aid, that it may be so. The family
difficulties are great; Wahnsdorf's rank is not ours; but he
persists in saying that to your management nothing is
impossible."

" His opinion is too flattering." said the Princess, with a
cold gravity of manner.

" But you surely will not refuse us your assistance? "

" You may count upon me even for more than you ask,"
said the Princess, rising. " How late it is! day is breaking
already! " And so, with a tender embrace, they parted.

CHAPTER XLII.

MADAME DE SABLOUKOFF inhabited "the grand apartment" of the Hôtel d'Italie, which is the handsomest quarter of the great hotel of Florence. The same suite which had once the distinguished honor of receiving a Czar and a King of Prussia, and Heaven knows how many lesser potentates! was now devoted to one who, though not of the small number of the elect-in-purple, was yet, in her way, what politicians calls a "puissance."

As in the drama a vast number of agencies are required for the due performance of a piece, so, on the greater stage of life, many of the chief motive powers rarely are known to the public eye. The Princess was of this number. She was behind the scenes, in more than one sense, and had her share in the great events of her time.

While her beauty lasted, she had traded on the great capital of attractions which were unsurpassed in Europe. As the perishable flower faded, she, with prudential foresight, laid up a treasure in secret knowledge of people and their acts, which made her dreaded and feared where she was once admired and flattered. Perhaps -- it is by no means improbable — she preferred this latter tribute to the former.

Although the strong sunlight was tempered by the closed jalousies and the drawn muslin curtains, she sat with her back to the window, so that her features were but dimly visible in the darkened atmosphere of the room. There was something of coquetry in this; but there was more, — there was a dash of semi-secrecy in the air of gloom and stillness around, which gave to each visitor who presented himself, — and she received but one at a time, — an impression of being admitted to an audience of confidence and

trust. The mute-like servant who waited in the corridor
without, and who drew back a massive curtain on your
entrance, also aided the delusion, imparting to the interview a character of mysterious solemnity.

Through that solemn portal there had passed, in and out,
during the morning, various dignitaries of the land, ministers and envoys, and grand " chargés " of the Court. The
embroidered key of the Chamberlain and the purple stock-
ings of a Nuncio had come and gone; and now there was a
brief pause, for the groom in waiting had informed the crowd
in the antechamber that the Princess could receive no more.
Then there was a hurried scrawling of great names in a
large book, a shower of visiting-cards, and all was over;
the fine equipages of fine people dashed off, and the courtyard of the hotel was empty.

The large clock on the mantelpiece struck three, and
Madame de Sabloukoff compared the time with her watch,
and by a movement of impatience showed a feeling of displeasure. She was not accustomed to have her appointments lightly treated, and he for whom she had fixed an
hour was now thirty minutes behind his time. She had been
known to resent such unpunctuality, and she looked as
though she might do so again. " I remember the day when
his grand-uncle descended from his carriage to speak to
me," muttered she; "and that same grand-uncle was an
emperor."

Perhaps the chance reflection of her image in the large
glass before her somewhat embittered the recollection, for
her features flushed, and as suddenly grew pale again. It
may have been that her mind went rapidly back to a period
when her fascination was a despotism that even the highest
and the haughtiest obeyed. " Too true," said she, speaking
to herself, " time has dealt heavily with us all. But *they*
are no more what they once were than am I. Their old
compact of mutual assistance is crumbling away under the
pressure of new rivalries and new pretensions. Kings and
Kaisers will soon be like bygone beauties. I wonder will
they bear their altered fortune as heroically? " It is but
just to say that her tremulous accents and quivering lip bore
little evidence of the heroism she spoke of.

She rang the bell violently, and as the servant entered she said, but in a voice of perfect unconcern, —

" When the Count von Wahnsdorf calls, you will tell him that I am engaged, but will receive him to-morrow — "

" And why not to-day, charming Princess?" said a young man, entering hastily, and whose graceful but somewhat haughty air set off to every advantage his splendid Hungarian costume. " Why not now?" said he, stooping to kiss her hand with respectful gallantry. She motioned to the servant to withdraw, and they were alone.

" You are not over exact in keeping an appointment, monsieur," said she, stiffly. " It is somewhat cruel to remind me that my claims in this respect have grown antiquated."

" I fancied myself the soul of punctuality, my dear Princess," said he, adjusting the embroidered pelisse he wore over his shoulder. " You mentioned four as the hour — "

" I said three o'clock," replied she, coldly.

" Three, or four, or even five, — what does it signify?" said he, carelessly. " We have not either of us, I suspect, much occupation to engage us; and if I have interfered with your other plans — if you have plans — A thousand pardons!" cried he, suddenly, as the deep color of her face and her flashing eye warned him that he had gone too far; " but the fact is, I was detained at the riding-school. They have sent me some young horses from the Banat, and I went over to look at them."

" The Count de Wahnsdorf knows that he need make no apologies to Madame de Sabloukoff," said she, calmly; " but it were just as graceful, perhaps, to affect them. My dear Count," continued she, but in a tone perfectly free from all touch of irritation, " I have asked to see and speak with you on matters purely your own — "

" You want to dissuade me from this marriage," said he, interrupting; " but I fancy that I have already listened to everything that can be urged on that affair. If you have any argument other than the old one about misalliance and the rest of it, I 'll hear it patiently; though I tell you beforehand that I should like to learn that a connection with an imperial house had some advantage besides that of a continual barrier to one's wishes."

"I understand," said she, quietly, "that you named the terms on which you would abandon this project, — is it not so?"

"Who told *you* that?" cried he, angrily. "Is this another specimen of the delicacy with which ministers treat a person of my station?"

"To discuss that point, Count, would lead us wide of our mark. Am I to conclude that my informant was correct?"

"How can I tell what may have been reported to you?" said he, almost rudely.

"You shall hear and judge for yourself," was the calm answer. "Count Kollorath informed me that you offered to abandon this marriage on condition that you were appointed to the command of the Pahlen Hussars."

The young man's face became scarlet with shame, and he tried twice to speak, but unavailingly.

With a merciless slowness of utterance, and a manner of the most unmoved sternness, she went on: "I did not deem the proposal at all exorbitant. It was a price that they could well afford to pay."

"Well, they refused me," said he, bluntly.

"Not exactly refused you," said she, more gently. "They reminded you of the necessity of conforming — of at least appearing to conform — to the rules of the service; that you had only been a few months in command of a squadron; that your debts, which were considerable, had been noised about the world, so that a little time should elapse, and a favorable opportunity present itself, before this promotion could be effected."

"How correctly they have instructed you in all the details of this affair!" said he, with a scornful smile.

"It is a rare event when I am misinformed, sir," was her cold reply; "nor could it redound to the advantage of those who ask my advice to afford me incorrect information."

"Then I am quite unable to perceive what you want with *me*," cried he. "It is plain enough you are in possession of all that I could tell you. Or is all this only the prelude to some menace or other?"

She made no other answer to this rude question than by a smile so dubious in its meaning, it might imply scorn, or pity, or even sorrow.

"You must not wonder if I be angry," continued he, in an accent that betokened shame at his own violence. "They have treated me so long as a fool that they have made me something worse than one."

"I am not offended by your warmth, Count," said she, softly. "It is at least the guarantee of your sincerity. I tell you, therefore, I have no threat to hold over you. It will be enough that I can show you the impolicy of this marriage, — I don't want to use a stronger word, — what estrangement it will lead to as regards your own family, how inadequately it will respond to the sacrifices it must cost."

"That consideration is for me to think of, madam," said he, proudly.

"And for your friends also," interposed she, softly.

"If by my friends you mean those who have watched every occasion of my life to oppose my plans and thwart my wishes, I conclude that they will prove themselves as vigilant now as heretofore; but I am getting somewhat weary of this friendship."

"My dear Count, give me a patient — if possible, an indulgent — hearing for five minutes, or even half that time, and I hope it will save us both a world of misconception. If this marriage that you are so eager to contract were an affair of love, — of that ardent, passionate love which recognizes no obstacle nor acknowledges any barrier to its wishes, — I could regard the question as one of those everyday events in life whose uniformity is seldom broken by a new incident; for love stories have a terrible sameness in them." She smiled as she said this, and in such a way as to make him smile at first, and then laugh heartily.

"But if," resumed she, seriously, · · "if I only see in this project a mere caprice, half — more than half — based upon the pleasure of wounding family pride, or of coercing those who have hitherto dictated to you; if, besides this, I perceive that there is no strong affection on either side, none of that impetuous passion which the world accepts as · the attenuating circumstance ' in rash marriages —"

" And who has told you that I do not love Ida, or that she is not devoted with her whole heart to *me?*" cried he, interrupting her.

" You yourself have told the first. You have shown by the price you have laid on the object the value at which you estimate it. As for the latter part of your question—" She paused, and arranged the folds of her shawl, purposely playing with his impatience, and enjoying it.

" Well," cried he, " as for the latter part; go on."

" It scarcely requires an answer. I saw Ida Della Torre last night in a society of which her affianced husband was not one; and, I will be bold enough to say, hers was not the bearing that bespoke engaged affections."

" Indeed!" said he, but in a tone that indicated neither displeasure nor surprise.

" It was as I have told you, Count. Surrounded by the youth of Florence, such as you know them, she laughed, and talked, and sang, in all the careless gayety of a heart at ease; or, if at moments a shade of sadness crossed her features, it was so brief that only one observing her closely as myself could mark it."

" And how did that subtle intelligence of yours interpret this show of sorrow?" said he, in a voice of mockery, but yet of deep anxiety.

" My subtle intelligence was not taxed to guess, for I knew her secret," said the Princess, with all the strength of conscious power.

" Her secret — her secret!" said he, eagerly. " What do you mean by that?"

The Princess smiled coldly, and said, " I have not yet found my frankness so well repaid that I should continue to extend it."

" What is the reward to be, madam? Name it," said he, boldly.

" The same candor on your part, Count; I ask for no more."

" But what have I to reveal; what mystery is there that your omniscience has not penetrated?"

" There may be some that your frankness has not avowed, my dear Count."

" If you refer to what you have called Ida's secret — "

" No," broke she in. " I was now alluding to what might be called *your* secret."

" Mine ! *my* secret ! " exclaimed he. But though the tone was meant to convey great astonishment, the confusion of his manner was far more apparent.

" Your secret, Count." she repeated slowly. " which has been just as safe in my keeping as if it had been confided to me on honor."

" I was not aware how much I owed to your discretion. madam," said he, scoffingly.

" I am but too happy when any services of mine can rescue the fame of a great family from reproach, sir." replied she, proudly ; for all the control she had heretofore imposed upon her temper seemed at last to have yielded to offended dignity. " Happily for that illustrious house — happily for you, too — I am one of a very few who know of Count Wahnsdorf's doings. To have suffered your antagonist in a duel to be tracked, arrested, and imprisoned in an Austrian fortress, when a word from you had either warned him of his peril or averted the danger, was bad enough ; but to have stigmatized his name with cowardice, and to have defamed him because he was your rival, was far worse."

Wahnsdorf struck the table with his clenched fist till it shook beneath the blow, but never uttered a word, while with increased energy she continued. —

" Every step of this bad history is known to me ; every detail of it, from your gross and insulting provocation of this poor friendless youth to the last scene of his committal to a dungeon."

" And, of course, you have related your interesting narrative to Ida ? " cried he.

" No, sir ; the respect which I have never lost for those whose name you bear had been quite enough to restrain me, had I not even other thoughts."

" And what may they be ? " asked he.

" To take the first opportunity of finding myself alone with you, to represent how nearly it concerns your honor that this affair should never be bruited abroad ; to insist upon your lending every aid to obtain this young man's liberation; to show that the provocation came from yourself; and, lastly, all-painful though it be, to remove from him the stain you have inflicted, and to reinstate him in the esteem that your calumny may have robbed him of. These were the other thoughts I alluded to."

"And you fancy that I am to engage in this sea of trouble for the sake of some nameless bastard, while in doing so I compromise myself and my own honor?"

"Do you prefer that it should be done by another, Count Wahnsdorf?" asked she.

"This is a threat, madam."

"All the speedier will the matter be settled if you understand it as such."

"And, of course, the next condition will be for me to resign my pretensions to Ida in his favor," said he, with a savage irony.

"I stipulate for nothing of the sort; Count Wahnsdorf's pretensions will be to-morrow just where they are to-day."

"You hold them cheaply, madam. I am indeed unfortunate in all my pursuit of your esteem."

"You live in a sphere to command it, sir," was her reply, given with a counterfeited humility; and whether it was the tone of mingled insolence and submission she assumed, or simply the sense of his own unworthiness in her sight, but Wahnsdorf cowered before her like a frightened child. At this moment the servant entered, and presented a visiting-card to the Princess.

"Ah, he comes in an opportune moment," cried she. "This is the Minister of the Duke of Massa's household, — the Chevalier Stubber. Yes," continued she to the servant, "I will receive him."

If there was not any conspicuous gracefulness in the Chevalier's approach, there was an air of quiet self-possession that bespoke a sense of his own worth and importance; and while he turned to pay his respects to the young Count, his unpolished manner was not devoid of a certain dignity.

"It is a fortunate chance by which I find you here, Count Wahnsdorf," said he, "for you will be glad to learn that the young fellow you had that affair with at Massa has just been liberated."

" When, and how?" cried the Princess, hastily.

" As to the time, it must be about four days ago, as my letters inform me; as to the how, I fancy the Count can best inform you, — he has interested himself greatly in the matter." The Count blushed deeply, and turned away to hide his face, but not so quickly as to miss the expression of scornful meaning with which the Princess regarded him.

" But I want to hear the details, Chevalier," said she.

" And I can give you none, madam. My despatches simply mention that the act of arrest was discovered in some way to be informal. Sir Horace Upton proved so much. There then arose a question of giving him up to us; but my master declined the honor, — he would have no trouble, he said, with England or Englishmen; and some say that the youth claims an English nationality. The cabinet of Vienna are, perhaps, like-minded in the matter; at all events, he is free, and will be here to-morrow."

" Then I shall invite him to dinner, and beg both of you gentlemen to meet him," said she, with a voice wherein a tone of malicious drollery mingled.

" I am your servant, madam," said Stubber.

" And I am engaged," said Wahnsdorf, taking up his shako.

" You are off to Vienna to-night, Count Wahnsdorf," whispered the Princess in his ear.

" What do you mean, madam?" said he, in a tone equally low.

" Only that I have a letter written for the Archduchess Sophia, which I desire to intrust to your hands. You may as well read ere I seal it."

The Count took the letter from her hand, and retired towards the window to read it. While she conversed eagerly with Stubber, she did not fail from time to time to glance towards the other, and mark the expression of his features as he folded and replaced the letter in its envelope, and, slowly approaching her, said, —

" You are most discreet, madam."

" I hope I am just, sir," said she, modestly.

" This was something of a difficult undertaking, too," said he, with an equivocal smile.

" It was certainly a pleasant and proud one, sir, as it always must be, to write to a mother in commendation of her son. By the way, Chevalier, you have forgotten to make your compliments to the Count on his promotion — "

" I have not heard of it, madam; what may it be?" asked Stubber.

" To the command of the Pahlen Hussars, sir, — one of the proudest ' charges ' of the Empire."

A rush of blood to Wahnsdorf's face was as quickly followed by a deadly pallor, and with a broken, faint utterance he said, " Good-bye," and left the room.

" A fine young fellow, — the very picture of a soldier," exclaimed Stubber, looking after him.

" A chevalier of the olden time, sir, — the very soul of honor," said the Princess, enthusiastically. " And now for a little gossip with yourself."

It is not " in our brief " to record what passed in that chatty interview ; plenty of state secrets and state gossip there was, — abundance of that dangerous trifling which mixes up the passions of society with the great game of politics, and makes statecraft feel the impress of men's whims and caprices. We were just beginning that era, " the policy of resentments," which has since pervaded Europe, and the Chevalier and the Princess were sufficiently behind the scenes to have many things to communicate ; and here we must leave them while we hasten on to other scenes and other actors.

CHAPTER XLIII.

THE dull old precincts of Downing Street were more than usually astir. Hackney-coaches and cabs at an early hour, private chariots somewhat later, went to and fro along the dreary pavement, and two cabinet messengers with splashed *calèches* arrived in hot haste from Dover. Frequent, too, were the messages from the House; a leading Oppositionist was then thundering away against the Government, inveighing against the treacherous character of their foreign policy, and indignantly calling on them for certain despatches to their late envoy at Naples. At every cheer which greeted him from his party a fresh missive would be despatched from the Treasury benches, and the whisper, at first cautiously muttered, grew louder and louder. "Why does not Upton come down?"

So intricate has been the web of our petty entanglements, so complex the threads of those small intrigues by which we have earned our sobriquet of the "perfide Albion," that it is difficult at this time of day to recall the exact question whose solution, in the words of the orator of the debate, "placed us either at the head of Europe, or consigned to us the fatal mediocrity of a third-rate power." The prophecy, whichever way read, gives us unhappily no clew to the matter in hand, and we are only left to conjecture that it was an intervention in Spain, or "something about the Poles." As is usual in such cases, the matter, insignificant enough in itself, was converted into a serious attack on the Government, and all the strength of the Opposition was arrayed to give power and consistency to the assault. As is equally usual, the cabinet was totally unprepared for defence; either they had altogether undervalued the subject, or they trusted to the secrecy with which they had conducted it; whichever of these be the right explanation, each minister could only say to his colleague, "It never came before *me;* Upton knows all about it."

"And where is Upton? — why does he not come down?" — were again and again reiterated; while a shower of messages and even mandates invoked his presence.

The last of these was a peremptory note from no less a person than the Premier himself, written in three very significant words, thus: "COME, OR GO;" and given to a trusty whip, the Hon. Gerald Neville, to deliver.

Armed with this not very conciliatory document, the well-practised tactician drew up to the door of the Foreign Office, and demanded to see the Secretary of State.

"Give him this card and this note, sir," said he to the well-dressed and very placid young gentleman who acted as his private secretary.

"Sir Horace is very poorly, sir; he is at this moment in a mineral bath; but as the matter you say is pressing, he will see you. Will you pass this way?"

Mr. Neville followed his guide through an infinity of passages, and at length reached a large folding-door, opening one side of which he was ushered into a spacious apartment, but so thoroughly impregnated with a thick and offensive vapor that he could barely perceive, through the mist, the bath in which Upton lay reclined, and the figure of a man, whose look and attitude bespoke the doctor, beside him.

"Ah, my dear fellow," sighed Upton, extending two dripping fingers in salutation, "you have come in at the death. This is the last of it!"

"No, no; don't say that," cried the other, encouragingly. "Have you had any sudden seizure? What is the nature of it?"

"He," said he, looking round to the doctor, "calls it 'arachnoidal trismus.' — a thing, he says, that they have all of them ignored for many a day, though Charlemagne died of it. Ah, Doctor," — and he addressed a question to him in German.

A growled volley of gutturals ensued, and Upton went on: —

"Yes, Charlemagne, — Melancthon had it, but lingered for years. It is the peculiar affection of great intellectual natures over-taxed and over-worked."

Whether there was that in the manner of the sick man that inspired hope, or something in the aspect of the doctor that suggested distrust, or a mixture of the two together, but certainly Neville rapidly rallied from the fears which had beset him on entering, and in a voice of a more cheery tone, said, —

"Come, come, Sir Horace, you'll throw off this as you have done other such attacks. You have never been wanting either to your friends or yourself when the hour of emergency called. We are in a moment of such difficulty now, and you alone can rescue us."

"How cruel of the Duke to write me that!" sighed Upton, as he held up the piece of paper, from which the water had obliterated all trace of the words. "It was so inconsiderate, — eh, Neville?"

"I'm not aware of the terms he employed," said the other.

This was the very admission that Upton sought to obtain, and in a far more cheery voice he said, —

"If I was capable of the effort, — if Doctor Geümirstad thought it safe for me to venture, — I could set all this to right. These people are all talking 'without book,' Neville, — the ever-recurring blunder of an Opposition when they address themselves to a foreign question: they go upon a newspaper paragraph, or the equally incorrect 'private communication from a friend.' Men in office alone can attain to truth — exact truth — about questions of foreign policy."

"The debate is taking a serious turn, however," interposed Neville. "They reiterate very bold assertions, which none of our people are in a position to contradict. Their confidence is evidently increasing with the show of confusion in our ranks. Something must be done to meet them, and that quickly."

"Well, I suppose I must go," sighed Upton; and as he held out his wrist to have his pulse felt, he addressed a few words to the doctor.

22

"He calls it 'a life period,' Neville. He says that he won't answer for the consequences."

The doctor muttered on.

"He adds that the trismus may be thus converted into 'Bi-trismus.' Just imagine Bi-trismus!"

This was a stretch of fancy clear and away beyond Neville's apprehension, and he began to feel certain misgivings about pushing a request so full of danger; but from this he was in a measure relieved by the tone in which Upton now addressed his valet with directions as to the dress he intended to wear. "The loose pelisse, with the astrakhan, Giuseppe, and that vest of *cramoisie* velvet; and if you will just glance at the newspaper, Neville, in the next room, I'll come to you immediately."

The newspapers of the morning after this interview afford us the speediest mode of completing the incidents; and the concluding sentences of a leading article will be enough to place before our readers what ensued: —

"It was at this moment, and amidst the most enthusiastic cheers of the Treasury bench, that Sir Horace Upton entered the House. Leaning on the arm of Mr. Neville, he slowly passed up and took his accustomed place. The traces of severe illness in his features, and the great debility which his gestures displayed, gave an unusual interest to a scene already almost dramatic in its character. For a moment the great chief of Opposition was obliged to pause in his assault, to let this flood-tide of sympathy pass on: and when at length he did resume, it was plain to see how much the tone of his invective had been tempered by a respect for the actual feeling of the House. The necessity for this act of deference, added to the consciousness that he was in presence of the man whose acts he so strenuously denounced, were too much for the nerves of the orator, and he came to an abrupt conclusion, whose confused and uncertain sentences scarcely warranted the cheers with which his friends rallied him.

"Sir Horace rose at once to reply. His voice was at first so inarticulate that we could but catch the burden of what he said, — a request that the House would accord him all the indulgence which his state of debility and suffering called for. If the first few sentences he uttered imparted a painful significance to the entreaty, it very soon became apparent that he had no occasion to bespeak such indulgence. In a voice that gained strength and fulness as he proceeded, he entered upon what might be called a

narrative of the foreign policy of the administration, clearly showing that their course was guided by certain great principles which
dictated a line of action firm and undeviating; that the measures
of the Government, however modified by passing events in
Europe, had been uniformly consistent, — based upon the faith of
treaties, but ever mindful of the growing requirements of the age.
Through a narrative of singular complexity he guided himself
with consummate skill, and though detailing events which occupied every region of the globe, neither confusion nor inconsistency ever marred the recital, and names and places and dates
were quoted by him without any artificial aid to memory."

There was in the polished air, and calm, dispassionate
delivery of the speaker, something which seemed to charm
the ears of those who for four hours before had been so
mercilessly assailed by all the vituperation and insolence of
party animosity. It was, so to say, a period of relief and
repose, to which even antagonists were not insensible. No
man ever understood the advantage of his gifts in this way
better than Upton, nor ever was there one who could convert the powers which fascinated society into the means of
controlling a popular assembly, with greater assurance of
success. He was a man of a strictly logical mind, a close
and acute thinker; he was of a highly imaginative temperament, rich in all the resources of a poetic fancy; he was
thoroughly well read, and gifted with a ready memory; but,
above all these, — transcendently above them all, — he was a
"man of the world;" and no one, either in Parliament or
out of it, knew so well when it was wrong to say "the right
thing." But let us resume our quotation : —

"For more than three hours did the House listen with breath-
less attention to a narrative which in no parliamentary experience
has been surpassed for the lucid clearness of its details, the
unbroken flow of its relation. The orator up to this time had
strictly devoted himself to explanation; he now proceeded to
what might be called reply. If the House was charmed and instructed before, it was now positively astonished and electrified
by the overwhelming force of the speaker's raillery and invective.
Not satisfied with showing the evil consequences that must ensue
from any adoption of the measures recommended by the Opposition, he proceeded to exhibit the insufficiency of views always
based upon false information.

" ' We have been taunted,' said he, ' with the charge of foment-
ing discords in foreign lands ; we have been arraigned as disturb-
ers of the world's peace, and called the firebrands of Europe ; we
are exhibited as parading the Continent with a more than Quix-
otic ardor, since we seek less the redress of wrong than the
opportunity to display our own powers of interference, — that quality which the learned gentleman has significantly stigmatized as
a spirit of meddling impertinence, offensive to the whole world of
civilization. Let me tell him, sir, that the very debate of this
night has elicited, and from himself too, the very outrages he has
had the temerity to ascribe to us. His has been this indiscriminate ardor, his this unjudging rashness, his this meddling impertinence (I am but quoting, not inventing, a phrase), by which, without accurate, without, indeed, any, information, he has ventured
to charge the Government with what no administration would be
guilty, of — a cool and deliberate violation of the national law of
Europe.

" ' He has told you, sir, that in our eagerness to distinguish
ourselves as universal redressers of injury, we have " ferreted out "
— I take his own polished expression — the case of an obscure boy
in an obscure corner of Italy, converted a commonplace and very
vulgar incident into a tale of interest, and, by a series of artful devices and insinuations based upon this narrative, a grave and
insulting charge upon one of the oldest of our allies. He has
alleged that throughout the whole of those proceedings we had
not the shadow of pretence for our interference ; that the acts
imputed occurred in a land over which we had no control, and in
the person of an individual in whom we had no interest : that
this Sebastiano Greppi — this image boy, for so with a courteous pleasantry he has called him — was a Neapolitan subject,
the affiliated envoy of I know not what number of secret societies ;
that his sculptural pretensions were but pretexts to conceal his
real avocations, — the agency of a bloodthirsty faction ; that his
crime was no less than an act of high treason : and that Austrian
gentleness and mercy were never more conspicuously illustrated
than in the commutation of a death-sentence to one of perpetual
imprisonment.

" ' What a rude task is mine when I must say that for even one
of these assertions there is not the slightest foundation in fact.
Greppi's offence was not a crime against the state ; as little was it
committed within the limits of the Austrian territory. He is not
the envoy, or even a member, of any revolutionary club ; he never
— I am speaking with knowledge, sir — he never mingled in the
schemes of plotting politicians : as far removed is he from sympathy with such men, as, in the genius of a great artist, he is elevated

above the humble path to which the learned gentleman's raillery would sentence him. For the character of "an image vendor," the learned gentleman must look nearer home; and, lastly, this youth is an Englishman, and born of a race and a blood that need feel no shame in comparison with any I see around me!'

"To the loud cry of 'Name, name,' which now arose, Sir Horace replied: 'If I do not announce the name at this moment, it is because there are circumstances in the history of the youth to which publicity would give irreparable pain. These are details which I have no right to bring under discussion, and which must inevitably thus become matters of town-talk. To any gentleman of the opposite side who may desire to verify the assertions I have made to the House, I would, under pledge of secrecy, reveal the name. I would do more: I would permit him to confide it to a select number of friends equally pledged with himself. This is surely enough?'"

We have no occasion to continue our quotation farther, and we take up our history as Sir Horace, overwhelmed by the warmest praises and congratulations, drove off from the House to his home. Amid all the excitement and enthusiasm which this brilliant success produced among the ministerialists, there was a kind of dread lest the overtaxed powers of the orator should pay the heavy penalty of such an effort. They had all heard how he came from a sick chamber; they had all seen him, trembling, faint, and almost voiceless, as he stole up to his place, and they began to fear lest they had, in the hot zeal of party, imperilled the ablest chief in their ranks.

What a relief to these agonies had it been, could they have seen Upton as he once more gained the solitude of his chamber, where, divested of all the restraints of an audience, he walked leisurely up and down, smoking a cigar, and occasionally smiling pleasantly as some "conceit" crossed his mind.

Had there been any one to mark him there, it is more than likely that he would have regarded him as a man revelling in the after-thought of a great success, — one who, having come gloriously through the combat, was triumphantly recalling to his memory every incident of the fight. How little had they understood Sir Horace Upton who would have read him in this wise! That daring and soaring nature

rarely dallied in the past; even the present was scarcely
full enough for the craving of a spirit that cried ever,
" Forward!"

What might be made of that night's success; how best
it should be turned to account! — these were the thoughts
which beset him, and many were the devices which his
subtlety hit on to this end. There was not a goal his
ambition could point to but which became associated with
some deteriorating ingredient. He was tired of the Continent, he hated England, he shuddered at the Colonies.
" India, perhaps," said he, hesitatingly, — " India, perhaps,
might do." To continue as he was, — to remain in office,
as having reached the topmost round of the ladder, — would
have been insupportable indeed; and yet how, without
longer service at his post, could any man claim a higher
reward?

CHAPTER XLIV

It was not till Sir Horace had smoked his third cigar that he seated himself at his writing-table. He then wrote rapidly a brief note, of which he proceeded to make a careful copy. This he folded and placed in an envelope, addressing it to his Grace the Duke of Cloudeslie.

A few minutes afterwards he began to prepare for bed. The day was already breaking, and yet that sick man was unwearied and unwasted; not a trace of fatigue on features that, under the infliction of a tiresome dinner-party, would have seemed bereft of hope.

The tied-up knocker, the straw-strewn street, the closely drawn curtains announced to London the next morning that the distinguished minister was seriously ill; and from an early hour the tide of inquirers, in carriages and on foot, passed silently along that dreary way. High and mighty were the names inscribed in the porter's book; royal dukes had called in person; and never was public solicitude more widely manifested. There is something very flattering in the thought of a great intelligence being damaged and endangered in our service! With all its melancholy influences, there is a feeling of importance suggested by the idea that for us and our interests a man of commanding powers should have jeoparded his life. There is a very general prejudice, not alone in obtaining the best article for our money, but the most of it also; and this sentiment extends to the individuals employed in the public service; and it is doubtless a very consolatory reflection to the tax-paying classes that the great functionaries of state are not indolent recipients of princely incomes, but hard-worked men of office, up late and early at their duties, prematurely old, and

worn out before their time! Something of this same feeling
inspires much of the sympathy displayed for a sick statesman, — a sentiment not altogether void of a certain misgiving
that we have probably over-taxed the energies employed in
our behalf.

Scarcely one in a hundred of those who now called and
" left their names" had ever seen Sir Horace Upton in their
lives. Few are more removed from public knowledge than
the men who fill even the highest places in our diplomacy.
He was, therefore, to the mass a mere name. Since his
accession to office little or nothing had been heard of him,
and of that little, the greater part was made up of sneering
allusions to his habits of indolence; impertinent hints about
his caprices and his tastes. Yet now, by a grand effort in
the " House," and a well got-up report of a dangerous illness
the day after, was he the most marked man in all the state,
— the theme of solicitude throughout two millions of people!

There was a dash of mystery, too, in the whole incident,
which heightened its flavor for public taste; a vague, indistinct impression — it did not even amount to rumor — was
abroad, that Sir Horace had not been " fairly treated" by
his colleagues; either that they could, if they wished it,
have defended the cause themselves, or that they had needlessly called him from a sick bed to come to the rescue, or
that some subtle trap had been laid to ensnare him. These
were vulgar beliefs, which, if they obtained little credence in
the higher region of club-life, were extensively circulated,
and not discredited, in less distinguished circles. How they
ever got abroad at all; how they found their ways into
newspaper paragraphs, terrifying timid supporters of the
ministry by the dread prospect of a " smash," exciting
the hopes of Opposition with the notion of a great seces-
sion, throwing broadcast before the world of readers every
species of speculation, all kinds of combination, — who
knows how all this happened? Who, indeed, ever knew how
things a thousand times more secret ever got wind and
became club-talk ere the actors in the events had finished an
afternoon's canter in the Park?

If, then, the world of London learned on the morning in
question that Sir Horace Upton was very ill, it also surmised

— why and wherefore it knows best — that the same Sir
Horace was an ill-used man. Now, of all the objects of
public sympathy and interest, next after a foreign emperor
on a visit at Buckingham Palace, or a newly arrived hippopotamus at the Zoölogical Gardens, there is nothing your
British public is so fond of as "an ill-used man." It is
essential, however, to his great success that he be ill-used
in high places; that his enemies and calumniators should
have been, if not princes, at least dukes and marquises and
great dignitaries of the state. Let him only be supposed to
be martyred by these, and there is no saying where his
popularity may be carried. A very general impression is
current that the mass of the nation is more or less "ill-
used," — denied its natural claims and just rewards. To hit
upon, therefore, a good representation of this hard usage,
to find a tangible embodiment of this great injustice, is a
discovery that is never unappreciated.

To read his speech of the night before, and to peruse the
ill-scrawled bulletin of his health at the hall door in the
morning, made up the measure of his popularity, and the
world exclaimed, "Think of the man they have treated in
this fashion!" Every one framed the indictment to his own
taste; nor was the wrong the less grievous that none could
give it a name. Even cautious men fell into the trap, and
were heard to say, "If all we hear be true, Upton has not
been fairly treated."

What an air of confirmation to all these rumors did it
give, when the evening papers announced in the most striking type: RESIGNATION OF SIR HORACE UPTON. If the
terms in which he communicated that step to the Premier
were not before the world, the date, the very night of the
debate, showed that the resolution had been come to
suddenly.

Some of the journals affected to be in the whole secret of
the transaction, and only waiting the opportune moment to
announce it to the world. The dark, mysterious paragraphs
in which journalists show their no-meanings abounded, and
menacing hints were thrown out that the country would no
longer submit to — Heaven knows what. There was, besides
all this, a very considerable amount of that catechetical

inquiry, which, by suggesting a number of improbabilities, hopes to arrive at the likely, and thus, by asking questions where they had a perfect confidence they would never be answered, they seemed to overwhelm their adversaries with shame and discomfiture. The great fact, however, was indisputable, — Upton had resigned.

To the many who looked up at the shuttered windows of his sad-looking London house, this reflection occurred naturally enough, — How little the poor sufferer, on his sick bed, cared for the contest that raged around him; how far away were, in all probability, his thoughts from that world of striving and ambition whose waves came to his door-sills. Let us, in that privilege which belongs to us, take a peep within the curtained room, where a bright fire is blazing, and where, seated behind a screen, Sir Horace is now penning a note; a bland half smile rippling his features as some pleasant conceit has flashed across his mind. We have rarely seen him looking so well. The stimulating events of the last few days have done for him more than all the counsels of his doctors, and his eyes are brighter and his cheeks fuller than usual. A small miniature hangs suspended by a narrow ribbon round his neck, and a massive gold bracelet adorns one wrist, — " two souvenirs" which he stops to contemplate as he writes; nor is there a touch of sorrowful meaning in the glance he bestows upon them, — the look rather seems the self-complacent regard that a successful general might bestow on the decorations he had won by his valor. It is essentially vainglorious.

More than once has he paused to read over the sentence he has written, and one may see, by the motion of his lips as he reads, how completely he has achieved the sentiment he would express. "Yes, charming Princess," said he, perusing the lines before him. " I 've once more to throw myself at your feet, and reiterate the assurances of a devotion which has formed the happiness of my existence." ("That does not sound quite French, after all," muttered he: "better perhaps: 'has formed the religion of my heart.'") " I know you will reproach my precipitancy; I feel how your judgment, unerring as it ever is, will condemn what may seem a sudden ebullition of temper; but, I ask, is this amongst the catalogue of my weaknesses? Am I of that clay which is always fissured when heated? No. *You* know me better, — *you* alone of all the world have the clew to a heart whose affections are all your own. The few explanations of all that has happened must be reserved for our meeting. Of course, neither the newspapers nor the reviews have any conception of the truth. Four words will set your heart at ease, and these you must have: 'I have done wisely;' with that assurance you have no more to fear. I mean to leave this in all secrecy by the end of the week. I shall go over to Brussels, where you can address me under the name of Richard Bingham. I shall only remain there to watch events for a day or two, and thence on to Geneva.

"I am quite charmed with your account of poor Lady G——, though, as I read, I can detect how all the fascinations you tell of were but reflected glories. Your view of her situation is admirable, and, by your skilful tactique, it is she herself that ostracizes the society that would only have accepted her on sufferance. How true is your remark as to the great question at issue, — not her guilt or innocence, but what danger might accrue to others from infractions that invite publicity. The cabinet were discussing t' other day a measure by which sales of estated property could be legalized without those tiresome and costly researches into title which, in a country where confiscations were frequent, became at last endless labor. Don't you think that some such measure might be beneficially adopted as regards female character? Could there not be invented a species of social guarantee which, rejecting all investigation into bygones after a certain limit, would confer a valid title that none might dispute?

"Lawyers tell us that no man's property would stand the test of a search for title. Are we quite certain how far the other sex are our betters in this respect; and might it not be wise to interpose a limit beyond which research need not proceed?

"I concur in all you say about G—— himself. He was always looking for better security than he needed, — a great mistake, whether the investment consist of our affections or our money. Physicians say that if any man could only see the delicate anatomy on which his life depends, and watch the play of those organs that sustain him, he would not have courage to move a step or utter a loud word. Might we not carry the analogy into morals, and ask, is it safe or prudent in us to investigate too deeply? are we wise in dissecting motives? or would it not be better to enjoy our moral as we do our material health, without seeking to assure ourselves further?

" Besides all this, the untravelled Englishman — and such was Glencore when he married — never can be brought to understand the harmless levities of foreign life. Like a fresh-water sailor, he always fancies the boat is going to upset, and he throws himself out at the first 'jobble'! I own to you frankly, I never knew the case in question ; 'how far she went,' is a secret to me. I might have heard the whole story. It required some address in me to escape it ; but I do detest these narrations, where truth is marred by passion, and all just inferences confused and confounded with vague and absurd suspicions.

" Glencore's conduct throughout was little short of insanity ; like a man who, hearing his banker is insecure, takes refuge in insolvency, he ruins himself to escape embarrassment. They tell me here that the shock has completely deranged his intellect, and that he lives a life of melancholy isolation in that old castle in Ireland.

" How few men in this world can count the cost of their actions, and make up that simple calculation, 'How much shall I have to pay for it?'

" Take any view one pleases of the case, would it not have been better for him to have remained in the world and of it? Would not its pleasures, even its cares, have proved better 'distractions' than his own brooding thoughts? If a man have a secret ailment, does he parade it in public? Why, then, this exposure of a pain for which there is no sympathy?

" Life, after all, is only a system of compensations. Wish it to be whatever you please, but accept it as it really is, and make the best of it! For my own part, I have ever felt

like one who, having got a most disastrous account of a
road he was about to travel, is delightfully surprised to find
the way better and the inns more comfortable than he looked
for. In the main, men and women are very good; our
mistake is, expecting to find people always in our own
humor. Now, if one is very rich, this is practical enough;
but the mass must be content to encounter disparity of
mood and difference of taste at every step. There is, therefore, some tact required in conforming to these ' irregulari-
ties,' and unhappily everybody has not got tact.

" You, charming Princess, have tact; but you have beauty,
wit. fascination. rank, — all that can grace high station,
and all that high station can reflect upon great natural gifts;
that *you* should see the world through a rose-tinted medium
is a very condition of your identity; and there is truth, as
well as good philosophy, in this view! You have often
told me that if people were not exactly all that strict moralists might wish, yet that they made up a society very pleasant and livable withal, and that there was also a floating
capital of kindness and good feeling quite sufficient to trade
upon, and even grow richer by negotiating!

" People who live out of the world, or, what comes to
the same thing, in a little world of their own, are ever craving after perfectibility, — just as, in time of peace, nations
only accept in their armies six-foot grenadiers and gigantic
dragoons. Let the pressure of war or emergency arise,
however, or, in other words, let there be the real business of
life to be done, then the standard is lowered at once, and the
battle is sought and won by very inferior agency. Now,
show troops and show qualities are very much alike; they
are a measure of what would be very charming to arrive at,
were it only praticable! Oh that poor Glencore had only
learned this lesson. instead of writing nonsense verses at
Eton !

" The murky domesticities of England have no correla-
tives in the sunny enjoyments of Italian life; and John
Bull has got a fancy that virtue is only cultivated where
there are coal fires. stuff curtains, and a window tax. Why.
then, in the name of Doctors' Commons, does he marry a
foreigner? "

Just as Upton had written these words, his servant presented him with a visiting-card.

" Lord Glencore!" exclaimed he, aloud. " When was he here?"

" His Lordship is below stairs now, sir. He said he was sure you'd see him."

" Of course; show him up at once. Wait a moment; give me that cane, place those cushions for my feet, draw the curtain, and leave the aconite and ether drops near me, — that will do, thank you."

Some minutes elapsed ere the door was opened; the slow footfall of one ascending the stairs, step by step, was heard, accompanied by the labored respiration of a man breathing heavily; and then Lord Glencore entered, his form worn and emaciated, and his face pale and colorless. With a feeble, uncertain voice, he said, —

" I knew you'd see me, Upton, and I wouldn't go away!" And with this he sank into a chair and sighed deeply.

" Of course, my dear Glencore, you knew it," said the other, feelingly, for he was shocked by the wretched spectacle before him; " even were I more seriously indisposed than — "

" And were you really ill, Upton?" asked Glencore, with a weakly smile.

" Can you ask the question? Have you not seen the evening papers, read the announcement on my door, seen the troops of inquirers in the streets?"

" Yes," sighed he, wearily, " I have heard and seen all you say; and yet I bethought me of a remark I once heard from the Duke of Orleans: 'Monsieur Upton is a most active minister when his health permits; and when it does not, he is the most mischievous intriguant in Europe.' "

" He was always straining at an antithesis; he fancied he could talk like St. Simon, and it really spoiled a very pleasant converser."

" And so you have been very ill?" said Glencore, slowly, and as though he had not heeded the last remark; " so have I also!"

" You seem to me too feeble to be about, Glencore," said Upton, kindly.

"I am so, if it were of any consequence, — I mean, if my life could interest or benefit any one. My head, however, will bear solitude no longer; I must have some one to talk to. I mean to travel; I will leave this in a day or so."

"Come along with me, then; my plan is to make for Brussels, but it must not be spoken of, as I want to watch events there before I remove farther from England."

"So it is all true, then, — you have resigned?" said Glencore.

"Perfectly true."

"What a strange step to take! I remember, more than twenty years ago, your telling me that you'd rather be Foreign Secretary of England than the monarch of any third-rate Continental kingdom."

"I thought so then, and, what is more singular, I think so still."

"And you throw it up at the very moment people are proclaiming your success!"

"You shall hear all my reasons, Glencore, for this resolution, and will, I feel assured, approve of them; but they'd only weary you now."

"Let me know them now, Upton; it is such a relief to me when, even by a momentary interest in anything, I am able to withdraw this poor tired brain from its own distressing thoughts." He spoke these words not only with strong feeling, but even imparted to them a tone of entreaty, so that Upton could not but comply.

"When I wished for the Secretaryship, my dear Glencore," said he, "I fancied the office as it used to be in olden times, when one played the great game of diplomacy with kings and ministers for antagonists, and the world at large for spectators; when consummate skill and perfect secrecy were objects of moment, and when grand combinations rewarded one's labor with all the certainty of a mathematical problem. Every move on the board could be calculated beforehand, no disturbing influences could derange plans that never were divulged till they were accomplished. All that is past and gone; our Constitution, grown every day more and more democratic, rules by the House of Commons. Questions whose treatment demands all the skill of a states-

man and all the address of a man of the world come to be
discussed in open Parliament; correspondence is called for,
despatches and even private notes are produced; and while
the State you are opposed to revels in the security of secrecy,
your whole game is revealed to the world in the shape of a
blue-book.

" Nor is this all: the debaters on these nice and intricate
questions, involving the most far-reaching speculation of
statesmanship, are men of trade and enterprise, who view
every international difficulty only in its relation to their
peculiar interests. National greatness, honor, and security
are nothing, — the maintenance of that equipoise which
preserves peace is nothing, — the nice management which,
by the exhibition of courtesy here, or of force there, is
nothing compared to alliances that secure us ample supplies
of raw material, and abundant markets for manufactures.
Diplomacy has come to this!"

" But you must have known all this before you accepted
office; you had seen where the course of events led to, and
were aware that the House ruled the country."

" Perhaps I did not recognize the fact to its full extent.
Perhaps I fancied I could succeed in modifying the system,"
said Upton, cautiously.

" A hopeless undertaking!" said Glencore.

" I'm not quite so certain of that," said Upton, pausing
for a while as he seemed to reflect. When he resumed, it
was in a lighter and more flippant tone: " To make short of
it, I saw that I could not keep office on these conditions,
but I did not choose to go out as a beaten man. For my
pride's sake I desired that my reasons should be reserved
for myself alone; for my actual benefit it was necessary
that I should have a hold over my colleagues in office.
These two conditions were rather difficult to combine, but
I accomplished them.

" I had interested the King so much in my views as to
what the Foreign Office ought to be that an interchange of
letters took place, and his Majesty imparted to me his fullest
confidence in disparagement of the present system. This
correspondence was a perfect secret to the whole Cabinet;
but when it had arrived at a most confidential crisis, I sug-

gested to the King that Cloudeslie should be consulted. I knew well that this would set the match to the train. No sooner did Cloudeslie learn that such a correspondence had been carried on for months without his knowledge, views stated, plans promulgated, and the King's pleasure taken on questions not one of which should have been broached without his approval and concurrence, than he declared he would not hold the seals of office another hour. The King, well knowing his temper, and aware what a terrific exposure might come of it, sent for me, and asked what was to be done. I immediately suggested my own resignation as a sacrifice to the difficulty and to the wounded feelings of the Duke. Thus did I achieve what I sought for. I imposed a heavy obligation on the King and the Premier, and I have secured secrecy as to my motives, which none will ever betray.

"I only remained for the debate of the other night, for I wanted a little public enthusiasm to mark the fall of the curtain."

"So that you still hold them as your debtors?" asked Glencore.

"Without doubt, I do; my claim is a heavy one."

"And what would satisfy it?"

"If my health would stand England," said Upton, leisurely. "I'd take a peerage; but as this murky atmosphere would suffocate me, and as I don't care for the latter without the political privileges, I have determined to have the 'Garter.'"

"The Garter! a blue ribbon!" exclaimed Glencore, as though the insufferable coolness with which the pretension was announced might justify any show of astonishment.

"Yes; I had some thoughts of India, but the journey deters me, — in fact, as I have enough to live on, I'd rather devote the remainder of my days to rest, and the care of this shattered constitution." It is impossible to convey to the reader the tender and affectionate compassion with which Sir Horace seemed to address these last words to himself.

"Do you ever look upon yourself as the luckiest fellow in Europe, Upton?" asked Glencore.

"No," sighed he; "I occasionally fancy I have been hardly dealt with by fortune.   I have only to throw my eyes around me, and see a score of men, richer and more elevated than myself, not one of whom has capacity for even a third-rate task, so that really the self-congratulation you speak of has not occurred to me."

"But, after all, you have had a most successful career —"

"Look at the matter this way, Glencore; there are about six — say six men in all Europe — who have a little more common sense than all the rest of the world: I could tell you the names of five of them." If there was a supreme boastfulness in the speech, the modest delivery of it completely mystified the hearer, and he sat gazing with wonderment at the man before him.

CHAPTER XLV

"Have you any plans, Glencore?" asked Upton, as they posted along towards Dover.

"None," was the brief reply.

"Nor any destination you desire to reach?"

"Just as little."

"Such a state as yours, then, I take it, is about the best thing going in life. Every move one makes is attended with so many adverse considerations, — every goal so separated from us by unforeseen difficulties, — that an existence, even without what is called an object, has certain great advantages."

"I am curious to hear them" said the other, half cynically.

"For myself," said Upton, not accepting the challenge, "the brief intervals of comparative happiness I have enjoyed have been in periods when complete repose, almost torpor, has surrounded me, and when the mere existence of the day has engaged my thoughts."

"What became of memory all this while?"

"Memory!" said Upton, laughing, "I hold my memory in proper subjection. It no more dares obtrude upon me uncalled for than would my valet come into my room till I ring for him. Of the slavery men endure from their own faculties I have no experience."

"And, of course, no sympathy for them."

"I will not say that I cannot compassionate sufferings, though I have not felt them."

"Are you quite sure of that?" asked Glencore, almost sternly; "is not your very pity a kind of contemptuous sentiment towards those who sorrow without reason, — the strong man's estimate of the weak man's sufferings? Believe me, there is no true condolence where there is not the same experience of woe!"

"I should be sorry to lay down so narrow a limit to fellow-feeling," said Upton.

"You told me a few moments back," said Glencore, "that your memory was your slave. How, then, can you feel for one like me, whose memory is his master? How understand a path that never wanders out of the shadow of the past?"

There was such an accent of sorrow impressed upon these words that Upton did not desire to prolong a discussion so painful; and thus, for the remainder of the way, little was interchanged between them. They crossed the strait by night, and as Upton stole upon deck after dusk, he found Glencore seated near the wheel, gazing intently at the lights on shore, from which they were fast receding.

"I am taking my last look at England, Upton," said he, affecting a tone of easy indifference.

"You surely mean to go back again one of these days?" said Upton.

"Never, never!" said he, solemnly. "I have made all my arrangements for the future, — every disposition regarding my property; I have neglected nothing, so far as I know, of those claims which, in the shape of relationship, the world has such reverence for; and now I bethink me of myself. I shall have to consult you, however, about this boy," said he, faltering in the words. "The objection I once entertained to his bearing my name exists no longer; he may call himself Massy, if he will. The chances are," added he, in a lower and more feeling voice, "that he rejects a name that will only remind him of a wrong!"

"My dear Glencore," said Upton, with real tenderness, "do I apprehend you aright? Are you at last convinced that you have been unjust? Has the moment come in which your better judgment rises above the evil counsels of prejudice and passion — "

"Do you mean, am I assured of her innocence?" broke in Glencore, wildly. "Do you imagine, if I were so, that I could withhold my hand from taking a life so infamous and dishonored as mine? The world would have no parallel for such a wretch! Mark me, Upton!" cried he, fiercely, " there is no torture I have yet endured would equal the bare possibility of what you hint at."

" Good Heavens! Glencore, do not let me suppose that selfishness has so marred and disfigured your nature that this is true. Bethink you of what you say. Would it not be the crowning glory of your life to repair a dreadful wrong, and acknowledge before the world that the fame you had aspersed was without stain or spot? "

" And with what grace should I ask the world to believe me? Is it when expiating the shame of a falsehood that I should call upon men to accept me as truthful? Have I not proclaimed her, from one end of Europe to the other, dishonored? If *she* be absolved, what becomes of *me* ? "

" This is unworthy of you, Glencore," said Upton, severely; " nor, if illness and long suffering had not impaired your judgment, had you ever spoken such words. I say once more, that if the day came that you could declare to the world that her fame had no other reproach than the injustice of your own unfounded jealousy, that day would be the best and the proudest of your life."

" The proud day that published me a calumniator of all that I was most pledged to defend, — the deliberate liar against the obligation of the holiest of all contracts! You forget, Upton, — but I do not forget, — that it was by this very argument you once tried to dissuade me from my act of vengeance. You told me — ay, in words that still ring in my ears — to remember that if by any accident or chance her innocence might be proven, I could never avail myself of the indication without first declaring my own unworthiness to profit by it; that if the Wife stood forth in all the pride of purity, the Husband would be a scoff and a shame throughout the world! "

" When I said so," said Upton, " it was to turn you from a path that could not but lead to ruin; I endeavored to deter you by an appeal that interested even your selfishness."

" Your subtlety has outwitted itself, Upton," said Glencore, with a bitter irony; " it is not the first instance on record where blank cartridge has proved fatal! "

"One thing is perfectly clear," said Upton, boldly, "the man who shrinks from the repair of a wrong he has done, on the consideration of how it would affect himself and his own interests, shows that he cares more for the outward show of honor than its real and sustaining power."

"And will you tell me, Upton, that the world's estimate of a man's fame is not essential to his self-esteem, or that there yet lived one who would brave obloquy without, by the force of something within him?"

"This I will tell you," replied Upton, "that he who balances between the two is scarcely an honest man, and that he who accepts the show for the substance is not a wise one."

"These are marvellous sentiments to hear from one whose craft has risen to a proverb, and whose address in life is believed to be not his meanest gift."

"I accept the irony in all good humor; I go farther, Glencore, I stoop to explain. When any one in the great and eventful journey of life seeks to guide himself safely, he has to weigh all the considerations, and calculate all the combinations adverse to him. The straight road is rarely, or never, possible; even if events were, which they are not, easy to read, they must be taken in combination with others, and with their consequences. The path of action becomes necessarily devious and winding, and compromises are called for at every step. It is not in the moment of shipwreck that a man stops to inquire into petty details of the articles he throws into a long-boat; he is bent on saving himself as best he can. He seizes what is next to him, if it suit his purpose. Now, were he to act in this manner in all the quiet security of his life on shore, his conduct would be highly blamable. No emergency would warrant his taking what belonged to another, — no critical moment would drive him to the instinct of self-preservation. Just the same is the interval between action and reflection. Give me time and forethought, and I will employ something better and higher than craft. My subtlety, as you like to call it, is not my best weapon; I only use it in emergency."

"I read the matter differently," said Glencore, sulkily; "I could, perhaps, offer another explanation of your practice."

"Pray let me hear it; we are all in confidence here, and I promise you I will not take badly whatever you say to me."

Glencore sat silent and motionless.

"Come, shall I say it for you, Glencore? for I think I know what is passing in your mind."

The other nodded, and he went on, —

"You would tell me, in plain words, that I keep my craft for myself; my high principle for my friends."

Glencore only smiled, but Upton continued, —

"So, then, I have guessed aright; and the very worst you can allege against this course is, that what I bestow is better than what I retain!"

"One of Solomon's proverbs may be better than a shilling; but which would a hungry man rather have? I want no word-fencing, Upton; still less do I seek what might sow distrust between us. This much, however, has life taught me: the great trials of this world are like its great maladies. Providence has meant them to be fatal. We call in the doctor in the one case, or the counsellor in the other, out of habit rather than out of hope. Our own consciousness has already whispered that nothing can be of use; but we like to do as our neighbors, and so we take remedies and follow injunctions to the last. The wise man quickly detects by the character of the means how emergent is the case believed to be, and rightly judges that recourse to violent measures implies the presence of great peril. If he be really wise, then he desists at once from what can only torture his few remaining hours. They can be given to better things than the agonies of such agency. To this exact point has my case come, and by the counsels you have given me do I read my danger! Your only remedy is as bad as the malady it is meant to cure! I cannot take it!"

"Accepting your own imagery, I would say," said Upton, "that you are one who will not submit to an operation of some pain that he might be cured."

Glencore sat moodily for some moments without speaking; at last he said, —

"I feel as though continual change of place and scene would be a relief to me. Let us rendezvous, therefore, somewhere for the autumn, and meanwhile I'll wander about alone."

"What direction do you purpose to take?"

"The Schwarzwald and the Höhlenthal, first. I want to revisit a place I knew in happier days. Memory must surely have something besides sorrows to render us. I owned a little cottage there once, near Steig. I fished and read Uhland for a summer long. I wonder if I could resume the same life. I knew the whole village, — the blacksmith, the schoolmaster, the Dorfrichter, — all of them. Good, kind souls they were: how they wept when we parted! Nothing consoled them but my having purchased the cottage, and promised to come back again!"

Upton was glad to accept even this much of interest in the events of life, and drew Glencore on to talk of the days he had passed in this solitary region.

As in the dreariest landscape a ray of sunlight will reveal some beautiful effects, making the eddies of the dark pool to glitter, lighting up the russet moss, and giving to the half-dried lichen a tinge of bright color, so will, occasionally, memory throw over a life of sorrow a gleam of happier meaning. Faces and events, forms and accents, that once found the way to our hearts, come back again, faintly and imperfectly it may be, but with a touch that revives in us what we once were. It is the one sole feature in which self-love becomes amiable, when, looking back on our past, we cherish the thought of a time before the world had made us sceptical and hard-hearted!

Glencore warmed as he told of that tranquil period when poetry gave a color to his life, and the wild conceptions of genius ran like a thread of gold through the whole web of existence. He quoted passages that had struck him for their beauty or their truthfulness; he told how he had tried to allure his own mind to the tone that vibrated in " the magic music of verse," and how the very attempt had inspired him with gentler thoughts, a softer charity, and a more tender benevolence towards his fellows.

"Tieck is right, Upton, when he says there are two natures in us, distinct and apart: one, the imaginative and ideal; the other, the actual and the sensual. Many shake them together and confound them, making of the incongruous mixture that vile compound of inconsistency where the beautiful and the true are ever warring with the deformed and the false; their lives a long struggle with themselves, a perpetual contest between high hope and base enjoyment. A few keep them apart, retaining, through their worldliness, some hallowed spot in the heart, where ignoble desires and mean aspirations have never dared to come. A fewer still have made the active work of life subordinate to the guiding spirit of purity, adventuring on no road unsanctioned by high and holy thoughts, caring for no ambitions but such as make us nobler and better.

"I once had a thought of such a life; and even the memory of it, like the prayers we have learned in our childhood, has a hallowing influence over after years. If that poor boy, Upton," and his lips trembled on the words, — "if that poor boy could have been brought up thus humbly! If he had been taught to know no more than an existence of such simplicity called for, what a load of care might it have spared *his* heart and *mine!*"

"You have read over those letters I gave you about him?" asked Upton, who eagerly availed himself of the opportunity to approach an almost forbidden theme.

"I have read them over and over," said Glencore, sadly; "in all the mention of him I read the faults of my own nature, — a stubborn spirit of pride that hardens as much as elevates; a resentful temper, too prone to give way to its own impulses; an over-confidence in himself, too, always ready to revenge its defeats on the world about him. These are his defects, and they are mine. Poor fellow, that he should inherit all that I have of bad, and yet not be heir to the accidents of fortune which make others so lenient to faults!"

If Upton heard these words with much interest, no less was he struck by the fact that Glencore made no inquiry whatever as to the youth's fate. The last letter of the packet revealed the story of an eventful duel and the boy's escape from Massa by night, with his subsequent arrest by the police; and yet in the face of incidents like these he continued to speculate on traits of mind and character, nor

even adverted to the more closely touching events of his
fate. By many an artful hint and ingenious device did Sir
Horace try to tempt him to some show of curiosity; but all
were fruitless. Glencore would talk freely and willingly of
the boy's disposition and his capacity; he would even speculate on the successes and failures such a temperament might
meet with in life; but still he spoke as men might speak of a
character in a fiction, ingeniously weighing casualties and
discussing chances; never, even by accident, approaching
the actual story of his life, or seeming to attach any interest
to his destiny.

Upton's shrewd intelligence quickly told him that this
reserve was not accidental; and he deliberated within himself how far it was safe to invade it.

At length he resumed the attempt by adroitly alluding to
the spirited resistance the boy had made to his capture, and
the consequences one might naturally enough ascribe to a
proud and high-hearted youth thus tyrannically punished.

"I have heard something," said Upton, "of the sever-
ities practised at Kuffstein, and they recall the horrible
tales of the Inquisition; the terrible contrivances to extort
confessions. — expedients that often break down the intellect
whose secrets they would discover; so that one actually
shudders at the name of a spot so associated with evil."

Glencore placed his hands over his face, but did not utter
a word; and again Upton went on urging, by every device
he could think of, some indication that might mean interest,
if not anxiety, when suddenly he felt Glencore's hand grasp
his arm with violence.

"No more of this, Upton," cried he, sternly; "you do
not know the torture you are giving me." There was a long
and painful pause between them, at the end of which Glencore spoke, but it was in a voice scarcely above a whisper,
and every accent of which trembled with emotion. "You
remember one sad and memorable night, Upton, in that old
castle in Ireland. — the night when I came to the resolution
of this vengeance! I sent for the boy to my room; we
were alone there together, face to face. It was such a scene
as could brook no witness, nor dare I now recall its details
as they occurred. He came in frankly and boldly, as he

felt he had a right to do. How he left that room, — cowed, abashed, and degraded, — I have yet before me. Our meeting did not exceed many minutes in duration; neither of us could have endured it longer. Brief as it was, we ratified a compact between us: it was this, — neither was ever to question or inquire after the other, as no tie should unite, no interest should bind us. Had you seen him then, Upton," cried Glencore, wildly, " the proud disdain with which he listened to my attempts at excuse, the haughty distance with which he seemed to reject every thought of complaint, the stern coldness with which he heard me plan out his future, — you would have said that some curse had fallen upon my heart, or it could never have been dead to traits which proclaimed him to be my own. In that moment it was my lot to be like him who held out his own right hand to be first burned, ere he gave his body to the flames.

" We parted without an embrace; not even a farewell was spoken between us. While I gloried in his pride, had he but yielded ever so little, had one syllable of weakness, one tear escaped him, I had given up my project, reversed all my planned vengeance, and taken him to my heart as my own. But no! He was resolved on proving by his nature that he was of that stern race from which, by a falsehood, I was about to exclude him. It was as though my own blood hurled a proud defiance to me.

" As he walked slowly to the door, his glove fell from his hand. I stealthily caught it up. I wanted to keep it as a memorial of that bitter hour; but he turned hastily around and plucked it from my hand. The action was even a rude one; and with a mocking smile, as though he read my meaning and despised it, he departed.

" You now have heard the last secret of my heart in this sad history. Let us speak of it no more." And with this, Glencore arose and left the deck.

CHAPTER XLVI.

THE FLOOD IN THE MAGRA.

WHEN it rains in Italy it does so with a passionate ardor that bespeaks an unusual pleasure. It is no " soft dissolving in tears," but a perfect outburst of woe, — wailing in accents the very wildest, and deluging the land in torrents. Mountain streams that were rivulets in the morning, before noon arrives are great rivers, swollen and turbid, carrying away massive rocks from their foundations, and tearing up large trees by the roots. The dried-up stony bed you have crossed a couple of hours back with unwetted feet is now the course of a stream that would defy the boldest.

These sudden changes are remarkably frequent along that beautiful tract between Nice and Massa, and which is known as the " Riviera di Levante." The rivers, fed from innumerable streams that pour down from the Apennines, are almost instantaneously swollen; and as their bed continually slopes towards the sea, the course of the waters is one of headlong velocity. Of these, the most dangerous by far is the Magra. The river, which even in dry seasons is a considerable stream, becomes, when fed by its tributaries, a very formidable body of water, stretching full a mile in width, and occasionally spreading a vast sheet of foam close to the very outskirts of Sarzana. The passage of the river is all the more dangerous at these periods as it approaches the sea, and more than one instance is recorded where the stout raft, devoted to the use of travellers, has been carried away to the ocean.

Where the great post-road from Genoa to the South passes, a miserable shealing stands, half hidden in tall osiers, and surrounded with a sedgy, swampy soil the foot

sinks in at every step. This is the shelter of the boatmen
who navigate the raft, and who, in relays by day and night,
are in waiting for the service of travellers. In the dreary
days of winter, or in the drearier nights, it is scarcely possible to imagine a more hopeless spot; deep in the midst of
a low marshy tract, the especial home of tertian fever, with
the wild stream roaring at the very door-sill, and the thunder
of the angry ocean near, it is indeed all that one can picture
of desolation and wretchedness. Nor do the living features
of the scene relieve its gloomy influence. Though strong
men, and many of them in the prime of life, premature age
and decay seem to have settled down upon them. Their
lustreless eyes and leaden lips tell of ague, and their sad,
thoughtful faces bespeak those who are often called upon to
meet peril, and who are destined to lives of emergency and
hazard.

It was in the low and miserable hut we speak of, just as
night set in of a raw November, that four of these raftsmen sat at their smoky fire, in company with two travellers
on foot, whose humble means compelled them to await the
arrival of some one rich enough to hire the raft. Meanly clad
and wayworn were the strangers who now sat endeavoring to
dry their dripping clothes at the blaze, and conversing in a
low tone together. If the elder, dressed in a russet-colored
blouse and a broad-leafed hat, his face almost hid in beard
and moustaches, seemed by his short and almost grotesque
figure a travelling showman, the appearance of the younger,
despite all the poverty of his dress, implied a very different
class.

He was tall and well knit, with a loose activity in all
his gestures which almost invariably characterizes the
Englishman; and though his dark hair and his bronzed
cheek gave him something of a foreign look, there was a
calm, cold self-possession in his air that denoted the Anglo-
Saxon. He sat smoking his cigar, his head resting on one
hand, and evidently listening with attention to the words
of his companion. The conversation that passed will save
us the trouble of introducing them to our reader, if he have
not already guessed them.

"If we don't wait," said the elder, "till somebody

richer and better off than ourselves comes, we'll have to pay seven francs for passin' in such a night as this."

"It is a downright robbery to ask so much," cried the other, angrily. "What so great danger is there, or what so great hardship, after all?"

"There is both one and the other, I believe," replied he, in a tone evidently meant to moderate his passion; "and just look at the poor craytures that has to do it. They're as weak as a bit of wet paper; they haven't strength to make themselves heard when they talk out there beside the river."

"The fellow yonder," said the youth, "has got good brawny arms and sinewy legs of his own."

"Ay, and he is starved after all. A cut of rye bread and an onion won't keep the heart up, nor a jug of red vinegar, though ye call it grape-juice. On my conscience, I'm thinkin' that the only people that preserves their strength upon nothin' is the Irish. I used to carry the bags over Slieb-na-boregan mountain and the Turk's Causeway on wet potatoes and buttermilk, and never a day late for eleven years."

"What a life!" cried the youth, in an accent of utter pity.

"Faix, it was an elegant life, — that is, when the weather was anyways good. With a bright sun shinin' and a fine fresh breeze blowin' the white clouds away over the Atlantic, my road was a right cheery one, and I went along inventin' stories, sometimes fairy tales, sometimes makin' rhymes to myself, but always happy and contented. There wasn't a bit of the way I hadn't a name for in my own mind, either some place I read about, or some scene in a story of my own; but better than all, there was a dog, — a poor starved lurcher he was, — with a bit of the tail cut off; he used to meet me, as regular as the clock, on the side of Currah-na-geelah, and come beside me down to the ford every day in the year. No temptation nor flattery would bring him a step farther. I spent three-quarters of an hour once trying it, but to no good; he took leave of me on the bank of the river, and went away back with his head down, as if he was grievin' over something. Wasn't that mighty curious?"

" Perhaps, like ourselves, Billy, he was n't quite sure of his passport," said the other, dryly.

" Faix, may be so," replied he, with perfect seriousness. " My notion was that he was a kind of an outlaw, a chap that maybe bit a child of the family, or ate a lamb of a flock given him to guard. But indeed his general appearance and behavior was n't like that; he had good manners, and, starved as he was, he never snapped the bread out of my fingers, but took it gently, though his eyes was dartin' out of his head with eagerness all the while."

" A great test of good breeding, truly," said the youth, sadly. " It must be more than a mere varnish when it stands the hard rubs of life in this wise."

" 'T is the very notion occurred to myself. It was the dhrop of good blood in him made him what he was."

Stealthy and fleeting as was the look that accompanied these words, the youth saw it, and blushed to the very top of his forehead. " The night grows milder," said he, to relieve the awkwardness of the moment by any remark.

" It's a mighty grand sight out there now," replied the other; " there's three miles if there's an inch of white foam dashing down to the sea, that breaks over the bar with a crash like thunder; big trees are sweepin' past, and pieces of vine trellises, and a bit of a mill-wheel, all carried off just like twigs on a stream."

" Would money tempt those fellows, I wonder, to venture out on such a night as this?"

" To be sure; and why not? The daily fight poverty maintains with existence dulls the sense of every danger but what comes of want. Don't I know it myself? The poor man has no inimy but hunger; for, ye see, the other vexations and troubles of life, there's always a way of gettin' round them. You can chate even grief, and you can slip away from danger: but there's no circumventin' an empty stomach."

" What a tyrant is then your rich man!" sighed the youth, heavily.

" That he is. ' Dives honoratus. Pulcher rex denique regum.' You may do as you please if ye 'r rich as a Begum."

"A free translation, rather, Billy," said the other, laughing.

"Or ye might render it this way," said Billy, —

> "If ye 've money enough and to spare in the bank,
> The world will give ye both beauty and rank.

And I 've nothing to say agin it," continued he. "The raal stimulus to industhry in life, is to make wealth powerful. Gettin' and heapin' up money for money's sake is a debasin' kind of thing; but makin' a fortune, in order that you may extind your influence, and mowld the distinies of others, — that's grand."

"And see what comes of it!" cried the youth, bitterly. "Mark the base and unworthy subserviency it leads to; see the race of sycophants it begets."

"I have you there, too," cried Billy, with all the exultation of a ready debater. "Them dirty varmint ye speak of is the very test of the truth I 'm tellin' ye. 'T is because they won't labor — because they won't work — that they are driven to acts of sycophancy and meanness. The spirit of industhry saves a man even the excuse of doin' anything low!"

"And how often, from your own lips, have I listened to praises at your poor humble condition; rejoicings that your lot in life secured you against the cares of wealth and grandeur!"

"And you will again, plaze God! if I live, and you presarve your hearin'. What would I be if I was rich, but an ould — an ould voluptuary?" said Billy, with great emphasis on a word he had some trouble in discovering. "Atin' myself sick with delicacies, and drinkin' cordials all day long. How would I know the uses of wealth? Like all other vulgar creatures, I 'd be buyin' with my money the respect that I ought to be buyin' with my qualities. It 's the very same thing you see in a fair or a market, — the country girls goin' about, hobbled and crippled with shoes on, that, if they had bare feet, could walk as straight as a rush. Poverty is not ungraceful itself. It 's tryin' to be what is n't natural, spoils people entirely."

"I think I hear voices without. Listen!" cried the youth.

"It's only the river; it's risin' every minute."

"No, that was a shout. I heard it distinctly. Ay, the boatmen hear it now!"

"It is a travelling-carriage. I see the lamps," cried one of the men, as he stood at the door and looked landward. "They may as well keep the road; there's no crossing the Magra to-night!"

By this time the postilions' whips commenced that chorus of cracking by which they are accustomed to announce all arrivals of importance.

"Tell them to go back, Beppo," said the chief of the raftsmen to one of his party. "If we might try to cross with the mail-bags in a boat, there's not one of us would attempt the passage on the raft."

To judge from the increased noise and uproar, the travellers' impatience had now reached its highest point; but to this a slight lull succeeded, probably occasioned by the parley with the boatman.

"They'll give us five Napoleons for the job," said Beppo, entering, and addressing his chief.

"Per Dio, that won't support our families if we leave them fatherless," muttered the other. "Who and what are they that can't wait till morning?"

"Who knows?" said Beppo, with a genuine shrug of native indifference. "Princes, belike!"

"Princes or beggars, we all have lives to save!" mumbled out an old man, as he reseated himself by the fire.. Meanwhile the courier had entered the hut, and was in earnest negotiation with the chief, who, however, showed no disposition to run the hazard of the attempt.

"Are you all cowards alike?" said the courier, in all the insolence of his privileged order; "or is it a young fellow of your stamp that shrinks from the risk of a wet jacket?"

This speech was addressed to the youth, whom he had mistaken for one of the raftsmen.

"Keep your coarse speeches for those who will bear them, my good fellow," said the other, boldly, "or mayhap the first wet jacket here will be one with gold lace on the collar."

"He's not one of us; he's a traveller," quickly inter-

24

posed the chief, who saw that an angry scene was brewing.
"He's only waiting to cross the river," muttered he in a
whisper, "when some one comes rich enough to hire the raft."

"*Sacre bleu!* Then he sha'n't come with us; that I'll
promise him," said the courier, whose offended dignity
roused all his ire. "Now, once for all, my men, will you
earn a dozen Napoleons, or not? Here they are for you
if you land us safely at the other side; and never were
you so well paid in your lives for an hour's labor."

The sight of the gold, as it glistened temptingly in his
outstretched hand, appealed to their hearts far more eloquently than all his words, and they gathered in a group
together to hold counsel.

"And you, are you also a distinguished stranger?"
said the courier, addressing Billy, who sat warming his
hands by the embers of the fire.

"Look you, my man," cried the youth, "all the gold in
your master's leathern bag there can give you no claim to
insult those who have offered you no offence. It is enough
that you know that we do not belong to the raft to suffer us
to escape your notice."

"*Sacristi!*" exclaimed the courier, in a tone of insolent
mockery. "I have travelled the road long enough to learn
that one does not need an introduction before addressing a
vagabond."

"Vagabond!" cried the youth, furiously; and he sprang
at the other with the bound of a tiger. The courier quickly
parried the blow aimed at him, and, closely grappled, they
both now reeled out of the hut in terrible conflict. With
that terror of the knife that figures in all Italian quarrels,
the boatmen did not dare to interfere, but looked on as,
wrestling with all their might, the combatants struggled,
each endeavoring to push the other towards the stream.
Billy, too, restrained by force, could not come to the rescue,
and could only by words, screamed out in all the wildness
of his agony, encourage his companion. "Drop on your
knee — catch him by the legs — throw him back — back into
the stream. That's it — that's it! Good luck to ye!"
shouted he, madly, as he fought like a lion with those about
him. Slipping in the slimy soil, they had both now come to
their knees; and after a struggle of some minutes' duration,

rolled, clasped in each other's fierce embrace, down the slope into the river. A plash, and a cry half smothered, were heard, and all was over.

While some threw themselves on the frantic creature, whose agony now overtopped his reason, and who fought to get free, with the furious rage of despair, others, seizing lanterns and torches, hurried along the bank of the torrent to try and rescue the combatants. A sudden winding of the river at the place gave little hope to the search, and it was all but certain that the current must already have swept them down far beyond any chance of succor. Assisted by the servants of the traveller, who speedily were apprised of the disaster, the search was continued for hours, and morning at length began to break over the dreary scene, without one ray of hope. By the gray cold dawn, the yellow flood could be seen for a considerable distance, and the banks too, over which a gauzy mist was hanging; but not a living thing was there! The wild torrent swept along his murky course with a deep monotonous roar. Trunks of trees and leafy branches rose and sank in the wavy flood, but nothing suggested the vaguest hope that either had escaped. The traveller's carriage returned to Spezia, and Billy, now bereft of reason, was conveyed to the same place, fast tied with cords, to restrain him from a violence that threatened his own life and that of any near him.

In the evening of that day a peasant's car arrived at Spezia, conveying the almost lifeless courier, who had been found on the river's bank, near the mouth of the Magra. How he had reached the spot, or what had become of his antagonist, he knew not. Indeed, the fever which soon set in placed him beyond the limit of all questioning, and his incoherent cries and ravings only betrayed the terrible agonies his mind must have passed through.

If this tragic incident, heightened by the actual presence of two of the actors — one all but dead, the other dying — engaged the entire interest and sympathy of the little town, the authorities were actively employed in investigating the event, and ascertaining, so far as they could, to which side the chief blame inclined.

The raftsmen had all been arrested, and were examined carefully, one by one; and now it only remained to obtain from the traveller himself whatever information he could contribute to throw light on the affair.

His passport, showing that he was an English peer, obtained for him all the deference and respect foreign officials are accustomed to render to that title, and the Prefect announced that if it suited his convenience, he would wait on his Lordship at his hotel to receive his deposition.

"I have nothing to depose, no information to give," was the dry and not over-courteous response; but as the visit, it was intimated, was indispensable, he named his hour to admit him.

The bland and polite tone of the Prefect was met by a manner of cold but well-bred ease which seemed to imply that the traveller only regarded the incident in the light of an unpleasant interruption to his journey, but in which he took no other interest. Even the hints thrown out that he ought to consider himself aggrieved and his dignity insulted, produced no effect upon him.

"It was my intention to have halted a few days at Massa, and I could have obtained another courier in the interval," was the cool commentary he bestowed on the incident.

"But your Lordship would surely desire investigation. A man is missing; a great crime may have been committed—"

"Excuse my interrupting; but as I am not, nor can be supposed to be, the criminal,—nor do I feel myself the victim,—while I have not a claim to the character of witness, you would only harass me with interrogatories I could not answer, and excite me to take interest, or at least bestow attention, on what cannot concern me."

"Yet there are circumstances in this case which give it the character of a preconcerted plan," said the Prefect, thoughtfully.

"Perhaps so," said the other, in a tone of utter indifference.

"Certainly, the companion of the man who is missing, and of whom no clew can be discovered, is reported to have uttered your name repeatedly in his ravings."

"My name,—how so?" cried the stranger, hurriedly.

"Yes, my Lord, the name of your passport.—Lord Glencore. Two of those I have placed to watch beside his bed have repeated the same story, and told how he has never ceased to mutter the name to himself in his wanderings."

"Is this a mere fancy?" said the stranger, over whose sickly features a flush now mantled. "Can I see him?"

"Of course. He is in the hospital, and too ill to be removed; but if you will visit him there, I will accompany you."

It was only when a call was made upon Lord Glencore for some bodily exertion that his extreme debility became apparent. Seated at ease in a chair, his manner seemed merely that of natural coolness and apathy; he spoke as one who would not suffer his nature to be ruffled by any avoidable annoyance; but now, as he arose from his seat, and endeavored to walk, one side betrayed unmistakable signs of palsy, and his general frame exhibited the last stage of weakness.

"You see, sir, that the exertion costs its price," said he, with a sad, sickly smile. "I am the wreck of what once was a man noted for his strength."

The other muttered some words of comfort and compassion, and they descended the stairs together.

"I do not know this man," said Lord Glencore, as he gazed on the flushed and fevered face of the sick man, whose ill-trimmed and shaggy beard gave additional wildness to his look; "I have never, to my knowledge, seen him before."

The accents of the speaker appeared to have suddenly struck some chord in the sufferer's intelligence, for he struggled for an instant, and then, raising himself on his elbow, stared fixedly at him. "Not know me?" cried he, in English; "'t is because sorrow and sickness has changed me, then."

"Who are you? Tell me your name?" said Glencore, eagerly.

"I'm Billy Traynor, my Lord, the one you remember, the doctor—"

"And my boy!" screamed Glencore, wildly.

The sick man threw up both his arms in the air, and fell backward with a cry of despair; while Glencore, tottering for an instant, sank with a low groan, and fell senseless on the ground.

CHAPTER XLVII.

A FRAGMENT OF A LETTER.

LONG before Lord Glencore had begun to rally from an attack which had revived all the symptoms of his former illness, Billy Traynor had perfectly recovered, and was assiduously occupied in attending him. Almost the first tidings which Glencore could comprehend assured him that the boy was safe, and living at Massa under the protection of the Chevalier Stubber, and waiting eagerly for Billy to join him. A brief extract from one of the youth's letters to his warm-hearted follower will suffice to show how he himself regarded the incident which befell, and the fortune that lay before him.

. . . .

It was a long swim, of a dark night too, Master Billy; and whenever the arm of a tree would jostle me, as it floated past, I felt as though that "blessed" courier was again upon me, and turned to give fight at once. If it were not that the river took a sudden bend as it nears the sea, I must infallibly have been carried out; but I found myself quite suddenly in slack water, and very soon after it shallowed so much that I could walk ashore. The thought of what became of my adversary weighed more heavily on me when I touched land; indeed, while my own chances of escape were few, I took his fate easily enough. With all its dangers, it was a glorious time, as, hurrying downward in the torrent, through the dark night, the thunder growling overhead, the breakers battering away on the bar, I was the only living thing there to confront that peril! What an emblem of my own fate in everything! A headlong course, an unknown ending, darkness — utter and dayless darkness — around me, and not one single soul to say, "Courage!" There is something splendidly exciting in the notion of having felt thoughts that others have never felt, — of having set footsteps in that untracked sand where no traveller has ever ventured. This impression never left me as I buffeted the murky waves, and struck out boldly through the surfy stream. Nay, more, it will never leave me while I live. I have now proved myself to my own heart! I have been, and for a considerable time too, face to face with death. I have regarded my fate as certain, and yet have I not quailed in spirit or flinched in coolness. No, Billy; I reviewed every step of my strange and wayward life. I bethought me of my childhood, with all its ambitious longings, and my boyish days as sorrow first broke upon me, and I felt that there was a fitness in this darksome and mysterious ending to a life that touched on no other existence. For am I not as much alone in the great world as when I swam there in the yellow flood of the Magra?

As the booming breakers of the sea met my ear, and I saw that I was nearing the wide ocean, I felt as might a soldier when charging an enemy's battery at speed. I was wildly mad with impatience to get forward, and shouted till my voice rang out above the din around me. How the mad cheer echoed in my own heart! It was the trumpet-call of victory.

Was it reaction from all this excitement — the depression that follows past danger — that made me feel low and miserable afterwards? I know I walked along towards Lavenza in listlessness, and when a gendarme stopped to question me, and asked for my passport, I had not even energy to tell him how I came there. Even the intense desire to see that spot once more, — to walk that garden and sit upon that terrace. — all had left me; it was as though the waves had drowned the spirit, and left the limbs to move unguided. He led me beside the walls of the villa, by the little wicket itself, and still I felt no touch of feeling, no memory came back on me: I was indifferent to all! and yet *you* know how many a weary mile I have come just to see them once more, — to revisit a spot where the only day-dream of my life lingered, and where I gave way to the promptings of a hope that have not often warmed this sad heart.

What a sluggish swamp has this nature of mine become, when it needs a hurricane of passion to stir it! Here I am, living, breathing, walking, and sleeping, but without one sentiment that attaches me to existence; and yet do I feel as though whatever endangered life, or jeoparded fame would call me up to an effort and make me of some value to myself.

I went yesterday to see my old studio : sorry things were those strivings of mine, — false endeavors to realize conceptions that must have some other interpreter than marble. Forms are but weak appeals, words are coarse ones; music alone, my dear friend, is the true voice of the heart's meanings.

How a little melody that a peasant girl was singing last night touched me! It was one that *she* used to warble, humming as we walked, like some stray waif thrown up by memory on the waste of life.

So then, at last, I feel I am not a sculptor; still as little, with all your teaching, am I a scholar. The world of active life offers to me none of its seductions; I only recognize what there is in it of vulgar contention and low rivalry. I cannot be any of the hundred things by which men eke out subsistence, and yet I long for the independence of being the arbiter of my own daily life. What is to become of me? Say, dearest, best of friends, — say but the word, and let me try to obey you. What of our old plans of 'savagery'? The fascinations of civilized habits have made no stronger hold upon me since we relinquished that grand idea. Neither you nor I assuredly have any places assigned us at the feast of this old-world life; none have bidden us to it, nor have we even the fitting garments to grace it!

There are moments, however, — one of them is on me while I write, — wherein I should like to storm that strong citadel of social exclusion, and test its strength. Who are they who garrison it? Are they better, and wiser, and purer than their fellows? Are they lifted by the accidents of fortune above the casualties and infirmities of nature? and are they more gentle-minded, more kindly-hearted, and more forgiving than others? This I should wish to know and learn for myself. Would they admit us, for the nonce, to see and judge them? let the Bastard and the Beggar sit down at their board, and make brotherhood with them? I trow not, Billy. They would hand us over to the police!

And my friend the courier was not so far astray when he called us vagabonds!

If I were free, I should, of course, be with you; but I am under a kind of mild bondage here, of which I don't clearly comprehend the meaning. The chief minister has taken me, in some fashion, under his protection, and I am given to understand that no ill is intended me; and, indeed, so far as treatment and moderate liberty are concerned, I have every reason to be satisfied. Still is there something deeply wounding in all this mysterious "consideration." It whispers to me of an interest in me on the part of those who are ashamed to avow it, — of kind feelings held in check by self-esteem. Good Heavens! what have *I* done, that this humiliation should be my portion? There is no need of any subtlety to teach me what I am, and what the world insists I must remain. There is no ambition I dare to strive for, no affection my heart may cherish, no honorable contest I may engage in, but that the utterance of one fatal word may not bar the gate against my entrance, and send me back in shame and confusion. Had I of myself incurred this penalty, there would be in me that stubborn sense of resistance that occurs to every one who counts the gain and loss of all his actions; but I have not done so! In the work of my own degradation I am blameless !

I have just been told that a certain Princess de Sabloukoff is to arrive here this evening, and that I am to wait upon her immediately. Good Heavens! can she be—? The thought has just struck me, and my head is already wandering at the bare notion of it! How I pray that this may not be so; my own shame is enough, and more than I can bear; but to witness that of — ! Can you tell me nothing of this? But even if you can, the tidings will come too late; I shall have already seen her.

I am unable to write more now; my brain is burning, and my hand trembles so that I cannot trace the letters. Adieu till this evening.

Midnight.

I was all in error, dear friend. I have seen her; for the last two hours we have conversed together, and my suspicion had no foundation. She evidently knows all my history, and almost gives me to believe that one day or other I may stand free of this terrible shame that oppresses me. If this were possible, what vengeance would be enough to wreak on those who have thus practised on me? Can you imagine any vendetta that would pay off the heart-corroding misery that has made my youth like a sorrowful old age, dried up hope within me, made my ambition to be a snare, and my love a mere mockery? I could spend a life in the search after this revenge, and think it all too short to exhaust it !

I have much to tell you of this Princess, but I doubt if I can remember it. Her manner meant so much, and yet so little; there was such elegance of expression with such perfect ease, — so much of the *finest* knowledge of life united to a kind of hopeful trust in mankind. that I kept eternally balancing in my mind whether her intelligence or her kindliness had the supremacy. She spoke to me much of the Harleys. Ida was well, and at Florence. She had refused Wahnsdorf's offer of marriage. and though ardently solicited to let time test her decision, persisted in her rejection.

Whether she knew of my affection or not. I cannot say; but I opine not, for she talked of Ida as one whose haughty nature would decline alliance with even an imperial house if they deemed it a condescension; so that the refusal of Wahnsdorf may have been on this ground. But how can it matter to *me* ?

I am to remain here a week. I think they said. Sir Horace Upton is coming on his way south. and wishes to see me; but you will be with me ere that time, and then we can plan our future

together. As this web of intrigue — for so I cannot but feel it
— draws more closely around me, I grow more and more impatient to break bounds and be away! It is evident enough that
my destiny is to be the sport of some accident, lucky or unlucky,
in the fate of others. Shall I await this?

And they have given me money, and fine clothes, and a servant
to wait upon me, and treated me like one of condition. Is this
but another act of the drama, the first scene of which was an old
ruined castle in Ireland? They will fail signally if they think so;
a heart can be broken only once! They may even feel sorry for
what they have done, but I can never forgive them for what
they have made me! Come to me, dear, kind friend, as soon as
you can; you little know how far your presence reconciles me to
the world and to yourself! — Ever yours,

C. M.

This letter Billy Traynor read over and over as he sat by
Glencore's bedside. It was his companion in the long,
dreary hours of the night, and he pondered over it as he sat
in the darkened room at noonday.

" What is that you are crumpling up there? From whom
is the letter?" said Lord Glencore, as Billy hurriedly endeavored to conceal the oft-perused epistle. " Nay," cried
he, suddenly correcting himself, " you need not tell me; I
asked without forethought." He paused a few seconds, and
then went on: " I am now as much recovered as I ever
hope to be, and you may leave me to-morrow. I know that
both your wish and your duty call you elsewhere. Whatever future fortune may betide any of us, you at least have
been a true and faithful friend, and shall never want! As
I count upon your honesty to keep a pledge, I reckon on
your delicacy not asking the reasons for it. You will,
therefore, not speak of having been with me here. To mention me would be but to bring up bitter memories."

In the pause which now ensued, Billy Traynor's feelings
underwent a sore trial; for while he bethought him that now
or never had come the moment to reconcile the father and
the son, thus mysteriously separated, his fears also whispered the danger of any ill-advised step on his part, and the
injury he might by possibility inflict on one he loved best on
earth.

" You make me this pledge, therefore, before we part,"
said Lord Glencore, who continued to ruminate on what he

had spoken. " It is less for *my* sake than that of another."
Billy took the hand Glencore tendered towards him respectfully in his own, and kissed it twice.

" There are men who have no need of oaths to ratify
their faith and trustfulness. You are one of them, Traynor," said Glencore, affectionately.

Billy tried to speak, but his heart was too full, and he
could not utter a word.

" A dying man's words have ever their solemn weight,"
said Glencore, " and mine beseech you not to desert one
who has no prize in life equal to your friendship. Promise
me nothing, but do not forget my prayer to you." And
with this, Lord Glencore turned away, and buried his face
between his hands.

" And in the name of Heaven," muttered Billy to himself
as he stole away, " what is it that keeps them apart and
won't let them love one another? Sure it was n't in nature
that a boy of his years could ever do what would separate
them this way. What could he possibly say or do that his
father might n't forget and forgive by this time? And then
if it was n't the child's fault at all, where 's the justice in
makin' him pay for another's crime? Sure enough, great
people must be unlike poor craytures like me, in their
hearts and feelin's as well as in their grandeur; and there
must be things that *we* never mind nor think of, that are
thought to be mortial injuries by *them*. Ay, and that is
raysonable too! We see the same in the matayrial world.
There 's fevers that some never takes; and there 's climates
some can live in, and no others can bear!

" I suppose, now," said he, with a wise shake of the
head, " pride — pride is at the root of it all, some way or
other; and if it is, I may give up the investigation at onst,
for divil a one o' me knows what pride is, — barrin' it 's the
delight one feels in consthruin' a hard bit in a Greek
chorus, or hittin' the manin' of a doubtful passage in ould
Æschylus. But what 's the good o' me puzzlin' myself?
If I was to speculate for fifty years, I 'd never be able to
think like a lord, after all!" And with this conclusion he
began to prepare for his journey.

CHAPTER XLVIII

"What can have brought them here, Stubber?" said the Duke of Massa, as he walked to and fro in his dressing-room, with an air of considerable perturbation. "Be assured of one thing, they have come for mischief! I know that Sabloukoff well. *She* it was separated Prince Max from my sister, and that Montenegro affair was all *her* doing also."

"I don't suspect —"

"Don't you? Well, then, *I* do, sir; and that's enough," said he, interrupting. "And as to Upton, he's well known throughout Europe, — a ' mauvais coucheur,' Stubber; that's what the Emperor Franz called him, — a ' mauvais coucheur,' one of those fellows England employs to get up the embarrassments she so deeply deplores. Eh, Stubber, that's the phrase: ' While we deeply deplore the condition of the kingdom,' — that's always the exordium to sending out a fleet or an impertinent despatch. But I'll not endure it here. I have my sovereign rights, my independence, my allies. By the way, haven't my allies taken possession of the Opera House for a barrack?"

"That they have, sir; and they threaten an encampment in the Court gardens."

"An open insult, an outrage! And have *you* endured and submitted to this?"

"I have refused the permission; but they may very possibly take no heed of my protest."

"And you'll tell me that I am the ruler of this state?"

"No, but I'll say you might, if you liked to be so."

"How so, Stubber? Come, my worthy fellow, what's your plan? You have a plan, I'm certain — but I guess it: turn Protestant, hunt out the Jesuits, close the churches, demolish the monasteries, and send for an English frigate down to the Marina, where there's not water to float a fishing-boat. But no, sir, I'll have no such alliances; I'll throw myself upon the loyalty and attachment of my people, and — I'll raise the taxes. Eh, Stubber? We'll tax the 'colza' and the quarries! If they demur, we'll abdicate; that's my last word, — abdicate."

"I wonder who this sick man can be that accompanies Upton," said Stubber, who never suffered himself to be moved by his master's violence.

"Another firebrand, — another emissary of English disturbance. Hardenberg was perfectly right when he said the English nation pays off the meanest subserviency to their own aristocracy by hunting down all that is noble in every state of Europe. There, sir, he hit the mark in the very centre. Slaves at home, rebels abroad, — that's your code!"

"We contrive to mix up a fair share of liberty with our bondage, sir."

"In your talk, — only in your talk; and in the newspapers, Stubber. I have studied you closely and attentively. You submit to more social indignities than any nation, ancient or modern. I was in London in '15, and I remember, at a race-course, — Ascot, they called it, — the Prince had a certain horse called Rufus."

"I rode him," said Stubber, dryly.

"*You* rode him?"

"Yes, sir. I was his jock for the King's Plate. There was a matter of twenty-eight started, — the largest field ever known for the Cup, — and Rufus reared, and, falling back, killed his rider; and the Duke of Dunrobin sent for me, and told me to mount. That's the way I came to be there."

"*Per Bacco!* it was a splendid race, and I'm sure I never suspected when I cheered you coming in, that I was welcoming my future minister. Eh, Stubber, only fancy what a change!"

Stubber only shrugged his shoulders, as though the alteration in fortune was no such great prize after all.

"I won two thousand guineas on that day, Stubber. Lord Heddleworth paid me in gold, I remember; for they picked my pocket of three rouleaux on the course. The

Prince laughed so at dinner about it, and said it was pure patriotism not to suffer exportation of bullion. A great people the English, that I must say! The display of wealth was the grandest spectacle I ever beheld; and such beauty too! By the way, Stubber, our ballet here is detestable. Where did they gather together that gang of horrors?"

"What signifies it, sir, if the Austrian Jägers are bivouacked in the theatre?"

"Very true, by Jove!" said the Duke, pondering. "Can't we hit upon something, — have you no happy suggestion? I have it. Stubber, — an admirable thought. We'll have Upton to dinner. We'll make it appear that he has come here specially to treat with us. There is a great coldness just now between St. James's and Vienna. Upton will be charmed with the thought of an intrigue; so will be La Sablonkoff. We'll not invite the Field-Marshal Rosenkrantz: that will itself offend Austria. Eh, Stubber, is n't it good? Say to-morrow at six, and go yourself with the invitation."

And, overjoyed with the notion of his own subtlety, the Prince walked up and down, laughing heartily, and rubbing his hands in glee.

Stubber, however, was too well versed in the changeability of his master's nature to exhibit any rash promptitude in obeying him.

"You must manage to let the English papers speak of this, Stubber. The 'Augsburg Gazette' will be sure to copy the paragraph, and what a sensation it will create at Vienna!"

"I am inclined to think Upton has come here about that young fellow we gave up to the Austrians last autumn, and for whom he desires to claim some compensation and an ample apology."

"Apology, of course, Stubber, — humiliation to any extent. I'll send the Minister Landelli into exile, — to the galleys, if they insist; but I'll not pay a scudo, — my royal word on it! But who says that such is the reason of his presence here?"

"I had a hint of it last night, and I received a polite note from Upton this morning, asking when he might have a few moments' conversation with me."

" Go to him, Stubber, with our invitation. Ask him if he likes shooting. Say I am going to Serravezza on Saturday; sound him if he desires to have the Red Cross of Massa; hint that I am an ardent admirer of his public career; and be sure to tell me something he has said or done, if he come to dinner."

" There is to be a dinner, then, sir? " asked Stubber, with the air of one partly struggling with a conviction.

" I have said so, Chevalier! " replied the Prince, haughtily, and in the tone of a man whose decisions were irrevocable. " I mean to dine in the state apartments, and to have a reception in the evening, just to show Rosenkrantz how cheaply we hold him. Eh, Stubber? It will half kill him to come with the general company! "

Stubber gave a faint sigh, as though fresh complications and more troubles would be the sole results of this brilliant tactique.

" If I were well served and faithfully obeyed, there is not a sovereign in Europe who would boast a more independent position. — protected by my bold people, environed by my native Apennines, and sustained by the proud consciousness — the proud consciousness — that I cannot injure a state which has not sixpence in the treasury! Eh, Stubber? " cried he, with a burst of merry laughter. " That's the grand feature of composure and dignity, to know you can't be worse! and this, we Italian princes can all indulge in. Look at the Pope himself, he is collecting the imposts a year in advance! "

" I hope that this country is more equitably administered," said Stubber.

" So do I, sir. Were I not impressed with the full conviction that the subjects of this realm were in the very fullest enjoyment of every liberty consistent with public tranquillity, protected in the maintenance of every privilege — By the way, talking of privileges, they mustn't play ' Trottolo ' on the high roads; they sent one of those cursed wheels flying between the legs of my horse yesterday, so that if I had n't been an old cavalry soldier, I must have been thrown! I ordered the whole village to be fined three hundred scudi, one half of which to be sent to the shrine of our Lady of Loretta, who really, I believe, kept me in my saddle! "

" If the people had sufficient occupation, they 'd not play
' Trottolo,' " said Stubber, sternly.

" And whose the fault if they have not, sir? How many
months have I been entreating to have those terraced gardens finished towards the sea? I want that olive wood, too,
all stubbed up, and the ground laid out in handsome par-
terres. How repeatedly have I asked for a bridge over that
ornamental lake; and as to the island, there 's not a magnolia planted in it yet. Public works, indeed; find me the
money, Stubber, and I 'll suggest the works. Then, there 's
that villa, the residence of those English people, — have we
not made a purchase of it? "

" No, your Highness; we could not agree about the
terms, and I have just heard that the stranger who is travelling with Upton is going to buy it."

" Stepping in between me and an object I have in view!
And in my own Duchy, too! And you have the hardihood
to tell me that you knew of and permitted this negotiation
to go on? "

" There is nothing in the law to prevent it, sir. "

" The law! What impertinence to tell me of the law!
Why, sir, it is I am the law, — I am the head and fountain
of all law here; without my sanction, what can presume
to be legal? "

" I opine that the Act which admits foreigners to possess
property in the state was passed in the life of your Highness's father."

" I repeal it, then! It saps the nationality of a people;
it is a blow aimed at the very heart of independent sovereignty. I may stand alone in all Europe on this point, but
I will maintain it. And as to this stranger, let his passport
be sent to him on the spot."

" He may possibly be an Englishman, your Highness;
and remember that we have already a troublesome affair on
our hands with that other youth, who in some way claims
Upton's protection. Had we not better go more cautiously
to work? I can see and speak with him."

" What a tyranny is this English interference! There is
not a land, from Sweden to Sicily, where, on some assumed
ground of humanity, your Government have not dared to
impose their opinions! You presume to assert that all men

must feel precisely like your dogged and hard-headed countrymen, and that what are deemed grievances in your land should be thought so elsewhere. You write up a code for the whole world, built out of the materials of all your national prejudices. your insular conceit, — ay, and out of the very exigencies of your bad climate; and then you say to us, blessed in the enjoyment of light hearts and God's sunshine, that we must think and feel as you do! I am not astonished that my nobles are discontented with the share you possess of my confidence; they must long have seen how little suited the maxims of your national policy are to the habits of a happier population!"

"The people are far better than their nobles, — that I 'm sure of," said Stubber, stoutly.

"You want to preach socialism to me, and hope to convert me to that splendid doctrine of communism we hear so much of. You are a dangerous fellow, — a very dangerous fellow. It was precisely men of your stamp sapped the monarchy in France, and with it all monarchy in Europe."

"If your Highness intends Proserpine to run at Bologna, she ought to be put in training at once," said Stubber, gravely; "and we might send up some of the weeds at the same time, and sell them off."

"Well thought of, Stubber; and there was something else in my head, — what was it?"

"The suppression of the San Lorenzo convent, perhaps: it is all completed, and only waits your Highness to sign the deed."

"What sum does it give us, Stubber, eh?"

"About one hundred and eighty thousand scudi, sir, of which some twenty thousand go to the National Mortgage Fund."

"Not one crown of it, — not a single bajocco, as I am a Christian knight and a true gentleman. I need it all, if it were twice as much. If we incur the anger of the Pope and the Sacred College, — if we risk the thunders of the Vatican, — let us have the worldly consolation of a full purse."

"I advised the measure on wiser grounds, sir. It was not fair and just that a set of lazy friars should be leading lives of indolence and abundance in the midst of a hard-worked and ill-fed peasantry."

"Quite true; and on these wise grounds, as you call them, we have rooted them out. We only wish that the game were more plenty, for the sport amuses us vastly." And he clapped Stubber familiarly on the shoulder, and laughed heartily at his jest.

It was in this happy frame of mind that Stubber always liked to leave his master; and so, promising to attend to the different subjects discussed between them, he bowed and withdrew.

CHAPTER XLIX

"WHAT an insufferable bore, dear Princess!" sighed Sir Horace, as he opened the square-shaped envelope that contained his Royal Highness's invitation to dinner.

"I mean to be seriously indisposed," said Madame de Sabloukoff; "one gets nothing but chagrin in intercourse with petty Courts."

"Like provincial journals, they only reproduce what has appeared in the metropolitan papers, and give you old gossip for fresh intelligence."

"Or, worse again, ask you to take an interest in their miserable 'localisms,'—the microscopic contentions of insect life."

"They have given us a sentry at the door, I perceive," said Sir Horace, with assumed indifference.

"A very proper attention!" remarked the lady, in a tone that more than half implied the compliment was one intended for herself.

"Have you seen the Chevalier Stubber yet?" asked Upton.

"No; he has been twice here, but I was dressing, or writing notes. And you?"

"I told him to come about two o'clock," sighed Sir Horace. "I rather like Stubber."

This was said in a tone of such condescension that it sounded as though the utterer was confessing to an amicable weakness in his nature.—"I rather like Stubber."

Though there was something meant to invite agreement in the tone, the Princess only accepted the speech with a slight motion of her eyebrows, and a look of half unwilling assent.

" I know he's not of *your* world, dear Princess, but he belongs to that Anglo-Saxon stock we are so prone to associate with all the ideas of rugged, unadorned virtue."

" Rugged and unadorned indeed ! " echoed the lady.

"And yet never vulgar," rejoined Upton, — " never affecting to be other than he is ; and, stranger still, not self-opinionated and conceited."

" I own to you," said she, haughtily, " that the whole Court here puts me in mind of Hayti, with its Marquis of Orgeat and its Count Marmalade. These people, elevated from menial station to a mock nobility, only serve to throw ridicule upon themselves and the order that they counter- feit. No socialist in Europe has done such service to the cause of democracy as the Prince of Massa ! "

" Honesty is such a very rare quality in this world that I am not surprised at his Highness prizing it under any garb. Now, Stubber is honest."

" He says so himself, I am told."

" Yes, he says so, and I believe him. He has been employed in situations of considerable trust, and always acquitted himself well. Such a man cannot have escaped temptations, and yet even his enemies do not accuse him of venality."

" Good Heavens ! what more would he have than his legitimate spoils? He is a Minister of the Household, with an ample salary ; a Master of the Horse ; an inspector of Woods and Forests ; a something over Church lands ; and a Red Cross of Massa besides. I am quite ' made up ' in his dignities, for they are all set forth on his visiting-card with what purports to be a coat of arms at top." And, as she spoke, she held out the card in derision.

" That's silly, I must say," said Upton, smiling ; " and yet, I suppose that here in Massa it was requisite he should assert all his pretensions thus openly."

" Perhaps so," said she, dryly.

" And, after all," said Upton, who seemed rather bent on a system of mild tormenting, — " after all, there is some- thing amiable in the weakness of this display, — it smacks of gratitude ! It is like saying to the world, ' See what the munificence of my master has made me ! ' "

" What a delicate compliment, too, to his nobles, which proclaims that for a station of trust and probity the Prince must recruit from the kitchen and the stables. To *my* thinking, there is no such impertinent delusion as that popular one which asserts that we must seek for everything in its least likely place, — take ministers out of counting-houses, and military commanders from shop-boards. For the treatment of weighty questions in peace or war, the gentleman element is the first essential."

"Just as long as the world thinks so, dear Princess; not an hour longer."

The Princess arose, and walked the room in evident displeasure. She half suspected that his objections were only devices to irritate, and she determined not to prolong the discussion. The temptation to reply proved, however, too strong for her resolution, and she said, —

"The world has thought so for some centuries; and when a passing shade of doubt has shaken the conviction, have not the people rushed from revolution into actual bondage, as though any despotism were better than the tyranny of their own passions?"

"I opine," said Upton, calmly, "that the 'prestige' of the gentleman consists in his belonging to an 'order.' Now, that is a privilege that cannot be enjoyed by a mere popular leader. It is like the contrast between a club and a public meeting."

"It is something that you confess these people have no 'prestige.'" said she, triumphantly. "Indeed, their presence in the world of politics, to my thinking, is a mere symbol of change, — an evidence that we are in some stage of transition."

"So we are, madame; there is nothing more true. Every people of Europe have outgrown their governments, like young heirs risen to manhood, ordering household affairs to their will. The popular voice now swells above the whisper of cabinets. So long as each country limits itself to home questions, this spirit will attract but slight notice. Let the issue, however, become a great international one, and you will see the popular will declaring wars, cementing alliances, and signing peaces in a fashion to make statecraft tremble!"

"And you approve of this change, and welcome it?" asked she, derisively.

"I have never said so, madame. I foresee the hurricane, that's all. Men like Stubber are to be seen almost everywhere throughout Europe. They are a kind of declaration that, for the government and guidance of mankind, the possession of a good head and an honest heart is amply sufficient; that rulers neither need fourteen quarterings nor names coeval with the Roman Empire."

"You have given me but another reason to detest him," said the Princess, angrily. "I don't think I shall receive him to-day."

"But you want to speak with him about that villa; there is some formality to be gone through before a foreigner can own property here. I think you promised Glencore you would arrange the matter."

She made no reply, and he continued: "Poor fellow! a very short lease would suffice for his time; he is sinking rapidly. The conflict his mind wages between hope and doubt has hastened all the symptoms of his malady."

"In such a struggle a woman has more courage than a man."

"Say more boldness, Princess," said Upton, slyly.

"I repeat, courage, sir. It is fear, and nothing but fear, that agitates him. He is afraid of the world's sneer; afraid of what society will think, and say, and write about him; afraid of the petty gossip of the millions he will never see or hear of. This cowardice it is that checks him in every aspiration to vindicate his wife's honor and his boy's birth."

"*Si cela se peut,*" said Upton, with a very equivocal smile.

A look of haughty anger, with a flush of crimson on her cheek, was the only answer she made him.

"I mean that he is really not in a position to prove or disprove anything. He assumed certain 'levities' — I suppose the word will do — to mean more than levities; he construed indiscretions into grave faults, and faults into crimes. But that he did all this without sufficient reason, or that he now has abundant evidence that he was mistaken, I am unable to say, nor is it with broken faculties and a wan-

dering intellect that he can be expected to review the past
and deliver judgment on it."

"The whole moral of which is: what a luckless fate is
that of a foreign wife united to an English husband!"

"There is much force in the remark," said Upton, calmly.

"To have her thoughts, and words, and actions submitted
to the standard of a nation whose moral subtleties she could
never comprehend; to be taught that a certain amount of
gloom must be mixed up with life, just as bitters are taken
for tonics; that *ennui* is the sure type of virtue, and low
spirits the healthiest condition of the mind, — these are her
first lessons: no wonder if she find them hard ones.

"To be told that all the harmless familiarities she has
seen from her childhood are dangerous freedoms, all the
innocent gayeties of the world about her are snares and pit-
falls, is to make existence little better than a penal servitude,
— this is lesson the second. While, to complete her education, she is instructed how to assume a censorial rigidity of
manner that would shame a duenna, and a condemnatory
tone that assumes to arraign all the criminals of society, and
pass sentence on them. How amiable she may become in
disposition, and how suitable as a companion by this training, *you*, sir, and your countrymen are best able to
pronounce."

"You rather exaggerate our demerits, my dear Princess,"
said Upton, smiling. "We really do *not* like to be so very
odious as you would make us."

"You are excellent people, with whom no one can live, —
that's the whole of it," said she, with a saucy laugh. "If
your friend Lord Glencore had been satisfied to stay at
home and marry one of his own nation, he might have
escaped a deal of unhappiness, and saved a most amiable
creature much more sorrow than falls to the lot of the least
fortunate of her own country. I conclude you have some
influence over him?"

"As much, perhaps, as any one; but even that says
little."

"Can you not use it, therefore, to make him repair a
great wrong?"

"You had some plan, I think?" said he, hesitatingly.

" Yes ; I have written to her to come down here. I have pretended that her presence is necessary to certain formalities about the sale of the villa. I mean that they should meet, without apprising either of them. I have sent the boy out of the way to Pontremoli to make me a copy of some frescoes there; till the success of my scheme be decided, I did not wish to make him a party to it."

" You don't know Glencore, — at least as I know him."

" There is no reason that I should," broke she in. " What I would try is an experiment, every detail of which I would leave to chance. Were this a case where all the wrong were on one side, and all the forgiveness to come from the other, friendly aid and interposition might well be needed; but here is a complication which neither you, nor I, nor any one else can pretend to unravel. Let them meet, therefore, and let Fate — if that be the name for it — decide what all the prevention and planning in the world could never provide for."

" The very fact that their meeting has been plotted beforehand will suggest distrust."

" Their manner in meeting will be the best answer to that," said she, resolutely. " There will be no acting between them, depend upon 't."

" He told me that he had destroyed the registry of their marriage, nor does he know where a single witness of the ceremony could be found."

" I don't want to know *how* he could make the *amende* till I know that he is ready to do it," said she, in the same calm tone.

" To have arranged a meeting with the boy had perhaps been better than this. Glencore has not avowed it, but I think I can detect misgivings for his treatment of the youth."

" This was my first thought, and I spoke to young Massy the evening before Lord Glencore arrived. I led him to tell me of his boyish days in Ireland and his home there; a stern resolution to master all emotion seemed to pervade whatever he said; and though, perhaps, the effort may have cost him much, his manner did not betray it. He told me that he was illegitimate, that the secret was

divulged to him by his own father, that he had never heard
who his mother was, nor what rank in life she occupied.
When I said that she was one in high station, that she was
alive and well, and one of my own dearest friends, a sudden
crimson covered his face, as quickly followed by a sickly
pallor; and though he trembled in every limb, he never
spoke a word. I endeavored to excite in him some desire
to learn more of her, if not to see her, but in vain. The
hard lesson he had taught himself enabled him to repress
every semblance of feeling. It was only when at last, driven
to the very limits of my patience, I abruptly asked him,
'Have you no wish to see your mother?' that his coldness
gave way, and, in a voice tremulous and thick, he said,
'My shame is enough for myself.' I was burning to say
more, to put before him a contingency, the mere shadow of
a possibility that his claim to birth and station might one
day or other be vindicated. I did not actually do so, but I
must have let drop some chance word that betrayed my
meaning, for he caught me up quickly, and said, 'It would
come too late, if it came even to-day. I am that which I
am by many a hard struggle; you'll never see me risk a
disappointment in life by any encouragement I may give to
hope.'

"I then adverted to his father; but he checked me at
once, saying, 'When the ties that should be closest in life
are stained with shame and dishonor, they are bonds of
slavery, not of affection. My debt to Lord Glencore is the
degradation I live in, — none other. His heritage to me is
the undying conflict in my heart between what I once
thought I was and what I now know I am. If we met,
it would be to tell him so.' In a word, every feature of the
father's proud unforgivingness is reproduced in the boy,
and I dreaded the very possibility of their meeting. If ever
Lord Glencore avow his marriage and vindicate his wife's
honor, his hardest task will be reconciliation with this
boy."

"All, and more than all, the evils I anticipated have
followed this insane vengeance," said Upton. "I begin to
think that one ought to leave a golden bridge even to our
revenge, Princess."

" Assuredly, wherever a woman is the victim," said she, smiling; " for you are so certain to have reasons for distrusting yourself."

Upton sat meditating for some time on the plan of the Princess; had it only originated with himself, it was exactly the kind of project he would have liked. He knew enough of life to be aware that one can do very little more than launch events upon the great ocean of destiny; that the pretension to guide and direct them is oftener a snare than anything else; that the contingencies and accidents, the complications too, which beset every move in life, disconcert all one's pre-arrangements, so that it is rare indeed when we are able to pursue the same path towards any object by which we have set out.

As the scheme was, however, that of another, he now scrutinized it, and weighed every objection to its accomplishment, constantly returning to the same difficulty, as he said, —

" You do not know Glencore."

" The man who has but one passion, one impulse in life, is rarely a difficult study," was the measured reply. " Lord Glencore's vengeance has worn itself out, exactly as all similar outbreaks of temper do, for want of opposition. There was nothing to feed, nothing to minister to it. He sees – I have taken care that he should see — that his bolt has not struck the mark; that her position is not the precarious thing he meant to make it, but a station as much protected and fenced round by its own conventionalities as that of any, the proudest lady in society. For one that dares to impugn her, there are full fifty ready to condemn *him*; and all this has been done without reprisal or recrimination; no partisanship to arraign his moroseness and his cruelty, — none of that 'coterie' defence which divides society into two sections. This, of course, has wounded his pride, but it has not stimulated his anger; but, above all, it has imparted to her the advantage of a dignity of which his vengeance was intended to deprive her."

" You must be a sanguine and a hopeful spirit, Princess, if you deem that such elements will unite happily hereafter," said Upton, smiling.

" I really never carried my speculations so far," replied she. " It is in actual life, as in that of the stage, quite suffi- cient to accompany the actors to the fall of the curtain."

" The Chevalier Stubber, madame," said a servant, enter- ing, " wishes to know if you will receive him."

" Yes — no — yes. Tell him to come in," said, she rapidly, as she resumed her seat beside the fire.

CHAPTER L.

NOTWITHSTANDING the strongly expressed sentiments of the Princess with regard to the Chevalier Stubber, she received him with marked favor, and gave him her hand to kiss, with evident cordiality. As for Upton, it was the triumph of his manner to deal with men separated widely from himself in station and abilities. He could throw such an air of good fellowship into the smallest attentions, impart such a glow of kindliness to the veriest commonplaces, that the very craftiest and shrewdest could never detect. As he leaned his arm, therefore, on Stubber's shoulder, and smiled benignly on him, you would have said it was the affectionate meeting with a long-absent brother. But there was something besides this: there was the expansive confidence accorded to a trusty colleague; and as he asked him about the Duchy, its taxation, its debt, its alliances and difficulties, you might mark in the attention he bestowed all the signs of one receiving very valuable information.

" You perceive, Princess," said he, at last, " Stubber quite agrees with the Duke of Cloudeslie, — these small states enjoy no real independence."

" Then why are they not absorbed into the larger nations about them?"

" They have their uses; they are like substances interposed between conflicting bodies, which receive and diminish the shock of collisions. So that Prussia, when wanting to wound Austria, only pinches Baden; and Austria, desirous of insulting Saxony, ' takes it out' on Sigmaringen."

" It's a pleasant destiny you assign them," said she, laughing.

" Stubber will tell you I'm not far wrong in my appreciation."

"I'm not for what they call 'mediatizing' them neither, my Lady," said Stubber, who generally used the designation to imply his highest degree of respect. "That may all be very well for the interests of the great states, and the balance of power, and all that sort of thing; but we ought also to bestow a thought upon the people of these small countries, especially on the inhabitants of their cities. What's to become of *them* when you withdraw their courts, and throw their little capitals into the position of provincial towns and even villages?"

"They will eke out a livelihood somehow, my dear Stubber. Be assured that they'll not starve. Masters of the Horse may have to keep livery stables; chamberlains turn valets; ladies of the bedchamber descend to the arts of millinery: but, after all, the change will be but in name, and there will not be a whit more slavery in the new condition than in the old one."

"Well, I'm not so sure they'll take the same comfortable view of it that you do, Sir Horace," said Stubber; "nor can I see who can possibly want livery stables, or smart bonnets, or even a fine butler, when the resources of the Court are withdrawn, and the city left to its own devices."

"Stubber suspects," said Upton, "that the policy which prevails amongst our great landed proprietors against small holdings is that which at present influences the larger states of Europe against small kingdoms; and so far he is right. It is unquestionably the notion of our day that the influences of government require space for their exercise."

"If the happiness of the people was to be thought of, which of course it is not," said Stubber, "I'd say leave them as they are."

"Ah, my dear Stubber, you are now drawing the question into the realm of the imaginary. What do any of us know about our happiness?"

"Enough to eat and drink, a comfortable roof over you, good clothes, nothing oppressive or unequal in the laws,— these go for a good way in the kind of thing I mean; and let me observe, sir, it is a great privilege little states, like little people, enjoy, that they need have no ambitions. They don't want to conquer anybody; they neither ask for

the mouth of a river here, or an island there; and if only
let alone, they'll never disturb the peace of the world at
large."

"My dear Stubber, you are quite a proficient at statecraft," said Upton, with the very least superciliousness in
the accent.

"Well, I don't know, Sir Horace," said the other, modestly, "but as my master's means are about the double of
what they were when I entered his service, and as the
people pay about one-sixth less in taxes than they used to
do, mayhap I might say that I have put the saddle on the
right part of the back."

"Your foreign policy does not seem quite as unobjection-
able as your home management. That was an ugly business
about that boy you gave up to the Austrians."

"Well, there were mistakes on all sides. You yourself,
Sir Horace, gave him a false passport; his real name turns
out to be Massy: it made an impression on me, from a
circumstance that happened when I was a young fellow
living as pad-groom with Prince Tottskoy. I went over
on a lark one day to Capri, and was witness to a wedding
there of a young Englishman called Massy."

"Were you, then, present at the ceremony?"

"Yes, sir; and what's stranger still, I have a voucher
for it."

"A voucher for it. What do you mean?"

"It was this way, sir. There was a great supper for
the country people and the servants, and I was there, and
I suppose I took too much of that Capri wine; it was
new and hot at the time, and I got into a row of some sort,
and I beat the Deputato from some place or t' other, and got
locked up for three days; and the priest, a very jolly fellow,
gave me under his handwriting a voucher that I had been a
witness of the marriage, and all the festivities afterwards,
just to show my master how everything happened. But
the Prince never asked me for any explanations, and only
said he 'hoped I had amused myself well;' and so I
kept my voucher to myself, and I have it at this very
hour."

"Will you let me see it, Stubber?"

" To be sure, sir, you shall have it, if I can lay my hand on't in the course of the day."

" Let me beg you will go at once and search for it; it may be of more importance than you know of. Go, my dear Stubber, and look it up."

" I'll not lose a moment, since you wish to have it," said Stubber; "and I am sure your ladyship will excuse my abrupt departure."

The Princess assured him that her own interest in the document was not inferior to that of Sir Horace, and he hastened off to prosecute his search.

" Here, then, are all my plans altered at once," exclaimed she, as the door closed after him. " If this paper mean only as much as he asserts, it will be ample proof of marriage, and lead us to the knowledge of all those who were present at it."

" Yet must we well reflect on the use we make of it," said Upton. " Glencore is now evidently balancing what course to take. As his chances of recovery grow less each day, he seems to incline more and more to repair the wrong he has done. Should we show on our side the merest semblance of compulsion, I would not answer for him."

" So that we have the power, as a last resource, I am content to diplomatize," said the Princess ; " but you must see him this evening, and press for a decision."

" He has already asked me to come to him after we return from Court. It will be late, but it is the hour at which he likes best to talk. If I see occasion for it, I can allude to what Stubber has told us; but it will be only if driven by necessity to it."

" I would act more boldly and more promptly," said she.

" And rouse an opposition, perhaps, that already is becoming dormant. No, I know Glencore well, and will deal with him more patiently."

" From the Chevalier Stubber, your Excellency," said a servant, presenting a sealed packet ; and Sir Horace opened it at once. The envelope contained a small and shabby slip of paper, of which the writing appeared faint and indistinct. It was dated 18—, Church of St. Lorenzo, Capri, and went to certify that Guglielmo Stubber had been present, on the

morning of the 18th August, at the marriage of the Most
Noble Signor Massy with the Princess de la Torre, having
in quality as witness signed the registry thereof; and then
went on to state the circumstance of his attendance at the
supper, and the event which ensued.   It bore the name of
the writer at foot, Basilio Nardoni, priest of the aforesaid
church and village.

" Little is Glencore aware that such an evidence as this
is in existence," said Upton.   " The conviction that he had
his vengeance in his power led him into this insane project.
He fancied there was not a flaw in that terrible indictment;
and see, here is enough to open the door to truth, and un-
do every detail of all his plotting.   How strange is it that
the events of life should so often concur to expose the
dark schemes of men's hearts; proofs starting up in un-
thought-of places, as though to show how vain was mere
subtlety in conflict with the inevitable law of Fate."

" This Basilio Nardoni is an acquaintance of mine," said
the Princess, bent on pursuing another train of thought;
" he was chaplain to the Cardinal Caraffa, and frequently
brought me communications from his Eminence.   He can be
found, if wanted."

" It is unlikely — most unlikely — that we shall require
him."

" If you mean that Lord Glencore will himself make all
the amends he can for a gross injury and a fraud, no more
is necessary," said she, folding the paper, and placing it
in her pocket-book; " but if anything short of this be intended, then there is no exposure too open, no publicity too
wide, to be given to the most cruel wrong the world has
ever heard of."

" Leave me to deal with Glencore.   I think I am about
the only one who can treat with him."

" And now for this dinner at Court, for I have changed
my mind, and mean to go," said the Princess.   " It is full
time to dress, I believe."

" It is almost six o'clock," said Upton, starting up.
" We have quite forgotten ourselves."

CHAPTER LI.

THE Princess Sabloukoff found — not by any means an unfrequent experience in life — that the dinner, whose dulness she had dreaded, turned out a very pleasant affair. The Prince was unusually gracious. He was in good spirits, and put forth powers of agreeability which had been successful in one of less distinction than himself. He possessed eminently, what a great orator once panegyrized as a high conversational element, "great variety," and could without abruptness pass from subject to subject, with always what showed he had bestowed thought upon the theme before him. Great people have few more enviable privileges than that they choose their own topics for conversation. Nothing disagreeable, nothing wearisome, nothing inopportune, can be intruded upon them. When they have no longer anything worth saying, they can change the subject or the company.

His Highness talked with Madame de Sabloukoff on questions of state as he might have talked with a Metternich; he even invited from her expressions of opinion that were almost counsels, sentiments that might pass for warnings. He ranged over the news of the day, relating occasionally some little anecdote, every actor in which was a celebrity; or now and then communicating some piece of valueless secrecy, told with all the mystery of a "great fact;" and then he discussed with Upton the condition of England, and deplored, as all Continental rulers do, the impending downfall of that kingdom, from the growing force of our restless and daring democracy. He regretted much that Sir Horace was not still in office, but consoled himself by reflecting that the pleasure he enjoyed in his society had been in that case denied him. In fact, what with insinuated flatteries, little

26

signs of confidence, and a most marked tone of cordiality, purposely meant to strike beholders, the Prince conducted the conversation right royally, and played "Highness" to perfection.

And these two crafty, keen-sighted people, did they not smile at the performance, and did they not, as they drove home at night, amuse themselves as they recounted the little traits of the great man's dupery? Not a bit of it. They were charmed with his gracious manner, and actually enchanted with his agreeability. Strong in their self-esteem, they could not be brought to suspect that any artifice could be practised on *them*, or that the mere trickery and tinsel of high station could be imposed on them as true value. Nay, they even went further, and discovered that his Highness was really a very remarkable man, and one who received far less than the estimation due to him. His flightiness became versatility; his eccentricity was all originalty; and ere they reached the hotel, they had endowed him with almost every moral and mental quality that can dignify manhood.

"It is really a magnificent turquoise," said the Princess, gazing with admiration at a ring the Prince had taken from his own finger to present to her.

"How absurd is that English jealousy about foreign decorations! I was obliged to decline the Red Cross of Massa which his Highness proposed to confer on me. A monarchy that wants to emulate a republic is simply ridiculous."

"You English are obliged to pay dear for your hypocrisies; and you ought, for you really love them." And with this taunt the carriage stopped at the door of the inn.

As Upton passed up the stairs, the waiter handed him a note, which he hastily opened; it was from Glencore, and in these words: —

Dear Upton, — I can bear this suspense no longer; to remain here canvassing with myself all the doubts that beset me is a torture I cannot endure. I leave, therefore, at once for Florence. Once there, — where I mean to see and hear for myself, — I can decide what is to be the fate of the few days or weeks that yet remain to — Yours,

GLENCORE.

"He is gone, then. — his Lordship has started?"

"Yes, your Excellency, he is by this time near Lucca, for he gave orders to have horses ready at all the stations."

"Read that, madame," said Upton, as he once more found himself alone with the Princess; "you will see that all your plans are disconcerted. He is off to Florence."

Madame de Sablonkoff read the note, and threw it carelessly on the table. "He wants to forgive himself, and only hesitates how to do so gracefully," said she, sneeringly.

"I think you are less than just to him," said Upton, mildly; "his is a noble nature, disfigured by one grand defect."

"Your national character, like your language, is so full of incongruities and contradictions that I am not ashamed to own myself unequal to master it; but it strikes me that both one and the other usurp freedoms that are not permitted to others. At all events, I am rejoiced that he has gone. It is the most wearisome thing in life to negotiate with one too near you. Diplomacy of even the humblest kind requires distance."

"You agree with the duellist, I perceive," said he, laughing, "that twelve paces is a more fatal distance than across a handkerchief: proximity begets tremor."

"You have guessed my meaning correctly," said she; "meanwhile, I must write to *her* not to come here. Shall I say that we will be in Florence in a day or two?"

"I was just thinking of those Serravezza springs," said Upton; "they contain a bi-chloride of potash, which Staub, in his treatise, says, 'is the element wanting in all nervous organizations.'"

"But remember the season, — we are in mid-winter; the hotels are closed."

"The springs are running, Princess; 'the earth,' as Moschus says, 'is a mother that never ceases to nourish.' I do suspect I need a little nursing."

The Princess understood him thoroughly. She well knew that whenever the affairs of Europe followed an unbroken track, without anything eventful or interesting, Sir Horace fell back upon his maladies for matter of occupation. She had, however, now occasion for his advice and counsel, and by no means concurred in his plan of spending some days, if not weeks, in the dreary mountain solitudes of Serravezza. "You must certainly consult Zanetti before you venture on these waters," said she; "they are highly dangerous if taken without the greatest circumspection;" and she gave a catalogue of imaginary calamities which had befallen various illustrious and gifted individuals, to which Upton listened with profound attention.

"Very well," sighed he, as she finished, "it must be as you say. I'll see Zanetti, for I cannot afford to die just yet. That 'Greek question' will have no solution without me. — no one has the key of it but myself. That Panslavic scheme, too, in the Principalities attracts no notice but *mine*; and as to Spain, the policy I have devised for that country requires all the watchfulness I can bestow on it. No, Princess," — here he gave a melancholy sigh, — "we must not die at this moment. There are just four men in Europe; I doubt if she could get on with three."

"What proportion do you admit as to the other sex?" said she, laughing.

"I only know of *one*, madame;" and he kissed her hand with gallantry. "And now for Florence, if you will."

It is by no means improbable that our readers have a right to an apology at our hands for the habit we have indulged of lingering along with the two individuals whose sayings and doings are not directly essential to our tale; but is not the story of every-day life our guarantee that incidents and people cross and re-cross the path we are going, attracting our attention, engaging our sympathy, enlisting our energies, even in our most anxious periods? Such is the world; and we cannot venture out of reality. Besides this, we are disposed to think that the moral of a tale is often more effectively conveyed by the characters than by the catastrophe of a story. The strange, discordant tones of the human heart, blending, with melody the purest, sounds of passionate meaning, are in themselves more powerful lessons than all the records of rewarded virtue and all the calendars of punished vice. The nature of a single man can be far more instructive than the history of every accident that befalls him.

It is, then, with regret that we leave the Princess and
Sir Horace to pursue their journey alone. We confess a
liking for their society, and would often as soon loiter in
the by-paths that they follow as journey in the more recognized high-road of our true story. Not having the conviction that our sympathy is shared by our readers, we again
return to the fortunes of Glencore.

When Lord Glencore's carriage underwent the usual
scrutiny exercised towards travellers at the gate of Florence,
and prying officials poked their lanterns in every quarter, in
all the security of their "caste," two foot travellers were
rudely pushed aside to await the time till the pretentious
equipage passed on. They were foreigners, and their effects,
which they carried in knapsacks, required examination.

"We have come a long way on foot to-day," said the
younger in a tone that indicated nothing of one asking a
favor. "Can't we have this search made at once?"

"Whisht! whisht!" whispered his companion, in English; "wait till the Prince moves on, and be polite with
them all."

"I am seeking for nothing in the shape of compliment,"
said the other; "there is no reason why, because I am on
foot, I must be detained for this man."

Again the other remonstrated, and suggested patience.

"What are you grumbling about, young fellow?" cried
one of the officers. "Do you fancy yourself of the same
consequence as Milordo? And see, he must wait his time
here."

"We came a good way on foot to-day, sir," interposed
the elder, eagerly, taking the reply on himself, "and we 're
tired and weary, and would be deeply obliged if you 'd
examine us as soon as you could."

"Stand aside and wait your turn," was the stern response.

"You almost deserve the fellow's insolence, Billy," said
the youth; "a crown-piece in his hand had been far more
intelligible than your appeal to his pity." And he threw
himself wearily down on a stone bench.

Aroused by the accent of his own language, Lord Glencore sat up in his carriage, and leaned out to catch sight
of the speaker; but the shadow of the overhanging roof

concealed him from view. "Can't you suffer those two poor fellows to move on?" whispered his Lordship, as he placed a piece of money in the officer's hand; "they look tired and jaded."

"There, thank his Excellency for his kindness to you, and go your way," muttered the officer to Billy, who, without well understanding the words, drew nigh the window; but the glass was already drawn up, the postilions were once more in their saddles, and away dashed the cumbrous carriage in all the noise and uproar that is deemed the proper tribute to rank.

The youth heard that they were free to proceed, with a half-dogged indifference, and throwing his knapsack on his shoulders, moved away.

"I asked them if they knew one of her name in the city, and they said ' No.' " said the elder.

"But they so easily mistake names: how did you call her?"

"I said 'Harley, — la Signora Harley,'" rejoined the other; "and they were positive she was not here. They never heard of her."

"Well, we shall know soon," sighed the youth, heavily. "Is not this an inn. Billy?"

"Ay is it. but not one for our purpose, — it's like a palace. They told me of the ' Leone d' Oro ' as a quiet place and cheap."

"I don't care where or what it be ; one day and night here will do all I want. And then for Genoa, Billy, and the sea, and the world beyond the sea," said the youth, with increasing animation. "You shall see what a different fellow I'll be when I throw behind me forever the traditions of this dreary life here."

"I know well the good stuff that 's in ye," said the other, affectionately.

"Ay, but you don't know that I have energy as well as pride." said the other.

"There 's nothing beyond your reach if you will only strive to get it," said he again, in the same voice.

"You 're an arrant flatterer. old boy," cried the youth, throwing his arm around him; "but I would not have

you otherwise for the world. There is a happiness even
in the self-deception of your praise that I could not deny
myself."

Thus chatting, they arrived at the humble door of the
" Leone d' Oro," where they installed themselves for the
night. It was a house frequented by couriers and *vetturini*,
and at the common table for this company they now took
their places for supper. The Carnival was just drawing
to its close, and all the gayeties of that merry season were
going forward. Nothing was talked of but the brilliant
festivities of the city, the splendid balls of the Court, and
the magnificent receptions in the houses of the nobility.

" The Palazzo della Torre takes the lead of all," said
one. " There were upwards of three thousand masks there
this evening, I 'm told, and the gardens were just as full as
the *salons*."

" She is rich enough to afford it well," cried another. " I
counted twenty servants in white and gold liveries on the
stairs alone."

" Were you there, then? " asked the youth, whom we may
at once call by his name of Massy.

" Yes, sir; a mask and a domino, such as you see
yonder, are passports everywhere for the next twenty-four
hours; and though I 'm only a courier, I have been chatting
with duchesses, and exchanging smart sayings with coun-
tesses, in almost every great house in Florence this evening.
The Pergola Theatre, too, is open, and all the boxes crowded
with visitors."

" You are a stranger, as I detect by your accent," said
another, " and you ought to have a look at a scene such as
you 'll never witness in your own land."

" What would come of such freedoms with us, Billy? "
whispered Massy. " Would our great lords tolerate, even
for a few hours, the association with honest fellows of this
stamp? "

" There would be danger in the attempt, anyhow," said
Billy.

" What calumnies would be circulated, what slanderous
tales would be sent abroad, under cover of this secrecy!
How many a coward stab would be given in the shadow

of that immunity! For one who would use the privilege
for mere amusement, how many would turn it to account for
private vengeance."

"Are you quite certain such accidents do not occur
here?"

"That society tolerates the custom is the best answer
to this. There may be, for aught we know, many a cruel
vengeance executed under favor of this secrecy. Many
may cover their faces to unmask their hearts; but, after
all, they continue to observe a habit which centuries back
their forefathers followed; and the inference fairly is, that
it is not baneful. For my own part, I am glad to have an
opportunity of witnessing these Saturnalia, and to-morrow
I'll buy a mask and a domino, Billy, and so shall you too.
Why should we not have a day's fooling, like the rest?"

Billy shook his head and laughed, and they soon afterwards parted for the night.

While young Massy slept soundly, not a dream disturbing
the calmness of his rest, Lord Glencore passed the night in
a state of feverish excitement. Led on by some strange,
mysterious influence, which he could as little account for as
resist, he had come back to the city where the fatal incident
of his life had occurred. With what purpose, he could not
tell. It was not, indeed, that he had no object in view. It
was rather that he had so many and conflicting ones that
they marred and destroyed each other. No longer under the
guidance of calm reason, his head wandered from the past
to the present and the future, disturbed by passion and
excited by injured self-love. At one moment, sentiments
of sorrow and shame would take the ascendant; and at the
next, a vindictive desire to follow out his vengeance and
witness the ruin that he had accomplished. The unbroken,
unrelieved pressure of one thought, for years and years of
time, had at last undermined his reasoning powers; and
every attempt at calm judgment or reflection was sure to be
attended with some violent paroxysm of irrepressible rage.

There are men in whom the combative element is so
strong that it usurps all their guidance, and when once they
are enlisted in a contest, they cannot desist till the struggle
be decided for or against them. Such was Glencore. To

discover that the terrible injury he had inflicted on his wife had not crushed her nor driven her with shame from the world, aroused once more all the vindictive passions of his nature. It was a defiance he could not withstand. Guilty or innocent, it mattered not; she had braved him, — at least so he was told, — and as such he had come to see her with his own eyes. If this was the thought which predominated in his mind, others there were that had their passing power over him, — moments of tenderness, moments in which the long past came back again, full of softening memories; and then he would burst into tears and cry bitterly.

If he ventured to project any plan for reconciliation with her he had so cruelly wronged, he as suddenly bethought him that her spirit was not less high and haughty than his own. She had, so far as he could learn, never quailed before his vengeance; how, then, might he suppose would she act in the presence of his avowed injustice? Was it not, besides, too late to repair the wrong? Even for his boy's sake, would it not be better if he inherited sufficient means to support an honorable life, unknown and unnoticed, than bequeath to him a name so associated with shame and sorrow?

"Who can tell," he would cry aloud, "what my harsh treatment may not have made him? what resentment may have taken root in his young heart? what distrust may have eaten into his nature? If I could but see him and talk with him as a stranger, — if I could be able to judge him apart from the influences that my own feelings would create, — even then, what would it avail me? I have so sullied and tarnished a proud name that he could never bear it without reproach. 'Who is this Lord Glencore?' people would say. 'What is the strange story of his birth? Has any one yet got at the truth? Was the father the cruel tyrant, or the mother the worthless creature, we hear tell of? Is he even legitimate, and, if so, why does he walk apart from his equals, and live without recognition by his order?' This is the noble heritage I am to leave him, — this the proud position to which he is to succeed! And yet Upton says that the boy's rights are inalienable; that, think how I may, do what I will, the day on which I die, he is the rightful Lord

Glencore. His claim may lie dormant, the proofs may be buried, but that, in truth and fact, he will be what all my subterfuge and all my falsehood cannot deny him. And then, if the day should come that he asserts his right, — if, by some of those wonderful accidents that reveal the mysteries of the world, he should succeed to prove his claim, — what a memory will he cherish of *me!* Will not every sorrow of his youth, every indignity of his manhood, be associated with my name? Will he or can he ever forgive him who defamed the mother and despoiled the son?

In the terrible conflict of such thoughts as these he passed the night; intervals of violent grief or passion alone breaking the sad connection of such reflections, till at length the worn-out faculties, incapable of further exercise, wandered away into incoherency, and he raved in all the wildness of insanity.

It was thus that Upton found him on his arrival.

Down the crowded thoroughfare of the Borgo d' Ognisanti the tide of Carnival mummers poured unceasingly. Hideous masks and gay dominos, ludicrous impersonations and absurd satires on costume, abounded, and the entire population seemed to have given themselves up to merriment, and were fooling it to the top o' their bent. Bands of music and chorus-singers from the theatre filled the air with their loud strains, and carriages crowded with fantastic figures moved past, pelting the bystanders with mock sweetmeats, and covering them with showers of flour. It was a season of universal license, and, short of actual outrage, all was permitted for the time. Nor did the enjoyment of the scene seem to be confined to the poorer classes of the people, who thus for the nonce assumed equality with their richer neighbors; but all, even to the very highest, mixed in the wild excitement of the pageant, and took the rough treatment they met with in perfect good-humor. Dukes and princes, white from head to foot with the snowy shower, went laughingly along, and grave dignitaries were fain to walk arm-in-arm with the most ludicrous monstrosities, whose gestures turned on them the laughter of all around. Occasionally — but, it must be owned, rarely — some philosopher of a sterner school might be seen passing hurriedly along, his severe features and contemptuous glances owning to little sympathy with the mummery about him; but even *he* had to compromise his proud disdain, and escape, as best he might, from the indiscriminate justice of the crowd. To detect one of this stamp, to follow, and turn upon him the full tide of popular fury, seemed to be the greatest triumph of the scene. When such a victim presented himself, all joined in the pursuit: nuns embraced, devils environed him, angels perched on his shoulders, mock wild boars rushed between his legs; his hat was decorated with feathers, his clothes inundated with showers of meal or flour; hackney-coachmen, dressed as ladies, fainted in his arms, and semi-naked bacchanals pressed drink to his lips. In a word, each contributed what he might of attention to the luckless individual, whose resistance — if he were so impolitic as to make any — only increased the zest of the persecution.

An instance of this kind had now attracted general attention, nor was the amusement diminished by the discovery that he was a foreigner and an Englishman. Impertinent allusions to his nation, absurd attempts at his language, ludicrous travesties of what were supposed to be his native customs, were showered on him, in company with a hailstorm of mock bonbons and lime-pellets; till, covered with powder, and outraged beyond all endurance, he fought his way into the entrance of the Hôtel d'Italie, followed by the cries and laughter of the populace.

"Cursed tomfoolery! Confounded asses!" cried he, as he found himself in a harbor of refuge. "What the devil fun can they discover in making each other dirtier than their daily habits bespeak them? I say," cried he, addressing a waiter, "is Sir Horace Upton staying here? Well, will you say Major Scaresby — be correct in the name — Major Scaresby requests to pay his respects."

"His Excellency will see you, sir," said the man, returning quickly with the reply.

From the end of a room, so darkened by closed shutters and curtains as to make all approach difficult, a weak voice called out, "Ah, Scaresby, how d' ye do? I was just thinking to myself that I could n't be in Florence, since I had not seen you."

"You are too good, too kind, Sir Horace, to say so," said the other, with a voice whose tones by no means corresponded with the words.

"Yes, Scaresby, everything in this good city is in a manner associated with your name. Its intrigues, its quarrels, its loves and jealousies, its mysteries, in fine, have had no such interpreter as yourself within the memory of man!

What a pity there were no Scaresbys in the Cinque Cento! How sad there were none of your family here in the Medician period! What a picture might we then have had of a society fuller even than the present of moral delinquencies." There was a degree of pomposity in the manner he uttered this that served to conceal in a great measure its sarcasm.

"I am much flattered to learn that I have ever enlightened your Excellency on any subject," said the Major, dryly.

"That you have, Scaresby. I was a mere dabbler in moral toxicology when I heard your first lecture, and, I assure you, I was struck by your knowledge. And how is the dear city doing?"

"It is masquerading to-day," said Scaresby, "and, consequently, far more natural than at any other period of the whole year. Smeared faces and dirty finery, — exactly its suitable wear!"

"Who are here, Major? Any one that one knows?"

"Old Millington is here."

"The Marquis?"

"Yes, he's here, fresh painted and lacquered; his eyes twinkling with a mock lustre that makes him look like an old po'-chaise with a pair of new lamps!"

"Ha, ha, ha!" laughed Sir Horace, encouragingly.

"And then — there's Mabworth."

"Sir Paul Mabworth?"

"Ay, the same old bore as ever! He has got off one of Burke's speeches on the India Bill by heart, and says that he spoke it on the question of the grant for Maynooth. Oh, if poor Burke could only look up!"

"Look down! you ought to say, Scaresby; depend upon 't, he's not on the Opposition benches still!"

"I hate the fellow," said Scaresby, whose ill-temper was always augmented by any attempted smartness of those he conversed with. "He has taken Walmsley's cook away from him, and never gives any one a dinner."

"That is shameful; a perfect dog in the manger!"

"Worse; he's a dog without any manger! For he keeps his house on board-wages, and there's literally nothing to eat! That poor thing, Strejowsky."

"Oh, Olga Strejowsky, do you mean? What of her?"

"Why, there's another husband just turned up. They thought he was killed in the Caucasus, but he was only passing a few years in Siberia; and so he has come back, and claims all the emeralds. You remember, of course, that famous necklace, and the great drops! They belonged once to the Empress Catherine, but Mabworth says that he took the concern with all its dependencies; he'll give up his bargain, but make no compromise."

"She's growing old, I fancy."

"She's younger than the Sabloukoff by five good years, and they tell me *she* plays Beauty to this hour."

Ah, Scaresby, had you known what words were these you have just uttered, or had you only seen the face of him who heard them, you had rather bitten your tongue off than suffered it to fashion them!

"Brignolles danced with her at that celebrated *fête* given by the Prince of Orleans something like eight-and-thirty years ago."

"And how is the dear Duke?" asked Upton, sharply.

"Just as you saw him at the Court of Louis XVIII.; he swaggers a little more as he gets more feeble about the legs, and he shows his teeth when he laughs, more decidedly since his last journey to Paris. Devilish clever fellows these modern dentists are! He wants to marry; I suppose you've heard it."

"Not a word of it. Who is the happy fair?"

"The Nina, as they call her now. She was one of the Della Torres, who married, or didn't marry, Glencore. Don't you remember him? He was Colonel of the Eleventh, and a devil of a martinet he was."

"I remember him," said Upton, dryly.

"Well, he ran off with one of those girls, and some say they were married at Capri, — as if it signified what happened at Capri! She was a deuced good-looking girl at the time, — a coquette, you know, — and Glencore was one of those stiff English fellows that think every man is making up to his wife; he drank besides."

"No, pardon me, there you are mistaken. I knew him intimately; Glencore was as temperate as myself."

"I have it from Lowther, who used to take him home at night; *he* said Glencore never went to bed sober! At all events, she hated him, and detested his miserly habits."

"Another mistake, my dear Major. Glencore was never what is called a rich man, but he was always a generous one!"

"I suppose you'll not deny that he used to thrash her? Ay, and with a horsewhip too!"

"Come, come, Scaresby; this is really too coarse for mere jesting."

"Jest? By Jove! it was very bitter earnest. She told Brignolles all about it. I'm not sure she didn't show him the marks."

"Take my word for it, Scaresby," said Upton, dropping his voice to a low but measured tone, "this is a base calumny, and the Duke of Brignolles no more circulated such a story than I did. He is a man of honor, and utterly incapable of it."

"I can only repeat that I believe it to be perfectly true!" said Scaresby, calmly. "Nobody here ever doubted the story."

"I cannot say what measure of charity accompanies your zeal for truth in this amiable society, Scaresby, but I can repeat my assertion that this must be a falsehood."

"You will find it very hard, nevertheless, to bring any one over to your opinion," retorted the unappeasable Major. "He was a fellow everybody hated; proud and supercilious to all, and treated his wife's relations — who were of far better blood than himself — as though they were *canaille*."

A loud crash, as if of something heavy having fallen, here interrupted their colloquy, and Upton sprang from his seat and hastened into the adjoining room. Close beside the door — so close that he almost fell over it in entering — lay the figure of Lord Glencore. In his efforts to reach the door he had fainted, and there he lay, — a cold, clammy sweat covering his livid features, and his bloodless lips slightly parted.

It was almost an hour ere his consciousness returned; but when it did, and he saw Upton alone at his bedside, he pressed his hand within his own, and said, "I heard it all, Upton, every word! I tried to reach the room; I got out of bed — and was already at the door — when my brain reeled, and my heart grew faint. It may have been malady, it might be passion, — I know not; but I saw no more. He is gone, — is he not?" cried he, in a faint whisper.

"Yes, yes, — an hour ago; but you will think nothing of what he said, when I tell you his name. It was Scaresby, — Major Scaresby; one whose bad tongue is the one solitary claim by which he subsists in a society of slanderers!"

"And he is gone!" repeated the other, in a tone of deep despondency.

"Of course he is. I never saw him since; but be assured of what I have just told you, that his libels carry no reproach. He is a calumniator by temperament."

"I'd have shot him, if I could have opened the door," muttered Glencore between his teeth; but Upton heard the words distinctly. "What am I to this man," cried he, aloud, "or he to me, that I am to be arraigned by him on charges of any kind, true or false? What accident of fortune makes him my judge? Tell me that, sir. Who has appealed to him for protection? Who has demanded to be righted at his hand?"

"Will you not hear me, Glencore, when I say that his slanders have no sting? In the circles wherein he mixes, it is the mere scandal that amuses; for its veracity, there is not one that cares. You, or I, or some one else, supply the name of an actor in a disreputable drama, the plot of which alone interests, not the performer."

"And am I to sit tamely down under this degradation?" exclaimed Glencore, passionately. "I have never subscribed to this dictation. There is little, indeed, of life left to me, but there is enough, perhaps, to vindicate myself against men of this stamp. You shall take him a message from me; you shall tell him by what accident I overheard his discoveries."

"My dear Glencore, there are graver interests, far worthier cares, than any this man's name can enter into, which should now engage you."

"I say he shall have my provocation, and that within an hour!" cried Glencore, wildly.

"You would give this man and his words a consequence that neither have ever possessed," said Upton, in a mild and subdued tone. "Remember, Glencore, when I left with you this morning that paper of Stubber's it was with a distinct understanding that other and wiser thoughts than those of vengeance were to occupy your attention. I never scrupled to place it in your hands; I never hesitated about confiding to you what in a lawyer's phrase would be a proof against you. When an act of justice was to be done, I would not stain it by the faintest shadow of coercion. I left you free, I leave you still free, from everything but the dictates of your own honor."

Glencore made no reply, but the conflict of his thoughts seemed to agitate him greatly.

"The man who has pursued a false path in life," said Upton, calmly, "has need of much courage to retrace his steps; but courage is not the quality you fail in, Glencore, so that I appeal to you with confidence."

"I have need of courage," muttered Glencore; "you say truly. What was it the doctor said this morning, — aneurism?"

Upton moved his head with an inclination barely perceptible.

"What a Nemesis there is in nature," said Glencore, with a sickly attempt to smile, "that passion should beget malady! I never knew, physically speaking, that I had a heart — till it was broken. So that," resumed he, in a more agreeable tone, "death may ensue at any moment — on the least excitement?"

"He warned you gravely on that point," said Upton, cautiously.

"How strange that I should have come through that trial of an hour ago! It was not that the struggle did not move me. I could have torn that fellow limb from limb, Upton, if I had but the strength! But see," cried he, feebly, "what a poor wretch I am; I cannot close these fingers!" and he held out a worn and clammy hand as he spoke. "Do with me as you will," said he, after a pause; "I ought to have followed your counsels long ago!"

27

Upton was too subtle an anatomist of human motives to venture by even the slightest word to disturb a train of thought which any interference could only damage. As the other still continued to meditate, and, by his manner and look, in a calmer and more reflective spirit, the wily diplomatist moved noiselessly away, and left him alone.

CHAPTER LIII.

A MASK IN CARNIVAL TIME.

FROM the gorgeous halls of the Pitti Palace down to the humblest chamber in Camaldole, Florence was a scene of rejoicing. As night closed in, the crowds seemed only to increase, and the din and clamor to grow louder. It seemed as though festivity and joy had overflowed from the houses, filling the streets with merry-makers. In the clear cold air, groups feasted, and sang, and danced, all mingling and intermixing with a freedom that showed how thoroughly the spirit of pleasure-seeking can annihilate the distinctions of class. The soiled and tattered mummer leaned over the carriage-door and exchanged compliments with the masked duchess within. The titled noble of a dozen quarterings stopped to pledge a merry company who pressed him to drain a glass of Monte Pulciano with them. There was a perfect fellowship between those whom fortune had so widely separated, and the polished accents of high society were heard to blend with the quaint and racy expressions of the " people."

Theatres and palaces lay open, all lighted *" a giorno."* The whole population of the city surged and swayed to and fro like a mighty sea in motion, making the air resound the while with a wild mixture of sounds, wherein music and laughter were blended. Amid the orgie, however, not an act, not a word of rudeness, disturbed the general content. It was a season of universal joy, and none dared to destroy the spell of pleasure that presided.

Our task is not to follow the princely equipages as they rolled in unceasing tides within the marble courts, nor yet to track the strong flood that poured through the wide thoroughfares in all the wildest exuberance of their joy.

Our business is with two travellers, who, well weary of being for hours a-foot, and partly sated with pleasure, sat down to rest themselves on a bench beside the Arno.

" It is glorious fooling, that must be owned, Billy," said Charles Massy, " and the spirit is most contagious. How little have you or I in common with these people! We scarce can catch the accents of the droll allusions, we cannot follow the strains of their rude songs, and yet we are carried away like the rest to feel a wild enjoyment in all this din, and glitter, and movement. How well they do it, too! "

" That's all by rayson of concentration," said Billy, gravely. " They are highly charged with fun. The ould adage says, ' Non semper sunt Saturnalia,' — It is not every day Morris kills a cow."

" Yet it is by this very habit of enjoyment that they know how to be happy."

" To be sure it is," cried Billy; " *they* have a ritual for it which *we* have n't; as Cicero tells us, ' In jucundis nullum periculum.' But ye see we have no notion of any amusement without a dash of danger through it, if not even cruelty ! "

" The French know how to reconcile the two natures; they are brave, and light-hearted too."

" And the Irish, Mister Charles, — the Irish especially," said Billy, proudly; " for I was alludin' to the English in what I said last. The ' versatile ingenium ' is all our own.

> He goes into a tent and he spends half a-crown,
> Comes out, meets a friend, and for love knocks him down.

There's an elegant philosophy in that, now, that a Saxon would never see! For it is out of the very fulness of the heart, ye may remark, that Pat does this, just as much as to say, ' I don't care for the expense!' He smashes a skull just as he would a whole dresser of crockery-ware! There's something very grand in that recklessness."

The tone of the remark, and a certain wild energy of his manner, showed that poor Billy's faculties were slightly under the influences of the Tuscan grape; and the youth smiled at sight of an excess so rare.

"How hard it must be," said Massy, "to go back to the workaday routine of life after one of these outbursts, — to resume not alone the drudgery, but all the slavish observances that humble men yield to great ones!"

"'Tis what Bacon says. 'There's nothing so hard as unlearnin' anything;' and the proof is how few of us ever do it! We always go on mixin' old thoughts with new, — puttin' different kinds of wine into the same glass, and then wonderin' we are not invigorated!"

"You're in a mood for moralizing to-night, I see, Billy," said the other, smiling.

"The levities of life always puts me on that thrack, just as too bright a day reminds me to take out an umbrella with me."

"Yet I do not see that all your observation of the world has indisposed you to enjoy it, or that you take harsher views of life the closer you look at it."

"Quite the reverse; the more I see of mankind, the more I'm struck with the fact that the very wickedest and worst can't get rid of remorse! 'Tis something out of a man's nature entirely — something that dwells outside of him — sets him on to commit a crime; and then he begins to rayson and dispute with the temptation, just like one keepin' bad company, and listenin' to impure notions and evil suggestions day after day; as he does this, he gets to have a taste for that kind of low society, — I mane with his own bad thoughts, — till at last every other ceases to amuse him. Look! what's that there; where are they goin' with all the torches there?" cried he, suddenly, springing up and pointing to a dense crowd that passed along the street. It was a band of music, dressed in a quaint mediaeval costume, on its way to serenade some palace.

"Let us follow and listen to them. Billy," said the youth: and they arose and joined the throng.

Following in the wake of the dense mass, they at last reached the gates of a great palace, and after some waiting gained access to the spacious courtyard. The grim old statues and armorial bearings shone in the glare of a hundred torches, and the deep echoes rang with the brazen voices of the band as, pent up within the quadrangle, the din of a large orchestra arose. On a great terrace overhead numerous figures were grouped, — indistinctly seen from the light of the *salons* within, — but whose mysterious movements completed the charm of a very interesting picture.

Some wrapped in shawls to shroud them from the night air, some, less cautiously emerging from the rooms within, leaned over the marble balustrade and showed their jewelled arms in the dim hazy light, while around and about them gay uniforms and costumes abounded. As Billy gave himself up to the excitement of the music, young Massy, more interested by the aspect of the scene, gazed unceasingly at the balcony. There was just that shadowy indistinctness in the whole that invested it with a kind of romantic interest, and he could weave stories and incidents from those whose figures passed and repassed before him. He fancied that in their gestures he could trace many meanings, and as the bent-down heads approached, and their hands touched, he fashioned many a tale in his own mind of moving fortunes.

"And see, she comes again to that same dark angle of the terrace," muttered he to himself, as, shrouded in a large mantle and with a half mask on her features, a tall and graceful figure passed into the place he spoke of. "She looks like one among, but not of, them. How much of heart-weariness is there in that attitude; how full is it of sad and tender melancholy! Would that I could see her face! My life on 't that it is beautiful! There, she is tearing up her bouquet; leaf by leaf the rose-leaves are falling, as though one by one hopes are decaying in her heart." He pushed his way through the dense throng till he gained a corner of the court where a few leaves and flower-stems yet strewed the ground; carefully gathering up these, he crushed them in his hand, and seemed to feel as though a nearer tie bound him to the fair unknown. How little ministers to the hope; how infinitely less again will feed the imagination of a young heart!

Between them now there was, to his appreciation, some mysterious link. "Yes," he said to himself, "true, I stand unknown, unnoticed; yet it is to *me* of all the thousands here she could reveal what is passing in that heart! I know it, I feel it! She has a sorrow whose burden I might help to bear. There is cruelty, or treachery, or falsehood arrayed against her; and through all the splendor of the scene — all the wild gayety of the orgie — some spectral image never leaves her side! I would stake existence on it that I have read her aright!"

Of all the intoxications that can entrance the human faculties, there is none so maddening as that produced by giving full sway to an exuberant imagination. The bewilderment resists every effort of reason, and in its onward course carries away its victims with all the force of a mountain torrent. A winding stair, long unused and partly dilapidated, led to the end of the terrace where she stood, and Massy, yielding to some strange impulse, slowly and noiselessly crept up this till he gained a spot only a few yards removed from her. The dark shadow of the building almost completely concealed his figure, and left him free to contemplate her unnoticed.

Some event of interest within had withdrawn all from the terrace save herself; the whole balcony was suddenly deserted, and she alone remained, to all seeming lost to the scene around her. It was then that she removed her mask, and suffering it to fall back on her neck, rested her head pensively on her hand. Massy bent over eagerly to try and catch sight of her face; the effort he made startled her, she looked round, and he cried out, " Ida — Ida! My heart could not deceive me!" In another instant he had climbed the balcony and was beside her.

"I thought we had parted forever, Sebastian," said she; "you told me so on the last night at Massa."

"And so I meant when I said it," cried he; "nor is our meeting now of my planning. I came to Florence, it is true, to see, but not to speak with you, ere I left Europe forever. For three entire days I have searched the city to discover where you lived, and chance — I have no better name for it — chance has led me hither."

"It is an unkind fortune that has made us meet again," said she, in a voice of deep melancholy.

"I have never known fortune in any other mood," said he, fiercely. "When clouds show me the edge of their silver linings, I only prepare myself for storm and hurricane."

" I know you have endured much," said she, in a voice of deeper sadness.

" You know but little of what I have endured," rejoined he, sternly. " You saw me taunted, indeed, with my humble calling, insulted for my low birth, expelled ignominiously from a house where my presence had been sought for; and yet all these, grievous enough, are little to other evils I have had to bear."

" By what unhappy accident, what mischance, have you made *her* your enemy, Sebastian? She would not even suffer me to speak to you. She went so far as to tell me that there was a reason for the dislike, — one which, if she could reveal, I would never question."

" How can I tell?" cried he, angrily. " I was born, I suppose, under an evil star; for nothing prospers with me."

" But can you even guess her reasons? " said she, eagerly.

" No, except it be the presumption of one in *my* condition daring to aspire to one in *yours;* and that, as the world goes, would be reason enough. It is probable, too, that I did not state these pretensions of mine over delicately. I told her, with a frankness that was not quite acceptable, I was one who could not speak of birth or blood. She did not like the coarse word I applied to myself, and I will not repeat it; and she ventured to suggest that, had there not appeared some ambiguity in her own position, *I* could never have so far forgotten mine as to advance such pretensions — "

" Well, and then?" cried the girl, eagerly.

" Well, and then," said he, deliberately, " I told her I had heard rumors of the kind she alluded to, but to *me* they carried no significance; that it was for *you* I cared. The accidents of life around you had no influence on my choice; you might be all that the greatest wealth and highest blood could make you, or as poor and ignoble as myself, without any change in my affections. ' These,' said she, ' are the insulting promptings of that English breeding which you say has mixed with your blood, and if for no other cause would make me distrust you.'

" ' Stained as it may be,' said I, ' that same English blood is the best pride I possess.' She grew pale with passion as

I said this, but never spoke a word; and there we stood, staring haughtily at each other, till she pointed to the door, and so I left her. And now, Ida, who is she that treats me thus disdainfully? I ask you not in anger, for I know too well how the world regards such as me to presume to question its harsh injustice. But tell me, I beseech you, that she is one to whose station these prejudices are the fitting accompaniments, and let me feel that it is less myself as the individual that she wrongs, than the class I belong to is that which she despises. I can better bear this contumely when I know that it is an instinct."

"If birth and blood can justify a prejudice, a Princess of the house of Della-Torre might claim the privilege." said the girl, haughtily. "No family of the North, at least, will dispute with our own in lineage; but there are other causes which may warrant all that she feels towards you even more strongly, Sebastian. This boast of your English origin, this it is which has doubtless injured you in her esteem. Too much reason has she had to cherish the antipathy! Betrayed into a secret marriage by an Englishman who represented himself as of a race noble as her own, she was deserted and abandoned by him afterwards. This is the terrible mystery which I never dared to tell you, and which led us to a life of seclusion at Massa. This is the source of that hatred towards all of a nation which she must ever associate with the greatest misfortunes of her life! And from this unhappy event was she led to make me take that solemn oath that I spoke of, never to link my fortunes with one of that hated land."

"But you told me that you had not made the pledge." said he, wildly.

"Nor had I then, Sebastian; but since we last met, worked on by solicitation, I could not resist; tortured by a narrative of such sorrows as I never listened to before, I yielded, and gave my promise."

"It matters little to *me!*" said he, gloomily; "a barrier the more or the less can be of slight moment when there rolls a wide sea between us! Had you ever loved me, such a pledge had been impossible."

"It was you yourself, Sebastian, told me we were never to meet again." rejoined she.

"Better that we had never done so!" muttered he.
"Nay, perhaps I am wrong," added he, fiercely; "this
meeting may serve to mark how little there ever was between
us!"

"Is this cruelty affected, Sebastian, or is it real?"

"It cannot be cruel to echo your own words. Besides,"
said he, with an air of mockery in the words, "she who lives
in this gorgeous palace, surrounded with all the splendors of
life, can have little complaint to make against the cruelty of
fortune!"

"How unlike yourself is all this!" cried she. "You of
all I have ever seen or known, understood how to rise above
the accidents of fate, placing your happiness and your
ambitions in a sphere where mere questions of wealth never
entered. What can have so changed you?"

Before he could reply, a sudden movement in the crowd
beneath attracted the attention of both, and a number of
persons who had filled the terrace now passed hurriedly
into the *salons*, where, to judge from the commotion, an
event of some importance had occurred. Ida lost not a
moment in entering, when she was met by the words:
'It is she, Nina herself is ill; some mask — a stranger, it
would seem — has said something or threatened something."
In fact, she had been carried to her room in strong convulsions; and while some were in search of medical aid for
her, others, not less eagerly, were endeavoring to detect
the delinquent.

From the gay and brilliant picture of festivity which was
presented but a few minutes back, what a change now came
over the scene! Many hurried away at once, shocked at
even a momentary shadow on the sunny road of their existence; others as anxiously pressed on to recount the incident
elsewhere; some, again, moved by curiosity or some better
prompting, exerted themselves to investigate what amounted
to a gross violation of the etiquette of a carnival; and thus,
in the *salons*, on the stairs, and in the court itself, the
greatest bustle and confusion prevailed. At length some
suggested that the gate of the palace should be closed, and
none suffered to depart without unmasking. The motion
was at once adopted, and a small knot of persons, the
friends of the Countess, assumed the task of the scrutiny.

Despite complaints and remonstrances as to the inconvenience and delay thus occasioned, they examined every carriage as it passed out. None, however, but faces familiar to the Florentine world were to be met with; the well-known of every ball and *fête* were there, and if a stranger presented himself, he was sure to be one for whom some acquaintance could bear testimony.

At a fire in one of the smaller *salons* stood a small group, of which the Duc de Brignolles and Major Scaresby formed a part. Sentiments of a very different order had detained these two individuals, and while the former was deeply moved by the insult offered to the Countess, the latter felt an intense desire to probe the circumstance to the bottom.

" Devilish odd it is ! " cried Scaresby; " here we have been this last hour and a half turning a whole house out of the windows, and yet there's no one to tell us what it's all for, what it's all about ! "

" Pardon, monsieur," said the Duke, severely. " We know that a lady whose hospitality we have been accepting has retired from her company insulted. It is very clearly our duty that this should not pass unpunished."

" Ought n't we to have some clearer insight into what constituted the insult? It may have been a practical joke, — a *mauvaise plaisanterie*, Duke."

" We have no claim to any confidence not extended to us, sir," said the Frenchman. " To me it is quite sufficient that the Countess feels aggrieved."

" Not but we shall cut an absurd figure to-morrow, when we own that we don't know what we were so indignant about."

" Only so many of us as have characters for the ' latest intelligence.' "

To this sally there succeeded a somewhat awkward pause, Scaresby occupying himself with thoughts of some perfectly safe vengeance.

" I should n't wonder if it was that Count Marsano — that fellow who used to be about the Nina long ago — come back again. He was at Como this summer, and made many inquiries after his old love ! "

A most insulting stare of defiance was the only reply
the old Duke could make to what he would have been
delighted to resent as a personal affront.

"Marsano is a *mauvais drôle*," said a Russian; "and if
a woman slighted him, or he suspected that she did, he's
the very man to execute a vengeance of the kind."

"I should apply a harsher epithet to a man capable of
such conduct," said the Duke.

"He'd not take it patiently, Duke," said the other.

"It is precisely in that hope, sir, that I should employ
it," said the Duke.

Again was the conversation assuming a critical turn, and
again an interval of ominous silence succeeded.

"There is but one carriage now in the court, your Excellency," said the servant, addressing the Duke in a low voice,
"and the gentleman inside appears to be seriously ill. It
might be better, perhaps, not to detain him."

"Of course not," said the Duke; "but stay, I will go
down myself."

There were still a considerable number of persons on foot
in the court when the Duke descended, but only one equipage
remained, — a hired carriage, — at the open door of which a
servant was standing, holding a glass of water for his master.

"Can I be of any use to your master?" said the Duke,
approaching. "Is he ill?"

"I fear he has burst a blood-vessel, sir," said the man.
"He is too weak to answer me."

"Who is it, — what's his name?"

"I am not able to tell you, sir; I only accompanied him
from the hotel."

"Let us have a doctor at once; he appears to be dying,"
said the Duke, as he placed his fingers on the sick man's
wrist. "Let some one go for a physician."

"There is one here," cried a voice. "I'm a doctor;"
and Billy Traynor pushed his way to the spot. "Come,
Master Charles, get into the coach and help me to lift him
out."

Young Massy obeyed, and not without difficulty they
succeeded at last in disengaging the almost lifeless form
of a man whose dark domino was perfectly saturated with

fresh blood; his half mask still covered his face, and, to screen his features from the vulgar gaze of the crowd, they suffered it to remain there.

Up the wide stairs and into a spacious *salon* they now carried the figure, whose drooping head and hanging limbs gave little signs of life. They placed him on a sofa, and Traynor, with a ready hand, untied the mask and removed it. "Merciful Heavens," cried he, "it's my Lord himself!"

The youth bent down, gazed for a few seconds at the corpse-like face, and fell fainting to the floor.

"My Lord Glencore himself!" said the Duke, who was himself an old and attached friend.

"Hush! not a word," whispered Traynor; "he's rallyin' — he's comin' to; don't utter a syllable."

Slowly and languidly the dying man raised his eyelids, and gazed at each of those around him. From their faces he turned his gaze to the chamber, viewing the walls and the ceiling all in turn; and then, in an accent barely audible, he said, "Where am I?"

"Amongst friends, who love and will cherish you, dear Glencore," said the Duke, affectionately.

"Ah, Brignolles, I remember you. And this, — who is this?"

"Traynor, my Lord, — Billy Traynor, that will never leave you while he can serve you!"

"Whose tears are those upon my hand, — I feel them hot and burning," said the sick man; and Billy stepped back, that the light should fall upon the figure that knelt beside him.

"Don't cry, poor fellow," said Glencore; "it must be a hard world, or you have many better and dearer friends than I could have ever been to you. Who is this?"

Billy tried, but could not answer.

"Tell him, if you know who it is; see how wild and excited it has made him," cried the Duke; for, stretching out both hands, Glencore had caught the boy's face on either side, and continued to gaze on it, in wild eagerness. "It is — it is!" cried he, pressing it to his bosom, and kissing the forehead over and over again.

"Whom does he fancy it? Whom does he suspect?"

"This is — look, Brignolles," cried the dying man, in a voice already thick with a death-rattle, — "this is the seventh Lord Viscount Glencore. I declare it. And now ——" He fell back, and never spoke more. A single shudder shook his feeble frame, and he was dead.

.   .   .   .

We have had occasion once before in this veracious history to speak of the polite oblivion Florentine society so well understands to throw over the course of events which might cloud, even for a moment, the sunny surface of its enjoyment. No people, so far as we know, have greater gifts in this way; to shroud the disagreeables of life in decent shadow — to ignore or forget them is their grand prerogative.

Scarcely, therefore, had three weeks elapsed, than the terrible catastrophe at the Palazzo della Torre was totally consigned to the bygones ; it ceased to be thought or spoken of, and was as much matter of remote history as an incident in the times of one of the Medici. Too much interested in the future to waste time on the past, they launched into speculations as to whether the Countess would be likely to marry again; what change the late event might effect in the amount of her fortune; and how far her position in the world might be altered by the incident. He who, in the ordinary esteem of society, would have felt less acutely than his neighbors for Glencore's sad fate, — Upton, — was in reality deeply and sincerely affected. The traits which make a consummate man of the world — one whose prerogative it is to appreciate others, and be able to guide and influence their actions — are, in truth, very high and rare gifts, and imply resources of fine sentiment as fully as stores of intellectual wealth. Upton sorrowed over Glencore as for one whose noble nature had been poisoned by an impetuous temper, and over whose best instincts an ungovernable self-esteem had ever held the mastery. They had been friends almost from boyhood, and the very worldliest of men can feel the bitterness of that isolation in which the "turn of life" too frequently commences. Such friendships are never made in later life. We lend our affections when young on very small security, and though it is true we are occasionally unfortunate, we do now and then make a safe investment. No men are more prone to attach an exaggerated value to early friendships than those who, stirred by strong ambitions, and animated by high resolves, have played for the great stakes in the world's lottery. Too much immersed in the cares and contests of life to find time to contract close personal attachments, they fall back upon the memory of school or college days to supply the want of their hearts. There is a sophistry, too, that seduces them to believe that then, at least, they were loved for what they were, for qualities of their nature, not for accidents of station, or the proud rewards of success. There is also another and a very strange element in the pleasure such memories afford. Our early attachments serve as points of departure by which we measure the distance we have travelled in life. "Ay," say we, "we were schoolfellows; I remember how he took the lead of me in this or that science, how far behind he left me in such a thing; and yet look at us now!" Upton had very often to fall back upon similar recollections; neither his school nor his college life had been remarkable for distinction; but it was always perceived that every attainment he achieved was such as would be available in after life. Nor did he ever burden himself with the toils of scholarship while there lay within his reach stores of knowledge that might serve to contest the higher and greater prizes that he had already set before his ambition.

But let us return to himself as, alone and sorrow-struck, he sat in his room of the Hôtel d'Italie. Various cares and duties consequent on Glencore's death had devolved entirely upon him. Young Massy had suddenly disappeared from Florence on the morning after the funeral, and was seen no more, and Upton was the only one who could discharge any of the necessary duties of such a moment. The very nature of the task thus imposed upon him had its own depressing influence on his mind; the gloomy pomp of death — the terrible companionship between affliction and worldliness — the tear of the mourner — the heart-broken sigh drowned in the sharp knock of the coffin-maker. He had gone through it all, and sat moodily pondering over the future, when Madame de Sabloukoff entered.

"She's much better this morning, and I think we can go over and dine with her to-day," said she, removing her shawl and taking a seat.

He gave a little easy smile that seemed assent, but did not speak.

"I perceive you have not opened your letters this morning," said she, turning towards the table, littered over with letters and despatches of every size and shape. "This seems to be from the King, — is that his mode of writing 'G. R.' in the corner?"

"So it is," said Upton, faintly. "Will you be kind enough to read it for me?"

"PAVILION, BRIGHTON.

"DEAR UPTON, — Let me be the first to congratulate you on an appointment which it affords me the greatest pleasure to confirm —

"What does he allude to?" cried she, stopping suddenly, while a slight tinge of color showed surprise, and a little displeasure, perhaps, mingled in her emotions.

"I have not the very remotest conception," said Upton, calmly. "Let us see what that large despatch contains; it comes from the Duke of Agecombe. Oh," said he, with a great effort to appear as calm and unmoved as possible, "I see what it is, they have given me India!"

"India!" exclaimed she, in amazement.

"I mean, my dear Princess, they have given me the Governor-Generalship."

"Which, of course, you would not accept."

"Why not, pray?"

"India! It is banishment, barbarism, isolation from all that really interests or embellishes existence, — a despotism that is wanting in the only element which gives a despot dignity, that he founds or strengthens a dynasty."

"No, no, charming Princess," said he, smiling; "it is a very glorious sovereignty, with unlimited resources and — a very handsome stipend."

"Which, therefore, you do not decline," said she, with a very peculiar smile.

" With your companionship, I should call it a paradise,"
said he.

" And without such? "

" Such a sacrifice as one must never shrink from at the
call of duty," said he, bowing profoundly.

The Princess dined that day with the Countess of Glencore,
and Sir Horace Upton journeyed towards England.

28

CHAPTER LIV.

YEARS have gone over, and once more — it is for the last time — we come back to the old castle in the West, beside the estuary of the Killeries. Neglect and ruin have made heavy inroads on it. The battlements of the great tower have fallen. Of the windows, the stormy winds of the Atlantic have left only the stone mullions. The terrace is cumbered with loose stones and fallen masonry. Not a trace of the garden remains, save in the chance presence of some flowering plant or shrub, half-choked by weeds, and wearing out a sad existence in uncared-for solitude. The entrance-gate is closely barred and fastened, but a low portal, in a side wing, lies open, entering by which we can view the dreary desolation within. The apartments once inhabited by Lord Glencore are all dismantled and empty. The wind and the rain sweep at will along the vaulted corridors and through the deep-arched chambers. Of the damp, discolored walls and ceilings, large patches litter the floors with fragments of stucco and carved architraves.

One small chamber, on the ground-floor, maintains a habitable aspect. Here a bed and a few articles of furniture, some kitchen utensils and a little bookshelf, all neatly and orderly arranged, show that some one calls this a home! Sad and lonely enough is it! Not a sound to break the weary stillness, save the deep roar of the heavy sea; not a living voice, save the wild shrill cry of the osprey, as he soars above the barren cliffs! It is winter, and what desolation can be deeper or gloomier! The sea-sent mists wrap the mountains and even the lough itself in their vapory shroud. The cold thin rain falls unceasingly; a cheerless, damp, and heavy atmosphere dwells even within doors; and the gray half light gives a shadowy indistinctness even to objects at hand, disposing the mind to sad and dreary imaginings.

In a deep straw chair, beside the turf fire, sits a very old man, with a large square volume upon his knee. Dwarfed by nature and shrunk by years, there is something of almost goblin semblance in the bright lustre of his dark eyes, and the rapid motion of his lips as he reads to himself half aloud. The almost wild energy of his features has survived the wear and tear of time, and, old as he is, there is about him a dash of vigor that seems to defy age. Poor Billy Traynor is now upwards of eighty; but his faculties are clear, his memory unclouded, and, like Moses, his eye not dimmed. "The Three Chronicles of Loughdooner," in which he is reading, is the history of the Glencores, and contains, amongst its family records, many curious predictions and prophecies. The heirs of that ancient house were, from time immemorial, the sport of fortune, enduring vicissitudes without end. No reverses seemed ever too heavy to rally from; no depth of evil fate too deep for them to extricate themselves. Involved in difficulties innumerable, engaged in plots, conspiracies, luckless undertakings, abortive enterprises, still they contrived to survive all around them, and come out with, indeed, ruined fortunes and beggared estate, but still with life, and with what is the next to life itself, an unconquerable energy of character.

It was in the encouragement of these gifts that Billy now sought for what cheered the last declining days of his solitary life. His lord, as he ever called him, had been for years and years away in a distant colony, living under another name. Dwelling amongst the rough settlers of a wild remote tract, a few brief lines at long intervals were the only tidings that assured Billy he was yet living; yet were they enough to convince him, coupled with the hereditary traits of his house, that some one day or other he would come back again to resume his proud place and the noble name of his ancestors. More than once had it been the fate of the Glencores to see " the hearth cold, and the roof-tree blackened ; " and Billy now muttered the lines of an old chronicle where such a destiny was bewailed : —

" Where are the voices, whispering low,
    Of lovers side by side ?
And where the haughty dames who swept
    Thy terraces in pride?
Where is the wild and joyous mirth
    That drown'd th' Atlantic's roar,
Making the rafters ring again
    With welcome to Glencore !

" And where 's the step of belted knight,
    That strode the massive floor ?
And where 's the laugh of lady bright,
    We used to hear of yore?
The hound that bayed, the prancing steed,
    Impatient at the door,
May bide the time for many a year —
    They 'll never see Glencore!

" And he came back, after all, — Lord Hugo, — and was taken prisoner at Ormond by Cromwell, and sentenced to death ! " said Billy. " Sentenced to death ! — but never shot ! Nobody knew why, or ever will know. After years and years of exile he came back, and was at the Court of Charles, but never liked, — they say dangerous ! That 's exactly the word, — dangerous ! "

He started up from his revery, and, taking his stick, issued from the room. The mist was beginning to rise, and he took his way towards the shore of the lough, through the wet and tangled grass. It was a long and toilsome walk for one so old as he was, but he went manfully onward, and at last reached the little jetty where the boats from the mainland were wont to put in. All was cheerless and leaden-hued over the wide waste of water; a surging swell swept heavily along, but not a sail was to be seen. Far across the lough he could descry the harbor of Leenane, where the boats were at anchor, and see the lazy smoke as it slowly rose in the thick atmosphere. Seated on a stone at the water's edge, Billy watched long and patiently, his eyes turning at times towards the bleak mountain-road, which for miles was visible. At last, with a weary sigh, he arose, and muttering, " He won't come to-day," turned back again to his lonely home.

To this hour he lives, and waits the " coming of Glencore."

THE END.

University Press : John Wilson & Son, Cambridge, U.S.A.